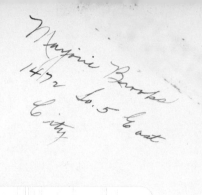

Marjorie Brooks
14½ So. 5 East
City

D1179846

WHITE BANNERS

White Banners

LLOYD C. DOUGLAS

BOSTON AND NEW YORK

HOUGHTON MIFFLIN COMPANY

The Riverside Press Cambridge

1936

The Riverside Press
CAMBRIDGE · MASSACHUSETTS
PRINTED IN THE U.S.A.

THIS BOOK TREATS OF PRIVATE VALOR
IT IS APPROPRIATELY
DEDICATED TO

BETTY DOUGLAS WILSON

WHITE BANNERS

Chapter I

AFTER so long a pause that Marcia felt sure whoever it was must have gone away, the front doorbell rang again, a courteously brief 'still waiting.'

It would be a neighbor child on the way home from school with a handful of basketball tickets. Or an agent tardily taking orders for cheap and gaudy Christmas cards.

The trip down to the door would be laborious. Doctor Bowen had wanted her to avoid the stairs as much as possible from now on. But the diffident summons sounded very plaintive in its competition with the savage swish of sleet against the windows.

Raising herself heavily on her elbows, Marcia tried to squeeze a prompt decision out of her tousled blonde head with the tips of slim fingers. The mirror of the vanity table ventured a comforting comment on the girlish cornflower fringe that Paul always said brought out the blue in her eyes. She pressed her palms hard on the yellow curls, debating whether to make the effort. In any event she would have to go down soon, for the luncheon table was standing exactly as they had left it, and Paul would be returning in half an hour.

Edging clumsily to the side of the bed, she sat up, momentarily swept with vertigo, and fumbled with her stockinged toes for the shapeless slippers in which she had awkwardly paddled about through two previous campaigns in behalf of humanity's perpetuity. When done with them, this time, Marcia expected to throw the slippers away.

Roberta eagerly reached up both chubby arms and bounced ecstatically at the approach of the outstretched

hands. Wallie scrambled up out of his blocks and deto-
nated an ominously sloppy sneeze.

'Hanky,' he requested, with husky solemnity.

'Well — I should say so,' agreed Marcia. 'Please don't
tell me you've been taking cold again.'

Wallie denied the accusation with a vigorous shake of
his head, whooped hoarsely, and began slowly pacing the
intermittent clatter of their procession down the dingy
stairway, the flat of his small hand squeaking on the cold
rail of the ugly yellow banister.

The bulky figure of a woman was silhouetted on the
frosted glass panels of the street door. Wallie, with a wobbly
index finger in his nose, halted to reconnoiter as they neared
the bottom of the stairs, and his mother gave him a gentle
push forward. They were in the front hall now, Marcia
irresolutely considering whether to brave the blizzard.
Wallie decided this matter by inquiring who it was in a
penetrating treble, reinforcing his desire to know by twist-
ing the knob with ineffective hands. Marcia shifted Roberta
into the crook of her other arm and opened the door to a
breath-taking swirl of stinging snow, the first real storm of
the season.

Outlandish in a shabby plush coat much too large for
her — though she was by no means a small person — and
an equally frowsy old fur hat drawn down over her brows,
the caller displayed a large red apple from which an in-
credibly long peeling dangled. Obviously expecting her
pantomime to speak for itself, the woman — heavy-eyed,
pale — silently produced another inch or two of apple-
skin tape projected through the slot of an ingenious little
knife firmly clutched in a blue-chapped, shivering fist.

'But I mustn't stand here in this storm,' protested
Marcia. 'You'll have to step inside. And please shut the
door quickly,' she added over her shoulder as she retreated
into the comparative warmth of the living-room, the apple-
person following with Wallie reeling alongside gazing up at
her inquisitively.

'Sorry to have bothered you,' regretted the peddler. It was a singularly low-pitched voice registering the last extremity of weariness, perhaps something of battered refinement too. The gray eyes were cloudy and seemed reluctant to draw a clear focus, though this might be attributed to fatigue rather than a calculated evasiveness.

Murmuring a non-committal acceptance of the apology, Marcia eased Roberta's undependable feet onto the sewing-machine table and stretched out a hand toward the magical tool.

'How much is it?'

'A quarter.'

'I'll take one,' said Marcia, glancing up to meet the gray eyes squarely for the first time. Then she added 'Please' with a slight inclination of her head which seemed to invest the trivial transaction with something like dignity. She was a little surprised at her suddenly altered attitude toward this taciturn woman with the pallid face, the puzzling eyes, and the impossible clothes. It had been habitual with Marcia to make short work of door-to-door canvassers.

Politely but without effusion the peddler produced a barely audible 'Thank you,' and began rummaging — rather ineffectually, for her hands were stiff with cold — in the depths of a capacious old shopping-bag bulging with demonstration apples, while Marcia studied the impassive face at close range. It appeared to mask a personality intended for and probably accustomed to better things than the house-to-house vending of a cheap kitchen gadget. Or perhaps it had a secret to conceal. The woman was a curious bundle of inconsistencies, the dowdy old hat and the rough hands being so shockingly unrelated to the disciplined voice and eyes which testified to a well-furnished mind.

'I shall have to go upstairs for the money,' said Marcia, when the merchandise had changed hands. 'Will you watch my baby?'

The cryptic eyes lifted, lighted, and a smile nervously twitched the corners of the drooping mouth. Muttering something about the snow on her coat, the woman un-buttoned the ill-fitting garment and tossed it aside. The uncouth hat was tugged off also, disheveling a thick mop of well-cared-for, blue-black hair and releasing a crackle of electricity. Without the hat and coat she was only forty, perhaps a little less than that if she were entirely well and contented.

'But I don't like to have you climb those steep stairs for me,' she protested. 'Perhaps you'd better not.'

'I really shouldn't,' confided Marcia. Then, impulsively, 'Would you mind? It's on my dressing-table, a brown leather purse, first door to the right at the head of the stairs.' She slipped her hands under Roberta's arms to reclaim her, but the caller ignored the gesture and cuddled the baby closer to her abundant breast. The gray eyes searched Marcia's youthful face for a moment discon-certingly.

'Do you think,' inquired the gently reproving voice, 'that you ought to let a stranger ramble about through your house hunting for your pocketbook?'

Marcia flushed a little and felt very young and foolish.

'It does sound reckless, when you put it that way,' she admitted, adding, with a naïveté that brought a puckery smile to the visitor's lips, 'What are we going to do about it?' Then, suddenly inspired, 'My husband will be here in a little while. Could you wait?'

'Gladly,' sighed the caller. 'I have been on my feet all day.' She sank into the nearest chair and softly rubbed her white chin against the top of Roberta's silky head.

'It's chilly in here.' Marcia stooped over the wood-bas-ket and dragged the metal screen aside from the cold grate. 'The furnace runs low at this time in the afternoon, and I can't do anything about it.'

'Let me make that fire for you. I'm bigger than you

are.' Again little Roberta was transferred and the stranger knelt before the grate.

'Nobody could be bigger than I am,' murmured Marcia. She sat interestedly surveying the slow but competent movements of her mysterious guest. The shoes were badly worn, but they had once been good — expensively good. Whoever had wanted that hat had not bought those shoes. Marcia felt that the shoes were authentic. So was the black crêpe frock. It was old, but it fitted.

The fire blazed, and with much difficulty the weary woman rose to her feet, clutching the mantel for support. Marcia tried to keep the pity out of her tone when she said cordially, 'Now draw up a chair close to it. You must be half-frozen.'

There was silence between them for some time, the stranger leaning forward with her elbows on her knees and her chin cupped in both hands, staring into the crackling flames. Presently she straightened and turning toward Marcia asked wistfully if she might hold the baby again.

Silently complying, Marcia went through the double doorway into the dining-room and began to clear the table, Wallie hovering close.

'Mum-mee!' he wheedled shrilly. 'Can I have a piece o' bread-n-butter-n-sugar?'

Marcia led the way into the diminutive pantry, Wallie gleefully chirping redundant comments on his good fortune while his mother laid out the makings of a snack. Suddenly his improvised refrain was broken off short. At the same instant Marcia sensed another presence, and glancing around was startled to see her strange visitor standing in the passage. She had Roberta closely nestled in her arms. Her pale lips were parted, slightly baring sound white teeth tightly locked. The gray eyes were importunate — and ashamed.

'Perhaps you would like some too.' Marcia tried to make the invitation sound half-playful, hoping to safeguard the woman's self-respect if she could.

'Oh — please! If you would.' The deep-pitched voice
was husky. 'I haven't had anything to eat since morning
and I'm not so very long out of the hospital.'

'You should have told me,' chided Marcia gently. 'Do
help yourself — and there's some cold tongue in the refrigerator. I'll make you a cup of tea. Not much wonder
you're fagged. Was it an operation?' Proceeding into the
cold kitchen, she lighted the gas under the kettle.

'I don't know,' replied the half-starved woman indifferently, surrendering Roberta and taking up the bread-knife
in a shaky hand. 'Maybe they do call it an operation.'
She began eating ravenously.

Shocked by the exhibition of such hunger as she had never
seen so candidly displayed, Marcia retreated a step, fumbling at her beads with agitated fingers. She felt rebuffed
too, for surely her solicitous query had deserved a better
reply than this casual impertinence.

'I mean,' explained the woman, her articulation muffled
by the food she was wolfing, 'is it an operation when you
have a baby? I know,' she continued, between spasmodic
swallowings, 'that it's an operation when you have something unhealthy that has to be cut out of you, but having
a baby is the most natural thing in the world, or at least
it would seem so seeing how long it was going on before
there were any surgeons or hospitals.'

Indisposed to debate whether childbirth should be considered as an institution or an operation, but personally
interested in babies as individuals, Marcia inquired, 'What
did you do with it?'

'He's at the hospital. They said he could be adopted.'

'Have you no friends?'

'No, that is — not here.'

'Relatives?'

'Well, none wanting a baby.' She turned to cut another
slice of bread.

'That's too bad,' sympathized Marcia. 'There's your
tea on the kitchen table. Come, Wallie. You run in now

and sit by the fire. Go on — quickly. Do as Mother tells you.'

'I don't want to,' squeaked Wallie. 'I want to watch the lady eat.'

Marcia was devastated with chagrin, wondering whether an apology on behalf of her unfortunate offspring would ease the strain, when the problem was solved for her by a good-natured laugh and a mumbled 'I don't wonder.'

Unable to think of anything appropriate to say, Marcia smiled faintly and led her reluctant child into the living-room, where she lowered Roberta into the perambulator and returned to her task at the dining-table, for some moments mechanically moving the dishes about, wishing this awkward situation had not arisen. She hoped the woman would go soon. Surely she had enough to worry her without adding anything more. Paul would be here at any moment. He would go popping through the kitchen immediately on his way to the furnace. He would discover this famished woman and interest himself in her predicament. Anyone could see at a glance that she shouldn't be turned out into the storm. And it would be quite right and proper to ask her to stay if they could afford it, or had a suitable place for her. Paul would think they had. He was so hopelessly impractical, so heart-breakingly in debt, so childishly indifferent to their plight. And in a month there was to be the hospital and the nurses and the doctor — without the slightest vestige of a plan for these imperative expenses. Poor Paul. He should have married someone who knew how to manage. . . . No — she would have to see to it that the unhappy creature was out of the house before Paul arrived. For the moment Marcia quite forgot the real reason for the woman's tarrying.

Resolutely she gathered up a double handful of dishes and carried them to the kitchen sink. The stranger promptly joined her there, turned back her sleeves, and began drawing hot water into the dishpan.

'You'll not need to help,' said Marcia crisply. 'There

aren't many. I can easily do them alone. Thanks — just the same.' She tried to make the dismissal significant without being unkind.

'Where do you keep the aprons?' inquired the woman, unimpressed by Marcia's rather stiff repudiation of her proffered services.

'But — really ——' Marcia was being very firm now. 'I prefer to do them myself.' She accented every word, secretly reproaching herself for having to offend the grateful tramp.

Pretending not to realize this sudden shift of mood, the stranger smiled indulgently and began washing the dishes. The food had braced her up and every motion testified to an amazingly prompt revival of latent energy. Marcia decided to make a last stand. Time was passing rapidly. On the verge of tearful exasperation, she said: 'You have your own work to do, and I'm keeping you from it. I'll go and get your money for you at once. My husband might be delayed. And it is getting dark. I mustn't detain you.'

Flicking the hot suds from her hands, the woman followed as far as the dining-room without comment and stacked up the rest of the dishes. Marcia made an impatient little gesture of bafflement, her knuckles digging into her forehead. Weak in the knees, she slumped into a chair by the grate, hoping to recover her strength for the painful trip upstairs. Minutes passed. The energetic clatter of dishes had subsided now and the unwelcome volunteer in the kitchen could be heard walking about. She was coming quietly into the living-room. Marcia glanced up dully, relieved to see the woman take up the frumpy old coat and the mangy hat and the preposterous shopping-bag from the chair where they had sprawled in an untidy pile.

'I'm going up for the money now,' said Marcia weakly. 'Thank you for doing the dishes.'

'I'll be in the kitchen,' replied the woman, draping her effects over her arm.

That was ever so good, thought Marcia. The poor dear

had caught the idea that she must go and was planning to leave by the back door to avoid a collision with the man of the house. Perhaps she had divined that she was expected to be gone when he came. Pulling herself together, Marcia dragged her burdensome body up the stairs and down again, wincing at every step of the return trip. There was a mighty stamping of snowy feet on the front porch as she hurried through the dining-room. Perhaps the worrisome incident could be closed in the nick of time.

At the kitchen doorway she stopped and speechlessly surveyed a dismaying scene. In apparent contentment, the woman was seated in the corner with a pan in her lap, peeling her experimental apples with one of her patent knives. She looked up brightly and smiled.

'Pie,' she explained — and then added irrelevantly, 'My name is Hannah.'

For all of fifteen minutes Hannah had the kitchen to herself. She was much perplexed. The girlish blonde had been so pleasantly kind — and then had suddenly gone into a panic of desire to get her out of the house. That would be because her husband was a brute. The pretty thing was clearly frightened about something, and undoubtedly that was it. Hannah thoughtfully stroked her chin with the back of her hand and wondered what she ought to do — stay and help get dinner and put the disordered kitchen to rights, in payment for her food, or take her quarter and vanish.

While she debated, half-intelligible wisps of conversation drifted through from the living-room where the nervous and distraught girl-wife was pouring out her story. Occasionally his soft voice offered a soothing comment. He wasn't a brute. Hannah continued to peel her apples. The situation was clearing up. She smiled and shook her head a little, compassionately, eavesdropping without compunction on the private talk, occasional phrases of which were becoming audible. They were stony-broke, their credit was exhausted, they were going to have another baby, they couldn't take on any more obligations — all this in the harassed voice of the lovely blonde — and here was this hungry person out in the kitchen peeling her own apples with the unquestionable expectation that her services would be recognized and rewarded.

'But' — the man was saying reassuringly — 'you need help, Marcia, and if she wants to do something for you, in return for your kindness, why not let her?'

'But we can't afford it, Paul.'

'Why can't we? We've been in tight corners before.'

Now they were just going around and around, getting nowhere. The apples were all peeled. Having intruded this far into their family complications, Hannah felt that a little more impudence on her part would not be likely to alter her status very much, so she decided to go to the basement and do something about the fire before it went out, if indeed it had not already done so. Then, if they were agreed that she mustn't stay and help, in return for the food she had eaten, they could say so — and she would go. She sincerely hoped they would not insist on this, for it was plain to be seen that the young woman was almost at the end of her physical resources.

The first door she tried unlatched with much difficulty, but when it did consent to let go it was generous enough, unexpectedly disgorging a great many of the larger articles which the shallow closet contained — an ironing-board, two brooms, a mop, and the long handle of a carpet-sweeper bounding violently out to assault her, attended by a covey of dust-cloths. The eruption caused a deal of racket and for a little while there was no sound of talk in the house. Then his father called Wallie to come back here, and Hannah coaxed the things into their lair again, all but the umbrella which had opened in flight and couldn't be closed without risk of a compound rib fracture.

She tried the other door. The stairs to the basement, now that Hannah had located them, were pitch-dark at the top, though a feeble yellow light glowed from one of the rooms in the cavern below. Just inside the door there was an electric bulb which did not respond when she turned the button. Groping her way cautiously down the narrow steps she found the furnace-room by the aid of the almost extinct lamp which presumably had been burning all day. The coal supply was low, but there was a plenty of everything else in the dingy room. Hannah vigorously shook down the ashes and clinkers, opened the drafts, and shoveled in a small quantity of coal, thinking it indiscreet to offer the fire very much nourishment until it was feeling better. While she waited for signs of its resuscitation there was time to glance about. She shook her head and whispered, 'Tsch, tsch.'

It was none of her business, of course, but there was a battered trunk with no lock, no hasps and one handle, a broken chair, a pile of magazines, a bicycle with two flat tires and a mildewed seat, a roll of old rugs and strips of carpet, a three-legged card-table, a hobby-horse with one ear, one rocker and no tail, a tall filing-cabinet, and a serviceable but very grimy office desk on which reposed two high stacks of old books covered with soot, a pile of folded chintz draperies, a gilt clock, a half-dozen flower-pots with earth in them, an unstrung tennis racquet, one roller-skate, and a cracked cut-glass berry-bowl containing three hickory nuts, a bunch of rusty keys, a doorknob, a spool of white silk thread, a monogrammed belt-buckle, five dominoes, a box of fish-food, a toothbrush, and a small gift copy of *Sartor Resartus*. Hannah threw in another shovelful of coal and wondered what they would be thinking overhead when they heard all the noise she was making.

Retracing her steps upstairs, she decided to carry on with the pie. Pulling open the flour-bin in the kitchen cabinet, she was pleased to find it nearly half full. It contained also the flour-sifter, a couple of little tin dies for cutting cookies, a rolling-pin, and a lead pencil which must have got in by accident. Hoping to be equally successful in locating the other ingredients for the pie, Hannah went to the refrigerator, taking pains to avoid the sluggish stream which ambled aimlessly across the pantry floor and whose headwaters, she knew, had their origin in an over-flowing pan beneath the icebox.

Opening the door she found a tin bucket filled with lard. Excellent luck, thought Hannah. There was a plentiful supply of almost everything. The refrigerator was stuffed to capacity; four quart milk-bottles, all partly used, but one which was empty, a highly ornamented glass jar with a few slices of cold tongue, the skeleton of a rib roast from which most of the choice meat had been cut, two asparagus tips in a saucer, a few stalks of discouraged celery, one candied sweet potato holding forth alone in a large bowl with the smugness of an old settler, three half-used glasses of jelly, and, side by side, a pound of unwrapped butter and a slice of Roquefort cheese. Hannah removed the cheese.

There was also a neat paper parcel. She argued with herself for a moment and opened it — four French lamb chops. Then she took the can of lard to the kitchen-cabinet where operations were resumed on behalf of the apple-pie. She was stooping over to light the gas in the oven when masculine footsteps commanded her attention. The man was in his middle thirties, slender, a little over average height, and very good-looking.

'How do you do,' he said pleasantly. 'Mrs. Ward tells me — I am her husband, by the way ——'

'I thought you might be,' replied Hannah, unperturbed. 'I knew she was expecting you.'

'Mrs. Ward has been just a bit upset. You see ——' He hesitated for an instant.

'Yes, I know,' assisted Hannah companionably. 'It's her condition. What with two little children on her hands and nobody to help her and another baby expected soon, she naturally would be nervous.'

'Of course,' he agreed. 'But the point is that Mrs. Ward

feels embarrassed over your remaining here to offer your services in this way. She says you have been earning your living by selling something and we are keeping you from it. We both appreciate your kindness, but — to put the matter frankly — Mrs. Ward doesn't want you to do anything further. She feels that we cannot afford to have kitchen help just now.'

'If you don't mind, Mr. Ward,' rejoined Hannah, plying the rolling-pin energetically, 'I'll keep right on with this pastry, so it won't get tough. Pardon me for interrupting.'

'Well — that was about all I had meant to say. We are greatly obliged for what you have done, and if we were able we should gladly keep you on, but — as I have tried to point out — we can't afford it.'

Hannah pinched the pie all the way around with an experienced thumb and holding it on a level with her eyes deftly trimmed the edge.

'I know you can't,' she said, and then added, lowering her voice confidentially, 'and I know why.'

He bridled a little at that, lighted a cigarette with an impatient gesture, and replied, clipping his words, 'At least — it's no responsibility of yours.'

'I'm not so sure about that,' countered Hannah. 'I got into your mess by accident and through no fault of mine. I was blown into your house by the blizzard. Your wife was very kind to me. I've been awfully knocked about lately, Mr. Ward, and she seemed to realize it. She is a darling. And then I found myself out here in your kitchen — and I just can't leave her in this dreadful state. I should worry myself to death about her.'

'Dreadful state?' he echoed woodenly.

Hannah pursed her lips and smiled a maternal reproof.

'Don't pretend you didn't know. This hand-to-mouth way you people live — everything at loose ends — spending so much and getting so little for it.' Hannah felt that she had burned most of her bridges now and might as well speak her mind plainly. 'That sweet girl ought to be hav-

ing good care — especially now. She shouldn't be doing
her own work — and she's doing it the hardest way there
is. I don't wonder she's discouraged and nervous, the way
this house is run. I hope I haven't offended you, but it's
true.'

He had been scowling darkly through Hannah's speech,
but her last conciliatory remark was so genuinely sympathetic that his face cleared a little.

'I know,' he admitted, with a rueful sigh, 'we aren't
very good at it.'

Hannah teased him with a sisterly grin.

'I'll bet you mean,' she drawled, 'that your wife isn't
very good at it. Men always think that. But you left the
furnace lamp on all day, I notice, and you've been buying
kindling all tied up in cute little bundles when the basement is running over with loose boards and broken boxes
enough to supply you for the winter. It isn't all her fault,
I can tell you.'

'Did I say it was?' he grumbled.

Hannah made no reply to that, being occupied at the
moment by her task of regulating the oven. He sauntered
to the door and stood there indecisively.

'Wouldn't you like to empty that refrigerator pan while
you're here?' asked Hannah, as if he were fifteen and she
was his mother. 'That's really a man's job, you know.
It's heavy.'

He complied good-naturedly enough, dragging the loath-
some thing out and slopping a great puddle of slimy water
on the floor. Hannah had anticipated this and was already
at his elbow with the mop.

'Sorry,' he muttered, trying to balance his burden on the
way to the sink. 'It's always full, no matter how often you
empty it.'

'You could remedy that in half an hour if you wanted
to,' scoffed Hannah, unwrapping the expensive chops.
'Bore a hole in the floor, put in a tin funnel, and run a
piece of hose down to a big bucket in the cellar.'

'And then the bucket would always be running over down there.'

Hannah glanced up and chuckled as she replied, 'Well — I don't think that would matter much. You aren't very particular how the cellar looks.' She raised her eyebrows so drollishly when she added, 'I was down there,' that he laughed a little in spite of his determination to be firm with her. The sound of it brought Marcia to the doorway, her wide blue eyes full of inquiry.

'If it's something funny ——' she began, with as much dignity as she could muster.

'If you will set the table now, Mrs. Ward,' interjected Hannah, quite unruffled, 'I'll have your dinner ready in a few minutes.'

Marcia turned away frankly annoyed, followed by Paul, who said, when they had reached the dining-room: 'She isn't a bad sort, dear. Bit of a character, I should say. No end amusing. Why not let her help you tonight if she wants to? Tomorrow you can tell her to go.'

'Tomorrow? You mean she is to stay here all night?'

'Why not? She doesn't seem dangerous. And there's a bed. She's probably clean — don't you think?' He grinned broadly. 'I gather that she's almost as fastidious as we are, judging from some comments she made about our cellar.'

'She didn't dare!' spluttered Marcia.

'Dare? You don't know our Hannah very well. She as much as said ——'

'That I was the worst housekeeper in the world, I suppose.'

'No, no, darling; nothing about you. She thinks you're wonderful.'

'Yes — aren't I?' muttered Marcia derisively. 'So — she's to sleep in the guest-room, I suppose. In that case, I'd better lay a place for her at the table.' She began taking the silver from the buffet.

Hannah, who had been significantly rattling dishes in

the pantry, came in at this juncture with a trayful, and, noting the preparations for three places, inquired, 'Does little Wallie eat at the table?'

'In his high-chair,' replied Marcia, still grim.

'Then we'll not need these,' said Hannah, restoring the extra silver to the buffet-drawer. 'I shall be serving the table.'

Marcia had gone early to bed after showing Hannah where she was to sleep — 'just for tonight' — and taking pains to specify that their hospitality was offered because of the very bad weather. She had admitted to herself — and, a bit reluctantly, to Paul also — that it was a welcome relief to be temporarily free of kitchen drudgery. Now that her burdens had been eased for a few hours, she realized the weight of them.

Having finished his pipe and the newspaper, and observing that a light still burned in the kitchen, Paul strolled out to see what Hannah was up to now. She had been reorganizing the contents of the refrigerator with a view to their consolidation. The neighboring cupboard ledge bore evidence to the number and variety of articles which she seemed to consider superfluous. He watched her for a while in interested silence as she sat squatting on her heels intent on her occupation.

'A refrigerator,' he said at length in the declamatory tone of one reciting the Commandments, 'is a nasty thing.'

Hannah looked up over her shoulder and nodded approval of this sentiment. 'It seems to me,' she said slowly, 'that whoever thought up a refrigerator might have had brains enough to give the thing legs, so you wouldn't have to sit on the floor or stand on your head to see what's in it.'

'Funny nobody ever thought of that,' ruminated Paul, reloading his pipe.

'Pooh — I'll bet every woman has. It's plain to see that it was a man planned it. It's too bad women aren't able to invent things.' Hannah's regret over the uninventiveness of her sex sounded sincere, and Paul puffed thoughtfully as he considered this curious biological fact. She rose with a wince from her tiresome posture and showed that she had something on her mind. 'If you are at liberty for a few minutes, Mr. Ward, I wish you would go down in the basement with me. I want to do something about that tomorrow.'

'I thought you were going away tomorrow,' he reminded her gently.

'That's why we have to decide tonight what ought to be done down there.'

He could think of no reasonable objection to this, so they descended the dark stairs, Hannah remarking en route that the electric lamp in the unfurnished storeroom on the second floor would be of more service here than there, and Paul consenting not very convincingly that he would see to it.

'How long has it been,' she inquired, 'since you used that desk?'

Welcoming any distraction from the threat of an unpleasant job, Mr. Ward scratched his head thoughtfully for the exact date while Hannah's fingers flexed restlessly. His averted eyes and oblique mouth predicted a reminiscence.

'Must have been 1908. It has been idle since we came here. My uncle gave me the desk when I received my doctorate.'

'Doctor it?'

'The degree, you know. Doctor of Philosophy.'

'Oh — do they have to doctor philosophy? I don't know much about such things.'

He eyed her narrowly for an instant and then nodded slowly, feeling that the query, whether asked in playful satire or honest ignorance, could properly be answered in the affirmative. Then he added, 'The desk is of no use to us. My office at the university is equipped with everything.'

'Is that what you do?' inquired Hannah compassionately. 'You're a professor?'

He nodded, tugging at the spluttering pipe.

'Well — I guess you know I'm sorry,' she said penitently, 'for talking to you the way I did. I was a little out of fix with you for being so helpless, but of course I didn't know what your business was. You'll excuse me, won't you?'

Paul laughed heartily and said she was priceless, but Hannah remained so contritely straight-faced that his laughter sounded to himself as if it had just a trace of incipient madness in it, and he suddenly sobered, blinking rapidly. If this woman was ragging him, she was making a good job of it, he reflected. He had visions of himself reporting the incident at luncheon tomorrow at the University Club. Then it occurred to him that it would be an awkward sort of story to tell — even to Fritz Manheim or Sandy Laughton. They wouldn't get it.

'So — you probably wouldn't miss the desk,' Hannah was saying, 'if you came down some morning and it wasn't here.' And when he admitted that this might easily be the case, Hannah pointed to the bicycle. 'Ever ride it?' she asked. He shook his head. 'It isn't in bad condition,' she observed, 'if the tires were mended. It's too good to sit here and rust. How about that filing-case?'

'I'll not be using it any more — at least so far as I know.'

'Well — that's far enough,' drawled Hannah, 'when you're cleaning junk out of a cellar. I suppose it's full of old papers and letters and things.'

Paul said he shared that supposition and promised to go through it, one of these days, when he had a spare minute; should have done so, he confessed, long ago.

Hannah shook her head and regarded him with one of her unanswerable grins. 'You — and your spare minutes,' she scoffed. 'What's the matter with right now? You're not doing anything else, are you?' Then, while he was trying to contrive an excuse for postponement of the un-

pleasant job, she told him to go up and find a couple of
good lamps. Returning, rather glumly, he found that she
had cleared a space around the cabinet and was wiping off
the soot.

'It's just as we thought,' she announced, as if the two of
them were conspirators engaged in dealing with the dis-
orderly clutter of a house they had unfortunately fallen
heir to; 'the thing is full. Better empty all the drawers into
that big clothes-basket, Professor, and then you can sort
out the stuff — and decide how much you want to keep.'

'I'd rather you didn't call me "Professor,"' he said
testily, dumping the contents of the top drawer into the
basket.

'Sorry,' murmured Hannah. 'I didn't know you were
sensitive about it.'

He had felt himself growing more and more surly over
the nasty task she had badgered him into, but Hannah's
ingenuous remark was quite too absurd to be received
irascibly. He laughed in spite of his irritation and pursued
the disgusting assignment without further grousing. In sober truth, these things should have been attended to long
ago. If this odd creature wanted to help, why not humor
her?

'Better see if the desk isn't full too,' advised Hannah.
'I've a notion, from all that's on top of it, there wasn't
any room left inside. . . . Are those rugs worth keeping? . . .
Does this lawnmower work? . . . Is that garden hose any
good? . . . Then what's the wheelbarrow for, if you haven't
a garden? You easily could have a nice garden, you know.'

It was long after midnight when they finished classifying
the basement's grimy hoard. The few papers which Paul
thought might have some future value had been tied up in
neat packages for temporary storage in a box Hannah had
found in the attic. Every scrap of paper that had been re-
jected she had stowed in a big burlap bag along with the
old magazines. 'It won't bring very much,' she admitted,
'but it's better business to sell it than to hire somebody to
cart it away.'

'You'd better go to bed now,' suggested Paul wearily. 'You must be very tired.'

'Bet your life I'm tired!' She rubbed back her damp, disordered hair with her forearm. 'And I never was this dirty before.'

He scowled a little at that and reminded her that nobody had asked her to do it. 'In fact,' he pursued stiffly, 'I can't understand why you did. You certainly don't owe us anything.'

'I owe the town something,' said Hannah. 'I have been a charity case in the University Hospital for three weeks.'

'That isn't owing the town,' growled Paul punctiliously. 'That's the state.'

'It's about the same thing. I don't even live in the state — if it comes to that. You are citizens and pay taxes. Perhaps I can square up a little if I do something for you. . . . I'm going to bed now. What time do you want your breakfast, and how do you like your eggs?'

'Er — poached, please, about half-past seven; but, look here, do you want me to believe that you actually feel under some sort of obligation to the town — or the state? Almost nobody does, you know. I'm mighty sure I don't!'

'Why not? The government of the town and the state is made up of the people, isn't it? I'm owing people. It's the same as any other debt, isn't it?' Hannah had one foot on the lower step, poised to go.

'Ummm — so you're paying back your debt to the state by helping the Ward family out of a scrape. Suppose the Ward family doesn't want you to. What then?'

She was thoughtful for a moment and a sudden inspiration came to the rescue. 'But the hospital did a lot of things to me that I didn't like either; though I suppose it was for my good.'

'So, you're intending to help us whether we like it or not. Is that it? You're just a little bit crazy, aren't you?'

'Perhaps,' confessed Hannah, mounting the stairs. 'You ought to know.' This last comment sounded saucier than she had intended, so she added respectfully, '— You being a professor,' which still left the colloquy lacking a satisfactory last line. To remedy this she said 'Good night' almost tenderly.

When she was at the top he called to her in a voice full of amusement under heavy compression.

'Hannah — would it be too much bother if you tried to sell this old stuff to a second-hand man? I don't know much about such business.'

'Yes, sir — I had expected to, tomorrow. You didn't think I'd go to all this trouble and then not finish it, did you?'

'I suppose,' he reflected, 'you could get more for it than I.'

Hannah chuckled a little, and then, suddenly deferential, replied, 'Yes, sir. I know that.'

'Well — you may sell it for us on one condition.' Paul was quite the man of the house, now, taking no nonsense from anybody. 'You are to keep ten per cent for your own. That is no more than fair. If you do not want to handle this job on these terms, you are not to do it at all. Understand? We are temporarily hard pressed here, but we are not paupers.'

'Thanks — and may I spend the ninety per cent on the house? I'm pretty good at making a dollar go a long way.'

'I dare say you are. Do what you please with it — in consultation with Mrs. Ward, of course.'

'Yes, sir. Don't forget to turn out the lights before you come up.'

Paul regarded his grimy hands with distaste and snapped off one of the lights. Then he turned it on again and ambled over to the empty fruit-cellar. For a long time he stood looking up at the raw joists under the pantry floor, speculating on a spot where a hole might be bored to let the seepage through from the icebox. What a clumsy arrangement; what an unsanitary, thoroughly objectionable apparatus it would be at its very best.

Why did people consent to the housing of such an abomination as a refrigerator, anyway? He fell into a brown study then and leaned against the wall, disregarding its coating of soot. After a while he sat down on a dusty box and slowly refilled his pipe.

The big packing-houses made their own ice: why shouldn't it be possible for private homes to have their own refrigeration plants? It might be worth looking into.

Stiff in every joint and dirty beyond description, he went up to bed at two o'clock, his head whirling with a new idea. This was the best hunch he'd ever had. He was determined to have a go at it, anyway. If it amounted to nothing — well, he wouldn't be any worse off, would he?

Chapter II

Marcia roused at nine with an oppressive sense of guilt such as a sentry might feel when caught asleep at his post. But no one came to reproach her. The house was very quiet.

She always depended on the children to waken her early. This morning there hadn't been a peep out of them. They must have been stealthily whisked away before they had had a chance to make a noise. That, she reflected, would be some more of this mysterious Hannah's doings. Hannah, for some unknown reason, had determined to make herself indispensable, though why she had decided it might be to her advantage to share their plight was a riddle that would take a lot of explaining.

Marcia sleepily conceded that if it really was the woman's ambition to become so useful they couldn't part with her, she was already well on the way toward success. One might try valiantly to be indignant over Hannah's obstinate generosity, but it was a sweet relief to know that some-body — no matter who or why — had temporarily shouldered the irksome load.

That the canny creature had managed to take Paul into camp was to have been expected. Marcia hoped Hannah would not consider this a feather in her cap, seeing how easily Paul could be taken in by almost anybody. Under her direction, doubtless — Marcia could reconstruct the self-assured tone in which the calm orders had been issued — Paul had slipped quietly out of the house to his eight-fifty class in Elizabethan Drama, after having breakfasted without haste or confusion. Paul would like that, nor was he the sort to worry over the future consequences of putting himself this much deeper into Hannah's debt.

Marcia interlaced her fingers behind her curly head and stared wide-eyed at the dingy ceiling. It wasn't exactly as if Paul was insensitive to debt. The humiliations of it hurt him. He was always very much subdued after a telephone conversation in which some impatient credit manager ruthlessly raked him over the coals. But after a pensive half-hour he would bob up like a cork. Knowing he was worried and wounded, she would go to him and sit on the arm of his chair. And he would look up brightly smiling, rub his cheek fondly against her arm, and say, 'Listen — I'll read you something funny.' She wished she had the same capacity for such prompt and painless recovery from a raw insult. There wasn't, she reflected with a deep sigh, very much bounce left in her. Paul was certainly a marvel of resilience, or else he was a master at concealing his thoughts, and she didn't think he was the latter. In fact, he was almost childishly frank. You could read him like a book. He was transparent as glass.

The oddest feature of his character was his undefeatable hope that things would soon be better for them. He had been nourishing himself on that faith ever since they were married. He had always talked about their predicament as if it was some sort of unforeseen emergency which ought to ease up by the tenth of the month at the latest. Every day since their honeymoon — on borrowed money, as she discovered six months later when he was savagely dunned for it — Paul had been counseling her to be patient and of good cheer. They wouldn't always be poor, no-sir-ee! Something would turn up. Once, ostensibly in jest but privately a little annoyed by his frequent use of this classic phrase, she had ventured to hint at the similarity between his optimism and that of Mr. Wilkins Micawber. After that, he usually beat a hasty retreat when he found himself about to recite this article of his creed, but he was apt at devising the equivalents of it. Something would turn up.

He believed that with a faith as bland as it was foolish and as dangerous as it was pathetic.

It wasn't as if he had just sat there serenely waiting for some benevolent angel to hand him a cornucopia. He had tried to do something to encourage Fortune to consider his need, rigged a little workshop in the attic, spent weary hours over clumsy models laboriously whittled out with flimsy tools. Sometimes Marcia would go up to show her interest. He would be humped over the bench, intently squinting at his product as if he had now arrived at the strategic moment, far too absorbed to stop even to value her good wishes. He would smile absently and wave her away — and she would answer his smile as courageously as possible. Then she would tiptoe down the attic stairs and cry her eyes out for him. Her throat ached now at the remembrance. Some days he would come home from the library with an armful of books about patents and sit up to all hours with them. He would abandon one project for another, casually dismissing the task he had toiled over for weeks and bravely taking on a fresh one with a cheerfulness that simply broke one's heart. Marcia wiped her eyes with the corner of the sheet. It was a darned shame! That's what it was! And things were never going to be any different. Paul's salary would never be very much larger than it was now.

Grimacing ironically at the mirror, Marcia sat at her vanity table and spent more than the usually allotted time with her hair. It was about the only thing she had left now to remind her of what she ought to look like, and she found comfort in concentrating her attention on it for a while, sweeping the brush through its spun gold almost caressingly. Paul had always been so proud of it.

And then, because she was playing the grand lady this morning, she drew on the pink negligee that he had given her on her birthday in June. They hadn't been able to pay the grocery bill in full that month or any part of the butcher's bill, but she couldn't summon the courage to chide him. Every time she had worn it, Marcia had experienced an uncomfortable feeling that the expensive garment wasn't really hers. It probably belonged by rights to the butcher, because she invariably thought of him whenever she looked at it. This would be an appropriate occasion to put it on. The voluntary assistance she was receiving wasn't rightfully hers either. She knew they would have all that to pay for sooner or later. High-grade service like this didn't just fall into your lap by magic. In the long run, the most expensive way to acquire anything was to get it for nothing. She pinned up her yellow hair and went leisurely down the stairs.

Wallie, with his hair wetted and slecked back off his forehead, giving him a detestable smart-alecky expression, was sitting at his little table by the fire so industriously engaged with his crayons that he barely glanced up when he mumbled, ''Lo, Mummy,' in preoccupied response to his mother's twice-repeated greeting. And how was her little boy's cold this morning, Marcia wondered, a query he answered promptly and fully with a resounding sneeze. Roberta was asleep in her perambulator on the other side of the grate, her thumb in her little rosebud of a mouth, as usual.

As she passed through the dining-room, Marcia noted that her place at the table was laid. It was a strange sensation to be cared for so thoroughly, somewhat perplexing but undeniably enjoyable. It was too good to be true; certainly too good to last very long.

Hannah had mounted the ironing-board on the backs of two kitchen chairs and was taking much pains with one of Roberta's little dresses. She smiled a salute.

'Sorry I overslept,' apologized Marcia. 'Someone should have called me.' She realized, in her unpremeditated choice of 'someone,' that she was still bracing herself against an admission of Hannah into the household.

'Are you ready for your breakfast, ma'am?' asked Hannah pleasantly.

'I'll get it. All I want is a cup of coffee and a piece of toast ... You're taking more trouble than I do with Roberta's clothes.'

'You would if you had the time, ma'am. What a sweet baby she is!'

'I wish I could make her stop sucking her thumb.'

'All babies do, more or less, don't they?' inquired Hannah serenely. 'Perhaps they have some good reason for it, ma'am.'

'What — for instance?' Marcia wondered. The woman was so capable. She might have an explanation. 'And I wish,' added Marcia kindly enough, 'you wouldn't tag all your remarks to me with "ma'am." I'm not accustomed to it. If you're going to do my ironing without wages, I don't care to be cast for the part of the duchess.'

'Thank you, ma'am,' stammered Hannah. 'As for Roberta's thumb, it has been so long since I was a baby that I've forgotten. But I think that Nature knows what she's up to, most of the time.'

'I wonder,' doubted Marcia. 'I see Wallie's cold is no better. I must telephone Doctor Bowen to come and look at him.'

Hannah peeled Roberta's fluffy white dress off the ironing-board and patted it down smoothly in a fresh place.

'Didn't he ever have a cold before?' she asked casually.

'Dozens! One right after another. Spring, summer, fall, and winter. He has been known to have two or three at the same time.'

'You always have the doctor?' inquired Hannah, amused.

'Of course! A cold is dangerous if you let it run on. You can't depend much on your wise old Mother Nature.'

'What does the doctor prescribe?'

'Oh, he doesn't usually give Wallie any medicine; tells me to keep him warm and see that he has plenty of liquids.'

'Well, can't we do that?' asked Hannah placidly. 'Not much use hiring the doctor to come here and say it over again. That four dollars would go a long way toward a ton of coal, if we're to keep the child warm. We are about out, you know.'

It was an odd thing, thought Marcia, what shocking impertinences this woman could commit without leaving you the slightest loophole for a suitable retort. And it was always done with a disarming smile that made it difficult for you to become indignant.

'Yes,' said Marcia, subdued, 'I must order some coal this morning.' Her face was perplexed. She wondered whether their coal-dealer would consent to send out any more until they had paid something on their old bill. Paul had said he would talk to him about it. It would be unpleasant. He always postponed such humiliations as long as possible.

'You needn't worry about Wallie. He will be all right. I gave him a big dose of castor oil awhile ago.' Hannah's calm report implied that any thought about sending for the doctor could now be prudently dropped.

'Did you have much trouble getting it into him?' asked Marcia, pouring her coffee. 'He does hate it so terribly.'

Hannah smiled reminiscently and admitted that there had been 'quite a struggle.' Marcia knitted her brows and pictured the little fellow frightened and overpowered by this domineering creature who seemed bent on having her own way with all of them. 'But I wouldn't give much,' Hannah went on, 'for a child who would take castor oil without some sort of fight. I'd expect him to wind up in a home for the feeble-minded.'

'I hope you didn't have to be rough with him,' said Marcia. 'He's very sensitive. Did you hold his hands? Did he cry?'

For some time Hannah was much occupied with her ironing and the tardiness of her reply brought a deepening expression of concern into Marcia's eyes.

'No,' she said at length, 'he didn't cry and I didn't have to hold his hands. When I saw how much he objected to the nasty stuff, I stood him up here on the table and talked

to him about you. I told him how sweet you were to him
— and to everybody — and how you were so very tired
that we mustn't make a noise, and if he didn't get over
his cold you would have to sit up at night with him when
you were sick yourself and ought to be in bed — and a lot
more things like that.' There was a long pause. 'And so'
— Hannah's voice lowered — 'he took it.'

Marcia's eyes grew misty.

'I didn't see him take it,' continued Hannah, bending
over her task. 'I put a big spoonful in orange juice and set
the glass down on the table, and I said, "There it is,
Wallie. Hannah's not going to make you do it — and Hannah's not even going to watch you do it."' The iron kept
on making deft little jabs into the ruffles, Hannah's eyes
intent on her work. 'And then I left him alone, and pretty
soon I came back — and he had taken it.'

'And what would you have done if he hadn't?' inquired
Marcia, frankly stirred by the report of her son's bravery.

'Oh — I would have started all over again, I suppose,
and promised to bake him some animal cookies, or some
such bribe as that. I'm glad I didn't have to. It's so — so
glorious, don't you think, when you find they've good
sound stuff in them?'

Marcia's pride shone in her eyes. She was quiet for a
moment and then remarked, with a little perplexity, 'But
you just said a child was probably feeble-minded who
would consent to take castor oil without a struggle. I hope
you don't think Wallie is.'

'Perhaps I didn't make myself clear, Mrs. Ward. I told
you there was a battle. Wallie put up a big fight, no doubt
about that, but it was on the inside, where all fights ought
to take place.... No' — she went on, half in soliloquy —
'Wallie gave himself a dose of something more important
than castor oil. He's a very stout little fellow.'

'And now you're going to make him the cookies,' said
Marcia childishly.

'Not today,' confided Hannah. 'It's ever so much better

if he can learn to fight battles without promise of pay.'
She tipped the iron up on its stern, and with one plump
bare arm akimbo, proceeded to elucidate her theory. 'That's
what ails so many people, Mrs. Ward. When they were
little tots they took their castor oil because somebody was
going to make animal cookies for them. And then, later
on, every time they do something fine and big and nobody
comes running up the next minute with animal cookies,
they go into tantrums and say, "Lookit! What's the good
taking nasty medicine if there aren't any animal cookies?"'
... Hannah took up the iron again. 'No — we mustn't
spoil this lad if we can help it. He's a thoroughbred, you
know. And they take a lot of handling.'

'You're funny,' observed Marcia, rather surprised to
find that she had made the thought audible.

'So they tell me,' admitted Hannah, 'but' — she hung
Roberta's dress on the drying-rack and reached into the
basket for another tiny garment — 'but, anyway, Wallie
got his castor oil, and that's the main thing.' She hesitated,
as if waiting for some rejoinder, and added, 'Isn't it?'

'No,' replied Marcia thoughtfully, 'I don't think that's
the main thing at all. And neither do you. I agree about
the importance of playing the game without bribes. I know
I've been peevish, plenty of times, because I wasn't paid
off promptly for some little voluntary hardship.'

'You do pretty well, Mrs. Ward — if I may say so.'

Marcia flushed a little and was annoyed at the very considerable pleasure she was experiencing in having been
commended by her new maid. She knew she had no business being affected, one way or the other, by Hannah's
opinions. It was impertinent of the woman to offer comments of this kind. Nevertheless, it was comforting. And
on what grounds could Marcia Ward predicate any snob-
bishness?

'Thank you, Hannah,' she said gratefully. 'You have
been very kind to us. I can't quite understand it. Just
why?'

Hannah ironed diligently for some time and then replied as from a distance, 'You took me in, Mrs. Ward, when I was a — when you didn't know me, or really want me.'

'I'm afraid I didn't do it very graciously. Certainly nothing I have done for you entitles me to any — any animal cookies.' They both laughed a little, and Marcia was rather glad now that she hadn't told Paul about Hannah's baby. At least she had been able to do that much for her: she had kept her secret. She wondered if it might not ease Hannah's mind to know that. Rather childishly she ventured upon the topic while it was fresh in her mind. 'By the way — I've been meaning to tell you that I haven't said anything to Mr. Ward about your baby.'

Hannah plied her iron industriously for a while and then inquired without looking up, 'Why didn't you?'

Marcia was slightly nettled. She declared to herself that she had never met anyone who could so utterly destroy a conversation and leave you sitting with the wreck of it in your hands — and no place to put it. She had a notion to say, 'Because I feared it might embarrass you to know that Mr. Ward knew.' But this would imply that Hannah really ought to be embarrassed, no matter who did or didn't know about the baby. After sparring mentally with several tentative replies, and finding something the matter with all of them, she said feebly, 'I just didn't — that's all.' And left the room.

After luncheon — Paul did not come home on Tuesdays — Hannah came upstairs to say that Mr. Ward had given her permission to dispose of some old furniture in the basement. She had telephoned to a second-hand dealer who would be there about three.

'I'm going down now to give the desk and the filing-cabinet a good polishing before the man comes. That's where I'll be if you want anything.'

'Seems to me you're putting yourself to unnecessary

bother,' said Marcia. 'The man will know what the furniture is worth, even if it is a little dusty.'

'Yes — that's the trouble. If the furniture is dusty, the man will know what it's worth *to us* and he'll offer a price to fit. But if it's clean and looks as if we thought something of it ourselves, the offer will be several dollars more.'

'Hannah,' said Marcia, laughing, 'I certainly shouldn't want to do any bargaining with you.'

'I was just coming to that, Mrs. Ward. How would you like to let me stay — at least until the baby arrives and you are well again? You need me, and I like it here.'

'I wish we could, Hannah. You've been such a help. But — as I told you — we haven't the money. How do you suppose it would make us feel — having you work for us without wages? No, we shouldn't consider it for a minute!'

'But if I figured some way,' persisted Hannah, 'so that you could pay me wages without spending any more money, would you let me stay? How much do you think it costs you a month for food?'

Marcia gave herself to some mental calculation and surmised that it might be about sixty-five dollars. 'Or seventy, at the outside,' she added prudently.

'If you'll let me have sixty dollars, I'll run the table and pay myself fair wages. . . . And I'll guarantee that we shall all have plenty to eat too.'

'It's a bargain,' declared Marcia. 'I hope you can do it. I'm sure I shouldn't be able to.'

An hour later there was a considerable stir in the basement, sound of voices, Hannah's and a man's. After much animated parley there was the screech and bump of furniture being dragged about. Marcia went to the window and watched a truck taking the load.

Hannah came up now attired in her ridiculous street outfit.

'We did pretty well, Mrs. Ward. Thirty-nine dollars. I'm going down to the market if you can spare me for a while.'

'But can't you use the telephone and save yourself a trip? It's snowing again.'

'My kind of shopping can't be done on the telephone, Mrs. Ward. I arranged for some coal to be here in a couple of hours. I asked this man where he bought his coal and he said there was a car in the railroad yards. People who are willing to go down there and shovel it out ——'

'Hannah! Don't tell me you're going to do that!' Marcia sat up in bed, wide-eyed.

'Of course not.' Hannah laughed heartily, almost girlishly, abandoning her reserve for an instant. Then, remembering the considerable difference in their status, she sobered and went on: 'If people shovel it out and haul it away themselves, it's about half-price. I told him to bring us two tons. We pay him well for the trucking. I guess we'll save enough on that coal to cover about all I'm likely to spend today at the market.'

At five, Hannah came back staggering under the weight of a large basket. Marcia, full of curiosity, went to the kitchen, found her sitting there panting, and reproached her for carrying such a load.

'It was only a block from the street-car,' defended Hannah. 'There were some good bargains today. I didn't want to let them go. I ordered enough at one place to have it delivered free — parsnips, potatoes, apples, and such things. There's a good storage-room in the cellar. I'll have some sand hauled in to keep the roots in fine condition.'

'What on earth, Hannah!' Marcia lifted the paper cover and looked into the basket.

'It's a hog's head. It cost seventy cents. A lot of meat on it. Very tasty, too, if you know how to make it up. There's almost everything in a hog's head — lard, sausage, mincemeat, scrapple ——'

Marcia's serious interest in this recital was so amusing to Hannah that she added a few more by-products, 'Chops, bacon, ham.'

'And eggs, I dare say,' assisted Marcia. 'But what are we going to do with all this canned corn?'

'Don't you like corn?'

'Yes — but here is a whole dozen — and a dozen tomatoes!'

'Well,' drawled Hannah, 'we shan't try to eat it all up today. It will be nice to have a few things on hand. These tomatoes cost eighty-four cents; exactly the same tomatoes that you buy on the telephone for a dollar-forty, except the label isn't quite so fancy. And there isn't much you can do with a lovely tin can but pay a man to haul it away.... I think you'll be satisfied with the food I'm going to give you, Mrs. Ward. There won't be any French chops with pink panties and a little bite of meat about the size of a peppermint lozenge, for we can't afford that, but we'll have things that stick to the ribs. Next week I'm going to buy a breast of mutton and let you see what can be done with another cheap cut.'

Marcia helped to put the supply away on the pantry shelves, finding herself quite enthusiastic over the prospect of these substantial economies.

'This will relieve my husband,' she confided impulsively. 'I know he worries — though he doesn't talk much about it.'

'It isn't any of my business, Mrs. Ward,' ventured Hannah, encouraged by this unpremeditated remark, 'but what does your husband make up in that room in the attic? I saw a lot of tools and funny bottles when I was up there hunting for a basket. There's a little lathe, too.'

'That's his workshop. He can't go up there in cold weather. It's a pity, too,' regretted Marcia, 'for it is the only recreation he has.'

'Well, all he needs is a half-dozen two-by-fours and some beaver-board to make a partition, and a small oil-stove. He could be snug and warm. But what's he trying to do? Little pieces of furniture, maybe?'

'No — it's an invention — or something,' said Marcia

vaguely. 'He hasn't really worked at it for a long time. Perhaps he has given it up. I haven't heard him say — not for weeks.'

Hannah began preparations for dinner.

'Maybe we can get him at it again,' she suggested. 'Maybe he has got something. You never can tell. But — I wouldn't have thought Mr. Ward was mechanical. He seems so sort o' helpless, and gentle. But then' — she repeated, half to herself — 'you never can tell.'

Marcia said she presumed that was true and left to look after the children.

'It isn't something that's going to make perpetual motion, is it?' called Hannah.

'No,' replied Marcia. 'I don't understand it, but I know it isn't that.... Something in chemistry, more likely.'

'Well,' said Hannah, in a tone of relief, 'that's good news, anyway. We couldn't afford to buy him a stove if he had anything like perpetual motion up his sleeve.'

Paul was in gay spirits at dinner. Marcia could not remember when he had been so unaccountably incandescent, certainly not for a year or more, and strongly hinted that she would be glad to rejoice with him if she knew what it was about. He seemed to be hugging a secret. It was not an unprecedented mood. Usually, as Christmas or her birthday approached, he slyly made pretense of torturing her curiosity with suppressed tidings of great joy, a boyish whimsy she tried to play up to with protestations that it wasn't fair, but privately alarmed for fear some preposterous extravagance, indulged in for her delight, would bring down on their hapless house a dismaying epidemic of bill-collectors representing the merchants whose monthly statements lay in her desk with a rubber band around them and a lot of menace in them.

And so often — how she despised herself for thinking this, but, my Sainted Uncle! wasn't it true? — the extravagant gifts were things utterly unusable. The fitted overnight bag, a-sparkle with silver-plated trinkets: how long had it been since she had had occasion to carry an overnight bag! The electric egg-boiler on a Sheffield tray! The morocco-cased traveler's clock! And the black velvet evening wrap with cheap white fur fuzzing. She had actually laughed at that: an evening wrap. She hadn't had an evening gown since their wedding. She pictured herself at a party, doffing her new black velvet coat and letting her hostess see what she had on under it. She laughed, and cried, after she had told Paul it was exactly what she had been wanting. Surely whatever old fellow it was had written in the Bible, 'Love beareth and endureth all things,' must have had a pretty good head — for a prophet.

Unfortunately, Paul would have to go back to the university tonight. Dean Oliver had been ill — Marcia knew this was true — and had been farming out his schedule of student interviews among the members of the staff. Not that Paul resented it. Indeed, he had found it rather pleasant to sit in the dean's chair for a couple of hours and play he was God for a procession of shamefaced athletes who had been a bit nonchalant in their attitude toward the 'Faerie Queen' or had thought erroneously, when they had registered for it, that Anglo-Saxon was 'a pipe.' But he would be back as soon as possible, and they would play a few games of Russian bank if Marcia was still up.

He had warmly felicitated Hannah on her successful merchandising, making no reservations in the sincere appreciation he felt. Fearing perhaps that he had not shown this plainly enough, he sauntered out to the kitchen and said, generously but just a bit condescendingly: 'It pleases us very much, Hannah, that you have decided to stay here. I hope we may make it worth your while — if not immediately, some day before too long.' His eyes were dreamily averted as he added, rather mysteriously, 'We might not always be so hard up.'

Hannah, who was now eating her own dinner on the porcelain table, looked him over appraisingly. Yes, that was it, all right: he was inventing something, poor devil. And spending the money already, no doubt. Giving her some of it. Probably arranging an annuity for her comfort in her old age.

Marcia, unfastening Wallie's bib and helping him down, involuntarily closed her eyes for a moment, as in prayer, and wished he wouldn't. This Hannah, who could see you through a stone wall and count the buttons on your coat, would probably grin when she had a chance. Really — you had to love someone very much indeed to put up with this sort of thing. Hannah could hardly be expected to view it sympathetically. For a moment, Marcia wished this woman had never come to look in on their grown-up playhouse; that's what it was.

Hannah smiled, rather grimly, and went on eating her dinner, listening, but taking stock of him as he stood there, his feet a little too wide apart for a professor. Excellent fellow — she liked him. But this was no time for him to be counting his chickens. Or hinting at what he was about to catch a pailful of at the end of a rainbow. And she didn't quite relish this air of benevolence with which he was filling her hands with the earnings of his dreams. She honestly hated to do it, but it would be good for him to get himself back on the ground again.

'How soon do you have to go?' she asked irrelevantly, in her throaty contralto.

He pursed his lips, dragged out his watch, studied it for a moment out of the tail of his eye, and said it would be about half an hour.

'If you'll go upstairs and take off those trousers,' she said, in the tone of sixty talking to six, 'I'll press 'em for you. They look sort o' jumpy, if you know what I mean. We've got to keep up appearances, you know,' she added, with one of her unanswerable smiles.

He stood for a moment, uncertain whether to be offended or grateful; then slowly turned and started on his errand. As he passed through the living-room, Marcia glanced up inquisitively, sensitive to a sudden change in his mood.

'Must you go?' she asked gently.

'Not for a few minutes. She's going to press my pants.' Hoping to give the episode a touch of drollery to save himself from abject abasement, he whispered behind his hand, 'She says they're jumpy — if you know what I mean.'

Marcia was tempted to laugh, but, divining the humiliation under his not very effective mask of clownishness, a wave of loyalty and compassion suddenly sobered her.

'Hannah had no business to say that to you.'

'Well — it's true, isn't it?' he growled, with a reluctant grin. 'They haven't been pressed for weeks. Hannah's impudent as the devil, I grant you, but she's right about the pants.'

He tossed the baggy trousers over the banister and Marcia carried them to the kitchen where Hannah was ready with the ironing-board. In a few minutes they were on him again, and he was leaving with his old gray felt hat set at a jaunty angle, his self-assurance entirely recovered. Hannah was clearing the table.

'Thank you, Hannah,' he called jovially. 'I'll do as much for you, sometime.' Then he kissed Marcia with more ardor than was customary at the hall door and left boyishly whistling.

Undoubtedly he was maneuvering himself into a grand state of expectation with a bitter disappointment waiting to smite the luster out of his eyes, but it was difficult to resist the contagion of his enthusiasm. Marcia returned to her needlework with a lighter heart than she had carried for months. After all — wasn't it better, she asked herself, to tarry for an hour occasionally in a Fool's Paradise, and pretend to enjoy it, than dwell perpetually in the more rational Valley of Bagdad which seemed to be their manifest destiny?

When the children had been put to bed, Marcia strolled out to the kitchen where Hannah was busy with the hog's head. It was interesting to watch her. Apparently she knew exactly what use was to be made of every particle: very

competent, no matter what she endeavored to do. Never
before had Marcia felt quite so helpless and inexperienced
as in the presence of this resourceful woman. It annoyed
her a little, and it annoyed her even more to realize that she
had permitted it to annoy her. She had fully realized her
own incompetency in dealing with the problems of home
management, but it had never been so startlingly called to
her attention. It wasn't simply that she didn't know how
to buy economically, didn't know how to utilize food ef-
ficiently when it was sent to her, didn't know how to organize her time: she was not resourceful. That was the one
word that told the whole story. Hannah knew how to con-
vert worthless cellar junk into money, she knew how to get
coal at half-price, she knew how to press trousers so they'd
look like new, she could fabricate three dollars' worth of
meat from a seventy-cent hog's head. Marcia admired her,
envied her, respected her — and disliked her for being so
capable.

And yet, in all honesty, she reflected, Hannah really
hadn't put on a show of superior knowledge. She had been
deferential enough. But the fact remained that she —
Marcia Wallace Ward, A.B. — lacked a very great deal of
being as capable as this enigma that had drifted in from
God knew where.

'What's your other name, Hannah?' she inquired, after
several minutes of silence between them. 'I don't remember
your telling us.'

'My family's name is Parmalee.'

'They don't live in this part of the country?'

'No. . . . Some people like the brains, too. Shall I have
some for breakfast?'

Marcia said she should do as she pleased. They could
try it, anyway, though somehow it didn't sound very good.
Hannah agreed to this, adding that if they didn't like it,
she would fry some sausage.

'Mr. Ward will probably like the brains,' speculated
Marcia.

'I expect so,' said Hannah. 'Men are always able to eat things like that. I think they just do it to show they're brave.'

'That sounds a little as if you might be a man-hater, Hannah,' ventured Marcia, with a chuckle to prove it was said in play.

'There's nothing wrong about bravery,' declared Hannah dryly. 'Everybody wants to be. Trouble with the average man is he doesn't get much chance to show his muscle, living in the city and working at a desk. That's what makes 'em have tough spells at home, and roar, "Who the hell's hid my pipe?" And his wife feels hurt. Doesn't realize that he's just out trotting his manliness around to see if it's still working. I think it's a pretty good thing to feed a man brains, once in a while, and say, "I really don't see how you can do it!" while he's eating. And kidneys, too. He should be fed kidneys and feet and tails and snouts and garter-snakes and praise — heaping spoonfuls of praise!'

'I suppose so,' said Marcia thoughtfully, wondering whether Hannah wasn't trying to give her a little indirect advice on how to manage a husband. 'I try to practice that, though perhaps I'm not very good at it. I think we all do better if we're encouraged.'

Hannah agreed to this so heartily that Marcia wished the supple-minded woman might find something in her worth a word of commendation. As she mentally called the roll of the brief conflicts of opinion they had had, one little episode invited debate.

'Hannah,' she said reminiscently, 'when you didn't want me to climb the stairs yesterday, I asked you to go up and get my purse, and you thought me very foolish. But — wouldn't you have done that yourself under the same circumstances?'

Hannah hacked hard with the cleaver and resumed her skillful operations with the butcher-knife. 'Yes,' she said at length, 'I would have — but that's a different matter.'

'You mean it would have been all right for you to do it,

but not for me?' Marcia's grin was slightly derisive. 'I think that's an odd thing for you to say.'

'I shouldn't have said it,' admitted Hannah, 'though I meant no offense, ma'am.'

'Just what did you mean, then?' Marcia challenged stiffly.

'I meant,' explained Hannah, quite undisturbed, 'that you would have done it without stopping to think it over — just on impulse, you know — and it might have turned out badly — and then you would have had nothing to show for it.'

'On impulse!' echoed Marcia. 'Well — how would you have done it, if not impulsively? Or perhaps it's a fixed habit with *you* to let people take advantage of you.'

Hannah nodded her head demurely. 'I'm afraid I do,' she confessed, 'but I wouldn't recommend the habit — that is, not generally. It costs more than most people would care to pay.'

Marcia moved toward the door, making no effort to conceal the fact that she was considerably ruffled. It was insufferable to be treated like a child. And anyway — what the woman had been saying was stuff and nonsense. She paused in the doorway.

'Now, look here, Hannah ——' Marcia didactically laid down a slim index finger in the exact center of her other palm. 'Let's get this straight. You said that if I allowed a stranger to go to my room for my purse, I would be doing it on impulse; and that if the stranger imposed on me, I would have nothing to show for it. Granted. I think that's correct. Well — suppose that you, who, it seems, do this sort of thing by habit and according to a program, should allow a stranger the same privilege and she imposed on you, what would *you* have to show for it? — I'd like to know.'

Hannah seemed so intent on her occupation for a while that there was no opportunity to talk. Presently she sat down with the large wooden bowl in her lap and began cut-

ting up the meat into very small pieces. Glancing up at
Marcia, still waiting, she gave her a tender little smile.

'Sorry I brought it up,' she said quietly. 'I'm afraid I
can't explain it very well. If I told you everything I believe,
you might think I was out of my head.'

She had spoken so gently and seriously that Marcia forgot her indignation.

'I think,' she ventured, 'that I understand you now. You
trust everyone. Isn't that it? Once in a while you are disappointed and defrauded, but you can afford to take the
loss because — because it usually turns out all right, and
balances up. Isn't that it?'

'Not quite. Not at all, in fact. No — that isn't it. When
you trust somebody and he lets you down, *you've something
to show for that, too.* I don't understand it myself, Mrs.
Ward, and it sounds very silly, but it's true.'

Marcia felt she had had about all of this that was good
for her. She nodded briefly, non-committally. Hannah
might interpret it to be a mildly indifferent assent either to
the truth or silliness of what she had been saying. Patting
a yawn, she said she would go to bed now, and proceeded to
the living-room, where she sat for some time looking into
the fire. Then she went back to the kitchen. Hannah
smiled inquiringly. Marcia searched her uplifted gray
eyes.

'Try to tell me, Hannah. Maybe I'm not as dumb as I
look. If you had sent me for your purse, and I had bolted
out of the house with it, you wouldn't have tried to catch
me, because — you'd have had something to show for your
trustfulness. How do you mean? *What would you have
had?*'

'More strength,' replied Hannah determinedly.

'It sounds a little like some kind of religion,' Marcia observed, 'but if it was you would probably be trying to bully
me into believing it, whether I wanted to or not; so — it
must be something else. And you won't tell me what you
get out of it?' Marcia was more than a little annoyed. 'I

don't suppose it would work for anyone as dull as I am, anyhow. So it would hardly be worth while telling me.'

Hannah continued at her work with downcast eyes.

'I'm not good enough, perhaps,' goaded Marcia.

Hannah looked up, smiled, sighed, and bent again over her task.

'Sorry,' muttered Marcia. 'I had no business to say that.'

'Oh — I don't mind,' said Hannah tranquilly. 'Once I would have said the same thing. I told you I couldn't make you see it. That's true. It's not because you're too dumb to understand. It's because I'm too dumb to explain. All that I know about it is this: if you find that you're related to people — all kinds of people — so closely that if you make war on them you're fighting yourself — and if you don't trust them you're not trusting yourself — there's a strange power that begins to give you more than you had lost by being defrauded, now and then. If you walk quietly and trustfully — you have something to show for it.'

'You mean — satisfaction; spiritual satisfaction: that sort of thing?' Marcia's little flick of the fingers dismissed the whole business. 'That's old stuff. They used to sing about it in Sunday School — when I was only so high.'

'Not by a jugful they didn't!' protested Hannah, so swiftly and sternly that the denial made Marcia blink in amazement. 'Nobody sings about *this*, I can tell you! This thing I'm talking about isn't easy to do. It's not baby-play. If you want to find out whether it's something you can set to a Sunday-School tune, *you just try it!* Make some experiments with it!' Hannah put the wooden mixing-bowl on the table and stood erect, her gray eyes lighted with an animation that held Marcia rigidly at attention. 'You make a resolution that when people revile you, and persecute you, and defraud you, you'll simply smile back and take it on the chin — and make that the fixed rule of your life — and refuse to quarrel or fight, no matter what they do to you — and you'll soon discover that you've tackled something with more teeth in it than a Sunday-School ditty!' She sat down again, took the bowl between her knees, rather abashed over the very long speech she had made.

'Why, Hannah!' Marcia's voice was half-frightened. 'Who'd ever have thought you could get stirred up like that.'

'I didn't mean to, ma'am, I don't — very often. You see — it has cost me a lot, and I didn't like to see it mixed up with something that people sleep over on Sunday mornings.'

'Do you think I ought to try it?' asked Marcia childishly. There was a long silence.

'That would be for you to decide. If you want to know anything more about it than I've told you, you may have to discover it for yourself.' Hannah paused so long that Marcia, thinking the strange talk ended, turned away. 'But — when you do discover it,' finished Hannah impressively, 'something will happen to you that you're not looking for. I can tell you that much. . . . *And you'll be surprised!*'

'I don't think I understand,' murmured Marcia, mystified.

'How many senses have you?' asked Hannah, in a low voice.

'Five — I've always believed,' answered Marcia, smiling.

'Well — you make an honest trial of this thing we've been talking about,' said Hannah meaningly, 'and you'll have six.'

'What a funny thing to say!'

'Yes — isn't it? . . . And when you get it — the sixth one — and I can promise you it won't be an easy thing to do — you'll be' — Hannah waited and groped, with questing eyes, for the right word, and failing to find it, she lamely fell back on what she had said before — '*you'll be surprised!*'

Chapter III

It was the hottest summer anybody could recall. In the country the corn parched in its husks, the wheat curled up and gladly died. Little was left stirring in the whole Mid-West but raucous political clamor and an unprecedented pest of grasshoppers.

The only comfortable place in the house was the basement. Marcia had said she wished she, too, could think of something important to do down there, and Paul had absently replied that there was plenty to be done, all right, if she had anything constructive to suggest. But he had not specified the nature of his dilemma or confided the objective of his relentless labor.

Had the Wards been penniless they might have contrived to borrow enough money to rent a cottage at some near-by lake, as they had always done in the days of their heart-breaking insolvency. Now that they were for the first time in their married life out of the woods financially (thanks to Hannah), it seemed imprudent to incur this unnecessary expense.

Their other reason for remaining in town during the summer vacation was Paul's intense application to his new project. He was inventing something again — something that was under construction in the basement, where he toiled for the greater part of every day with a zeal at once amazing and pathetic, for it was absurd to hope that a professor of English Literature could accomplish very much with a plumber's wrench. Even he, serious as he was over it, had ventured a little joke about the novelty of converting the lamp of learning into an acetylene torch.

Paul Ward had matured perceptibly in the past six months. It was a new and comforting sensation to be free of bill-collectors. The nervous flicker of the parasitical smile that had ineffectually draped his chagrin and foreboding was no longer in evidence. And when he had occasion to answer the telephone, you would have thought him another person than the half-frightened, half-furtive apologizer and time-beggar who had abased himself before the raw impudence of brassy whippersnappers in the credit departments of the stores and the utilities.

'Oh, yes — well — I'll be taking care of that on the tenth of the month,' he had been accustomed to saying, deferentially.

'Tenth of *what* month? That's what we want to know. And let me tell you sumpin more! ——' And then the surly dunner would tell him 'sumpin more,' while the sensitive, tortured fellow ground his teeth in helpless humiliation. That was all over now and Paul was showing the effects of his emancipation.

Whatever satisfaction Hannah had experienced in her successful management of the household's business affairs, her greatest happiness was derived from the splendid flowering of Paul's disencumbered personality. Of course she enjoyed watching the beautiful Marcia's achievement of radiance and poise, but the more spectacular change had occurred in the spirit of Paul. Hannah had grown to like him with an honest affection so disarmingly forthright in its protectiveness that Marcia, observing it, was moved rather to gratitude than jealousy. It delighted Hannah to see the gradual straightening of Paul's broad shoulders which gave him the effect of added height, the new pick-up to his words that had disposed of the old indecisive drawl. She had been amused a little, too, over his boyish glee in discovering how much more value there was in the same old dollar, now that his credit had been restored.

'We are always two months behind in our rent,' she had said in March. 'This time you can pay up one of them.

First of May we will take up the other. Then we are going to ask Mr. Chalmers for fresh wallpaper in the bedroom, repairs on the front steps, and a complete overhauling of the furnace.'

When, in May, they were on an even keel, Mr. Chalmers came in breezily one afternoon to have them go through the usual formalities of renewing their lease. Hannah was invited to participate in the interview. We need some repairs, she said. The front steps were falling down. The upstairs rooms required new paper. The furnace was wasteful and must have a heavier fire-pot and new grates. But Mr. Chalmers drew a long face. He was barely breaking even on this property. If he made these repairs, he would have to increase the rent.

'But,' said Hannah, 'aren't you making a pretty good thing out of this investment? At least twelve per cent, I should say.'

Mr. Chalmers was amazed. He even chuckled a little over the utter ludicrousness of Hannah's remark. The property was worth thirteen thousand dollars! And there were the frightful taxes!

'You people who rent don't realize,' spluttered Mr. Chalmers.

'Let's be calm, please,' said Hannah gently. 'I looked it all up in the tax reports. This house is assessed at fifty-eight hundred dollars. I know what taxes you pay.' Having serenely dropped this bomb, she excused herself and returned to the kitchen, Paul following her shortly after.

'Hannah,' he whispered, with a childish concern that made her laugh, 'what did you run away for?'

'I thought we'd better let that soak in for a minute or two before we rub on any more. It's a pretty tough hide, but we don't want to raise a blister. You go back and tell him we're moving on the last day of August.'

'But suppose he consents to the improvements.'

'Well — even at that, let's tell him there's no rush about renewing. And if he says he has another family anxious to

take it — which is, of course, the first thing he will think
of to use as a club — you tell him to go ahead and let the
other people have it.'

'But what if he should let someone else take the house?
We can't move now, Hannah. I've some very important
experiments to do here.' He lowered his voice impressively.
'You don't know just how important it is.'

'That's true, I don't. I've often wondered. Maybe you
have, too. This will be a good way to find out. If it happens
that we are to stay, we can be encouraged to hope that ——'

'If I were that superstitious, I'd ——'

Hannah shook her head.

'It isn't superstition. It's just hefting the thing a little
to see how much it weighs. If it's too flimsy to stand
a simple test like this, maybe you'd better not spend any
more time on it. You go back and tell Mr. Chalmers we're
moving out.'

Paul hesitated, then a light came into his eyes.

'Hannah,' he said solemnly, 'you have forgotten your pet
theory. We mustn't argue, or quarrel, or haggle, or go to
battle with anyone — including, of course, Mr. Chalmers.'

'Well — we're not fighting, in this case. We're just
retreating.'

Paul returned to the living-room where Mr. Chalmers had
the new lease spread out on the table.

'Right there, Professor.' Mr. Chalmers handed him the
pen. 'And I'll be running along.'

'We're not renewing the lease, Mr. Chalmers. You can't
afford to make the improvements, and we can't afford
a higher rent. So — we will be moving, end of August.'

Mr. Chalmers was astounded, wounded, admonitory.
They would have trouble finding another place. Houses
were scarce. It was always expensive to move. But Professor Ward gently mumbled that this would be their own
lookout.

'Now see here,' entreated Mr. Chalmers, 'let's go over
this matter again. I certainly don't want you fine people

to be put to a lot of inconvenience. Just what is it that you've got to have?'

'I'll call Hannah,' said Paul, somewhat to Mr. Chalmers's dismay.

The lease was signed a half-hour later. Hannah had suggested that the specifications for improvements should be drawn up and signed too; the front steps, the furnace, the wallpaper, a new porcelain sink, repair of the hot-water machine, kalsomining in the kitchen, and new screens upstairs.

'But I see no reason for a signed statement,' objected Mr. Chalmers. 'I keep my word.'

'So do we,' said Hannah, 'but you had us sign your lease.'

Mr. Chalmers boisterously disdained the thought that he wasn't trusting them. 'Just a formal matter,' he declared with a gesture that made a very small thing of it. 'Simply for purposes of — of record.' But he complied with Hannah's wish for a memorandum of all he was to do for them. At the front door he tarried, and, jerking a fat thumb over his shoulder toward the general direction of the disappearing Hannah, he growled, 'Who is that lady?'

Paul grinned amiably and replied, 'That's Hannah.'

'Relative?'

'No — the maid.'

'Do you let your maid attend to your business?'

'Yes. Does it fairly well, don't you think?'

'I'll say,' muttered Mr. Chalmers. 'She's a-wastin' herself doin' housework.' They both chuckled a little, and Paul went back to his work, pausing in the kitchen to say, 'You got more out of that chap than you had planned on, didn't you?'

'No,' said Hannah. 'If you don't raise your voice and holler, or put on a big bluster, but just sit tight and wait, you usually come out on top of the heap. If you simply refuse to fight, you get what's coming to you, maybe not right away, but in time. Once in a while it's hard to do, but you'll find it pays. Here we were refused the wallpaper and the new steps and the furnace, and we admitted we were licked. After that we got it all handed to us, plus the hot-water thing, the kitchen paint, the screens, and the new sink. The sink I really hadn't counted on, Mr. Ward,' she confided. 'I shouldn't have been much disappointed if that hadn't come through.'

'But, Hannah,' accused Paul, with mock piety, 'you always trust everyone, and you made poor Mr. Chalmers sign a paper. How could you?'

'Oh — *that*!' She busied herself for a moment with the bread she was kneading, rolling it furiously. 'Well — you see, we had caught Mr. Chalmers cheating, and it wouldn't be a bit kind to him to encourage him to do it again.'

'Yes, I see that,' laughed Paul. 'You just wanted to protect him against doing himself a bad turn.'

'Yes, sir,' agreed Hannah, diving again into her dough — 'something like that ... and we really did need the new sink,' she added, half to herself, as if she might be entertaining some lingering misgivings on the subject.

'I'll do as you say hereafter,' promised Paul, amused by her flustration. 'You're always right — really you are.'

She straightened, with both fists deep in the dough, and facing him squarely, said, 'I ought to make you sign a paper too. "Hannah is always right."' Her lips were significantly tight, after she had delivered this challenge, though there was a companionable twinkle in her eyes.

He knew what she meant. They had had several brisk arguments recently. About the rug, for instance. It had suddenly occurred to him that the living-room rug was shabby. Without consulting Marcia's taste or Hannah's budget, he had dropped in at a department store and bought an atrociously ugly magenta rug.

'If you don't mind my saying so,' Hannah had remarked, 'you'd be a happier man if you didn't have these buying spells. That rug! First one you saw, I expect. You should have had Mrs. Ward along.'

'I'll not buy anything more, Hannah,' he had promised.

But he did. It wasn't a week before he had appeared in a new gray suit, despite Hannah's injunctions that there mustn't be any further spending that month.

Privately Hannah forgave him for getting the new clothes. They had set back his clock five years. There was also a new red tie and a gray felt hat. He was stunning. So was the bill.

Hannah didn't want to scold, but they were such an improvident pair. Mrs. Ward never bought anything for herself, but she was forever making suggestions for unnecessary expenditures on the table.

'Hannah' — a typical remark — 'we've had breast of lamb three times in the past two weeks. I'm afraid Mr. Ward will tire of it.'

'Sorry,' said Hannah. 'I'll have a pot roast tomorrow.'

'How about a steak?'

'We'll have to wait, Mrs. Ward, until we get squared away. We're running a little behind, this month.'

'Look, Daddy, what a man gave me!' shouted Wallie, from halfway down the stairs. 'And Hannah says I mustn't wear it. Can't I, Daddy? Why can't I?'

Paul reluctantly tugged his eyes away from the mechanism he was working on and said absently, 'What y' got there? Oh — you're a Bull Moose, are you?'

Wallie set the gaudy little cap at a rakish angle and hopped up and down, shouting gleefully, 'I'm a Bulmus! I'm a Bulmus!'

'You're worse than that. You're a pest. Run along now and play.'

'But Hannah says I mustn't wear it.'

'Then do as Hannah says.'

The lad went sniffling up the stairs and for some minutes could be heard shrilly badgering Hannah. Then the racket subsided, indicating that some sort of agreement had been arrived at. The incident really amounted to nothing, but it excited Paul's curiosity to the extent that he presently found himself wanting a drink of water. National politics had never given him much concern, but he had to admit to himself that this was a bit different. There was a good deal of the sporting in it.

'Hannah,' he said, setting down the empty glass on the table where she was at work, 'I gather you're not a Bull Mooser.'

'Just between us, Mr. Ward,' she said in an undertone, 'I think I am. But we're university, you know, and the large majority of the regents are standpatters. I've been reading that in the papers.'

'Well — we've got a right to our private opinions, haven't we?'

'So long as they're private, yes. You can go to the ballot box in November and do whatever you like. But when your little boy romps up and down the street with a campaign cap on, there's nothing very private about that, is there?'

'Don't you believe in a man's having the courage of his convictions?' asked Paul, making elaborate pretense of moral indignation.

'If you have any — yes. But isn't this just a brawl among rival cliques? We may as well keep out of it, don't you think?'

'But, Hannah!' protested Paul, 'you believe in good government.'

'Quite so. But you can't make me believe that anything good can come of organizations that scream at the people and call each other bad names and try to drown out every calm word with a big noise. They're all doing that, which means that they're all wrong. If any one of them was right, it wouldn't have to be done that way.'

Paul seated himself astride a chair and lighted a cigarette, squinting against the smoke.

'You're so nearly always right, Hannah, that I don't like to leave you in this deplorable condition. Suppose a group of people who actually knew their theories of government were right and just, and disliked racket, were to sit with folded hands and permit the noise-makers to run the country anyhow they pleased, would you say that was very patriotic?'

'Well — if you ask *me*, Mr. Ward, I think that word "patriotic" has had a pretty rough time of it. Perhaps you know exactly what it means. I don't. But I do know this: whenever you hear a great lot of noise — bands playing, rockets shooting, and fat men yelling through megaphones, you want to look out, for they're trying to put something over on you. I claim that anybody who really *is* right and honest can live his whole lifetime without ever raising his voice above the tone of ordinary conversation. When the Truth begins to screech and whack the desk with its fist, it always makes me think of Little Red Ridinghood's long-eared grandmother.'

'You may be all wrong this time, Hannah, but you're consistent. I'll say that for you. You're always for non-resistance.'

She knew he was teasing her, but ignored his spoofing and carried on as if their talk was wholly serious.

'I don't like that word,' she said thoughtfully. 'Maybe that's what ails this idea — just the dull title the people have for it. You can't blame them much. Nobody should be expected to take much interest in a kind of power whose name begins with "Non."'

Paul took a turn up and down the little kitchen before replying.

'No matter what you call it, Hannah, the name won't help it. It's a dreadfully silly theory. It might seem to work once in a blue moon, but you'd soon be utterly crushed out if you tried to apply it as a principle in business or politics.'

She parted her lips to answer, but Paul raised a hand and went on — quite seriously now.

'I know, I know — you have a visionary notion that the meek are going to inherit the earth. It's a pretty thought, especially for the people who haven't very much, like you and me. And perhaps it will all come to pass sometime, but not now; somewhere, but not here. It isn't practical.'

Hannah grinned slyly.

'I don't think I'm impractical, Mr. Ward. Or, if I am, someone else had better accuse me of it besides you. Fancy *you* calling *me* impractical!' They both laughed. It wasn't often that Hannah let herself go in this manner. Customarily her remarks to Paul were phrased in terms of the respect due him as her superior. Occasionally they waived the conventions, by common consent, and indulged in some man-to-man talk. Paul quite liked it.

'And I'm not the sort that sees visions, either,' continued Hannah. 'I don't take any stock in such things. But I believe that after all the big noises are over, and the pushers and slappers and pounders have mauled one another to a pulp, the meek will inherit the — whatever is left to inherit. But if this idea of waiting in quietness and hope until the things we really ought to have are put into our hands' — there was a momentary pause during which her gray eyes widened and traveled past him as she tried to attach words to her thoughts — 'if this idea really has the sort of stuff in it to make it win in the long run, I believe it must have enough soundness in it to work pretty well *now* for the people who think it's true. My own experiments with it don't amount to much because I have so little to lose, if it doesn't work for me.'

'Say that last again, Hannah. I didn't get it.'

'I mean — if I had a million, and somebody tried to take it away from me, and I gave in rather than fight, it's natural that I should have more to show for it — if this thing works at all — than I should if someone had stolen my umbrella or my pocketbook which has about nine dollars in it.'

'Hannah — that's the biggest lot of nonsense I ever saw heaped up in one pile.'

'I think most men would feel that way about it,' she admitted. 'It's harder for men to let go of things — property, money. Men think of themselves as successful if they have lots of *things*. Women are always thinking of success as something that makes them admired and liked as *persons*. That's natural. You watch two small children playing at make-believe. Along comes a stylish woman on a thorough-bred horse. The boy says, "That's *mine!*" — meaning the horse; but his little sister says, "That's *me!*" — meaning the lady. And as long as they live, he is always saying "Mine!" and she is saying "Me!" It isn't much wonder if more women than men catch this idea — this idea about ——'

'About personality being more important than property?' suggested Paul, when she seemed to be mired.

'I guess so.' Hannah's brows contracted studiously while the blueberries she was cleaning ran for a moment uninspected through her fingers. 'I don't know that I ever thought about it just that way. But women are always tinkering with their faces, trying to make themselves over into something more beautiful, because it's a woman's self, after all, that she sets the most store by. A man doesn't try to prettify himself very much, or make himself over to look different. He wants to be important for owning something rather than being something.... I'm afraid I'm not saying this very well.... But, seeing that's the way we're made, it must be pretty hard for a man to let go his grip on things. I've often wondered if farmers didn't hate to bury their good corn and wheat in the dirt when it was always a gamble how much they'd get back.'

'Yes' — broke in Paul — 'but that is quite a different matter from letting someone make off with your property because you haven't courage enough to press your rightful claim to it. This soft theory that invites a second slap in the face, and hands over its overcoat to the extortioner who has already taken one's coat — it's really too silly to be talked about seriously by rational people. I'm rather sur-prised that you do it, Hannah. You're so sensible on most matters.'

'Thanks,' said Hannah dryly. 'To be crazy on only one subject isn't such a bad score.... But I object to your say-

ing that the people who hold to this idea haven't any courage. If you ever try it out, you'll find that it's something
the nervous and easily scared had better keep away from.
It calls for a kind of reckless bravery that isn't necessary
in a fight. When you fight there's a lot of excitement, and
even if you're getting the worst of it, you at least can be
hitting back. They say a pestered worm will do that. But
just to sit still and take it, believing that if you do you will
come out of the mess better off than if you had fought —
well, that isn't easy to do. If you want to make fun of it
because it's foolhardy, I shan't contradict you. But if you
say it's cowardly, then I'm afraid you don't understand....
But you'd better let me make this cake.... How's your new
toy coming along today?'

'Oh — not too badly,' sighed Paul, stretching his long
arms to full torsion. 'But I fear that the thing — even if it
does what I want it to do, which isn't any too sure — is
going to make a terrible noise.'

'Can't you box it up so the racket will all stay in the
basement?'

'That's what I'm trying to do. I say' — he added, with
a perplexed scowl — 'what makes you think I expect to
operate this machine in the basement? That's just my
workshop, you know. Because the weather's hot.'

Hannah nodded, winked rather disquietingly, resumed
her dignity, and remarked, 'Well, be that as it may, I
think you've got a good idea there, Mr. Ward.'

It was the first time she had expressed herself seriously
about his mysterious job in the cellar. He paused, en route
to the door, and said, 'You mean that?'

'Of course I do,' replied Hannah confidently. 'I believe
you're going to put it over. I've thought so all along.'

Paul strolled back to the table, his eyes bright with interest in her comment.

'Why didn't you say so?' he demanded almost crossly.
'It would have helped.'

'Partly because it was none of my business,' retorted

Hannah archly, 'but mostly because I thought you'd work better if nobody else messed into it with an opinion.'

'Then why are you telling me now?'

'Because my opinions are no good. You just said that the biggest idea I have is too silly to talk about. So — I can say almost anything now without upsetting you.'

'Now you *are* being silly,' reproved Paul. 'Hannah — if you're right about this little invention of mine, and it succeeds, I'm going to — to ——' He paused to contrive something important enough to be worth a promise.

'You'll then believe me right about the other idea: was that what you were trying to say? Well — I can tell you this much: it will be a whole lot easier for you to invent that new refrigerator ——'

'What's that?' Paul's voice was a guttural growl as he barged into her words. 'How did you know that's what I'm trying to make?'

Hannah touched the tips of her fingers to her puckered lips, and whispered, 'I won't tell anybody.'

'Well — I'll be damned!' he muttered.

'I wouldn't count very much on that if I were you,' commented Hannah judicially. 'The Devil's pretty busy, from all reports, and it isn't likely he has time to make that big a fuss over everybody. But — as I was saying — it will be much easier for you to make this — Psst! — this thing you are making than to understand that it takes more courage to wait and hope for your wishes to come true when almost everybody else is getting what he wants by clawing it out of other people's hands.... Now if you want any blueberry cake, you'd better get out of my way.'

At the door he flung back at her boyishly, 'Hannah — you're a peach!'

'And a nut,' she snapped. 'I guess I must be living a double life.'

Regularly every other Thursday, rain or shine, Hannah left immediately after the breakfast work was finished and did not return until late in the evening. This had been her custom for months, beginning about the time Marcia was up and resuming her usual activities after the arrival of little Sally.

They had made no secret of what Hannah had meant to them during Marcia's absence in the hospital and the longer period of her convalescence at home. Hannah had been everything — cook, nurse, housekeeper, treasurer, purchasing agent, attorney, anchor, propeller, and pilot, all rolled into one. Indeed, it was through those days that she quietly assumed the complete management of the Ward family's affairs, handling them with such ease and skill that they were quite content to permit it. Sometimes they explained again to each other how they had happened to lean so heavily on Hannah, implying that if it hadn't been for Marcia's six weeks off duty they would never have come to rely on their maid for advice about everything.

It never occurred to the Wards to question the woman's right to keep her own counsel in regard to the use she made of these bi-weekly days off, but there was no denying the curiosity they felt. Marcia had ingenuously opened the way for any confidence Hannah might wish to extend, several times elaborately setting up conversational machinery well adapted to this purpose, devices which the intended victim examined with an exasperating leisureliness before turning away. Sometimes, after Hannah had quietly nibbled all the bait off a particularly attractive lure and drifted nonchalantly out of reach, Marcia found herself wondering whether the canny creature might not have laughed about it a little in private. It wasn't always easy to tell, from the expression on Hannah's face, whether she was serious or spoofing.

On the third occasion of her late arrival home after having been gone since early morning, they were still up and reading in the living-room as she passed through.

'Did you have a pleasant day?' asked Marcia, brightly expectant. And Paul had lowered his book as if to say he would be glad to hear all about it.

Hannah had smiled, nodded graciously enough, and said, 'Thanks, Mrs. Ward.... We will be having buckwheat cakes in the morning.'

After that, Marcia quite gave up hinting. It was simply taken for granted that the inexplicable Hannah, who had discouraged all inquiries about her past and this particular feature of her present, would disappear on alternate Thursdays as completely as if the earth had swallowed her up.

She permitted herself no extravagances — had nothing to be extravagant with, indeed — but when spring came Hannah had found a very becoming little hat and had made a light coat on Marcia's machine. They were surprised to see how pretty she was in her new outfit, in striking contrast to her pathetic dowdiness in the old plush coat and the frighteningly ugly hat of the winter. There was something very attractive about Hannah. She was shapely and carried herself with a confident air. The casual passer-by wouldn't have picked her for the rôle in which she was cast. It would be natural enough if, on these unexplained excursions, she met some man friend. Marcia often wondered if this were not so, out of her imagination fabricating long stories which never had a very happy ending, for they couldn't spare Hannah now, even to serve the interests of a delayed romance.

Once, when a kitchen conversation had drifted into the vicinity of matrimony in general, Marcia had said, half playfully, but alert to the effect of it, 'You'll be married yourself, some day, Hannah' — which earned the non-committal rejoinder, 'Think so, Mrs. Ward?' — after which the talk suddenly veered off in another direction.

The fact was that Hannah, in that brief pause before replying, had impulsively considered saying, 'What makes you think I haven't been married?' But that would inevitably have demanded the telling of her story. There was nothing discreditable about it, but it was painful to remember. And Hannah was not in the market for pity. Sometimes she entertained misgivings over her own calm indifference to Marcia's friendly curiosity. Perhaps, if an occasion had invited it, she might have been able to tell Paul. He would have said, 'That's tough, Hannah' — after which he would appear to have forgotten all about it. But Marcia would be bringing it up and wishing something might be done about it.

So — Hannah's days off remained a mystery and after a few months all inquisitiveness on the subject subsided. If she didn't want to tell them where she went, surely it was her right to keep her affairs a secret.

Only once had there been any variation of her routine. Late one Thursday night in August she had called up to say it would be difficult for her to return until Sunday. She offered no explanations either then or afterward. On Sunday night, Paul decided, rather impulsively, to take the ten-forty that night for Chicago and spend the next day in the refrigeration department at Armour's.

When the train thundered in, screeching to an impatient stop, Paul walked past the day coaches toward his Pullman. Among the disembarking passengers he recognized Hannah. It was quite plain that she had been crying, for her eyes were red and swollen. It was dismaying, almost frightening, to see the well-poised Hannah in this state. She seemed on the point of hurrying away, though their eyes had met. Apparently thinking better of it, she paused, nodded, and tried a not very successful smile.

'Why, Hannah!' he exclaimed. 'You've been out of town?'

'Yes, sir.' She made a valiant effort to steady her voice.

He studied her face anxiously for an instant and she averted her swimming eyes. Impetuously taking her arm, he said, 'Hannah — is there anything I can do?'

She shook her head, gratefully pressed her fingers against the hand he had laid on her arm, and murmured, 'Thank you, Mr. Ward.'

'B-o-a-r-d!' shouted a trainman.

'I'm awfully sorry, Hannah.'

'Yes, sir — I know. Good night, Mr. Ward.'

Chapter IV

MARCIA experienced no disappointment and expressed no surprise when Paul bluntly announced, late one Sunday night in November, that he was now definitely done with mechanical inventions; that he would never again — so help him — fritter away precious time trying to do something for which he had neither training nor talent; that he wasn't cut out for any such business and had been a blithering idiot ever to have thought he was.

Having long since arrived at this conclusion herself, Marcia drew a discreetly inaudible sigh of satisfaction and privately hoped her husband might remain faithful to this resolve, though her relief was disturbingly conditioned by the mounting threat that Paul already bore in his bonnet the larva for another bee which might turn out to be as time-destroying and unproductive as any of its futile predecessors. The signs were unmistakable. During his hours at home he was restless, remotely inattentive, moody, sure symptoms that the embryonic idea — whatever it was — had passed through most of its metamorphoses and could be counted upon to begin buzzing at almost any time now.

It was clear that the decision he had just declared was in response both to a push and a pull. As for the push, he had made no substantial progress on his affair in the basement for all of two months, in spite of the fact that he had doggedly continued to spend his days there almost to the very moment of the university's reopening in mid-September.

His zeal had gradually ebbed as the momentum previously generated by his ecstatic hope declined through the successive stages of a katabasis which had reduced it from the stratosphere of hysterical hallelujahs to the more modest level of sanguine expectation, after which it had stepped down through a period of mere wistful hankering to fretful day-dreams featuring the prospect of some accidental discovery — popping up out of nowhere — to reward his patient toil. But no miraculous discovery had popped. No amiable angel had suggested a gas at once noninflammable and non-poisonous which might be used in the compressor, and no fairy's wand had pointed to an airtight joint between a stationary and a moving part in the machine that now lay neglected on his workbench.

As for the pull, a distraction had arrived in the form of an unexpected invitation to read a paper at the first monthly round-up of the University Club. It pleased Paul to have been thus honored. Seeing he was chiefly concerned vocationally with the life and works of the late (or early, rather) Edmund Spenser — for had he not won his doctorate at Columbia with a thesis on 'The Shepheardes Calender'? — it was natural that he should turn to his authentic trade for the makings of this important speech.

The assignment to display one's wit and wisdom before the bored and brittle membership of the University Club was always taken very seriously, not only by the younger fry on the faculty who hoped to win the favorable attention of their critical overlords, but by these grizzled oldsters themselves who, though they were practically guaranteed a glutton's helping of applause because of their influential seniority, nevertheless considered these exacting occasions worth an extra effort and prepared for them with a cleverness and cunning out of all proportion to their activities in the classroom where it was considered unprofessional to be interesting.

Indeed, this sentiment which exalted the dignity of dullness was so generally accepted that any sparkling pedagogue whose lectures proved entertaining enough to require the migration of his classes to a more spacious hall was

covertly referred to as 'a boundah.' On all other words
containing *r*, the faculty — mostly Western-tongued —
bore down on this guttural with the savagery of a bulldog
disturbed at his dinner, but when any one of them classified
an ambitious colleague whose happy *bons mots* had won
acclaim on the campus, it was customary to call him 'a
boundah,' probably out of respect for the word's more
frequent British usage. And it was to ensure against being
reviled with the unpleasant designation which lacked an *r*
that many a professor, who might have enjoyed the exercise of an adroit and piquant wit, abstained from it in his
classroom as he avoided oysters in months similarly distinguished.

This inhibition made it all the more imperative that when
a faculty man was invited to speak before his peers at the
University Club, where he was at liberty to let himself go
in the indulgence of button-popping persiflage, he must take
pains to do a good job. It was just as important for him to
be funny on such occasions as to be unfunny while engaged
in quenching the undergraduate thirst for knowledge. Well-
to-do alumni, booked as sacrificial victims to the endow-
ment fund or the projected stadium, were sometimes asked
to attend these functions; and, recalling with what glassy
eyes and distended throats they had swallowed one pro-
digious yawn after another while lounging in their chairs
utterly stupefied by the apathetic mumble of these learned
men, were now amazed that so much effulgence could be
radiated from stars commonly supposed by them to be
extinct.

Sensitive to the peculiar nature of his task, Paul had
turned to the composition of his essay with a concentration
that had driven what was left of his hope for the home
manufacture of ice into an eclipse not only total, but probably permanent. He enjoyed banter and relished repartee,
but it had not previously occurred to him in digging up the
bones of Spenser that he might strike a mine of merriment.
It was a new and stimulating sensation. Night after night

he sat at Marcia's desk in the living-room, chuckling over
neatly tipped-up phrases which, he felt, should be good for
a genial haw-haw. Occasionally he broke forth into open
laughter at some delicious bit which might even evoke an
appreciative hear-hear! He imagined he heard the eminent
satirist Wembel condescending to say, after adjournment,
'That was jolly good, Ward. You'll be doing a book on
Spenser, sometime. Put me down for one.'

Tonight, having sat for some minutes meditatively tapping his front teeth with the top of his pen, Paul slowly
pushed back his chair, regarded Marcia as an object of
great interest and, clearing his throat, solemnly abjured
invention — his recent invention in particular and all inventions in general. It wasn't his job. He would never
attempt it again.

'I can't say I blame you much, dear, for deciding to give
it up. After all, you could hardly have expected ——' Marcia had tried to put just the right degree of approval into
her remarks, knowing that if she joined too heartily in his
own pooh-poohing of his experiments he was likely to attempt a defense of them. And fearing she had already
begun a comment which might involve her in an argument,
she dropped it suddenly, en route, as being a bit too hot to
hold, and gave herself to a diligent recovery of a lost stitch
in the sweater she was knitting for Wallie.

'Do you know — Marcia ——' Paul rose, thrust his
hands deep into the pockets of his smoking-jacket, and
leaned against the mantel. 'You know ——' he repeated
dreamily. Marcia could see it coming — the new idea! It
was galloping toward her with harness a-jingle and hoofs
a-pounding and red nostrils distended. Always when Paul
was about to plunge into some fresh adventure, he thus
gave her due notice. With the unfocused, opalescent eye
of the enraptured he would begin — after an impressive
pause, 'Do you know — Marcia ——'

'Marcia — something tells me there's a great chance
here for a biographical novel. Nobody has ever done a

Spenser for popular consumption. I doubt if more than one out of a hundred know who he was.'

'One out of a hundred what?' inquired Marcia, unwilling to assist in the reckless inflation of his already turgid bubble. 'College professors, maybe?'

'There really could be made of it,' he soliloquized, disregarding her query, 'a great story.'

'But don't you have to presuppose a certain amount of general interest before you can hope to popularize a character? I should think a book on Spenser frankly intended for literary workers might do better.'

'Now that's where you're wrong, Marcia.' Paul was kind, but unbudgable. 'You've always insisted that I should stick to my job as a teacher and try to make something big out of that. It can't be done. Suppose I keep on doing what I'm doing. Suppose I do it a little better every year. When I'm fifty my salary will have been increased by a few hundreds; granted. But Marcia, darling, there's so much we want to do that can never be done unless I make some money — much more money than my position will ever provide.'

'I know, dear,' sympathized Marcia gently, 'and I want you to, of course.'

'So we can travel.... By the way' — he chuckled a little to signify that this needn't be taken too seriously, but his eyes showed he could easily be serious enough about it if given the slightest encouragement — 'I stopped in at the railroad station today and picked up some cruise literature.'

'Paul! How silly!' laughed Marcia. 'Fancy us planning a cruise.'

'I don't know that it's so silly,' he said half-petulantly. 'It certainly can't do any harm to talk about it. We've just got to do it, some day!'

Marcia unfolded the gaudy advertising and studied the pictures of familiar European scenes.

'It would be wonderful if we could, Paul,' she agreed softly. 'I do hope, for your sake, that we're able to. You've always been so keen on it.'

He reloaded his pipe and paced up and down the room for a while, quite lost in his dreams.

'Do you know — Marcia' — he paused to say impressively — 'if I can get this thing done by the middle of May — and I don't see why not, for I have all the stuff in hand with practically no research to do — the book might be accepted for publication within a month ——'

'Oh — do you think they would bring it out that soon?'

'I said "accepted,"' explained Paul, waving his pipe impatiently. 'As soon as it's accepted, we should be entirely justified in raising some cash on the strength of what would be coming to us, or perhaps they might make me a liberal advance. I understand that's done, sometimes, if the book is sure-fire. Well — if that came to pass, we could ——' He broke off to do a little mental arithmetic. 'Let's see. We should know by the middle of June. We could have made our boat reservations. Then we could plan to sail early in July for at least a two-months' trip. Hannah would look after the children. You know that. I'll show you. Look — sail to Southampton, up to London same day. Think what all it would mean to me; literary shrines in London, Stratford, Oxford. Think what it would mean to me to be able to ramble about in old East Smithfield — where Spenser was born, you know, and of course we should want to see Cambridge where he went to school. Think of it, Marcia, three centuries and a half ago!... It would certainly do me a lot of good in my work,' he added, hopeful that this practical feature of the trip might stimulate Marcia's interest to the point where she would forget to be prudent.

'Well — you write your book, dear,' she said, in the tone she used when recommending spinach to Roberta, 'and you know I'll be glad enough to take the trip with you. I'll keep the house as quiet as I can while you're working.'

'That's the way to talk! We'll plan on it! Dream of a lifetime! You better have a little chat with Hannah. Tell her what we're going to do.'

'There'll be plenty of time for that, dear. Let's make a little secret of it — and not tell anybody.'

'I don't believe you're as confident as I am,' said Paul, a bit disappointed. 'You've got to have a will to make things happen. That's the way to succeed.'

'Sounds like Hannah,' observed Marcia, amused.

'Well — you notice that Hannah generally gets what she wants. You tell her what we have in mind, and see if she doesn't think it a good idea.'

It was not a good idea, at all. Flushed with plaudits — for the speech at the University Club was a distinct success — Paul gave himself to the new book with a devotion that deserved a high reward. Impatient to take off a trial balance on his account with fame and fortune, he asked permission of a publisher to send on the first half of his work (that was about the middle of February) and having had a favorable response he posted the manuscript, after which it was difficult to write, his nervous eagerness for a reply from the East having distracted his attention. In this pitiful state of anxiety he waited for six weeks, at first regarding the postman as an angel of light who would one day bring him a certificate to the new freedom, but eventually coming to consider the chap as a venomously unscrupulous churl.

One day a letter came, on April first it was, as if to add a neat touch of derision to the casual unconcern with which the publisher doubted whether a work of this sort could expect to be commercially practical.

It was a heavy blow, and Paul was in poor condition to meet it, for his wanton day-dreaming over the favorable reply he had so blandly anticipated had already dulled his capacity for earnest work. Marcia had sensed this danger, one day saying to him, playfully, but with conviction, 'You'd better stop spending that money now — and carry on with the book.'

Unable to reconcile himself to the catastrophe, he girded

up his loins after a week of heavy sulking, revised the early part of his manuscript and sent it off again to another publisher. It was easy enough to understand how the judgment of one house might not coincide with another. Had not *Ben-Hur* knocked about the country for a whole year before it found a firm far-sighted enough to appreciate its merit?

The next rejection was more prompt and more briefly stated. They were grateful for his courtesy in wanting them to see his book, but it did not fit into their publication program.

After that, the manuscript journeyed to three more publishers, the last of whom replied, 'We have examined so much of the work as you have sent us ——' Ah — perhaps that was the trouble, thought Paul. They didn't want to pass on a mere fragment of a book. He would complete it!

And he did complete it by working zealously all summer, autumn, and into early winter. It was sent the rounds of the front-rank publishers. Not until the next May did Paul decide that he had added another failure to the rather formidable array of defeats which had terminated the various projects of recent years. He did not trust himself to talk much about it to Marcia; and she, aware how deep was his hurt, and herself devastated with pity for him, tried to beguile his attention from this latest and most painful of his disillusions.

Foster, who had charge of the University Extension lectures, asked him one day if he would like to go out, occasionally, to near-by towns for evening addresses. There was a small fee attached to these excursions — averaging about twenty dollars. Paul assented, and in February he was sent out twice, once to Milburn and again to Deshler, where he was quite royally entertained and his lectures were handsomely received, especially in Deshler, the local paper covering his appearance with a flattering column that put more lime in his spine than anything that had ever happened to him. Marcia was rejoiced at his expansive

mood. That night, after he had read the account of his
triumph at Deshler for the dozenth time (he had not realized until now to what extent he had covered himself with
glory on that occasion), he sat gazing at the ceiling for a
long time, and then, in the awed huskiness of one making
an astounding discovery, he said, 'Do you know — Marcia ——'

She put down *The Woman Thou Gavest Me*, which everybody was talking about, and gave him her full attention,
thinking she knew what was on his mind. 'Yes, dear,' she
said invitingly.

'Marcia — do you know there's a lot of money to be
made by lecturing for the chautauquas? I've had a little
taste of it now and I know I could do it. I mean to ask
Foster tomorrow how one breaks into this game. They
can't very well pay you less than fifty dollars a day and you
are booked for a five-day week all summer.' He scribbled
some figures on the back of an envelope. 'There would be
probably eight weeks of it. Expenses very small. Country
towns mostly. Short jumps. Not much paid out for travel.
Ought to net fifteen–sixteen hundred dollars. Put it away
in the savings bank and the interest on eight months would
be — let's see — forty-two dollars more.'

In spite of her resolution to see this through with comradely seriousness, Marcia grinned.

'Well — every little helps, doesn't it? That forty-two
dollars would be just as good to us as to anybody. It would
come nearly staking us to a week's board and lodging in
London, if we thought we had to be frugal. I'm going in for
it, darling. Here's one thing I know I can do — for I've
done it! I'm going on the lecture platform.' He pursed his
mouth and grew confidential, lowering his tone as against
possible eavesdropping. 'And some of those boys get fees
running into big figures, after they've been properly pub-
licized. It might turn out to be a great thing for us.'

But it didn't, Foster explaining that a man had to bring,
even to so unexacting an institution as the chautauqua

circuit, a platform reputation of more ample dimensions than Paul could boast. He said it kindly enough and promised to give his ambitious colleague some more extension dates next winter. By the time winter had come, however, all Europe was in the grip of war and there was not much of a market for lectures on the life and times and works of Edmund Spenser or anyone else with whose history Paul was conversant.

He did not confide the stories of his successive misadventures to Hannah, but she knew without being told that he had been ruthlessly victimized by his own enthusiasms. Her heart ached for him. She wasn't quite sure whether she suffered more in his behalf when he was deep in the doldrums of despair or during the hilarious periods when he was rigging up the machinery for the production of his assorted tragedies; for it was obvious that the higher he flew his various kites, the more painful was his chagrin when they came careening down, a handful of broken sticks.

Paul's state of mind in respect to the almost incredible disaster in Europe puzzled Hannah. He had always seemed so eager to go over there and see for himself the tombs and shrines and monuments which represented the best things we ourselves had fallen heir to — laws, letters, manners, arts, ideals. To hear him talk you would have thought that nothing we had ever accomplished over here was worth comparison to the greatness and glory of the achievements across the sea. The war somehow didn't take hold of him. True, he was interested in the newspapers. And he had pinned up a map on the living-room wall with a row of brass tacks across it to indicate the long crooked line of battle. Every day he moved the tacks, seeming much gratified when the side he thought he was cheering for had made a little indentation. But that was about as far as his interest seemed to go. The war was just a row of brass-headed tacks making ugly holes in the plaster.

'Awful! Isn't it?' he would say. But the tone of it was

about the same as it would have been if someone had remarked that it was a mighty hot day.

To Hannah, through those tragic years, the world was smashing up everything that was good. It was of no satisfaction to her when reports came of victories for the Allies. What mattered it which side had shed more blood in yesterday's 'big push'?

'Cheer up, Hannah!' Paul would say. 'We're making some good gains now.'

'No good gains ever came that way, Mr. Ward,' she would reply sadly. 'They're all wrong. They'll all lose. There will be no gains for anybody.'

Sometimes Hannah wondered — reproaching herself for this thought — whether the dear chap wasn't unconsciously getting a certain satisfaction out of it all. He had made such a muddle of his own affairs and had been so depressed over his defeats that the exciting reports of other people's more serious difficulties had diminished the gravity of his own. It was not that he took any pleasure in the war; rather that the war had made his little losses insignificant. He didn't fret now about being poor. The daily stories of starvation in Belgium had made his own food more appreciated. Perhaps he would have been indignant if anyone had said as much to him. One evening at dinner Wallie — nine now — had helped himself to a larger ration of candied sweet potatoes than he could use, and his father said, 'Some small boy in Belgium would probably be glad to have what you've left there, Wallie,' to which the child replied, after a moment's thought, 'But if I had eaten it, then he wouldn't have it either, would he?' Paul laughed. And Marcia laughed. It made Hannah sick that they could laugh at that — or anything. On his birthday, they gave Wallie an air-gun. He proudly showed it to Hannah. She closed her eyes tightly, shook her head, and with a blindly groping gesture motioned him away.

'But Daddy gave it to me,' explained Wallie, quite hurt.

'I don't like guns,' said Hannah.

'This is only an air-gun.'
'Could you kill anything with it?'
'Birds, maybe, or a squirrel.'
'Then I don't like air-guns.'

As the months passed, all mention of the war was scrupulously avoided in Hannah's presence. She was so unhappy that her sorrow seemed to permeate the whole establishment. In midsummer of '16 Paul suggested to Marcia that it was time their faithful Hannah had a little vacation. They would send her to the country for a week. It was obvious she needed a bit of relief from the long-continued devotion to her job. Incidentally, he remarked, it would be good for all of them. Pretending gratitude, Hannah had gone, half aware that the Wards would also be taking a vacation in her absence. She resolved to control her feelings, realizing that she had been at fault in permitting the gloominess of her heart to shadow their house. On her return, she seemed almost cheerful.

'That's exactly what she needed,' said Paul. 'She had stuck too close to it here. We must insist on her taking a little more time off.' And having expressed this belief to Marcia he went to the kitchen where Hannah was ironing, and repeated it — in altered phrasing — to her.

'Yes, sir,' she agreed pleasantly, 'a change of — of scenery is good for everybody. You can work at one thing too long. I was just thinking today about your — about what you were working on in the basement for many weeks.'

'I certainly did waste a great lot of time on that thing,' he grumbled with sour distaste for the subject.

'Well — of course that's up to you,' she murmured without looking up from her work.

'Up to me?'

'Yes — whether it was wasted time or not. You've had a good rest now. If you go at it again, fresh like, you might succeed. And then the time you have spent on it wouldn't be wasted. Isn't that so? I mean, it isn't decided yet whether you wasted your time. If you finished the job, everything you did on it before would have been time well spent. . . . Of course,' she added ruefully, 'as the matter stands now, you did waste a lot of time — and a lot of yourself, too.'

'Myself?'

'Yes. A disappointment like that is pretty bad for a person, don't you think? That is, if he doesn't make some good use of it.'

'Good use of a disappointment?' Paul sat down on the edge of a chair and lighted a cigarette. 'I can't see what use you could make of a disappointment. If you can, I'd be glad to hear about it. I've had a plenty.'

'Well — a disappointment,' ventured Hannah, feeling her way, cautiously, conscious of his half-derisive grin — 'sometimes a disappointment closes a door in a person's face, and then he looks about for some other door, and opens it, and gets something better than he had been hunting for the first time.'

'I tried several,' said Paul glumly. 'I think I tried 'em all.'

'I know.' Hannah reinforced her remembrance with a half-dozen quick little consolatory nods. 'I know you did, Mr. Ward.' Her voice lowered until it was barely more than a whisper. 'I could have cried for you. I think I did, sometimes.'

'Oh — well ——' He affected a jaunty tone that dismissed his many failures *en bloc*. 'I tried some things that weren't in my line. This one — for instance,' jerking his head toward the despicable refrigerator. 'I had no training for it. Involved a lot of chemistry. I didn't know enough — though I really did do three years of it in college. But it wasn't sufficient for this job.'

'That's one reason I always thought you might be able to do it,' remarked Hannah irrationally. 'I hoped maybe it was going to be handed to you, like. Sort of a gift from — from the outside.'

'Outside?' echoed Paul, screwing up his face.

'Yes.' Hannah ironed industriously for some minutes and then admitted, rather flustered, that it was of course 'a funny way to say it' — Paul continuing to regard her with a puzzled gaze that she found quite embarrassing.

'I know you don't believe in such things,' she went on diffidently. 'The other day — at my friend's house where I spent my vacation — she has a large library, left her by her husband — I was reading about the discovery of — of the law of — of ——' Finding herself bogged, Hannah tipped the iron up on end, rested both outspread hands on the table, intently searching Paul's eyes for assistance. 'You know. About the peas — so many white and so many yellow and so many tall and so many dwarfs ——'

'Oh — you mean the law of heredity — the Mendelian scheme for figuring out the results of scientific mating.'

'Yes — something like that. Well — do you know that this Mr. Mendel was a monk who found out all about it in his little garden in the monastery. He'd never been trained to be a scientist.'

'I see what you're driving at now, Hannah,' laughed Paul. 'Mendel was illuminated; is that it? Had a vision from on High, or something of the sort; is that what you mean? Well — why shouldn't he, being a monk? If Heaven doesn't look after the monks ——' Noting from the hurt look in her eyes that his teasing was ill-timed, he broke off and mumbled an apology.

'The book told about another case,' proceeded Hannah, apparently uninjured. 'There was a man named Michael Faraday.'

'Famous English chemist — I know — invented the dynamo, too; didn't he? Well — did he get his from the — from the "outside"?' Paul had resolved not to do any more spoofing, but the temptation was too strong. He grinned and waited for Hannah's rejoinder.

'I don't know,' she replied seriously. 'His father wanted him to be a blacksmith, but he didn't like it and got a job as a bookbinder. Maybe that is a good way to train for discovering a dynamo, but it doesn't sound as if it was. And he wasn't a monk. But the book said he did believe that there was something *outside*.'

'I'm afraid I'll never get anything that way,' said Paul, suppressing a yawn. 'That's out of my line, too.... So — young lady — that's what you were doing on your vacation, eh? Here we send you away for some fresh air and a little playtime, and you sneak off into a corner to post yourself on the Mendelian theory of genetics and the early life of Faraday. Well — you'll never cease being a surprise to me, Hannah.'

'That wasn't all I found out, Mr. Ward.' She smiled cryptically as to say she had a super-secret which might have to be tortured out of her. 'I had whole days — and nights, too — for reading, and the shelves were full of books on chemistry. I heard you say, one time, that you had to find a gas that wouldn't poison anybody and wouldn't take fire, and I just kept leafing through those books until I found one. I really did,' she added confidentially. 'You may think it was silly for me to be looking — me not knowing a blessed thing about it — but ——'

Paul was touched.

'No,' he muttered, 'I don't think it was silly. I think it was splendid of you, Hannah. I don't deserve that kind of fidelity. It was a wonderful thing for you to do for me. I can't tell you just how I feel about it. You are certainly a good friend.'

There was a long pause in their talk. Then he rose, patted Hannah on the shoulder, and walked toward the door.

'Don't you want to know,' asked Hannah, 'what I found?'

'Well — you see ——' Paul fumbled for words that wouldn't hurt too much. 'You see, Hannah, it wasn't just finding a gas that wouldn't poison anyone and wasn't inflammable. I expect there are a hundred gases like that. There's a lot more to it, my dear, than you thought. But I do honestly appreciate your trying. It was mighty fine of you.'

Hannah drew a slip of paper from the pocket of her apron and handed it to him. 'There's the name of it,' she said, with a little sigh. 'It may be no good, but the book said it was not poisonous and wouldn't burn — and there's something else about it that I copied there. I didn't understand, but I thought you would.'

Indulgently Paul took the crumpled paper and read, 'Sulphur dioxide . . . not corrosive on copper or iron.' Then he stood for a long time flicking the paper against his thumb, his eyes narrowing. He walked to the window and stood looking out, drumming with his fingers against the casement. After a while he turned and said, 'Were you talking to anybody about this, Hannah?'

She shook her head and continued ironing.

'You know I wouldn't have done that, Mr. Ward,' she said.

'And you don't know anything about chemistry, at all?'

'No, Mr. Ward. Of course not. How could I?'

'You just accidentally stumbled onto this while leafing through a textbook you found in somebody's library?'

'Yes, Mr. Ward.'

'Well, by God, I believe *you* have been getting hunches from the "outside"! I don't see how it could be explained any other way.' In the doorway he paused, regarded her with serious scrutiny for a moment, and said, 'Now let's get this straight, Hannah. You were simply browsing around among these books, and ——'

'Yes, sir. It's just as I told you. I don't think it was an accident. I was really hunting for it, you know. Do you believe,' she asked wistfully, 'that perhaps I found something?'

'Either that — or, as you say, you were *handed* something.'

Hannah nodded, her eyes shining.

'I would much rather you thought that, Mr. Ward.'

Chapter V

WHEN it was nearing time for Peter to start to the public school kindergarten — he would be five in November — the two women he erroneously believed to be his mother and his aunt debated for an hour one afternoon in latter August what name he should bear.

The discussion was entirely amicable, as befitted the talk of intimate friends, and was carried on in prudent undertones because the object of their interest was playing in his small tent only a few feet from where they sat, slowly swaying in the garden swing, shaded by a thick mesh of maple.

This question had not been at issue before. The child had never needed any other name than Peter. Lydia could not recall that he had ever inquired. But it was imperative now that the boy should be specifically identified. Whatever name he carried to school would be permanent. A mistake at this juncture might be regretted in the days to come.

Of course the easiest way to handle the problem (and the way they did handle it when the time came) was to enroll the little chap as Peter Edmunds. It would spare them a lot of explaining. So far as the neighbors knew, Peter was the only child of Mrs. Lydia Edmunds, who had lately bought the old Conklin home at the corner of Birch and Lincoln. There wasn't a birch within two hundred miles, but the memorabilia of Lincoln were everywhere about.

It was nearly four years since Mrs. Edmunds had acquired the stately house whose white columns and broad verandas gave the place an air of dignity and self-assurance, which even the nervous fussiness of a busy scroll-saw had been unable to dispute.

In almost any midwestern town a four years' residence would be ample to establish a well-behaved citizen's solid position in the esteem of the neighbors, but there were about five blocks on Lincoln Avenue where one might live for a decade and still be considered a newcomer.

Lydia had grinned and written back to Carrie in Virginia, 'If you've a notion it is easy to make friends out here in the corn belt, I suggest you come to Waterloo and try slapping a few backs on Lincoln Avenue.' Not that Lydia resented the exclusiveness of her neighbors, for she was not much of a back-slapper herself.

Waterloo knew nothing about Mrs. Edmunds except that she was a comely and prudent widow in her early forties who paid cash, drove her own small car, grew expensive dahlias, repainted the green shutters and white portico pillars of her solemn brick house every spring, attended the diminutive Episcopal Church on Sunday mornings, and effortlessly minded her own business. She carried a respectable balance in her current and savings accounts at the Citizens National Bank and maintained a safety deposit box there which she occasionally visited. Mr. Jennings, the president, had negotiated the purchase of conservative bonds for her on a few occasions, and Mrs. Jennings had called in company with Mrs. Morris, the doctor's wife. And several other ladies of excellent social rating had come to see her, though their calls usually turned out to be errands of solicitation for various philanthropic projects in the town.

But Lydia was not lonely. The standoffishness of Lincoln Avenue did not worry her. The days were well filled with the care of her little boy, her flower-garden, and the upkeep of the old brick house, where the famous Senator Conklin had lived up to his distinction and a little beyond his means, leaving at eighty a maiden daughter to whose insolence the bank and the merchants were lenient while she quietly went to seed, considerately passing away before their patience had been overtaxed.

Lydia had never bothered to explain to any of her new

acquaintances in Waterloo that little Peter was not of her own flesh and blood. A few casual friends in Rattoon, two hours away by train, could have recalled the circumstances of the child's acceptance into the Edmunds home, remembering Mrs. Edmunds's grave illness when her own baby had died at birth, and her return from the University Hospital, thirty miles distant, with an infant obviously intended for adoption.

The fact that this baby had not been adopted by Mr. and Mrs. Edmunds would have been of little interest to anyone in Rattoon. The Edmundses had not lived there long enough for their domestic affairs to stir very much curiosity. Jasper Edmunds, as a competent chemical engineer, had been employed on many widely spaced projects. The few immobile relatives they had left in Virginia and New Jersey were not in close contact with the migratory Jasper and Lydia. Except for infrequent and increasingly sketchy letters from Lydia, now in Nevada, now in Guatemala, Oregon, Brazil, Wyoming — all equally remote in the provincial mind of her sister Carrie and her brother Henry and the smug little huddle of stiff-corseted cousins — the Edmunds pair were remembered back home much as they are recalled who are not expected to return at all.

So when Jasper Edmunds, the ungregarious, had been suddenly snuffed out in a laboratory explosion, shortly after coming onto the chemical engineering staff at the big glass works in Rattoon, there were very few to be inquisitive about the future plans of his widow when she departed a month later for Waterloo.

The three women who for humanity's sake as well as the sheer look of it had expressed an interest in her, as they sat on the edge of their chairs in the funerary reek of fading roses which Lydia hadn't wanted to throw away, were told that she thought of moving to some quiet residential community where the taxes were low and a desirable house might be had at a bargain. The trio of glass wives — Alicia Colton, Maude Frazer, and Ella Osborne, whose husbands were

respectively Sales, Purchasing, and Publicity — consoled
Lydia the best they could, deeming her lucky to have been
left so securely provided for, the rumor having drifted about
that Jasper had carried a sizable life insurance. And while
no one of them directly mentioned the fact that the manner
of the taciturn chemist's departure had doubled the insurance his widow would have received in the event of his having died less newsworthily, Mrs. Osborne remarked that it
was certainly better, if a person's time had come, for him to
be spared the tedium of a protracted illness.

Maude and Alicia, a bit shocked by this bland confession
of Ella's envy (Fred Osborne had been living at his club for
months), hastily rectified her covetous comment by conceding that it was a serious blow, nevertheless, to have a
loved one take himself off with such dispatch. But it was
easy to see that the general consensus was that Lydia might
have met any number of calamities more severe than the in-
voluntary exchange of the stolid and uncommunicative
Jasper for one hundred and fifty thousand dollars in cash.
Whereupon the cloying scent of *Ce Soir ou Jamais* that
always tagged along after Ella gradually disentangled itself
from the withering roses that remained to certify to Jasper's
recent decease, and Lydia returned to the hot closets (it was
August) to prepare for the Salvation Army in its quest of
cast-off clothing.

In becoming black but not in weeds the widow drove to
Waterloo, with little Peter beside her on his knees reporting
the progress of the big moving-vans careening along behind
them, their husky crews still reekingly wet from handling
the huge boxes of books; for Lydia had resolved not to part
with Jasper's professional library, a quite magnanimous
decision when one reflected that it had occupied much more
of his time and thought than had Lydia herself. And after
that Rattoon, a nervous and noisy town of rapidly shifting
population, quickly resumed its former contour almost as if
the Edmundses had never lived there at all.

It is possible that Lydia might have returned to her

ancestral home in Virginia, where Carrie lived in the old house and Henry dwelt hard by. She had thought of it just a little, until her brother had insisted upon it with an urgency out of all proportion to his normal interest in her welfare. Henry's suggestion that he might be of some assistance in the prudent investment of her considerable windfall brought Lydia to a prompt decision. But the chief reason for her wanting to remain in the general vicinity of the university town was her attachment to an all-but-indispensable friend she had found during her convalescence at the University Hospital. In Waterloo, she would be close enough to her friend for frequent meetings.

Anybody but Lydia herself might have thought that she and her new comrade were miles apart socially, but in respect to congeniality they might have been sisters. Lydia was the elder by three years, appearing older than that, for her hair had turned quite gray. It was an unusual friendship, not only because of their mutual affection but because Lydia's cherished friend was little Peter's mother.

'Of course the time might come,' conceded Lydia, guarding her voice, 'when he would prefer to be known by his rightful name, though I can't think of any possible advantage it could ever be to him. It isn't likely,' she went on, a bit reluctantly — for her remark was going to be painful — 'it isn't likely that Peter will lose any property by not being a Bradford, now that his father has another wife. You've never pressed a claim for yourself or the boy, and by the time Peter is old enough to do it on his own account ——'

'But he wouldn't!'

'I know, dear. I was just thinking of the possibilities, not the probabilities.'

Lonely for their attention, Peter came toward them, dragging his little red cart filled with sand.

'Don't spill it on the grass, son,' said Lydia gently. 'Take it over there closer to the box. That's a good boy.'

'But I don't want you to talk any more,' he remonstrated, wrinkling up his freckled face into a lugubrious expression of outraged patience. 'Why can't Aunt Hannah come and play with me? You said you would, an awful long time ago.'

Lydia watched them with brooding affection, Hannah sitting on the grass with a shapely arm hooked over the board that boxed the sandpile on three sides, listening attentively to her child's chatter about the plight of a beleagured party of wooden clothespins who were hiding in a cave fearful of an attack from the formidable bandit-troupe of chess pieces, four of whom were mounted and ready to go into action.

'I do wish,' remarked Hannah over her shoulder, 'that Peter would play at something besides battles.'

'You don't want him to be a sissy, do you?' murmured Lydia, adding, with sly satisfaction, 'not that there's much danger of it, the little ruffian.'

While they played, Lydia, bending over her needlework, drifted into the favored reminiscence which so often occupied her mind, living over again the days when she had first met Hannah — because of Peter.

'Look, Mrs. Edmunds,' the nurse was saying. 'Isn't he cunning?' Lydia had been sitting apathetically in the hospital solarium, her inert hands empty as her cloudy eyes, not caring much whether she lived or died. In response to the girl's voice she had looked up, slowly. Had she been asked if she wanted to see a pretty baby she would have shaken her head. Baby? After having lost her own, less than a month ago? Certainly not. But here was the tiny fellow at arm's reach.

'I've an errand on this floor,' said the nurse. 'Want to hold him until I come back?' Without waiting for consent, she had deposited the warm little bundle in Lydia's lap. 'This,' she announced, affecting a formal introduction, 'is Master Peter Parmalee Bradford, whose mother isn't quite ready to take charge of him and whose other parent is — is out of town.'

'So they weren't married, then,' Lydia couldn't help saying. She had always considered it desirable for a child's existence to be properly authorized by the state.

'Oh, yes. Parentage all straight. I saw the certificate. The mother is darling. I suppose she picked a lemon ... Isn't he the best looking little thing you ever saw?'

Next day Lydia had asked to see Peter's mother, and Hannah came, on her first day off, straightforward, sincere, sensible, gratified that her baby's welfare was assured. As soon as she was earning anything she would pay what she could toward the child's care, hopeful of reclaiming him when her circumstances permitted. Lydia liked her honesty. It was pleasant now to recall those days when the doctors and nurses were amazed over their difficult patient's rapid recovery.

Then came Hannah's fortnightly visits; to Rattoon first, where, when Jasper died, Lydia had leaned full weight against her resourceful new friend for a couple of days when the first impact of the blow was dizzying — and then to quiet little Waterloo.

In fragments, and with no intent to tell the story of her life chronologically, Hannah had reviewed enough of her past to interpret her present. She had remembered almost nothing of her native Surrey and only an episode or two of the steerage voyage with her parents and three brothers, all older. There still swam vaguely before her eyes the kaleidoscope that had been New York in 1880, not quite so noisy and tremendous as it was to be later, but confusing enough to bewilder a shy little tot from the English countryside.

Thence to the large estate of the Raymonds on the North Shore in New England to which Dan Parmalee had come — all the way from Reigate in Surrey — to be the head gardener in an expensive fairyland of lilacs and laurel, tulips and rhododendrons, hawthorn and azaleas, with acres of green velvet bounded by weathered stone walls and shaded by magnificent elms.

There had been no rancor in Hannah's memories of her

childhood; and a wonder it was, too, Lydia often thought, for old Dan's family discipline must have been a frightfully cruel regimentation of their home. Proudly she stressed her industrious father's honesty, loyalty, obedience, but there was no doubt that Dan was hard, so hard that little Dannie had run away at thirteen. No — they never heard from him. Perhaps he went to Vancouver: he had often asked questions about the Canadian Northwest. The other boys — James and William — when half grown had gone back to England, working their passage on a freighter. It was easy to gather that Hannah's patience and poise dated back to her enforced self-containment as a child sitting calmly at the table of irascible old Dan, waiting to speak until she was spoken to, and outwardly conducting herself with a fair imitation of her mousey little mother's experienced docility.

The next phase of Hannah's life was worth a book. Lydia had never heard a story so tender. They had known each other a long time before Hannah ventured upon it, one rainy Sunday afternoon, during a week's vacation in Waterloo.

As a young girl she had seen very little of Philip, the Raymonds' only child. Either he was abroad with his mother or in a boys' school in Andover. Hannah met him occasionally on summer days, and sometimes he would stop and talk to her briefly, kindly, always amused over the little curtsies she made when shyly replying to his friendly questions.

'You don't have to bob like that when you talk to me,' Philip had teased. 'All men are created equal in this country.'

'Yes, sir,' Hannah had replied, dipping a curtsy, 'Thank you, sir.'

'But it makes me nervous!' protested Philip. 'Stop it!'

'Yes, sir,' agreed Hannah, bobbing. And then Philip had laughed until the embarrassed little girl's tears came.

'I'm sorry, Hannah,' he said contritely. 'I didn't mean to

hurt your feelings.' They had both smiled and Hannah had murmured, 'No, sir. Thank you, sir,' with a final jerk of her round little knees.

As they grew up, Philip's attitude, on the infrequent occasions of their meeting in the garden or elsewhere on the grounds, always conveyed the impression that there wasn't very much difference in their social stations, but Hannah had never humored him in this. It had been rubbed into her very bones that she belonged to the servant class and would be at her best while keeping that fact steadily in mind. Remembering your place had been part of old Dan's religion. And Hannah's too.

Once when they were talking about the life of a servant, Lydia had said, 'I've often wondered if it isn't rather debasing to have to wear a uniform.'

'I never felt that way about it,' Hannah replied with spirit, 'and I don't believe the king does, either.'

Lydia had smilingly reminded her that there was a world of difference between the two liveries but Hannah shook her head decisively. 'Not if the king and the housemaid are both doing their duty,' she said, 'and keeping in their rightful place.'

At sixteen — Hannah had not ventured to tell Lydia that she had been an uncommonly pretty girl but had shown her an old group photograph including an attractive young brunette with a shy smile and promising curves — she had been asked to come to the big house as a parlor-maid. She had gone willingly enough, though rather regretful to be done with school, where she had been happy, partly because she wanted an education but mostly for the freedom from the stultifying exactions at home. Work at the big house (she still called it that) was not heavy. For months on end only the servants were in possession. In summers it swarmed with guests and social events. In the winter there was almost nothing to do and Hannah had spent most of her uncharted time in the well-stocked library.

'I was so glad afterwards,' she told Lydia, 'for it helped

me to understand so many of the things he wanted to talk about.'

She couldn't remember exactly when she began worshipping Philip. Looking back on it all from this distance Hannah thought it must have dated from the time when she was a spindle-shanked, pigtailed, ratty little thing of twelve, secretly admiring the handsome fifteen-year-old boy in white flannels on the tennis court.

'I know my feeling for Philip kept me from being silly over other boys,' she said. 'Doubtless I should be thankful for that.'

'I wonder,' Lydia had replied. 'You might have had a happier life if you had married one of your schoolmates.'

Hannah had doubted that, proceeding with the story of her difficulty in concealing her love for Philip when, after she had gone to work in the big house, they would occasionally meet in the hall or she would have some small service to do for him.

'Once the housekeeper sent me to his room to gather up his linen. I thought he had gone away for the day and went into his room without knocking. "I'm sorry," I said, when I ran into him with his hair wet and tousled and himself all muffled up in a big Turkish bathrobe. And he said, "What have you got to be sorry about? You don't look as if you were ever sorry in your life." Of course he was just trying to put me at ease. But I couldn't forget what he had said. Perhaps he really did think I looked like that. So I always tried to look that way for him — as if I'd never been sorry. I suppose it was awfully silly . . . Sometimes when the house was full of company I helped serve the table. It seemed that no matter how many guests there were, or how much help we had, I always was assigned to serve Philip. My hand would tremble until I was afraid he might notice it. But I'm sure he didn't. I don't think he ever once looked me squarely in the eyes until he was sick. Probably he didn't know I was there at all — not until then.'

During the Christmas holidays of his junior year at

Harvard, Philip had been visited by some college friends. They had spent almost every daylight hour for a week in the snow. He had taken a severe cold. It had developed into a serious pleurisy.

Hannah had not seen him often, and then only for brief glimpses when she was sent to his room with messages to one or the other of the nurses, until warm spring days came. Once, while the nurse had gone in to bring his lunch out to the garden where he sat in his wheel-chair, they had sent her out with the morning paper, which had just arrived.

'And how have you been, Hannah?' he had inquired kindly. 'I haven't seen you for a long time. Want to stay a bit and read me the news? The sun dazzles my eyes.'

She had sat down on the stone bench near his chair to read to him in a voice that she remembered was very unsteady. He was so pale and his long hands were so thin. Presently she faltered in the middle of a sentence and he said: 'You mustn't do that, Hannah. It's because you always seem so happy that I want you to read to me. Don't disappoint me, please.'

And she had rubbed her fists hard into her wet eyes, smiling the best she could. 'I'm sorry,' she had murmured thickly. 'The sun is awfully bright today.'

Hannah believed it had been this remark of hers that had made Philip want to keep her with him. The family had been so depressed. He was hoping to find someone who wouldn't cry. He had smiled into her eyes and said, 'After you've had your lunch I wish you would come out here again and read me this book.' Hannah remembered what it was — The Flute and Violin, by James Lane Allen, which had just been published.

Well — that was the real beginning of it, not counting the way she had felt toward him before. Hannah was a bit self-conscious, at first, over all the attention she was receiving. Apparently the whole household realized that she was becoming important to Philip's welfare and deferred to her as they did to the nurses. She wasn't asked to do anything after nine in the morning, so that she would be at liberty to read to Philip if he wanted her, which he always did on pleasant days and sometimes on rainy ones too, in his room.

That had been a memorable summer. Hannah had read to Philip a full score of the current books that people were discussing. She would call up the Old Corner Book Store, and because the people there knew about Philip's illness they would hasten the deliveries. She recalled the names of some of the books they read; *The Master of Ballantrae*, which Philip liked, she thought, mostly because it had been written by a sick man almost as badly off as himself; *A Hazard of New Fortunes*, which he admired for its superb composition and she disliked because it seemed to make him pensive and restless; *The Light That Failed*, a story she felt wasn't a bit good for him; and *The Little Minister*, in the very middle of which he had stopped her to say, 'You could do a very good Babbie yourself, Hannah.' But it wasn't often he said anything like that. Not that first summer.

'I never knew just why he said that to me,' Hannah had reflected. 'Babbie was such an impudent little piece.'

'And were you still bobbing curtsies to Philip, through those days?' Lydia had inquired, to which Hannah had replied, with a puckery little smile: 'No — he didn't want me to. But I was very respectful.'

When winter came, Mrs. Raymond had taken him to Arizona. The house seemed very large and empty. Mr. Raymond was living at a hotel in town and did not come out. The snow was deep and there was little to do but read. Hannah had made good use of her leisure, hoping to be an acceptable companion to Philip on his return. The days seemed very long, but eventually they all passed.

The Arizona sun had tanned him brown, parchment brown, but the sharply defined bones in his hands and the keen outlines of his face made one wonder whether the baking had done him very much good. Hannah had thought it best not to put in an appearance at once upon his arrival. He might not want her. It would be more prudent to wait until she was sent for. They had come at noon. At three, she was called. Mr. Philip was out in the garden, said the nurse, and wanted to speak to her. Hannah's heart was in her mouth. She hoped Philip and his mother, who stood beside him holding a flower-basket half filled with iris, would not notice how flustered she was. Philip had smiled, the smile full of tiny little wrinkles, millions of them, in semicircles about his mouth, and had reached out a sadly emaciated hand.

'Hello,' he said, almost as if they had not been separated at all. And Hannah had taken the lean hand and said, 'Hello,' without meaning to be so forward. But Mrs. Raymond hadn't seemed to resent the liberty. She had smiled. 'I think Philip will be wanting you to read to him again, Hannah,' she said. It was the first time Mrs. Raymond had ever referred to Philip in Hannah's presence without the 'Mr.'

'And what did Mrs. Raymond think of Philip's having you with him so much?' Lydia had asked.

'I don't know. She seemed anxious that he should be humored in every way.'

'Didn't she suspect you were in love with him?'

'No,' said Hannah assuredly. 'Not then.'

'But you were — then?'

'I would have died for him,' whispered Hannah.

They had talked more than they read, that summer. Philip was much more serious than he had been. It wasn't as if he had lost all interest in current news and contemporary books, but he had the mood of one who, as Hannah expressed it, had 'backed off a long way to look at things through a telescope.' He wanted her to read history to him, especially English history dating from Restoration days, and France of the period when America was just beginning to be ambitious for a national life of her own.

But she would no more than get started on the tale of another costly conflict until Philip would say:

'Now there it is again, Hannah. Every time they fought

they came out of it with more problems on their hands than
they'd had before, plus the loss of the best and bravest
people. More problems, and fewer brains left to deal with
them.'

And then he would discuss this odd idea that seemed to
be influencing his thoughts about everything, his queer belief that any sort of conflict was unprofitable.

'I thought at first that his illness was making him religious,' Hannah had reflected. 'But I don't believe that had
much to do with it. He didn't talk about the evil of fighting;
just the uselessness of it. Perhaps it was because I loved
him so dearly that everything he said sounded reasonable,'
she would admit.

'One day he remarked, "If I have to back up my opinions
with a club, it's not much of a compliment to my opinions.
It really means that my opinions aren't good enough to
stand on their own merits. I don't even trust them myself
when I lay in a supply of gunpowder to anticipate somebody
else's disbelief in them. When people fight, they give their
whole case away. I think they fight because they have no
case."'

'Did you remind him,' Lydia had ventured, 'that slavery
would still be a legalized institution in this country if we
hadn't fought it out?'

'Philip said we could more profitably have bought it out.'

'Well, naturally,' Lydia had laughed. 'I think that too,
being a Virginian. But isn't it generally believed that there
were some principles involved beyond the mere commercial
part of it?'

Hannah had shaken her head vigorously. 'Philip thought
all wars were avoidable, including that one. The worst of
all the bad things about war, he believed, was the humiliation of defeat. He used to talk much, that summer, about
saving face. You know — the Chinese idea. He felt that
the bravest thing you could do, in any conflict, was to
help your enemy save his self-respect. So long as he hadn't
lost face, he was likely to act with dignity and remember

that he was a gentleman. But if you demolished that, you made a brute of him; and you really couldn't blame him much if, after having lost his self-respect, he turned on you and forced you, too, into using your teeth and claws. Philip said, "If you ever want to know how much distance we've put between ourselves and the animals, force your enemy to admit that he is no longer a free creature."'

Lydia's brows contracted studiously, and then she smiled a little over her remembrance of Hannah's zealous but amusing efforts to interpret the more difficult articles of young Philip Raymond's strange creed. Sometimes she had been tempted to remark, 'Perhaps the dear fellow's frail health may have influenced his opinions.' But she never actually said it. Hannah would have resented the implication that her hero disbelieved in fighting because he himself was not physically up to it.

'It's a nice enough theory,' Lydia had conceded politely. 'Only you do not take any stock in it yourself; do you?'

'What I think, Hannah, is beside the point. Nobody has made war on me and I have no cause to do battle. My opinion is worthless. But, honestly, we wouldn't have had any progress at all, would we, if our ancestors had not fought for their rights? Hasn't our history been just one long string of battles — from the very beginning of things?'

And then Hannah would try to repeat what Philip had said about that, though it wasn't easy to do. Lydia grinned as she wondered what Hannah's Professor Ward might have thought of their ill-informed discussion. She herself was no historian, much less a philosopher, for all her reading and the lectures she had heard in the finishing school in Baltimore. And Hannah's vocabulary in this field was limited to a little handful of Philip's phrases which sounded strange indeed when sprinkled through her simple speech.

'Philip said it was never the fighting that produced progress,' insisted Hannah, feeling her way cautiously. 'He said that all our progress had come about through adaptation.'

'Adaptation?'

'Yes — to circumstances, conditions, environment.

Then they had both laughed. 'Adaptation' and 'environment' were quite a mouthful for Hannah. She tried her best to explain, realizing that she was making a poor job of it but eager to justify Philip's odd ideas. In her own words — and with many long pauses for reorganization of her argument — Hannah had proceeded to her task, employing the illustrations he had used.

It was this way, she said. When the people of one tribe had worn out their soil, fished out their streams, and frightened away the game, they could do one of two things: make war on a neighboring prosperous tribe, or migrate to a new locality. The usual thing was to make war. If victorious, they captured the land and enslaved the people. The slaves were forced to do the work while their new masters grew fat, lazy, and stupid. Presently another army of invaders would come in and repeat the story. History was uncertain about many things but quite sure on this point: to acquire property by capture endangered the life of the victors. *The possession of anything you hadn't earned was a constant menace.*

Or the restless tribe could migrate to an undeveloped country and claim it for their own without contesting for it. In the strange land they would meet unfamiliar conditions. Perhaps the climate would be colder, requiring heavier clothing. They would learn to trap for furs. They wove firmer cloth on stronger looms with more skillful hands, taking pride in their craft and inventing artistic designs to distinguish their fabrics. The new foods were cultivated with better tools and cooked in a better pottery. Soon the people were creating art-forms in clay. Every new condition drove the tribe forward mentally. Swifter rivers demanded tougher boats. Hard woods dulled the old axes. Minds became more supple under the daily challenge. And so the people moved forward into greatness, not by looting and enslaving, but by yielding, conforming, adapting themselves to difficult circumstances.

'Of course I see that,' Lydia had agreed. 'Naturally it's better to work out something for oneself than to twist things out of other people's fingers. But — look here! Suppose some greedy tribe makes war on *you*. Are you supposed to sit there and let them hack you into cat's meat, or are you to drop everything you own and run away — so's to avoid a fight?'

Hannah had admitted that this was, indeed, the hard part of Philip's theory. He had sat for hours thinking about it. Sometimes he would speak fragments of his thoughts, as if Hannah had been following along and knew exactly where he was in his speculations.

'Almost anyone would say it wasn't common sense, I think,' Philip would confess. 'And it isn't. People with common sense, when their property is threatened, fight back just as furiously as they can. Maybe they are defeated and lose all. Maybe they are victorious, after having been maimed, impoverished, and loaded with debt. But the common sense thing to do is to fight back, and protect your rights. Besides — it's the brave thing to do and you're probably hissed if you don't. Only a little minority could be expected to stand out against public sentiment and display the uncommon sense of handing everything over, after which they could be free to move out into a new country — new set of conditions. Speaking of courage, Hannah, this program of living would test a man's valor more severely than any mere war. Only a few would be able to venture upon it. Fewer would be able to see it through. The rank and file wouldn't have the stuff in them to obey its hard demands, and probably shouldn't be asked to undertake it. But — I wonder if this isn't the way men become great.

'Imagine the case of a man who had used all his ingenuity to build up something for himself, and after he had succeeded to the point of being able to sit down and enjoy the rewards of his work some circumstance stripped him of everything he had, requiring him to take up the struggle again in a different field. Wouldn't he be much more valuable to himself — and society — for having had such an experience? Suppose a man consented to give up everything and make a new place for himself under conditions that forced him into new habits of mind, wouldn't it be a wonderful developer?'

Really, it was about all that Philip wanted to discuss as the summer days lazily passed. Hannah said the thing had taken such a grip on him that it was impossible not to be affected by it, even if the whole theory was so difficult that it seemed — on first hearing — to be mere nonsense.

'It's funny,' Hannah had reflected, 'how an idea will grow on you if you give it enough room. The time came when I believed it myself.'

'That was because you were in love with Philip,' Lydia had remarked gently. 'If he had said the moon is made of green cheese, you would have believed it.'

'I suppose so,' confessed Hannah. 'And for all I know,' she added, 'maybe it is.'

'I want an ice-cream soda, Aunt Hannah, a chocolate one,' Peter was saying.

'Very well, darling. We'll ask mother.' Hannah was struggling to her feet. 'Want to go with us, Lydia?'

'You take Peter. I'll stay and see what Susie is having for dinner. Run along, you two, and have a good time.' She would have been glad to go, but felt that Hannah had a right to be alone with her child as much as possible.

The beloved pair moved toward the house, probably to put Peter into a clean suit and brush Hannah's tangled hair. Lydia's needle lagged as she watched them cross the shaded lawn, Peter shrilly impatient to be off at once on their important errand. She glanced down at her chatelaine watch. It was only four-thirty. The swing swayed gently. The slim needle gathered up another loop of white silk . . .

And so it was October again, and Philip was to return to

Arizona with his mother, leaving in a few days. Mrs. Raymond had called Hannah into the library that morning and closed the door.

'Hannah,' she began, 'we have a very sick boy. I am afraid he is not going to be with us long. Anything he wants, he should have. Now he thinks you should go along to Arizona and help entertain him this winter. He finds your company congenial. I believe too, that you are good for him. Would you like to go?'

'Yes, ma'am — if you both want me to, ma'am.'

Philip's mother had found it difficult to continue with what she felt was necessary to be said. After a long pause, during which she absently rearranged the various writing materials on the desk, she glanced up, and searching the girl's eyes, said:

'You seem to be an understanding person, Hannah. We must have an honest talk. If you go with us to Arizona you will not be a nurse or a maid, but neither will you be a part of the family. Let us have all that understood. Philip likes you very much and has found you a great comfort. He may even be a little bit in love with you. I don't know . . . do you?'

Hannah shook her head and knew that her cheeks were scarlet.

'He has never talked to me about such things, ma'am. . . . He likes me to be with him — to read and talk . . . I think that's all.'

'And you?' asked Mrs. Raymond, seriously but kindly. 'Is that all — with you?'

Lydia, remembering how deeply affected Hannah had been when she told this part of the story, felt that it must have been a very touching moment.

Mrs. Raymond had risen from her chair and walked across the room, facing the perplexed girl, who, for answer to the candid question, had cupped her face in both hands and suddenly given way to a long sobbing intake of breath.

Putting her arm around Hannah, she murmured, 'That's what I was afraid of, dear. You're going to be dreadfully hurt.'

'I didn't want anybody ever to know,' confided Hannah, when she could speak. 'I tried not to, Mrs. Raymond — honestly, I did!'

'You are telling the truth, Hannah. I believe you. This is a very hard position we have made for you. And considering how you feel toward Philip, I think you have done very well.'

'Of course, Mrs. Raymond,' said Hannah, trying to control her voice, 'I knew I never could have him. I'm not good enough for him. But — I couldn't help loving him; could I?'

And then Mrs. Raymond had drawn Hannah into her arms and said thickly: 'You needn't be ashamed of your love, dear. It's quite high grade, I should say. I'm glad you were willing to tell me.' Hannah had pressed her forehead hard against the older woman's shoulder, reluctant to turn away.

'Please, Mrs. Raymond,' she whispered, 'I think you're — wonderful. I'll promise you — I won't ever let him know.'

'I'm not quite sure,' said Mrs. Raymond, slowly, 'that I want you to make such a promise. We are all going to do everything we can to make Philip happy.' She tightened her embrace of Hannah's girlish figure, while her tears ran unchecked. 'And if it brightens one single day for him to know that he has your affection, you may tell him. You will not do it unless he asks. And keep it in mind that your love for my son — whether he lives or dies — is quite hopeless. It's too bad the world is organized that way, but — but that's the way it is organized, and you know it.'

For a moment longer they clung to each other in silence. Then Mrs. Raymond suddenly disengaged herself, dabbed the tears out of her eyes, walked dignifiedly to her desk, consulted her engagement pad, and said in a crisp, business-

like tone, 'You will accompany me into town tomorrow.
I shall get you some suitable clothes and a trunk. We will
start at nine.'

'Thank you, ma'am,' replied Hannah, deferentially at
attention.

'We leave on Thursday noon for the West. I have spoken
to your father. You will be in readiness for the trip. I need
hardly say that you are not to discuss this with any of the
other servants. Meantime, you are relieved of your usual
duties.'

'Yes, ma'am.' Hannah made a prim little curtsy.

'That will be all, then. You may go.'

'Yes, ma'am.' Hannah turned and walked quickly
toward the door.

'Hannah!' Mrs. Raymond's voice was military.

'Yes, ma'am.' The girl straightened and waited.

'Very well done!'

'Thank you, ma'am. The same to you, please, if I may
say so.'

And so they went to Arizona, where Philip sat all day in
the sun with Hannah beside him, reading, talking; listening
mostly. One afternoon he said to her, after an extended
silence, 'You know I'm not going to be here much longer,
don't you?'

'Please, Philip,' she begged

'It's not that I care greatly,' he went on, listlessly.
'Life, the way I've been living it, isn't much of a treat. I
would have liked to have had a real go at it, Hannah. Just
between us, I wanted to see if that little idea of mine was
sound.'

'Want *me* to try it, Philip? ... in case — you can't?'

His face was puzzled, and for some time he did not reply.

'No, dear. It might make life very hard for you. I
wouldn't want you to do that. I'm too fond of you.'

'But I really believe in it, Philip.'

Then he had reached out a pathetically slim hand which

she took in both of hers and held tightly against her high
youthful breasts.

'I love you, Hannah,' he said softly.

With the utmost resolution Hannah had replied, as if
she considered his love but a dear comradeship, 'Isn't it
sweet, Philip, that we do like each other so much ... And
we always will — won't we?'

And so Philip Raymond had been brought home again,
weaker by far but rallying emotionally to the summons of
a New England spring that strained at its leash with an
impatience almost articulate. It was the gayest, brightest
of springs. It recklessly splashed every conceivable variant
of adolescent green and waxy yellow on a palette of woods
and gardens bounded by the hills and the sea, coaxing
many a discouraged, frozen, brittle thing to rise from the
seeming dead with a gallant resolve to bring forth foliage
and flowers. Philip was almost merry, those afternoons in
latter May and June, so responsive to the revitalizing urge
that Hannah often wondered — with her heart more than
her head — if he might not really renew his strength.

Surely it was a valorous last stand that he made in defense of his youth and its natural urges as Nature posted
her demand for the resurrection of everything that held
the faintest pulse. Hannah had thought it the most heart-
breaking thing of all — Philip's sending for his tailor and
standing dizzily to be measured for natty sports clothes.
He even ordered a new pair of riding-boots, and stroked
their softness with gaunt fingers.

Late one afternoon — she had been reading Whitman's
Leaves of Grass, rather wishing Philip had asked for something else — he laid a white hand on the open pages, his
signal that he wanted to make a remark, and said huskily,
'Hannah, dear, *if* I should get well ——'

'You must say "when," Philip. You're ever so much
better.'

'Would you, darling?' he entreated.

Hannah's training steadied her and counseled prudence. 'I'm not of your class, dear,' she said gently.

'And I'm the mere shadow of a man. Let's resolve to forget all that and obey good old Walt's challenge. You forget your silly notions about caste and I'll forget I'm sick.' He took up the book from her lap and in a wobbly scrawl wrote in the wide margin opposite the brave declaration, ' *From this hour freedom! From this hour I ordain myself loosed of limits!* ' — 'June twenty-third — 1892 — this is our resolve. Philip Raymond.' He handed the book back to her, and the pen, and she wrote underneath his name, 'Hannah Parmalee.'

'And if that meant we were engaged,' Hannah had said to Lydia, 'I suppose we were engaged.'

'I don't see what else,' Lydia had replied. And it was all true enough. Lydia had seen it in the book. The ink was faded, but the joint declaration was clear, significant.

But as the pastures browned and the locusts came and the blue smoke of burning leaves was scattered into grayish wisps by October rains, Philip gave up the brave fight, not conscious of any particular act of surrender or wittingly determined to quit; but, without meaning to do so, he quietly withdrew from the institution he had called Life. There was nothing dramatic about his actual departure. It was on a raw sleety afternoon of November, while the first surly swish of winter lashed the windows. Sleet, ever afterward, Hannah had said, swept her courage all away. It became the sign of defeat, sign of everything lost.

Philip had been unconscious for two days. Mr. Raymond sat with his head in his hands by the bed. Mrs. Raymond came and went softly, knowing that her boy had already pushed out to sea and would not be back. Hannah was not needed and no one seemed to remember. It was just as well. She was incapable of any more suffering, and there was nothing she could do for the quiet form that gradually melted away. When the starched nurse came down to the kitchen and said, 'Well — it's all over — at

last,' Hannah had no tears left to shed. She went home to
the rather grim cottage of Dan Parmalee, took a book from
under her pillow, and on the margin, above Philip's name,
opposite the courageous line '*From this hour, freedom!*'
Hannah wrote, 'Five P.M. November nineteenth, 1892.'

Lydia had thought it very unfortunate indeed that
Mrs. Raymond had died a few months afterward, for
no one else knew certainly how much Philip had cared for
Hannah.

'Unfortunate for her, yes,' agreed Hannah. 'But, for
me, no. They would have been embarrassed to have me on
their hands. I did not belong to them — and yet they
would have felt under some sort of obligation to me, I suppose. Mr. Raymond may not have known anything about
it. I fear they had become just a little bit estranged. He
was always very courteous, but there was a thick wall
between them. I don't believe I would have felt right about
taking anything from Mr. Raymond ... It was all for the
best, so far as I was concerned. Mrs. Raymond didn't have
anything more to do — so she died. It would be nice if
Nature was always that kind and showed as much good
taste.'

Lydia had smiled over that, and Hannah had defended
her droll remark seriously. 'Why not, indeed?' she insisted.
'Haven't we a right to expect that Nature will exhibit some
good taste?'

'Pish!' Lydia had replied. 'I wouldn't give three cents
for a double cord of wise books that try to give a mind and
feelings to Nature ... Good taste! Pooh! Nature? Good
taste? Nonsense!'

And so, after that, the big house was sold. Hannah
stayed on. When the new people, the Coopers, came, she
was employed as housekeeper. Adele, seventeen, was given
the room Philip had occupied. Every morning Hannah
filled a tall vase with flowers and took it to Adele's room.
And the girl said, 'Thank you, Hannah. It is sweet of you
to do that. Is there anything nice that I can do for you?'

'No, Miss Adele. I have everything I want.'

But the girl was always giving Hannah presents; expensive silk lingerie, books, bags, ornaments. Hannah would back off from them, but Adele would seem hurt if she did not accept them. Once when Adele was in town for the day and not expected until night she came home early and found Hannah sitting beside her bed, her face buried in her hands.

The girl had drawn the embarrassed Hannah to her feet and said, 'Tell me! You've got to! I want to know! If there's anything — anything *funny* about you, I'm going to know it! Let's have it! Why are you mooning in my room?'

And Hannah had told her — very briefly — very softly.

'You won't tell anyone, please?'

And Adele had buried her face on Hannah's shoulder and shaken her head and whispered, 'No, dear ... God! — I'm sorry for you, Hannah. ... But it must have been wonderful to have loved anyone — that much.'

There was an expensive wedding when Adele was twenty-three. Hannah had doubted the success of the match, for Martin Moore was all of a dozen years her senior and a century older in point of worldly experience. The best you could say for it was that it was 'a desirable match.' Hannah understood that phrase to mean an alliance between a rich and jaded old bachelor and a young girl who had been induced to believe that the things you could buy were more worth having than the fulfillment of a romantic dream. And perhaps the fact that they were going to live in Paris may have added a touch of greatly needed glamor to the sacrifice. Martin had business there, representing an American bank.

Adele had taught Hannah how to dress, and had turned her own modiste loose on the supple and graceful form of her friend. Hannah's black crêpe uniforms with white piping fitted like an expensive glove. 'Don't be foolish,' Adele would exclaim when Hannah protested about the costly elegance of the frocks she wore every day. 'Wouldn't you rather look the way God made you than wear some dowdy thing that deforms you? I've a lot of satisfaction looking at you in gowns that fit.'

So Hannah had felt well dressed at the wedding of her dear Adele, which was really the last event she ever attended that was worth thinking about; for old Dan Parmalee had a stroke, that winter, and as her mother was too frail for the necessary lifting of the big fellow, Hannah was obliged to go back to the cottage.

For a time it seemed that Dan, now definitely out of the picture so far as any further usefulness was concerned, would soon die — if not of apoplexy, of querulousness and surly sulking. Meek little Mother Parmalee broke a hip, and thus added one more good reason for Hannah's remaining at home. With surprising tenacity of life, the fragile Emma Parmalee shakily drank her tea and knitted woolen socks for Dan, over a period of more than two years before pneumonia carried her off. Dan stayed on, alternately playing the rôle of spoiled baby and pensioned giant.

Lydia had said to Hannah: 'It is a pity your father couldn't have gone when your mother passed away. It would have set you free. Everything since might have been different.'

'But then — I mightn't have had Peter.'

They were coming now, down the back steps from the kitchen, the little fellow clutching a big handful of lettuce, Hannah closely following him. Lydia waved to them.

'The rabbits,' called Hannah, as they proceeded toward the far corner of the spacious yard. 'Want to see them eat their dinner?'

'When I've reached a good stopping-place,' said Lydia . . .

So, then, Adele had come home, that next summer. Within an hour after her arrival she had appeared at the Parmalee cottage, breezily affectionate, but frankly disturbed to find Hannah so inexorably tied to her uninteresting responsibility.

'Maybe I've come back to stay,' confided Adele with the old impulsive candor. 'It isn't decided yet... But, Hannah, you've simply got to get away for a little while. This isn't right. I'll tell you what!' Adele exclaimed. 'I want to go with you. We'll go to Bar Harbor.'

'I couldn't,' declared Hannah. 'It's sweet of you — but I mustn't do that. Unless you want to take me as your maid.'

'How about going as my companion?'

'What does a companion have to do?' Hannah asked. 'I never noticed.'

'I'm not quite sure myself,' confessed Adele, 'for I never had one. I think, though, that a companion is just a person with better manners and more sense who goes along to buy the tickets and read the papers to her mistress and take the dog out for short walks, and is willing to be snubbed when the old lady wants to show off a little.'

'Sounds like a pleasant job,' observed Hannah.

'That's settled, then. And you'll be wanting some nice clothes. I'll see to it.' Adele was full of enthusiasm over her new scheme.

'I don't think a companion is expected to be very modish,' Hannah said, to which Adele whimsically replied, 'This one is. I'm not old enough yet to demand my companion's looking a frump just to set off my fine feathers.'

So they went to Bar Harbor, where Thomas Bradford joined them on a morning stroll, the second day. When he left them Adele muttered, 'There's something the world could get along without.'

Hannah laughed, but privately rose to his defense, for he had been pleasantly attentive to her, and it had been a long time since any man had regarded her with an appraising interest.

'Too much mother,' explained Adele. 'Thomas has paddled along beside that old girl's beach chair ever since he left college fifteen years ago. If all the fools in the world would have a convention, I feel sure she would be nomi-

nated by acclamation to swing the gavel — and Thomas,'
she added as an afterthought, 'would stand beside her and
hold it for her while she wasn't swinging it.'

And Hannah laughed again, but couldn't help remembering that he had looked her squarely in the eyes with an
expression of pleasure and interest. That afternoon Adele
had slept and Hannah had walked and Thomas had fallen
into step with her. Perhaps his charge slept also, temporarily freeing him to admire the shapely and genteel companion of feather-headed Adele Cooper — 'What's her
married name?' he asked. 'I never knew the chap... But
no matter. Tell me all about *you* — and where you've
been all my life. Let's sit down here.'

The tide was out and the sea was unusually quiet. They
lounged in the sand and talked, but not much about
Hannah, which pleased her, for there wasn't much to tell,
and Thomas was delightfully entertaining. He had been
everywhere. Hannah reclined on an elbow and looked far
out into the blue where it seemed to rise to meet a gray
sky, quite intoxicated with the reminiscent voice of the
widely traveled Thomas.

'Blue, yes, and very lovely, as you say. But you'll never
know how blue the bluest blue can be until you've seen a
sunrise on the Bay of Naples, from Capri, preferably... I
could wish I might be the one to show it to you, and watch
the wonder in your eyes.'

That sort of thing. And — when Hannah had confessed
how very much she wished to travel, but first wanted to see
the Surrey of her fathers ——

'You will, of course,' answered Thomas confidently. 'I
would like to be along with you when you stroll down the
garden paths. It would be like walking in a dream, wouldn't
it?'

It was an important afternoon for Hannah. Thomas
luxuriated in his recollective excursions, always insisting,
either directly or by implication, that they were reviewing
these enchanted scenes together, with something like a

veiled suggestion that they might do it in reality one of these days — who knew? And Hannah was enjoying herself far too much to banish the illusion. She listened, dreamily, and made no effort to check Thomas as he prattled on, increasingly reckless with his use of 'we,' and 'us,' and 'our,' until it was almost as if they were actually planning a trip together.

She had loved Philip with an undying devotion; but it was, she knew, a protective love that experienced a kind of curious ecstasy while performing tender little ministries to his weakness. Thomas was hinting — whether in earnest or merely to entertain himself — at a relationship which, if it ever came to pass, would make her the protected, nourished, indulged. It was a new sensation, and highly enjoyable, even if nothing ever came of it. They walked back to the Gables together, saying little on the return trip. Thomas smiled down into her uplifted eyes, as they parted.

'Tomorrow?' he inquired. 'About the same time?'

'If you want to,' said Hannah.

'I certainly am not going to interfere the least bit with your amusement, Hannah,' Adele had remarked, a few days afterward. 'It's your vacation, and God knows you've a little fun coming to you. But I do hope you're not planning to burn your fingers.'

Hannah had slumped down into a low chair beside Adele's bed. 'I'm afraid I've already done it,' she murmured. 'He thinks he's in love with me.'

'Well, maybe he is. And maybe you're infatuated with him. It certainly looks like it. But I'd hate to see you get tangled up with that mess. Thomas doesn't know whether his life's his own. Until the old lady is nice enough to die ——'

'He has had an awfully hard life,' defended Hannah.

'Now, *hasn't* he!' scoffed Adele. 'Lounging on the Riviera all winter and sprawling in the sun up here all summer like a lizard. However, it must have been a rough job, at that. Does he think he wants to marry you?'

Hannah nodded, with averted eyes. 'I couldn't now, of course. Not while Father lives.'

'Well, that's encouraging. Let's hope your father lives to be a hundred. Or you'll find yourself on the other side of the old gal's wheel-chair with about as much liberty as her little chow.'

'Do you think I would be much worse off than I am now?' asked Hannah. 'It won't be very exciting for me just to sit there, in that little cottage, and knit — all the rest of my life.' She was on the verge of tears but Adele refused to be sympathetic.

'No, that wouldn't be very exciting, Hannah, but at least you could knit when and what you wanted to, without asking permission of a vain old tyrant.'

Hannah had been quite right about Thomas's feeling toward her. He had been almost independent of his mother for the two whole afternoons and evenings before they parted. Adele, with heavy misgivings over this turn of affairs, was insisting that they return. Reluctantly, Hannah resumed her dull and thankless task. But Thomas, with nothing much else to do, enlivened her routine with letters, letters, and more letters. Seeing it was the only avocation he had, he pursued it in a manner that idealized and glorified him in the imagination of the lonely and love-starved Hannah.

When the gusty, slanting, autumn rains began to splash the fading shrubbery, Adele one day impetuously decided to go back to Martin Moore, or back to Paris rather, which was putting it less unattractively, she said. Her final words to Hannah, who had accompanied her as far as the South Station, were:

'Good-bye, dear, and please don't be a damned fool! There are too many of us now. One more would be crowding.'

In September, old Dan suffered another stroke and was gracious enough to everyone — including himself — to regard it as final. And to the utter amazement to all who had known him, Thomas Bradford — after a serious quarrel with his mother, who had gone a few steps too far, even for him, in making him feel a fool — wired Hannah to meet him in New York, where they were married, after which he defiantly led her into the old lady's sumptuous apartment and exhibited her with a truculent air of boastful disobedience on parade.

'She even stopped payment on the check she had just given him for that month's allowance,' said Hannah, when Lydia had inquired about their resources. 'I had about five hundred dollars. Thomas had almost nothing but his clothes and golf-sticks.'

They thought it would be better to get quite out of hearing of the tempest that Mother Bradford had stirred up, leaving for Chicago, where Thomas thought he had some friends who might think of something he could do. The friends were mildly glad to see him until he stammered out the truth about his need.

Unused to seeing how far a dollar could be spun out — never having earned one — Thomas quickly disposed of the little money they had. With his weak little show of self-reliance wasting to a mere glassy-eyed resignation, he wired to his mother, and she telegraphed him a ticket and instruction to come and see her — alone. He left Hannah nearly penniless in a shabby hotel room and obeyed his mother's command. She waited for three weeks, expecting word from him. It came, then, addressed from Reno. The letter was fourteen pages long, contrite, abject, disgustingly but very properly self-loathing. He had no other recourse, he said. He didn't know how to do anything. His mother would take him back only on condition that he get a divorce. Would Hannah understand the whole pitiful mess, and let him go free?

Hannah did not protest, nor did she assert her rightful claims, though she had just confirmed her mounting fear that her problem was to be still further complicated.

'It seemed to me, through those days,' Hannah had confided, 'that Philip was very near to me. No — I don't mean anything spooky. But the things Philip had said sounded in my ears as plainly as if he had just spoken them.'

'But Philip had not expected you to live by his queer theories,' Lydia had reflected. 'Surely you had a right to ask for your living expenses while you were having that baby. I think that was carrying things a bit too far.'

'Maybe so,' Hannah conceded, 'but it was a great satisfaction to feel that I was doing something Philip would have thought brave.'

At first it wasn't hard to find a good position as a maid, but the time came when they said they would have to let her go. They said they were sorry and doubtless they were, Hannah thought. She couldn't blame them much.

The doctor at the free clinic thought she would be better off at the University Hospital and sent her down there. When it was all over and done with, she went out to meet the winter that had arrived in the meantime. Her clothing was insufficient. With the last few dollars she had left ——

'Why didn't you tell me, dear?' Lydia had cried. 'How gladly I would have done something about it if I had known.'

With the last of her small resources Hannah visited a near-by used-clothes shop and bought the only heavy coat they had. It was too big for her and she despised it. Seeing there was no pride left, she also bought the old plush hat. Sitting in the railroad station to be protected from the cold, for her vitality was low, she studied the advertisements in the *Morning Star*. There was nothing but a chance to sell some little kitchen tool on commission. . . .

They were calling Lydia now, and rising from the swing she sauntered over to the far corner of the garden and joined them.

'How are the rabbits?' she asked.

'Stuffed,' said Hannah.

'But *I'm* not!' piped Peter.

'Very well, son.' Lydia and Hannah exchanged smiles. 'Mother will go in and see if dinner isn't nearly ready.'

Chapter VI

In HIS first blind fury over the ruinous telegram reporting the theft of his invention by the unscrupulous Ellises, Paul Ward went completely berserk. Absurdly miscast for so hectic an exhibition of emotional stampede, he was a shocking spectacle.

All of his previous disappointments had been accepted quietly. He had even been able to draw a tilted smile on these frequent occasions of failure, admitting that he hadn't counted much on the success of the thing anyway and would hope for better luck next time. With a seemingly boundless capacity for taking it on the chin, he had seen one scheme after another go the way of all their predecessors, and presently had bobbed up to invite Fate to rap him again.

But now, with fortune and freedom practically in his pocket, the Ellis message from Pittsburgh had driven him into a rip-roaring frenzy that stunned and stilled everyone in the house — except little Sally, who, terrified by this incredible storm, wept inconsolably and threw up two chocolate bars and a maple nut sundae purchased out of the recently established weekly allowance of spending money which she had not yet attempted to budget.

At the onset of Paul's purple rage, Marcia had ineffectively tried to do something about it, tagging him from room to room, dodging his eloquent gestures, and begging, 'Please, dear! Oh — please don't!' But when it became evident that he wasn't hearing or seeing her, she went to a window in the dining-room and turned her back on the sorry scene, the knuckles of both hands pressed hard

against her ears. Roberta's slim, sallow face was pasty
with horror. Wallie, who had imprudently ventured a
soothing comment, stood straight and snug in a corner,
wearing the blinking surprise of the unexpectedly slapped.
Even Hannah, who thought she knew Paul Ward in all his
moods, stared at this wild-eyed stranger in utter con-
sternation. And when she heard him in the basement
smashing to bits the machinery that was to have made
him rich, she made no effort to dissuade him, though every
crash of the hammer was as painful as if she herself had
been struck.

The racket subsided after a while, and then there was
complete silence. Apparently the tempest had spent itself.
Hannah decided to reconnoiter. In the living-room she
paused to suggest to Wallie and Roberta that they had
better go for a walk and come back in an hour.

'And don't worry,' she added, complacently. 'Your
father has had good reasons for being terribly upset. He'll
be all right again soon.'

Tiptoeing upstairs, Hannah peeked through the partly
open door and saw Marcia at full length on her bed, face
down, with Sally cuddled close beside her. Quietly retracing her steps to the kitchen, she began the concoction of a
pitcher of lemonade. At the door of the refrigerator she
paused, meditated for a moment, shook her head slowly,
and abandoned the lemonade project. She wasn't quite
sure what was needed in this case, but obviously it wasn't
anything involving ice.

There was a bottle of brandy upstairs in the medicine
cabinet. Hannah poured a liberal libation into a small
glass and carried it down to the basement, her heart pounding hard. She didn't believe Paul would have gone to the
length of destroying himself, but you couldn't tell what a
person might do in such a fit of passion. It took quite a
little courage to venture into the gloomy cubicle where she
knew she would find him.

He was sitting on the edge of the grimy workbench,

slumped over in an attitude of hopeless dejection, his face white and drawn, his hands limply dangling. One of them had been hurt and was bleeding.

Paul did not glance up when Hannah approached. She stepped toward him and silently held the brandy within range of his downcast eyes, but he made no move to accept it. Putting the glass down on the bench beside him, she went upstairs again, returning presently with a basin of warm water, a towel, a bottle of iodine, and the makings of a simple bandage. Paul had not stirred.

He permitted her to take up the bloody hand and dully watched her sponge it. After a while he slowly raised his head and their serious eyes met in an exchange of unspoken inquiry. Paul's were suddenly suffused with tears, and Hannah bent energetically over her task, half-blinded by her own. She knew he would not thank her for any display of pity, but it was very difficult not to offer some tender proof of her feeling for him in this quite desperate emergency. With a brave show of casualness she proceeded very practically with the necessary repairs.

When the bandage had been secured with adhesive tape, Hannah renewed her offer of the brandy, which her patient drank at one swallow. Gasping over the fiery dose, he restored the glass. Then their eyes met again, Hannah's moist, but holding the faintest suggestion of a gently reproving twinkle that matched the little pucker of her expressive lips. He had been — her look said — a very naughty boy, but she was definitely on his side and he could count on her, no matter how badly he behaved.

Paul laid his good hand on her shoulder, tightening his fingers on it slightly as if to say that he appreciated her understanding of his need. Although she well knew the exact value of this grateful caress and accepted it for what it was worth, the warmth of his impulsive grasp raced Hannah's heart-beats for a moment. It meant a great deal to her, this spontaneous evidence of sincere friendship. She had long been aware of Paul's deep regard for her as a

loyal employee who had been largely responsible for estab-
lishing the family's affairs on a sound basis. Today she
had been promoted to the rank of comrade. His hand on
her shoulder, in this moment of grave emergency, had con-
ferred the degree.

Not a word had been spoken. It was ever so much better
that way. She was glad he hadn't tried either to defend
or deplore his conduct. And she was glad to have avoided
the natural temptation to murmur some sympathetic
platitude.

Quietly gathering up the things she had brought, Hannah
moved toward the doorway, and giving him a swift, re-
assuring, backward glance slowly groped her way up the
dingy basement stairs, her eyes swimming with uncon-
trollable tears.

It was two o'clock Wednesday afternoon. Mrs. Ward
hadn't wanted luncheon and was up in her room, probably
in bed with her face buried in the pillows. The children
were at school. Paul was downtown in conference with his
attorney. He had restlessly roamed the house most of the
night, and had eaten almost nothing. The prevailing
gloom couldn't have been heavier if some member of the
family lay dead in a coffin.

Hannah was ironing. She could always think more
clearly when she ironed, and there was much need for clear
thinking in this house today. Besides, she always ironed
on Wednesday. Reaching into the basket, she drew out
Roberta's dimity and patted it smoothly onto the board.
The simple little dress didn't seem to belong to Roberta.
It was intended for an eight-year-old, which was, of course,
Roberta's age: eight and a half; only she was ever so much
older than that — older than Wallie, by far. Hannah had
never known a child like her; reserved, almost as if she were
a guest rather than a member of the household; serious
when others smiled, smiling when others laughed, courteous
but plainly annoyed over demonstrations of affection.

Even as a mere tot of four, when taken up to be cuddled Roberta would submit to it only for an instant. 'Too tight!' she would say, and wriggle out of the embrace.

The only doll she had ever taken any interest in was a Chinese coolie with a pair of little baskets dependent from a shoulder-yoke. And it wasn't as if she was precocious. Roberta's marks in school weren't especially good, except in drawing; and even there the teacher's disapproval of her tendency to take liberties in copying the patterns was frequently recorded in red ink on the margins of her sketches.

'I never saw a cat like that,' Hannah had playfully remarked one day, glancing over the child's shoulder as she sat by the kitchen window, doubled over her drawing-board.

'Didn't you?' mumbled Roberta absently, which was exactly the sort of reply you might expect. She wouldn't go to the bother of defending the cat. Nor would she have volunteered a criticism of your cat, had you been drawing one. Very odd child, elfish, remote. Mrs. Ward had been baffled over her strange ways and, unable to think of anything better to do in the straightening out of Roberta's queer kinks, had dosed her with cod liver oil until the sulky little enigma fairly gagged at the bare mention of the nasty stuff.

Hannah carefully hung up Roberta's dress on the rack and drew out of the basket a gray blouse of Wallie's, and if they weren't very careful they were going to spoil Wallie, which would be a pity; for he was a fine lad, so ridiculously like his father that his unconscious imitations of Paul's tricks of gesture and posture made you laugh. They were so much alike, indeed, that they didn't always get along very well. Doubtless that was because it got onto Paul's nerves sometimes to have this small mirror following him about, unintentionally grotesquing the little pomposities which Paul could have done very nicely without. And whenever Mrs. Ward wanted to dust off her husband a little, she attended to it by brushing Wallie, who would

rise to his own defense by offering sound precedent for
whatever he happened to have been doing, thus putting
his father to the necessity of repudiating the flattery,
which would hurt the boy's feelings so badly that he would
leave the table, everyone wondering who had started the
row, anyway. However, the tiffs never lasted very long.
Wallie, like his father, had a short memory. Lovable boy.
She wished he didn't have these awful colds. They frightened her.

Hannah's mobile lips curved in a tender smile as she
stretched Sally's little pajama suit out on the padded
board. It was natural, perhaps, that she loved Sally best
of all, for Peter was almost of the same age, and Sally had
been born when Hannah was desperately longing for her
own baby. But that didn't quite explain all of her feeling
for this child. Sally was going to be a beauty, and sweet as
she was pretty. Hannah had some misgivings about Sally's
undisguised affection for her, much as the little girl's ardent
attentions warmed her heart. Home from school, Sally
would come racing through the house shouting: 'Hannah!
Hannah — see what I did! Hannah — look what I've got!'
If Sally fell down and bumped her knee, she ran to Hannah.
If something happened to hurt her feelings, she told
Hannah.

'Better go and tell mother, too, hadn't you?' Hannah
would say, to ease her own conscience. And she could feel
the round little gold head nodding obediently against her
breast. But Hannah was always told first. Sometimes
Sally would be so anxious to resume her play that she
would leave her summer luncheon almost untasted. Her
mother would insist. Sally would protest.

'Hannah,' Mrs. Ward would say, 'don't you think it
would be better for Sally if she ate her rice?'

So, really, Mrs. Ward couldn't blame Hannah too much
if Sally was more prompt to obey her than her mother.
She had made an open bid for that dilemma — if it was a
dilemma; Hannah often wondered if it might not turn out

to be a dilemma, some day. Oh, well — you could deal with that when the time came. There were plenty of things, much more important than that, to fret about now.

She picked up a dainty handkerchief edged with lace. How many times a day, this past half-dozen years, had Hannah said to herself that it really wasn't any of her business; that she hadn't the slightest right to judge her or criticize her, even in her own private thoughts. Mrs. Ward — funny how she always thought of her as 'Mrs. Ward,' when Mr. Ward was invariably 'Paul,' probably because his wife spoke his name so frequently, while he usually called her 'Darling,' or some other term of endearment — Mrs. Ward was doing the very best she could. Now — let that settle it, once and for all! She's a sweet girl who never grew up, and if she isn't quite able to be of any help in a mess like this, it isn't her fault! Hannah took particular pains with the handkerchief. The lace was breaking a little and she resolved to mend it. But — wasn't it too bad about yesterday's performance; utterly helpless, running up to her room to have a private cry when he needed something or somebody to lean against. Maybe he hadn't missed her. Maybe he had been so frantic over his calamity that he hadn't given a thought about her slipping away, shy and scared and ashamed, at the moment when she might have shown a little strength. Perhaps she was really afraid of him. If so, that was too bad, for it might have killed something in her that could never be revived. Perhaps she was as much disappointed as Paul over the loss of their promised fortune and had gone to bed lamenting it.

But, no — Mrs. Ward wouldn't be caring so much about that. She wasn't the least bit greedy for money. No — her concern was for Paul. But what a way to show it! She'd lose him if she wasn't careful. All she had was her girlish beauty, and she wasn't even going to have that if she didn't stop fretting herself into a state of swollen-eyed, tear-smeared, red-nosed dejection. She wasn't the type that could do that without damage. Florid, peaches-and-cream blondes weren't intended for long hauls of worry. If they missed a couple of meals and cried themselves to sleep for a night or two they did their looks more harm than an olive-skinned brunette would suffer by a month's continuous grilling. Adele Cooper had once delivered a few remarks on this subject, and Hannah had never forgotten them. Adele was always making up odd rules like that, stating them so convincingly that you almost had to believe her, even while you were thinking, 'How silly!'

Hannah tugged a shirt out of the basket. There were some brown blotches on the sleeves, stains made by chemicals. She hadn't been able to wash out the spots. But no matter; it was an old working shirt anyway. Perhaps he would never wear it again. And if he didn't pull himself together pretty soon he would get in wrong at the University. Two whole days now he had missed all of his classes; sent word he was sick. Well — that was nearly enough to the truth, counting from yesterday afternoon. Who would ever have thought of him going into such a violent tantrum!

He had been waiting more than two weeks for word from that Mr. Ellis. A couple of times he had phoned home between classes, asking Mrs. Ward if there had been any news — wires or letters. And Mrs. Ward would reply: 'Sorry, Paul. Not a thing. You'll surely hear tomorrow.' Then, more often than not, Mrs. Ward would come on out to the kitchen and say, 'Dear, dear — if he doesn't have some word from Mr. Ellis very soon, I don't know what we're going to do with him.'

Paul had not talked to Hannah about it at all, which was strange. Not very much had happened in the course of his work on the new refrigerator that she hadn't known about. All but this unfortunate affair with Mr. Ellis. The little she knew about this was what Mrs. Ward had said. It was the morning after Hannah's customary day off. She had gone to Waterloo as usual to see Lydia and little Peter.

Paul had been in gay spirits at breakfast. Something very important was in the air. When he had left the house, Mrs. Ward had strolled out to the kitchen, bright-eyed and full of happy excitement.

'Well, Hannah,' she began, impressively and just a bit condescendingly, 'it will not be long now. Mr. Ellis — you know, the man who built the motor for Paul's invention — was here yesterday to see the machine in operation. His brother has a big manufacturing plant in Pittsburgh and is practically certain they will want to put Paul's refrigerator on the market. So our Mr. Ellis is going at once to explain it all to his brother, and they can be making their plans for the promotion and production while Paul is doing the tedious business of securing the patent. That way they can save months of time, Mr. Ellis says, and naturally Paul is anxious to get something out of it at the earliest possible moment.'

Of course. You wouldn't have expected anything else from Paul. Now that the machine had actually worked, the next move was to find a producer who would begin at once to turn them out by the thousand.

Hannah had expressed her joy over the promptness of this offer, adding, as a cautious afterthought, 'I suppose this Mr. Ellis is reliable.'

'Oh, yes, indeed,' Mrs. Ward had replied confidently. 'Paul says there isn't an abler mechanic this side of Chicago.'

'That wasn't quite what I meant,' explained Hannah. 'I was just wondering about his honesty.'

Mrs. Ward had laughed, teasingly.

'Fancy your raising that question, Hannah; you who believe in trusting everybody.'

And Hannah had said nothing more, except that she certainly hoped it would all turn out happily. It had worried her more than a little, as the days passed. She hoped that her own beliefs hadn't influenced Paul to be inexcusably foolhardy. But no — Paul wouldn't have given her ideas on that matter an instant's thought. Nevertheless, Hannah had some serious moments, through those days of waiting, in which she re-examined her own philosophy and cross-questioned it earnestly. It would be a quite dreadful thing if Paul were to be disappointed now when the reward for all his hard work was in sight.

That had been a wonderful day — that memorable Wednesday when the success of the machine was demonstrated for the first time. Paul had cut all of his classes on Tuesday and worked until far into the night. Hannah had taken a plate of scrambled eggs, bacon, and toast down to the basement at one o'clock. He had mumbled his thanks, but seemed anxious not to be bothered. Early in the forenoon he had started the motor and had come bounding upstairs with the expression of one who had seen a bright vision. Dragging up a chair to the open door of the refrigerator he had sat silently watching the coils. Hannah had held her breath. Something very important, she felt, was about to happen. The minutes ticked by. Presently Paul turned and glanced up at her over his shoulder.

'Come here, Hannah,' he had said huskily. 'Touch that pipe! Do you know what that means? *I've done it!*'

'Wonderful!' she had murmured. 'I'm so glad!'

And then he had run out of the room to find Mrs. Ward. She had come quickly. The three of them had gathered about the refrigerator, almost speechless with amazement and happiness. Paul had gone upstairs after a while, and hastily changed to his street clothes. With nothing but a cup of coffee for breakfast he had left the house, doubtless to go down to the Eureka Tool and Machine Company. And the next day Mr. Ellis had come while Hannah was away.

That had been a little over two weeks ago. When the noisy storm had broken over them yesterday, nobody had bothered to tell Hannah exactly what was in the devastating telegram, but she could guess. In Paul's frenzied raving, he had snarled out enough of it to explain it all.

'Oh, yes!' he growled, between clenched teeth. 'They had been working on the same project — and were all ready to promote it! Like hell they had! I'll show them whether they'll steal it from me! By God — I'll let them see whether they can get away with it, the low-lived thieves! Wait till I get my fingernails into the neck of that double-crossing, lying ——' Hannah had tried not to hear the rest of it. She didn't like to know that Paul could use such vulgar phrases, even in this stress; sorry to learn that he had access to them.

And today he was making plans to sue Mr. Ellis and Mr. Ellis's rascally brother. He was downtown talking to a lawyer about it. He wouldn't stop to ask who was the best lawyer in town, but would plunge into the first office he came to and splutter his story. And the lawyer would take the case, of course. And the Pittsburgh Ellis, who would have a smarter lawyer, would win it. What a beastly shame! He had counted on it with so much confidence, and had worked so long, and hoped so bravely. But that was Paul's trouble — he couldn't wait; just had to see his invention on the market immediately, so the money would begin to flow in. He had begun spending it already. Mr. Chalmers had driven them out to see the new house he was building on Edgewood Road, and Mrs. Ward had been asked to make suggestions about the decorations.

'I told him,' Mrs. Ward had remarked upon their return, 'that we weren't sure yet about our ability to buy a home, and he said, "But the house has to be decorated anyway, and I'll trust your taste."' She had taken a frightful cold out there in that unheated house. And now Wallie had it, too; had complained of a sore throat this morning. Hannah thought he was running a bit of a temperature and had advised against his going to school today, but there was to be a big rally this afternoon to encourage the basketball team for the Thanksgiving Night game, and he mustn't miss it. If she could only persuade him to stay in bed for a day or two.

Mr. Chalmers had called up again this morning, but Hannah had said that neither Mr. or Mrs. Ward could come to the phone now. He wouldn't be quite so attentive — his voice had sounded so sugary — when he learned that the Wards had given up the idea of buying a house. Poor Paul. He not only wasn't going to have a new home; he was arranging matters so as to lose even the little savings deposit at the bank. The lawyer would want that — all that and a promissory note for more.

They shouldn't have begun spending their fortune yet. How foolish of them to have encouraged the children to talk about a car. And the weekly allowance. Imagine! — little Sally! An allowance!

Hannah drew a long sigh. She had five irresponsible children on her hands — not counting her own. She smiled complacently at the precious remembrance. At least, she didn't have to worry about dear little Peter.

Wallie was definitely sick tonight, and they were all anxious. Yesterday had been Thanksgiving Day, and he had been so keen on going to the game that he had kept himself up, stoutly denying that he felt badly. He was so hoarse he could hardly speak, but insisted he had 'sprained' his voice by yelling so much at the rally. Hannah had suggested the clinical thermometer, to which he objected with such a noisy display of annoyance that she desisted, with many misgivings. Paul was sulky and remote, seemingly taking no interest in anything, not even in Wallie's imprudence, and Mrs. Ward was too bothered about Paul's mood to give full attention to any other worry; so the boy had gone to the game, returning at ten, fairly on fire with fever.

Hannah had dosed him with hot drinks and the simple household remedies which he made a feint of resisting, probably because he still wanted to defend his decision to go to the game in the face of her urgent protest. When she went into his room to look at him about five o'clock,

Hannah was frightened. Doctor Bowen came at eight and again at four. Mrs. Ward wondered if they should have a nurse, and the doctor said they would see in the morning. Wallie would have to be watched carefully tonight. Hannah had sat in his room from ten to midnight, Mrs. Ward relieving her then.

It had been a trying day, and Hannah thought she would be the better for a cup of tea. In the kitchen she found Paul munching a snack of cheese and crackers.

'How is he now?'

'Asleep, but restless,' Hannah said. 'He's a sick boy.'

'You mean' — Paul's eyes widened with sudden apprehension — 'you're seriously worried about him? Wallie has been through this again and again, you know.'

'We usually have been able to check it earlier. He kept going too long when he should have been in bed.'

'Yes — and part of that was my fault,' growled Paul remorsefully. 'I was too much occupied with my own troubles.' He regarded her with contracted brows. 'But where were you, Hannah? Why didn't you do something about it? You knew Mrs. Ward and I were at our wits' end . . . didn't you?'

Hannah nodded, but made no reply.

'Don't you realize that I'm ruined?'

'Well,' replied Hannah thoughtfully, 'I don't think you're ruined yet, but I'm awfully afraid you're planning on it.'

'Now just what does that mean?' he rasped.

'You're arranging to fight back, aren't you?'

'Still harping on that silly idea of yours, eh?'

'We can easily change the subject,' said Hannah gently. 'I am sorry if I neglected Wallie. I did try my best to keep him in, but ——'

'But what? Why weren't you firm with him?'

Remembering the tension of Paul's nerves and the reasons he had for being irritable, Hannah ventured no response to this, though she thought of several things she might have said if she had felt it necessary to defend herself. Her failure to reply annoyed him.

'I suppose your silence means that you are practicing your sweet gospel of non-resistance again. I'd much rather you talked, even if you scolded. I hate sulking.'

Hannah poured two cups of tea. He drew his chair up to the table, and shakily fumbled in the sugar-bowl.

'Sit down,' he commanded gruffly. 'I want to tell you about it; should have done so before. On the surface it looks as if we're demolished, but there's the ghost of a chance that we can bring these Ellis people to time. I talked to Barney Harrison about it. He has taken the case, and means to push it to the limit. I intend to fight 'em with every nickel I can raise!'

Hannah drew a long sigh and shook her head.

'You think,' snapped Paul, 'I haven't a fighting chance?'

'I think,' replied Hannah, 'you haven't a chance — fighting.'

'I suppose' — Paul's tone was bitter — 'I suppose you would just sit here and say nothing and let them defraud you ... wouldn't you?' he added, challengingly, when the pause had lengthened.

'No,' said Hannah, without raising her eyes. 'I wouldn't fight, but neither would I just sit here and do nothing about it. The choice of things one might do isn't quite that narrow. First, I should decide not to fight back. And then' — there was a long pause — 'I would hope that — somehow ——'

'An angel from heaven would stroll in,' assisted Paul, with elaborate mockery, 'and hand you full directions for recovering your property by magic.'

Hannah smiled a little, the same smile he had often seen on her lips in acknowledgment of some babyish remark of Sally's.

'That would be very pleasant,' she agreed obligingly. 'May I pour you another cup of tea?'

'Well — I don't believe in magic,' he muttered, pushing his cup toward her.

'Nor do I. But it's a very convenient word to use when something happens that we can't understand. I suppose there are sound laws and rules for everything that occurs — or ever occurred.'

'Now that's much more sensible, Hannah,' approved Paul, in a tone that tried to imitate her recent humoring of him as if he were a child. 'I thought you believed in miracles, and all manner of hocus-pocus. So — you don't take any stock in angels, after all.'

'I never saw one,' admitted Hannah. 'Of course,' she added prudently, 'that does not mean there aren't any. I never saw mountains on the moon, either.'

'Yes, yes, I know; and you never saw any spots on the sun, though they are there and everybody knows it ... but, seriously, you have something in the back of your head, Hannah, that you've been hinting at. No matter how foolish it is, I'll promise to listen.'

'Perhaps I'll try to tell you some day, after you have tried everything else — if you ask me nicely.'

'Have I been so rude to you?'

'What do *you* think?'

'I'm sorry ... I say, Hannah, tell me what's in your mind? What would you do if you were in my place?'

'I would' — she was meditative for a long minute, her eyes averted, her full lips puckered with indecision — 'I would drink that cup of tea while it is still hot, and go to bed, and try to get a couple of hours' sleep. You might relieve Mrs. Ward about two o'clock. No use of everybody's sitting up.'

'How about you?'

'I'm not sleepy.'

'Hannah, forgive me for being snappish with you. I've hardly been myself for days.' He pushed back his chair and rose.

'I think I had noticed that,' she said, amiably enough.

Paul paused in the doorway, not quite satisfied with the close of their conversation.

'You're a deep one, Hannah,' he drawled. 'I'd give a great deal of money to examine the inside of your head.'

Hannah was facing the porcelain sink, pouring hot water over the tea dishes, and without turning replied, 'You'll not have any money to spend on things that are only to be looked at — and not used. Your Mr. Harrison will be wanting your money.'

Paul made no reply, but continued to wait in the doorway. Suddenly penitent over having nagged him when he was wretched with worry, Hannah glanced toward him and added gently: 'But I'll be thinking about you, Mr. Ward. And if there's any way I can help, I'll do it.'

'I know that, Hannah,' he said warmly. 'I had hoped we might soon be in a position to show you how much we have valued your service — and your loyalty. I intended to do something for you.'

She allowed a whole minute to pass before she said quietly, 'Money — you mean?'

'Yes — and freedom from hard work.'

Hannah faced him now with serious eyes.

'I haven't minded the work, Mr. Ward. And I'm not particularly anxious to have more money. But I do very much want us all to be happy, and I'm afraid — I'm afraid we aren't going to be. The track we seem to be on now doesn't point in that direction.'

Paul made an impatient gesture with a flick of his fingers.

'If you think you have a better plan than mine for seeing us out of this mess, why not tell me what it is?'

Leaning back against the edge of the sink, Hannah folded her arms and stared at the floor with studious eyes. Presently she raised her head and with parted lips waited for the right words to organize themselves.

'It isn't a bit easy to talk about,' she began hesitatingly. 'It's something that has to be built up gradually by trying it out and thinking it over. I am sure you couldn't get anywhere with it unless you had some reason for believing and hoping it might succeed. I'm afraid it would sound very foolish to anyone who hadn't experimented with it, at least a little.' Hannah's low voice carried a note of entreaty as she continued, still groping for her words.

'Let me try to tell you what I mean, Mr. Ward. If — if some person, a few years ago, had ordered you to build a refrigerator that made its own ice, and had wanted it delivered at his house within a month, you would have laughed at him. Your invention didn't come that way. I wonder how many hours and miles you tramped back and forth, back and forth, down in that little room in our basement, trying to figure this thing out. And how many times you gave it all up and quit, disgusted. And then went at it again because something kept telling you it was not impossible.

'Well — here is another job for you. If anyone tried to tell you what results you might expect from it when it is finished, you would probably laugh. But if you thought seriously about it for a while, and made a few experiments, it might not seem so silly.' She walked slowly toward the doorway, where he stood listening with a patient but not very encouraging smile. 'Would you be willing to make a little adventure?' she asked earnestly.

'Blindfolded?'

'Something almost like that,' admitted Hannah. 'I'll tell you what you want to know, but first you must invest a little interest in it, or it will seem ridiculous. If you will go downtown in the morning and inform Mr. Harrison not to do anything more about the suit against Mr. Ellis until he hears from you further — *I'll tell you!*'

'Perhaps you'd better tell me first, and if it's a good idea I can easily stop Harrison.'

Hannah shook her head obdurately.

'No — if you haven't enough confidence in me to do that much in advance, my idea wouldn't seem worth bothering about. This will be no easy thing to do, I can tell you, even if you believed in it with all your heart.'

Paul shifted his position uneasily and lighted a cigarette. 'You're making all this sound dreadfully mysterious, Hannah ... I think we had better understand each other. If I am expected to do some preliminary spade-work, preparatory to a grand display of faith, you're — you're putting your money on the wrong horse,' he finished lamely, aware that he would have laughed over such a sentence if a student had executed it in an essay.

'We'll just forget it, then,' said Hannah quietly. 'I'll call you about two o'clock.' She turned and went back to her dishes. Paul remained standing there for a while; then with a long sigh of fatigue and perplexity he moved off through the dining-room, tarried uncertainly for some minutes in the living-room, and slowly mounted the stairs.

Hannah listened attentively to his receding footsteps and tried to interpret them. She had hoped, when they hesitated, that Paul might return and say: 'Very well then. I'll try it.' Perhaps she should have reminded him of the occasions when he had accepted her 'hunches' — as he called them — and had found them useful. Maybe Paul would think of that himself.

But suppose she did contrive to win his consent to make the adventure. It would be risky business. She had never tried out her theory on anything so important as this. What if Paul experimented with it — just to humor her — and failed?

Doctor Bowen had arrived in the morning as Roberta and Sally were leaving for school. After five minutes upstairs he had telephoned for a nurse, who came very soon in a taxi. Hannah, who had been anxiously on the alert, admitted her before she had a chance to ring.

'Gregory,' barked the nurse, handing Hannah her suitcase. She was forty, tall, lean, grim, and businesslike.

Hannah led the way to her own room and Miss Gregory began changing into her uniform, indicating by the careful timing of a sniff and a shrug that she disliked the idea of sharing the maid's quarters, even briefly. Promptly aware that nothing was wanted of her but her departure, Hannah went quietly downstairs and tried to busy herself with the usual morning's work. Her hands trembled.

Presently Paul came through, attended to the furnace, and said, 'I'm going down to a pharmacy to have some prescriptions filled.'

'How is he?' asked Hannah, trying to steady her voice. Paul did not reply. She followed him to the hall door and held his overcoat. He avoided her eyes. She softly closed the door behind him and watched his uneven, half-shuffling steps as he hurried jerkily toward the corner where he would take the street-car.

Mrs. Ward came down for a spoon. She had been crying. Hannah saw that she did not wish to be queried.

Then Doctor Bowen drove away, returning in a half-hour with another doctor. Miss Gregory came down with a handful of instruments and boiled them in a pan. Unable any longer to restrain her anxiety Hannah asked, in a half-whisper, 'Is it pneumonia?'

Without turning, Miss Gregory replied crisply, 'Doctor Bowen will probably tell Mr. and Mrs. Ward whatever he thinks they ought to know about the case.'

So — that was that, and now we knew exactly where we stood. Hannah felt a moment's resentment, but after a while she thought differently about Miss Gregory's surliness. The nurse wasn't here to express her own opinions, certainly not to an inquisitive maid-of-all-work who might try to be chummy unless promptly squelched. And Miss Gregory couldn't be expected to know the peculiar relation which this one maid sustained to the family.

Of course, reflected Hannah, it could have been done a little less unkindly. Miss Gregory probably had no personal sentiments about face-saving. Or, perhaps she had lost face herself, and was hoping to get it back by making other people lose theirs.

Miss Gregory called for a towel, and supporting the hot

pan in it she left the kitchen, intent on her occupation and
without a backward glance. After a while Doctor Bowen
left, but the younger doctor remained. Miss Gregory came
down then and said, 'I want a cup of strong coffee, a
poached egg, and a piece of toast.' Hannah complied
quickly, laying a place at the dining-table while the coffee
was brewing.

'Never mind — I'll have it right here in the kitchen —
standing.'

Hannah hoped Miss Gregory was as competent as she
was impolite. Too bad that poor little Wallie had to be
nursed by a person with such bad manners, though he
probably wouldn't notice, at least not today. She poured
the coffee and arranged the other things on the porcelain
table.

'Thanks,' said Miss Gregory.

Mrs. Ward came into the kitchen.

'Having lunch?' she asked, a bit annoyed.

'Breakfast,' replied Miss Gregory.

'Oh. You didn't have your breakfast?'

'There wasn't time. I was just going off night duty
when Doctor Bowen called, and — there wasn't time.'

Hannah brightened a little. Miss Gregory had good reasons for being snappish. She was worn out. Perhaps she
was a decent sort when properly treated. Stepping to the
range after Mrs. Ward had left the room, Hannah said
companionably: 'I'm going to fix you another egg. It will
be ready in a minute.'

'Thanks,' replied Miss Gregory, slightly thawed.

'Too bad you had to go so long without your coffee.'
Hannah's tone was genuinely sympathetic.

Miss Gregory nodded.

'Too bad for you, too,' she remarked dryly. 'I'm mean
as hell when I'm tired and hungry.'

Hannah regarded her with one of the puckery little smiles
which she often employed in condoning the small blunders
of the children, and Miss Gregory, glancing up, interpreted
it.

'What's your name?' she asked, with a brief grin.

'Hannah.'

'Is that all?'

'Usually.'

Miss Gregory's grin broadened a little.

'Been here long?'

'Since Wallie was about four.'

'Well, in that case you have a right to know that he is a very, very sick boy. It looks bad. We're going to know more about it before tomorrow morning, I think. Doctor Rogers gave him a serum. We can't do much now but wait.'

'Thanks for telling me,' murmured Hannah, rubbing away the tears.

'There's another nurse relieving me presently. Where do I sleep? I must have some rest — if I'm to be of any use tonight.'

'You're not going away, then?' Hannah's voice carried so much spontaneous gratitude that Miss Gregory sensed it.

'No — I am going to see it through.'

'May I make up my bed for you? It's really all we have to offer.'

'Please. You look tired too, Hannah. How long since you slept?'

'I'm quite all right, Miss Gregory.' Hannah tried to prove it by straightening her shoulders.

'Don't want any pity, eh?' Then, after a pause, 'Are you somehow related to — to these people?'

Hannah shook her head.

'Just the maid?' pursued Miss Gregory.

'That's all.'

Regarding Hannah for a moment with studious interest, and seeming about to venture a comment which, on second thought, she vetoed, Miss Gregory stretched her arms to full length, gave way to an undisguised yawn, smiled, shook her head slowly, and murmured a mystified little 'Humm-humm — humm,' deep in her throat, inflected as if she were saying, 'Funny world.'

Hannah had carefully tiptoed up and down the stairs a half dozen times between ten and eleven, but because there was nothing she could do she had resolved to remain in the kitchen now and try to be patient. The long strain was beginning to tell on her strength. Her heart-beats bumped in her dry throat.

Doctor Bowen was in with Wallie, and Miss Gregory too. Paul and Mrs. Ward were in their own room with the door ajar. Doubtless the doctor had advised them to remain outside the sickroom. Roberta, pale and frightened but composed, had consented to go to bed. Sally had sobbed herself to sleep at nine. The ominous sound of Wallie's labored breathing tugged at Hannah's chest and made her draw long, deep breaths in his behalf. Occasionally there was a little stir upstairs — the tinkle of ice in a glass, the moving of a chair, the creak of a door-hinge; but mostly it was quiet — except for Wallie's mounting battle with the Thing. His disease had taken on something like personality, in Hannah's overwrought mind. The Thing had Wallie by the throat and was trying to strangle him. You wanted to rush into the room and tug the Thing's talons out of his slim, throbbing neck. Hannah clenched her agitated hands into white-knuckled fists, closed her eyes tightly, and tried to endure.

A little before midnight Paul came down. Hannah recognized his steps on the stairs and met him in the kitchen doorway. He had eaten nothing all day but a brief breakfast of coffee and toast, and looked indescribably fagged. When he spoke, the words came wearily, woodenly.

'The doctor gave Mrs. Ward a sedative and she's having a little sleep . . . I don't see how my boy can stand this strain much longer. His heart, you know.'

Hannah could not trust herself to offer any comment. Lighting the gas in the range, she began to prepare a lunch for him.

'Perhaps Dr. Bowen and Miss Gregory would like something to eat, too,' she said.

Paul shook his head.

'I asked them and they said "No — not now."' He took Hannah's chair at the kitchen table and sat in silence while she went about her task. Presently, as she stood waiting for the coffee, he faced her with an odd expression as if he had something to say that required resolution.

'Hannah ——' Paul's voice sounded remote and spent but the tone predicted an important announcement. 'Hannah — I have been doing a great deal of thinking to-night... emergency thinking... I've never taken much interest in the idea that the things we do and the things we believe can — influence, in any way, whatever powers there may be — outside and beyond ourselves... and I'm not sure, even now, that I have any faith to offer. My mind is upset, and I know I'm not using it according to its habits. But so many people have believed — and do believe. I've been groping about to see if I could do it too. I have even tried to pray — but it has seemed an awfully caddish thing for me to do.'

'Not when you were doing it for Wallie,' suggested Hannah softly. 'You weren't asking anything for yourself.'

'Of course I was,' he contradicted. 'I want my boy to live — more than I want to live myself... but I couldn't pray. Not with the slightest hope that anything might come of it... And then it occurred to me that I might at least *do* something... So — I have decided, Hannah, that if Wallie gets well I'll drop the whole business of suing the Ellises... That's a definite *promise!*'

Hannah's eyes widened with an apprehension that was almost terror.

'Oh!' she pleaded, 'you mustn't do that!' She stepped toward him and clutched his shoulder. 'Oh, Paul, please don't say that again!' Her words tumbled over each other breathlessly. 'I'm so afraid! Oh — don't do that! You mustn't! It's dangerous! We might lose him!'

As she stood there shaken with convulsive sobs, Paul stared up at her with an expression of utter amazement.

He rose, and tugging her hands from her eyes, muttered, 'What do you mean? What have I done? Tell me!'

Hannah made a brave effort to recover her composure.

'Do you think They would let you drive a bargain with Them?' she said, huskily.

'They?' echoed Paul.

Hannah made a little gesture of impatience.

'They — or He — or It — or Whoever. I don't know anything about it — except — I know you mustn't trifle with Them! Risky business!'

She was a new Hannah, with whom Paul had had no previous acquaintance. He had never seen her stirred before. Her hands were trembling and her harassed eyes looked suddenly old — in years, experience, prescience.

'But — Hannah!' he asked, perplexed. 'Isn't that what you have been wanting me to do?'

'Oh, yes — but not *that way!* You mustn't try to bring your offering *to market!* ... If you want to make this adventure you will have to come the whole way with it!'

'Meaning — I'll not sue — no matter what happens to Wallie?'

'Exactly that! *Say it! Swear it!*' Hannah reached out her hand. There was a long moment of waiting.

'Very well, Hannah,' said Paul, steadying his voice. 'I give you my hand on it. If anybody knows about these things, I believe you do. I promise. Whatever may happen to my boy — I'll do nothing more to get my property back from the Ellises.'

She searched his face with shining eyes.

'I'm glad,' she whispered, clinging to his hand.

'You honestly believe in this — *don't* you?'

'Yes.'

'I wish I could — as you do.'

Hannah's forehead lined with perplexity, and a moment passed before she replied.

'I don't think that matters so much. You might have had plenty of belief that didn't cost you anything. But now you have pledged yourself to something that may cost you thousands. You might have fought this Mr. Ellis and won the case. And you might have filled your pockets with money. You have given that up. Why shouldn't They respect what you have done? . . . But — how are you going to feel' — she hesitated, her questing eyes searching his at close range — 'and how are you going to act — *if They don't?*'

'I'll try not to complain, Hannah, and I intend to keep my word . . . Honestly — do you think They will let us keep Wallie?'

She closed her tired eyes, unable to meet his challenge with the kind of assurance he sought. What had she done to her friend? Out of her agony and wistfulness she had suggested the surrender of his only hope to salvage a long-cherished dream. And who was she — old Dan Parmalee's daughter, maid-of-all-work, with almost no education — who was she to be committing a university professor to a test that might fail? What right had she to be talking so confidently about what They might do? What did she know about the mysterious ways of Them — or Him — or Who-ever-it-is? She didn't even go to church on Sundays.

'I hope so, Paul,' she said earnestly. 'But I do not know.'

He turned away and went back to his post of waiting. Hannah sank into the chair and listened to his footsteps ascending the stairs, wondering whether it was merely her own imagination that made them sound like the steady stride of a hopeful spirit. The echoes of the strange conversation lingered . . . Well — it was now up to Them! How would They feel about this unusual transaction? So far as this present adventure was concerned, it wouldn't make much difference how Paul felt about it. The question was: What would *They* think?

The talk with Hannah had done something to him. The new sensation was difficult to define. Of course, he reflected, at a time like this one's mind could be expected to cut some queer capers. You couldn't subject yourself to the neural strains and drains of the past few days and expect to remain normal. He had been plowed and harrowed in all directions, up and down and criss-cross. He sat in Marcia's boudoir chair and gazed out into the night, amazed that the darkness did not depress him.

This strange feeling of calmness was probably an hallucination. Hannah's faith had acted hypnotically on him at a moment when he was too far spent, neurally, to offer any resistance or point out any of the fallacies in her philosophy. But the most remarkable phenomenon of this curious emotional experience was the sheer fact that he found it comforting. His mind had been in a tumult. Now it was at peace. And the 'peace' was not the mere inertia and indifference of exhaustion: rather was it in the nature of a dynamic, a stimulant! It wasn't as if he had simply lost his spirit of stormy revolt against a sinister Fate that had robbed him of his right to a fortune and was now burning up his child. It wasn't a mere surrender. No — it was a *positive* thing! This new sensation seemed to have been produced not by the letting go of anything but by the laying hold on something! The inexplicable 'peace' — if that was the word — was not in the nature of a resignation: it was an *accretion!* Not an abdication, but an *accession!*

From the moment he had given Hannah the promise, this peculiar experience had begun to operate. The fiddle-string tension of his nerves had relaxed. The sense of foreboding and fear and dejection had been put to rest as if by some benign narcotic.

For a little while he tried to analyze his mood; but he soon discovered that he was content to accept the new 'peace' on its own terms without examining it too closely, fearing he might rationalize it away.

As he passed the open door of Wallie's room, the sickish feeling of fear that had come to him when, an hour ago, he had looked in on the flushed, swollen, almost unrecognizable face of his boy, did not recur.

Marcia was still asleep. He sat quietly in the low chair by the window. Doubtless this feeling would pass presently. It had arisen out of extraordinary circumstances and when the immediate problem had been solved — one way or the other — he might expect this remarkable experience to come to an end, perhaps never to be recaptured.

Some day, a month from now, he might resume his passionate wish for the retrieve of the fortune he had lost. At the moment, the loss was of no consequence at all. Doubtless he would again find himself hating and despising the Ellises with a contempt that embittered his very food, but he did not hate them now. It was a relief to ease this strain and unload this burden. He had not realized what an amount of energy had been required to sustain that galling weight.

It would pass, of course. It was a mere phantom. But for the hour it offered a healing for his spirit.

At three o'clock Miss Gregory came down. Hannah, who had been sound asleep with her head on her arms, roused at the sound of the competent steps. Something in the Gregory manner speeded Hannah's pulse. She glanced up inquiringly.

'He's — he's a little better?' she asked, entreaty in her eyes.

'By God — the boy may pull it over. He's perspiring.' Miss Gregory dragged the kettle over the gas-flame and signaled Hannah not to rise. 'Now — don't get me wrong,' she cautioned, suddenly blunt. 'Wallie has a chance — that's all. He is a stout young fellow. It's a good pump he has. Maybe it will pull him through. That — and the serum. He seems to be responding to the serum.'

Hannah stared up at her with parted lips and wide eyes swimming with tears. A mysterious smile slowly lighted her face.

'Serum?' she repeated, hardly above a whisper.

'The antitoxin. It works about once in a blue moon. Where do you keep the coffee?'

Chapter VII

CHRISTMAS was more tender than merry. Wallie's convalescence had proceeded slowly. For a full week after the acute crisis of his pneumonia had been reached, his recovery was still in doubt. Paul went to no classes. The doctor came twice a day. Miss Gregory was constantly on the alert. The family moved about softly, silently, haggard with worry.

It was a great day when Doctor Bowen said Wallie might sit up for a little while, and a greater one when his father carried him downstairs and carefully deposited him in a big leather chair by the grate, where they all clustered about him with a wide-eyed devotion that made him grin selfconsciously. Embarrassed, the boy broke the silence by swallowing noisily, deep in his thin white neck, and saying in a weak voice, 'Well — here we all are,' which made them laugh through their tears. Hannah promptly retired to the kitchen, followed by Miss Gregory. Sally went also, returning presently with a hot doughnut generously sprinkled with powdered sugar. She put it in Wallie's bony hand.

'Of all things, Sally!' said their mother gently. 'A doughnut — for a sick man!'

'You ought to see your face,' giggled Wallie, pointing a shaky finger. Then they all laughed at Sally, with powdered sugar on her plump cheeks, her round chin, and the tip of her nose. Even Roberta laughed, and detaching herself from the group wound up the phonograph for some Christmas hymns and carols. And when Trinity Choir sang 'Unto

Us a Son is Given,' Marcia, deeply moved, groped for
Paul's hand.

A little later in the kitchen she said to Hannah, who was
cutting out cookies in shapes of stars and trees and angels,
'We could very well get along without any other Christmas gifts this year, now that Wallie is safe.' And Hannah
rather wished they might all feel that way about it, for expenses had been high and it would be difficult to meet their
current bills in full, even if no more money was spent for
presents.

But Paul seemed to think that Wallie's recovery deserved
a special celebration. The child had been through a harrow-
ing experience, and this Christmas should be made a joyful occasion for him. If it cost a little more than they might
have spent under normal circumstances, so be it. It was no
time to count nickels.

And if Wallie was to have nice presents, the others should
have them too. Indeed, they all merited gifts, after the long
strain they had endured. It had been a frightful milling,
reiterated Paul, and they were going to make something of
Christmas this time, and the expenses, he continued, could
be damned. All this to Hannah, on the day Wallie sat up
for the first time. She hadn't the courage to caution him,
and promptly surprised both Paul and herself by conceding
the point, adding, however, that she wished the expenses
could realize that they were damned, to which he laughingly
replied that she was priceless. She then gave him one of
those half-teasing, puckery smiles which always left him
guessing what retort she had resolved not to make. 'It's
a good thing I am priceless,' thought Hannah, 'if we are to
have a grand spree of spending.'

'I've got Wallie the best bicycle to be had in town,' said
Paul.

'He'll love that,' Hannah heard herself saying. 'I hope it
will be an early spring, so he won't have to wait too long to
enjoy it.'

'You know, Hannah' — Paul's face was perplexed —

'I hadn't thought of that. However' — he brightened
quickly — 'he'll have fun owning it — and it will be something to look forward to.'

Hannah nodded. 'Just like the doll perambulator,' she
observed.

'It's a wonder I didn't think of that,' regretted Paul.
'But Sally can play with the doll, at least. It's quite a
novelty, you know.'

And so it was. It was a talking doll. Paul had made a
great event of showing it to Mrs. Ward and Hannah. He
had stored it in the attic. Hannah thought she knew why
he had asked them to view it together. Mrs. Ward had not
been consulted about these expensive gifts for the children;
had had no part in selecting them. Hannah knew exactly
how it had come about. Paul had been downtown on an errand the day Wallie had sat up for the first time. Beside
himself with joy and relief, he had impulsively decided on a
noteworthy Christmas celebration. Of course it would have
to be arranged for at once, on the spot, without a moment's
further consideration. It wouldn't occur to him until afterward that this was a selfish, childish, silly thing to do. Anyone else in the whole wide world, reflected Hannah, would
have paused to wonder if these extravagant gifts might not
make Mrs. Ward's discreet purchases for the children seem
cheap and beggarly by comparison. Now that Paul had
done it, perhaps he was a little bit ashamed.

So that was why, with much hush-hushing, he had tiptoed Mrs. Ward and Hannah to the attic, after the children
were in bed, to see the talking doll in a perambulator, big
and sturdy enough for a live baby. He knew Hannah
wouldn't chide him for the expense — not when the three
of them were together. And he knew Mrs. Ward wouldn't
be able to inquire, in Hannah's presence, why he hadn't
asked his wife to lend a hand in this adventure.

They shivered in the cold, exhaling spouts of steam,
while he unwrapped the bulky parcel. They looked and listened. In an impassive face, the doll's mouth gasped like

an expiring fish, and from somewhere in its abdomen a series of mechanical squawks was audible. By the use of a little imagination, one suspected that the doll said 'Papa — Mamma — Baby.'

'She hasn't been talking long,' Paul observed wittily, when the silence had begun to pile up.

Hannah was so full of unrelieved laughter that her side ached. She couldn't risk opening her mouth to offer a comment, and hoped Mrs. Ward would have something to say very soon, which she did.

'No — she hasn't a very wide vocabulary, has she?'

To this crisp observation Paul replied defensively that he thought the doll did very well to be able to talk at all. Then they looked at the expensive outfit of artists' supplies which were to be Roberta's, and Mrs. Ward remarked that a professional portrait painter would be happy to have it. It was too cold to linger very long, so they clattered down the narrow attic stairs, and by the time they were on the first floor Mrs. Ward had resumed her good nature. Hannah was glad. You had to forgive this fellow. After all, he was a grand person, if you knew how to take him. Mrs. Ward was behaving very well, Hannah thought, especially when she remarked that the paints and brushes would be quite an inspiration to Roberta.

After she had returned to her room, Paul came out to the kitchen with a beautifully ornamented round box and said it was the gift he had bought for Mrs. Ward. Hannah was afraid it was a hat, at first, but it turned out to be a dozen Cauldon service plates.

'Worth twelve dollars apiece,' said Paul impressively. 'Had them for eight because Bowker's was a bit overstocked. The man said they were really an extraordinary buy.'

'Yes,' agreed Hannah, 'I think that too.'

Paul beamed on her appreciatively. 'Beautiful, aren't they?' he demanded.

'Exquisite!' breathed Hannah.

He had never heard her use the word before, and admiration shone in his eyes, maybe because she had pronounced it correctly. He didn't think much of the mentality of women who said 'ex*quis*ite.' He always told the freshmen, early in the year, that a woman who would say 'ex*quis*ite' always had an untidy mind, and was likely to begin every other paragraph with 'Well — anyway.'

'You think she will like them?' insisted Paul, more confidently.

'Of course. Why not? They're lovely.'

After a moment more of silent admiration, Paul carefully stowed the plates in the silk-lined box. Drawing out his worn wallet, he extracted two tens and a five. Hannah could not help noticing that it left the pocketbook flat.

'For you,' he said gently. 'I wish it was more.'

'Thank you, Mr. Ward. You are all very kind to me.' Hannah's voice was tender. She looked up into his eyes and smiled. He returned the smile, and then they shook hands, wondering a little why they were doing so. Upon the bestowal of gifts, in the Ward household, it was customary for the beneficiary to kiss the donor. Maybe that was why they were shaking hands, Hannah thought. She could have kissed him, she knew, without affecting their relation the least bit; but perhaps it was better to shake hands. On second thought, it was ever so much better.

'We are all going to have a merry Christmas, aren't we?' she said, slipping the money into her apron pocket. He nodded, and made quite a ceremony over the lighting of a cigarette. Hannah poured him a glass of milk and cut a slice of cake. There would be an after-Christmas sale of canned vegetables at the stores. One could do a great deal with twenty-five dollars. It would relieve the strain of the next monthly statements.

'Funny thing,' said Paul, putting down the empty glass, 'I never felt just this way about Christmas before. The spirit of it, you know. I feel as if I knew what it is all about, this time. It's Wallie, of course. But the good-will part of it — that never struck me so forcibly. Peace and good-will toward men — and all that sort of thing. I don't even despise the Ellises.'

'You know why, don't you?' said Hannah gently.

'Well, I know what you're thinking, of course. I promised not to fight them. But that didn't mean I was going to stop hating them. Just now it doesn't seem to matter much. I can't quite understand my own feelings, though I've tried to analyze them. Some of the factors to the problem are clear enough. The emotional part of it is simple: Wallie's recovery. My home has suddenly become the most important fact in the world. And that's not hard to see through. I was defeated on the outside, and have been driven back. I'm in the position of the prodigal who, having lost his fortune, hurried home and found it a more interesting institution than it ever was before.'

'You know, Hannah,' he went on, choosing his words with a view to their simplicity, 'back in the Middle Ages a feudal lord would build a huge wall around everything he owned: houses, barns, shops, mills, fields, orchards, groves — everything. Then he would dig a deep ditch around his estate and run it full of water. Occasionally he would organize his men and go out to stage a big fight. Whether he won or lost, there was always a home-base to return to. Whenever he had had enough of fighting he could go back, pull up the sturdy old drawbridge, and thumb his nose at the whole world. Everything he really needed was snug inside the wall. Well, that's the way I feel now. I made an excursion, and I've been licked. Now I'm home again. It's a good place to be.'

Hannah had been listening with wide-eyed interest. A great deal of what Paul had been saying stirred memories of Philip's frequent references to modes of life long, long ago. She made no comment, realizing that Paul hadn't finished what he wanted to say. She nodded encouragingly, and waited.

'But here is the thing that mystifies me, Hannah. Why

did I stop hating the Ellises? The reason for my hating
them has not changed in the slightest degree. They stole
my only chance to set myself free and live a privileged life.
They have not given my property back. And I have promised not to exercise my lawful right to it. But I don't
care. I am entirely satisfied.'

Hannah's eyes sparkled.

'That's the best news I've heard for a long time. I don't
think there is anything so mysterious about it. You loathed
and despised the Ellises because you felt they had beaten
you. Now you've left off hating them. Can't you understand what that means? Down inside yourself, somewhere,
you have decided that the Ellises have not beaten you.
That's the explanation of this feeling of safety, security,
same as the lord behind the high wall and the what-you-
may-call-it. Philip used to talk about it.'

'Moat,' supplied Paul, with a grin. 'Who was Philip?
I never heard you speak of him before . . . But — look here!
You aren't meaning to imply that I have got the better of
the Ellises just because I've stopped wanting to bite them?'

Hannah's face had suddenly sobered.

'I'll tell you all about Philip — sometime. It's a long
story. Maybe you would be interested . . . I'm not sure
just how you have overcome the Ellises. It's enough to
know that you really have. It will all come out, I suppose,
and then we'll know. This much is sure: when a person
makes a costly giving-up, he gets something for it. I don't
pretend to understand it. I just know that one gets a new
power to — to deal with things.'

Paul regarded her with fresh interest and curiosity for
some minutes, then paced slowly back and forth, hands
deep in his coat-pockets.

'Hannah' — he stopped and faced her with the severity
of a prosecutor — 'I'm going to ask you a direct question.
Do you honestly believe that my decision, that night,
accounted for Wallie's recovery?'

'I do not know,' replied Hannah, so softly that the words

were barely audible. 'But I think it had everything to do with yours.'

'Was I sick, too?'

'Very.'

'Well — be that as it may.' Paul seemed impatient to settle the case of Wallie's rescue. 'The doctor and the nurse think the serum saved my boy's life. What do you think?'

'It might have been the serum,' conceded Hannah. 'They ought to know.'

'Yes, but didn't you get yourself all stirred up when you thought I was dickering with Them — or Him — or It? Don't you remember?'

'I didn't want you to take the risk of doing Wallie some damage,' explained Hannah weakly.

'Ah — there you are!' Paul leaned over the table and searched her eyes. 'The wrong way to have done it might have hurt Wallie. That means that the right way to have done it might have helped Wallie. And now you admit that you don't know.'

'That's because I am trying to be honest,' declared Hannah, accenting her words. 'We're dealing with something here that nobody knows very much about. I'm sure I don't. I hoped you might do Wallie some good. He was so very sick that anything was worth trying. We tried it — and Wallie got well. Wallie also had fine care, all the way through his sickness, and there was the serum. Why should I be asked to say whether I thought the serum had anything to do with Wallie's getting well? How could I know? Perhaps I have some private ideas on the subject — but maybe they're not worth much. I'm not a doctor.'

Paul nodded his head several times and pursed his lips tightly.

'So you think it may have been the serum, after all, now that we're calm enough to look at the affair unemotionally.'

'Yes — it might have been the serum that cured Wallie, but — my friend' — Hannah's voice took on a confident

tone — 'it was something else than serum that cured *you!*
You hated the Ellis brothers because they had power over
you. Now you've stopped hating them because *you* have
been given power. I haven't the faintest idea what you're
going to do with it, but it's there to be used for something —
if you want to. I'm quite sure of that.'

'Now, Hannah, you're getting beyond my depth again,'
growled Paul.

'I mean, you've been given something that makes you
feel secure again. Perhaps you could put this power to work
on some other big problem.'

Paul shrugged a shoulder and muttered that he supposed
she meant he could do something about his debts. Hannah
shook her head. 'Nonsense!' she exclaimed. 'We paid the
debts before. We can do it again. That's simple enough.
I'm thinking about something *important!*'

'Another invention, maybe,' scoffed Paul. 'Well, let me
tell you something, Hannah. It's beyond hope that I'll
ever think up another invention — and see it through to
the end.'

Hannah rubbed her temples hard with her strong fingers
and after a long silence replied, as from a distance, 'Maybe
you didn't see this one through to the end.'

'It made ice, didn't it? That's all it was for — wasn't
it?' Paul's voice rose a little, half testily. 'I never thought
it would shovel snow, or mow the lawn, or answer the doorbell. How do you mean, I didn't see it through to the
end?'

She motioned to him to sit down.

'I'm going to tell you about Philip Raymond, Paul.'
Her voice was very low and the words came slowly. 'When
I was a young girl I was very much in love with a boy who
was sick. He was the son of the people I worked for. He
liked me and I often read to him. And he used to talk to
me. In fact, everything I believe that is worth believing
I owe to Philip. He knew he was going to die. Things close
at hand didn't interest him.'

'Thinking about the future?' asked Paul, wanting to seem interested.

'Not the least bit. He was always talking about the past, same as you were a while ago. Sometimes he would ramble on for a whole afternoon about the history of ancient people; how they would be driven from one country to another by fierce tribes. And every time they had to face the hard conditions of living in a new land they became more powerful.'

'Of course! "Root, hog — or die!"'

'Yes. Came to a country where there were no natural caves to live in and the rocks were too heavy to lift. So — one of them invented a pulley. And — after that — they could lift anything they pleased, no matter how big it was. Philip said they never could have done it if they hadn't been driven out of the safe and pleasant country they had owned. They had to give up everything they possessed for that pulley, but it was the pulley that made it possible for them to erect great buildings and monuments. And it was these buildings and monuments that gave them a feeling of natural pride.

'And then the windlass. And when their stone chisels were too soft for dealing with such great blocks of granite, a man made a heavier tool of metal. Philip said they never would have discovered the use of metal back in the old country where their food grew wild on the trees and the days were never cold. And then there was always a new sense of freedom when they were forced to leave everything and run for their lives. You see, they would have gathered up a great lot of things that held them fast; herds of cattle to be fed, sheep to be sheared, corn to be harvested, furniture and pottery to be guarded against thieves. The things they owned had made slaves of them. And then they would be lashed and slapped and kicked out of their country by invaders. They would hurry away with nothing but their knapsacks, leaving all their property behind. Everything they had would be lost — but they would have come into

a new freedom. It was the very things they had owned
that had kept them from coming into new power. They
found their lives by losing them.'

Paul drew a long sigh and chuckled.

'That's all very well, Hannah, as an explanation of
dawn-man development. I'm afraid your Philip would have
had a rough time trying to apply it to our own affairs
today.'

Hannah's eyes lighted.

'But that's what Philip was trying to get at, you see!
He said that if a man, today, would resolve to disarm and
let the greedy people rob him of everything he owned,
occasionally, forcing him to adopt new habits and new
methods of work, he might expect to become great! The
same difficult conditions that led to the invention of the
needle and the compass and the saw and the lever, Philip
thought, would develop a man *now!*'

'Of course I see what you're trying to say, Hannah,' said
Paul cannily. 'The Ellises steal my invention and strip
me of a fortune that was all but in hand. My job now is
to leave it, without protest, and build something else —
spider fashion. There's nothing new about that doctrine.
Children have been speaking pieces about it on Friday
afternoons at school for five thousand years.'

Hannah was quiet for a moment, and then remarked
dryly that if people had been teaching this to their children
for five thousand years perhaps there was some truth in it.
This made Paul laugh. He rose, stretched his long arms,
and signified that the lengthy discussion — so far as he was
concerned — had reached the time for adjournment.

'Very well, Hannah,' he said drollishly. 'The Ellises
having cleaned me out I'll take up my bag and pilgrim's
staff and seek a new country ... But — I really can't think
of anything more to be done to the refrigerator.'

'Maybe not,' replied Hannah. 'Somebody will. Why
not you?'

Something had been cautioning Hannah that it was all too good to be true; that a reaction would set in; that this calm spirit of Paul's might be expected to boil over one of these days.

Wallie had gone back to school on the tenth and the customary routine of the house was resumed almost as if nothing had ever happened to disturb it. Perhaps all the attention he had received for five weeks had given him some odd ideas about his relation to the other objects of creation. If so, what else could you expect? He was only a boy, and at a period of life when being a boy was a difficult job, even if the conditions were entirely normal.

There was quite a spirited discussion at the table on Saturday noon, Wallie having announced that he was going skating with Billy Prentice, and his father having forbidden it because there had been a thaw.

'But the ice is three feet thick, Dad,' pursued Wallie.

'I don't believe it. And you're not to go. We've had all the worry about you that the traffic will stand. You mustn't give us any more of it — not for a while.' Paul's voice was hard. But then, he had had a rough morning — going through his bills. There wasn't much he could do about them, but there they were. It wasn't a suitable time for Wallie to rub him the wrong way. Hannah wished she might get the boy off in a corner and give him a word or two on the subject.

'It wasn't my fault if I took sick — and pretty near died, was it?' demanded Wallie, still capitalizing the seriousness of his recent disability, and rather surprised that so grave a matter could be viewed otherwise than with the greatest tenderness.

'I'm not so sure,' muttered Paul. Marcia broke in to inquire if he wanted a little Worcester sauce for his Spanish omelet, but he merely shook his head in the general direction of her distracting inquiry. 'You would go to that basketball game, in spite of everything that was done to dissuade you. You knew that I was in a serious business difficulty, and had no time or thought for anything but that. So you defied everybody and went to the game when you were sick and should have been in bed.'

Roberta said, 'Excuse me, please,' and began edging off her chair.

'Better finish your luncheon, dear,' advised Marcia, in a low voice. 'You'll be hungry after a while.'

'Let her go,' growled Paul. 'If Roberta is too sensitive to bear with her father while he announces a few simple truths, let her go. She'll have more fun sulking than eating. ... What I am trying to say, Wallie, is that you are not to go skating this afternoon. It's much too risky. You take a chance on coming home drenched to the skin, or drowned, maybe.'

'I have some work to do,' mumbled Roberta, leaving the table.

'Never mind, Daddy, I'll stick,' promised Sally amiably. 'I love quarreling, so long's I'm not in it.' She passed her plate. 'A little more please ... Now, Wallie, you say, "But Billy's father is letting *him* go."'

'You shut up,' snarled Wallie. 'And stop being so darn cute.'

'Oh — children!' pleaded Marcia.

Paul dealt severely with an incipient grin, and gave Sally a private wink along with another helping of the omelet.

'I saw you do that,' grumbled Wallie.

'Bright eyes,' remarked Sally, to her plate.

'That will be all,' decided Paul. 'Wallie, you may plan to amuse yourself some other way this afternoon.' His voice softened. 'We can't have you sick any more, you know.'

With her palms upturned idly in her lap Marcia gazed woodenly out at the dazzling sunshine, her impassive face registering quiet, resigned disgust for the whole affair. She couldn't think where the children had derived their snappishness. Certainly not from her. Nor her people. As she had often said, the Wallace home was a peaceful haven. By unspoken agreement they rose and left the table, Marcia

going up to her room. Wallie left by the front door, which
he closed after him with a significant emphasis. Sally joined
Hannah in the kitchen.

'They're all so funny,' she said, munching a cookie.

'You shouldn't laugh at people when they're disturbed
about something,' admonished Hannah.

'You said sometimes a laugh would stop a quarrel,
Hannah. You know you did,' defended Sally, trying to play
at being misunderstood.

'It's better to make a little joke about yourself, dear, and
have them laugh at *you*.'

'But I don't know any jokes on myself,' protested Sally.

'Then you should find some. People who can't remember
at least a few good jokes on themselves aren't very well-
to-do — inside.'

Their talk was interrupted by Paul's passing through the
kitchen to look at the furnace. His face was gloomy. He
closed the door after him at the top of the stairs, as if to say
he'd had enough family and wished to put the whole outfit
behind him for an interval.

He had always despised Saturdays, even as a lad. Always there were unpleasant chores to be done. Sunday
was dull enough, but you didn't have to chop kindling or
sort spotty apples. Out in rural Iowa they had always
remembered the Sabbath Day to keep it holy. He had
remembered it ever since, Sunday for its holiness. Saturday
was a day to be remembered too   for its grubbiness.

It occurred to him that he might run over to the University Club and play billiards. But that would mean tea and
cakes. The bills were plenty large. It was high time he was
economizing. He stirred the furnace savagely and a huge
puff of smarting smoke belched forth. Not very good coal,
this time. Some of Hannah's doings, probably. Trying
to save money. He threw in two shovelfuls of coal and
banged the hot door shut with his foot.

At the entrance of the little fruit-cellar he paused. The
wreck of his motor lay exactly where he had left it. Leaning

a shoulder against the door-jamb, he regarded the thing with sour reproach. No new thoughts occurred to him in respect to this smashed machine. He could face it now without loathing. It was no longer the pitiful corpse of a cherished dream, but the dried skeleton. His interest in it seemed remote, impersonal.

After all, there wasn't much to live for when you came to look at human existence rationally. You began with the idea that you were, potentially, a very remarkable fellow. At twelve, you recited 'Excelsior,' and learned your syntax by performing anatomical dissections of classic prose inviting you to make a better mouse-trap. When you graduated from high school, you made a speech largely compiled from the advices of inspirational authors and wound up at the end with a hoarse sentence from the 'Message to Garcia.' The old man who talked at your college Commencement dared you to go out and run circles around the whole bunch, both ancient and contemporary. So, you let them dazzle you with that kind of prattle from the time you were able to blow your own nose until the drudgeries of daily work completely swamped you.

You went into the groove-shop and looked them all over carefully and picked out a nice smooth groove that you thought was about your size. Then you sat yourself neatly into it and started on your ring-around-a-rosy, making the groove a little deeper with every revolution until the sleek walls of it began to compress your elbows against your ribs. That was the worst part of it — the surrender of elbow-room. You felt stifled. Your wife was devoted and you adored her, but she clung to you like the drowning, shutting off your air, so it was impossible for you to rescue either her or yourself. Your children acquired longer legs and worse manners. They used you for a beast of burden and ridiculed you for putting up with it. Your monthly bills — Good God!

There were footsteps on the stairs. That would be Hannah, coming down on one pretext or another to satisfy her curiosity about him. Hannah had done wonders for them, and it would be caddish to resent her affectionate interest, but even Hannah occasionally smothered him with too much attention.

He glanced at her over his shoulder, observing that she carried a basket full of empty cans and bottles presumably intended for the big box where such accumulations were deposited.

'Speaking of rubbish' — he gave her a cynical smile and jerked his head toward the wrecked motor — 'next time the man comes you'd better have him cart this thing away.'

'Isn't any part of it worth saving?' Hannah stood beside him, viewing the machine appraisingly. 'Perhaps it would bring a little more than just that much scrap-iron.'

She was taking it mighty coolly, he thought. Considering how much grief the whole thing had caused him, it was rather casual to be discussing whether the symbol of his disaster should be sold for junk or hauled to the city dump.

'It wasn't a very good job, anyhow. I think Ellis cheated me when he made it. I might have known what sort of person he was. People like that ought to be shown up for what they are. I'm not sure but it's a public duty.' Paul found this new thought absorbing. Odd it hadn't struck him before. 'You're something of an authority on morals, Hannah. Doesn't it look as if I were an accessory to Ellis's grand larceny when I know all about it and do nothing?'

She grinned understandingly.

'That's *your* affair,' she replied, unhelpfully. '*Mine* is to keep myself from being mixed up with a much bigger crime.'

His eyes inquired what she meant, though it was difficult for him to dissemble when dealing with Hannah.

'You're wanting me to encourage you in the breaking of your promise; isn't that it? Suppose we talk about that a little.'

'Very well — go ahead!' rasped Paul. 'You're the one

who engineered that promise, so you probably know the most about it.'

'You mustn't be unkind,' murmured Hannah. 'We can talk about it calmly — can't we? It isn't as if you had promised *me*. If it had been only to me, I could let you off.'

'You mean ——' Paul raised his eyes and pointed a finger skyward. 'You mean Them — or It — or Him — or — or What?' He chuckled dryly.

She nodded. 'And you were quite in earnest about it, too. It wasn't a bit funny when you did it.' Her words were spoken gently but very soberly. 'I'd be afraid.'

Paul made a gesture of impatience.

'Now that kind of talk, Hannah, is all very well for people who honestly believe in such things. I know you do and I respect you for it. But it leaves me cold. I don't accept it. I haven't any room in my thinking for ghosts — not even a Holy Ghost. That's my calm, considered opinion in broad daylight. Of course, when a man is at the tip-end of his resources and emotionally upset, you can't blame him for grabbing at any idea, however irrational. It's like a drowning man clutching at a straw. He doesn't clutch the straw because he thinks highly of it as a life-preserver. He doesn't think about it at all! His brains aren't working.'

'Maybe so,' sighed Hannah. 'But, all the same, I don't believe you would ever feel right about it if you broke that promise. You say you doubt whether there is' — she hesitated for an instant and then pointed upward as Paul had done — 'anything Up There. But that doesn't quite let you out. There's something *down here* ——' Hannah tapped him lightly on his chest. 'Maybe *They* are not real — but *You* are! If you want to break your promise to me, I'll forgive you and understand. And if you want to break the promise you made to Him or Them, because you don't believe there is any such thing, maybe you can do it and never hear from it again. But if you break the promise you made to *yourself* — well — that's another matter. You'll be sorry!'

Hannah slowly turned away and walked to the foot of the stairs, where she stood for a moment abstractedly swinging her empty basket, not at all satisfied with the manner in which their talk had ended. The echo of her final remark lingered unpleasantly in her ears.

Returning, she found Paul seated on the dusty workbench in a posture of deep concentration. Laying her hand on his arm she said contritely, 'I didn't mean to be impudent. I'm sorry.'

'That's all right, Hannah,' he muttered. 'No offense.' His tone conveyed an obvious dismissal, but she made no move to go. There was an extended silence.

'You've had so many serious losses, Paul. I couldn't bear to see you have the greatest one of all — the giving up of your pride.'

He glanced up, and their eyes met in a long look of mutual appraisal.

'And is that so valuable?' he queried. 'Seems to me a good deal has been said, from time to time, about the damaging effects of pride.' His lips twisted in a rather surly grin. 'If you want to know how highly pride is esteemed by the people who are supposed to pass on such matters, you might look in the Bible.'

'Maybe it means something else in the Bible. Pride, to me, isn't showing off. Pride is what makes me feel comfortable when I'm by myself. There are plenty of things I wouldn't do, not because they're prohibited by the Commandments, but because I'm too proud to do them. All I want is the approval of myself.' She paused, smiled, and added, 'That's why I came back. I didn't quite approve of what I had said to you.'

'It was all true enough,' confessed Paul, glumly. 'We both know that.'

'I'll go now,' said Hannah.

'And leave me to stew in my own juice, eh?'

'I'm afraid so.' Her tone was tender, almost maternal. 'It distresses me when you are unhappy. You've had a great deal to bear. I can't think of your doing this cruel thing to yourself.'

Impulsively he rose from the bench and reached out his hand.

'Very well, Hannah,' he declared firmly. 'I shall stick to my bargain. You win.'

She took his hand in both of hers and clasped it tightly, her eyes shining. She shook her head slightly.

'No, Paul, it's *you* who've won! And it is a very important victory.'

'Victory? Nonsense! It's just a final giving up; that's all. Just the swan song. I've been doing nothing lately but run up white flags.'

'No — not white flags, Paul. *White banners!*' Hannah's voice was vibrant with emotion. 'You haven't surrendered. You have just taken a new position. You'll be able to see your way — from here. I'm not going to worry about you any more.'

Chapter VIII

PAUL was unable immediately to recapture his former interest in his profession. The assorted distractions of many months were no longer claiming his time and mind, but it was not easy to concentrate on classroom lectures, student interviews, quiz-papers, and seminars after so long a period of perfunctory obedience to the mere letter of the law respecting his university obligations.

It was only after weeks of honest diligence that he regained enough sincere regard for his job to realize the extent of his abandonment of it. Occasionally he flushed with chagrin as the fact dawned on him that but for Dean Oliver's patience he might have been asked to quit altogether.

By the close of the second semester the old habits of work had been resumed and something like enthusiasm had developed. His chief ambition now was to show good old Oliver how much he appreciated the forbearance exercised in his behalf. They had had no conversation about the matter, but Paul observed, from the approving twinkle in the Dean's eye, that these earnest efforts to reinstate himself in the esteem of his chief had been duly noted.

As an additional testimony that he was again at his post of duty and meant business, Paul commenced work on a solid biography of Spenser intended for scholars. When he composed the preface his mood was that of a man writing a personal letter to Dean Oliver. And the Dean, when he had read the first three chapters, said warmly, 'Now you have struck your stride, Ward. This book will do you good, perhaps not in cash but in professional advancement.'

That same night Mrs. Oliver called up Marcia to invite them to the dinner they were giving on the twenty-third for Springer of Cambridge, who had just arrived as an exchange lecturer.

From that time forward Paul sensed a new attitude toward him on the part of his colleagues. More and more frequently did the Dean call him in for conference on minor administrational problems. And when Commencement impended, half of his evenings were spent at the office, to the improvement of his next salary check by seventy-five dollars. At one o'clock on Commencement Day he went home with his soggy black gown over his arm, hot and weary but pleased to believe that he had amply atoned for a long period of slackness and inattention by giving the University full measure, now that he was back in the running.

The new Ellis refrigerator appeared on the market, backed by an expensively vivid campaign of publicity. Paul was gratified that the announcement caused him so little distress. Marcia had laid the magazine on his desk, open at the page. He pursed his lips, glanced briefly at the picture, ran his eye over the text, grinned sourly, and pushed the offending thing off the end of the table into the waste-basket. Then he took up his pen and finished the sentence he was composing. Marcia observed, 'You certainly have yourself well in hand, dear.' And this made Paul glow with satisfaction. He had never thought of himself that way. It made him ambitious to achieve poise, balance, ballast.

Marcia took the children to the lake cottage where they had spent other summers, leaving Hannah to run the house. Paul joined the family at week-ends and for a fortnight in August.

The book was having a marked effect on Paul. It was steadying him. For seven hours every day his potential audience gathered about his desk; post-graduates, for the most part, their imagined presence influencing his rhetori-

cal style. A sprinkling of the faculty was in this fancied
audience, with Dean Oliver in the middle of the front row,
his head tipped a little to one side as if he might be doubt-
ing the accuracy of the current statement.

It was not Paul's nature to dramatize himself, but he was
becoming aware of his new acquisition. He observed that
he was walking with a more regular and deliberate step.
His gestures were fewer. His decisions, even in small matters, were carefully considered and calmly spoken. The
book might not shed much new light on Edmund Spenser,
but it was illuminating the unevaluated stability of Paul
Ward.

Hannah remarked this change in his tempo from a volatile six-eight to a ponderous four-four, and wasn't quite
sure that she approved. Whatever might have been the
liabilities of his effervescent temperament — his proneness
to go off at half-cock, his sudden, gusty, unpredictable
seizures of irritability and forthright rudeness, followed by
brief remorses — he was certainly more interesting than
this solemn owl who tramped about the house with the
impressive tread of a Major Prophet. Hannah would have
welcomed a wild outcry from the bathroom, addressed to
nobody in particular, 'What in hell has become of my
razor-blades?'

And, speaking of razor-blades, it was observed that the
professor had not shaved for a week. Jockeying a conversation about his tireless diligence to a point where he might
say he had been too busy to shave, Hannah was alarmed to
learn that he contemplated a Van Dyke. She was serving
breakfast when he dryly offered this information and
glanced up to note its reception.

'You'll never be able to run any more,' declared Hannah,
in a tone of warning.

'Perhaps I don't want to run,' replied Paul, stroking his
bristles. 'I think a little dignity would be to my advantage.'

'At times — yes,' she agreed reminiscently. 'It would be

nice if you had a dignified beard with wires on it — to be
hooked over your ears. And then, whenever you felt you
were sort of spluttery ——'

Paul rewarded her persiflage with a feeble grin. Really,
Hannah went a bit too far sometimes with her impudence;
meant it as a little pleasantry, of course, but shouldn't be
encouraged in it. He reflected, however, there was no sense
or justice in hurting her feelings.

'Quite a fantastic idea, Hannah,' he admitted.

'And you could take it off when you wanted to play.'

Paul said 'Umm' rather inattentively, and Hannah
vouchsafed a few remarks on personality. It didn't do
people much good to try to alter themselves into something
else.

'A red-headed woman,' she continued, 'can say and do
things that make her charming, but if a black-haired woman
dyes her hair red and then tries to say and do red-headed
things, she is sure to fail because, after all, she hasn't a red-
headed character. You can't dye a personality.'

'I presume what you're trying to get at, Hannah,' observed Paul crisply, 'is that I haven't a Van Dyke personality.'

'If I may say so, I think you would tire of it.'

'Well, now that you have said so, I think you may say
so. If I don't like it I can take it off.'

'Not so well,' objected Hannah. 'When you put it on,
people will think you did it because you weren't pleased
with yourself. They will suppose you have found something the matter with yourself and have decided to try to
look like someone else. That's risky enough. But if you
take it off again, it's the same as saying you're still displeased with yourself and that the remedy you tried was
no good.' She was so sober about it that Paul laughed.

The next morning he appeared at breakfast with his
face clean and pink.

'That's better,' approved Hannah, pouring his coffee.
'Now you can dance jigs — and everything.'

With the opening of the fall semester, Paul found himself booked for a considerable number of University Extension lectures, most of the dates in larger towns, one in Chicago. It was being demonstrated that his new devotion to his duties had earned him this bonus.

One Thursday night in early November he lectured in Waterloo. There was a large and genial audience out to hear him and he was at his best. In high spirits and well satisfied with what he had done, he went to the train, walking with an elastic step. Life, he reflected, might be worse. He had foozled some of his opportunities, but the future still held out a promise of fair reward for zealous application to his job. His trouble had been that he had tried to accomplish something in another field than his own. He would make it a point to avoid a repetition of such time-wasting excursions. He would never be rich, but he would be increasingly recognized as a sound workman in his profession.

Not many were waiting at the small brick station. Paul sauntered up and down the platform, the best periods of his lecture still echoing pleasantly in his memory. To interpret an ancient bard and reconstruct an almost forgotten era was worth doing. To make the versatile Spenser live anew was a feat comparable to an act of resurrection. Then he got to thinking about the reality of resurrection and wondered if a well-turned phrase, pivoting on this concept, might not brighten one sentence of the preface for his new book.

Presently he saw Hannah. She was in company with a woman slightly older than herself and a sturdy little boy of seven or eight. For a moment it occurred to him that Hannah, consistently secretive about her movements when off duty, might not wish to be recognized, and he had decided not to approach her when she glanced in his direction and their eyes met. Hannah smiled an unmistakable welcome and he advanced to speak. Unflustered, she presented her friend Mrs. Edmunds, who graciously accepted Professor Ward's acquaintance, but gave no sign whether the name meant anything to her.

'And this is Peter,' added Hannah.

Paul greeted them amiably, exchanged the inevitables with the comely Mrs. Edmunds, whom he promptly appraised as a person of undoubtable refinement, and, when the preliminary amenities had been attended to, turned his attention to the lad. He had a strong, determined face; quite an arresting face, indeed, for a child of his years. You weren't sure what manner of approach to make, but it was reasonably certain you should not try talking down to him.

'You know my Aunt Hannah?' asked Peter quietly.

'Very well — but I did not know she was your Aunt Hannah.' Paul wished he knew just where he stood in this matter. Hannah's well-balanced, non-committal smile offered no aid. One fact was fairly evident. The boy knew nothing of Hannah's employment. This Mrs. Edmunds knew, of course, or Hannah would not have risked a possible bean-spilling by inviting him to speak to them. He glanced into Mrs. Edmunds's disciplined eyes for a clue to this little mystery, but she did not oblige him.

'Are you a really-truly professor?' Peter's uplifted eyes squinted incredulously.

Paul laughed merrily, partly because he was amused, partly to assure the lad's mother — who would probably be distressed — that her child's innocent impudence had not annoyed him. But Mrs. Edmunds, not in the least abashed, laughed too. Hannah, with a half-apologetic smile, said, 'Why, Peter — whatever made you ask that question?'

Aware that he had blundered, the boy replied defensively, 'I thought professors were old men.'

'Nice recovery, Peter!' approved Paul. 'You've the makings of a statesman.'

'No' — drawled Mrs. Edmunds — 'I think Peter was entirely honest.'

'Thanks, then' — said Paul — 'to both of you.'

At this Hannah smiled her relief over the pleasant termination of an awkward moment. It was rather odd, thought

Paul. Hannah had seemed to feel more responsibility for
the lad's remark than had his mother. It was easy to see
how deep was her devotion to this boy. He was on the point
of saying, 'You must come and spend a day with your
Aunt Hannah, Peter' — but decided against it. Something
told him there was a little riddle here.

The noisy arrival of the train ended their conversation.
Paul had expected to find a seat in the parlor-car, but when
Hannah stopped at the steps of the day coach he decided
to join her. She seemed calmly undisturbed by their
chance meeting and made room for him beside her on the
seat as if it were quite natural for them to be traveling together.

'So — *this* is where you come — on your days off,' he
observed; adding slyly, 'You've always been so mysterious
about your holidays that I wondered if ——' He hesitated.

'You wondered if I was up to something I was ashamed
of?' assisted Hannah. 'Well — now you know.' She faced
him with steady, smiling eyes.

'Exceptionally attractive boy — young Peter,' said Paul
warmly. 'What does his father do?'

'Mr. Edmunds is dead; died when Peter was too little
to remember him clearly. He is a great comfort to Lydia.'

'You're related to her — some way?'

'No — just very close friends. It's a long story. Mr.
Edmunds was a chemist. He was killed in an accident.
Lydia's relatives live in the East. Circumstances threw us
together. I had no family within easy reach. Naturally,
we became friends.' Hannah busied herself, during this
recital, with a search in her handbag for her ticket, though
the conductor had not yet appeared. 'That's about all
there is to be told.'

'Pleasant for both of you, I'm sure,' commented Paul.
'No necessity for any secrecy. You should assure Mrs.
Edmunds that she is very welcome at our house whenever
she wishes to come and see you.'

'Well — it's better, I think, that she doesn't,' said

Hannah, measuring her words. 'It doesn't bother Lydia that I am a servant, but she has her own social position to think of. No one in Waterloo knows how or where I am employed. It's better so.'

Paul nodded understandingly. 'I see,' he agreed. 'And that's why you kept it a secret.'

'Yes. . . . Not even Peter knows. He thinks I'm his aunt.'

'So I noticed. You're very fond of him.'

'Naturally — he was a mere infant when I first saw him.'

The conductor came then and caused a brief interruption in their talk.

'Edmunds, Edmunds,' muttered Paul, searching his memory. 'Seems to me I recall the case of a chemist ——'

'That's the one,' said Hannah. 'He was killed in an explosion at the glass works in Rattoon.'

Paul's eyes suddenly lighted.

'I suppose he left quite a few books on chemistry.'

'Yes — Lydia kept them all.'

'So that's where you ——'

Hannah nodded.

'Lydia thought I was quite foolish.'

'I don't wonder. By any normal rule of reckoning, it was utterly silly. The discovery you made was sheer accident.'

Hannah drew a long sigh and said 'Maybe.' Then, shifting her position so she might face Paul more directly, she proceeded, with considerable animation, to relate the day's adventures. She and Lydia and Peter had gone downtown, bought him a new suit, a pair of roller-skates, 'and ice cream, of course,' she added.

Paul chuckled. 'I'm surprised,' he said dryly, 'your being a party to the outright purchase of ice cream. You're forever making it at home in that clumsy old freezer. I've always maintained it was cheaper to buy it.'

'You need the exercise, Mr. Ward. Turning that crank is good for you. Besides — it's ever so much better when you make it at home.'

'Don't you want little Peter to have good ice cream?' Paul searched her eyes.

Hannah stroked the fingers of her gloves and did not at once reply.

'I agree,' she said, at length, 'there really ought to be an easier way to make ice cream at home. I'll not ask you to do it, any more. I thought ——' There was a long pause. 'You'll forgive me, won't you, Mr. Ward, but I've kept hoping that if you were faced, now and then, with this ice problem, maybe you would — maybe you would do something about it.'

'I'm not in the ice business, not any more,' growled Paul.

'That's the pity of it,' rejoined Hannah. 'Why aren't you?'

It was a busy winter for Marcia Ward. Paul's conspicuous zeal at the University was earning them rewards in the form of invitations to teas, dinners, and receptions.

Beyond doubt, the marked attentions shown them by Dean and Mrs. Oliver had everything to do with it. The Dean had announced that Paul would be officially appointed his assistant at the end of the year, which meant nothing else than that Paul's succession to the deanship, upon the retirement or resignation of Oliver, was practically assured.

The importance of rank at the University was of a seriousness unmatched even in the army. It was no trivial matter to be made an assistant dean under any circumstance, but to be assistant to fagged old Oliver, who frankly fretted under the onerous duties of his office and wished himself well out of it, was a weighty responsibility carrying with it a deal of power over the professional welfare of many faculty men. Naturally the 'Lits' began to view Professor Ward with a new respect. It was important to keep in his good graces, and one easy and pleasant way to achieve this end was by showing social courtesies to his wife.

Marcia was dressing with more care and carried herself with a new confidence. For the first time in her life she was realizing that she possessed social gifts. Presently she ventured upon a program of discharging the obligations incurred by their acceptance of favors. As a hostess she was a surprising success. Paul was proud of her; proud also of the admiration she won by her beauty and charm. But however delightfully exciting was the new life on which they had embarked — or, more correctly, into which they had been thrust — it was playing the deuce with the family budget. Their creditors were not quite so rude as in the days of their utter obscurity, but eventually arrangements would have to be made to catch up with their bills.

Paul remarked one evening in April as he and Marcia discussed their perplexities, 'The butcher will not call up to dun us for filet mignons, as he would for pot roasts, but one of these days he will want us to pay the bill.'

When another Commencement had come and relaxation had set in, the restless fellow began to be so acutely distressed over the situation that he found it very difficult to concentrate on his book. He could easily finish it, this vacation, if his mind were free of worry, but now — instead of facing an imaginary audience of specialists in Early English, as he sat at his desk — the little amphitheater was filled entirely with tradesmen who would occasionally yelp out, in the very middle of a learned remark from the rostrum, 'That's all very well, perfesser, but how about paying me fer that coal?' And sometimes a voice from the audience would snarl, 'Nobody's going to buy yer dry book. Why don't yuh write sumpin snappy? Then yuh c'd pay yer honest debts!'

Again Marcia and the children were at the modest lake cottage, Paul asserting that they could live more economically there than in town, what with Wallie's daily catches of perch and the easy access they had to inexpensive farm products. It wasn't true, but it was comforting to say it. Anyway, the children's clatter would be out of the house.

He would be able to pursue his writing without distraction.
But it was very slow going, this summer. Paul walked
the floor, smoked until his throat was raw, gazed unseeing
out at the windows. Spenser — in mid-July — was approximately at the same place where he had paused to rest
on Independence Day.

One forenoon, when things were practically at a stand-
still, Paul went out to the kitchen to have a word with
Hannah. She inquired, interestedly, how the book was
going today, though the query was superfluous, as they both
knew. The book wasn't going, at all.

'For a long time I have been wondering,' said Hannah
thoughtfully, 'why you've made no effort to claim your
rights in that refrigerator business.'

Paul regarded her with speechless astonishment, unable
to believe his own ears. What indeed had come over Hannah?

'That's an odd thing for you to say,' he muttered. 'It
was you who badgered me into letting the whole thing slip
through my fingers. Are you suggesting that I press a suit
against these people now?'

'Oh — by no means! But when you let them carry off
your property without a fight, you had a right to expect
some manner of reward for your investment. So far as I
know you have never tried to use the power that is surely
in your hands. When the Ellises stole your invention, what
really happened was this: they set you free to do something
more important. Why haven't you done it? I think your
case is just like that of the people who had their land and
herds and houses taken from them, and instead of fighting
went out to a new country and made themselves great.
It wasn't as if they were going out entirely empty-handed.
They had lost their land, but they could find other land.
They had lost their houses, but they could build better
houses. Nobody could steal their experience or their knowing how to do things. In the new country they could im-
prove on all the work they had done before. Losing the old

stuff was fine for them. It set them free to do bigger things.'

Paul nodded, absently, and said it was an interesting thought, adding that he distinctly recalled her having gone over all this moonshiny argument once before.

'Yes, but why don't you experiment with it?' entreated Hannah. 'They've stolen your goods and set you free to go out and put your experience to work in a new and better way. All you've done is to give up everything. You have been set free, but you've never stirred hand or foot to use your freedom. I've so often wondered.'

'I suppose you mean that I could now make a better refrigerator than the one they stole from me. Is that it?' Paul's tone was slightly ironical, but betrayed a good deal of interest. 'What more do you think I could do to it?'

'I don't know,' admitted Hannah. 'I have had you turning the handle of that heavy old freezer every few days for a long time, hoping you might sweat out an idea.'

'Oh — I have gone into all that,' said Paul, annoyed to have been considered stupid. 'It would be too expensive. Nobody would want one. The cost of a machine for the exclusive purpose of freezing ice cream in a private home would more than equal the expense of buying ice cream to be served three times a day for the rest of their natural lives. No, no — that idea is foolish. Not meaning' — he added, genially — 'that I don't appreciate your motive. It's mighty good of you to be thinking about my welfare.'

'Well — would it cost so frightfully much if it was combined with the other refrigerator, the one that keeps things merely cool?'

Paul shook his head.

'That wouldn't work. You couldn't have two temperatures in there, and the process that would freeze the ice cream and sherbets would also freeze your milk and fruit.' His eyes widened, stared, and then narrowed. 'Unless — of course — perhaps ——' he mumbled, half-incoherently.

Hannah smiled and left him sitting there astride a kitchen chair. Paul did not see her go. She went upstairs and on his

bed she placed two long discarded garments — a neatly
folded shirt with elbow sleeves bearing the indelible stains
of chemicals, and a worn but clean pair of khaki trousers.
Returning, she found Paul standing before his desk in the
living-room, squaring up the loose pages of his book manuscript.

'Want a box for that?' asked Hannah, pausing beside
him and looking up companionably into his eyes.

'If you have one — thanks,' assented Paul casually.

Hannah quite liked the dialogue of this little drama. A
momentous decision had been arrived at, but it was accomplished without hysteria. That, she felt, was the proper
way to accept a high moment — with quietness. She
brought a strong pasteboard box and a long piece of express
cord and laid them on the desk. Paul chuckled a little.

'I'm surprised you didn't bring a padlock,' he drawled.

The steadying effect of the work Paul had done on Edmund Spenser proved to his advantage as he deliberately
laid out plans for the new refrigerator. The two projects
were not of the same category, but were similar in their
demand for patient precision. There was no wasteful haste
and a minimum of lost motion. But because he had been
over a great deal of this ground before, the task went forward with so little delay that within two weeks he was
almost up to the point where he had been when the unscrupulous Ellis had viewed the device and made off with its
secret. The motor had not been built yet. Paul was still
casting about for the best place to have it made.

One afternoon Hannah heard her name called peremp-
torily and made haste to the stuffy little workshop in the
fruit-cellar. Paul, with the light of an unexpected triumph
in his eyes, motioned to her to come in.

'Hannah!' he shouted jubilantly. 'I'm going to put the
whole damned thing in one box — motor and all!'

'That's great! How did you ever happen to think of
it?'

'Well — I was just wishing I had a better place to work, and then I said to myself, "Why am I planning to put the motor in the cellar, anyhow? It would be more effective if it was built right into the refrigerator." I think we *have* something now!'

'And we wouldn't have had it, would we,' reflected Hannah, 'if the other one hadn't been stolen. The Ellises set you free to do a finished job.'

'Hannah,' said Paul, in a troubled tone, 'there is something worrying me a little. Naturally I am using the same chemical formula as in the first one. The Ellises are unquestionably using that solution. Suppose they claim I've no right to it. I don't believe they would risk suing me in the face of all the facts — but what if they did? You think it would be quite right for me to defend myself, don't you?'

She shook her head emphatically. 'No, sir,' she declared, 'if they won't let you use that formula, *you'll find a better one!* I tell you, my friend, you've been forced out into a new country. They're not able to compete with you now! You know everything they know, plus the advantage of the freedom they gave you! I'm not sure but you really owe them something for stealing your other invention.'

'I suppose you think this vindicates your Philip,' said Paul soberly. 'And if you think that — well — you've certainly good grounds for it. It's a very fair and reasonable demonstration. You can depend on it, Hannah, I'll never debate this matter with you again.'

'You believe it — then?' she asked hopefully.

He was silent for some time.

'It's very mysterious,' he admitted. 'It's quite beyond me. I just know that I have hit upon a big idea after having given up a little idea. And I presume that it was necessary to give up the little one before I was eligible to have the big one.... Or something like that,' he concluded vaguely.

Hannah drew a cryptic smile, and when Paul's eyes had

queried her for its meaning, she replied, 'I don't think of myself as a religious person, but something you just said, and the way you said it, reminded me of a story in the Bible about a man who was magically cured of blindness. They asked him all manner of questions and tried to talk him out of it, and all he would say was, "I know only one thing about it: I was blind, and now I can see."'

'Yes,' said Paul, 'I remember that story. Do you believe it, may I inquire?'

'I think ——' Hannah hesitated for a long moment. 'I think I do — now. But I never did before. I see no reason, now, for not believing it — not after what has just happened to *you*.'

Paul gave a little gesture of dismissal to the matter and began tossing his tools into a basket.

'I'm going to move my trinkets upstairs, Hannah. We're done working in the basement.'

'To the attic, you mean? Won't it be hot up there?'

'We'll open the windows and run a fan. There's more room — and, besides, I don't care to take any chances on this secret getting away from me.'

Marcia received the news of Paul's resumed activities on the refrigerator with dismay. This, she said to herself, was really too, too much!

For years on end she had been a little nobody while Paul Ward had fiddled with one invention after another. And she had kept hoping that some day he would stop trying to do the impossible and make something of himself at the University.

Now he had done so, and with such success as she had hardly anticipated. Life for Marcia had expanded immeasurably. It was pleasant to bask in the reflected light of Paul's new distinctions. They promised an increasing security. She had quietly, inarticulately envied the few faculty wives whose husbands had arrived at positions of influence. Sometimes, when she and Paul went to the University auditorium to attend a concert or a lecture, and there was a genial buzz of admiration and interest when the deans and their wives came in, and the ranking professors of large renown attended by well-gowned spouses, Marcia would wonder how it might feel to be the object of such attention.

It had now begun to look as if all this might sometime come to pass. Paul had it in him, and he had been lucky enough to put himself in line for advancement. And it wasn't, Marcia kept telling herself, that she merely wanted to gratify her own vanity and cuddle the thrill of these flattering preferments. No; she coveted them for the children's sake. It was no small matter, the social advantages accruing to the families of distinguished professors. There was Roberta, for instance. Sally, no doubt, would contrive to make friends, but Roberta would be all the better off for some sort of propulsion.

Seated on the veranda of the cottage, with a writing-pad on her knee, Marcia was in the very act of telling Paul again how happy she was over the fine place he had been making for himself — and all of them. She pictured him, she wrote, sitting at his desk in the living-room (which she did hope was not too uncomfortable on these hot days) doing the book that was to give him another boost in the esteem of the University.

At that juncture, Wallie, who had been down to the village post-office, rode up across the brown lawn on his bicycle, expertly tossed a letter in her lap, and resumed his progress toward the dusty road. The letter was brief. Edmund Spenser had been carefully stowed away for the present. And work had been started again on the refrigerator.

Now we were to have all this misery to endure, once more. It would be the same old story, of course. Something would happen to make a fizzle of it. The whole summer would be squandered, the book would be left unfinished, Paul would be plunged into a fit of moody sulking.

He would go into the fall semester tired, beaten, disinterested.

Marcia started her letter again.

'I *do most sincerely* wish you well, Paul,' she began, 'but what a lot of agony you have had in trying to do something you have admitted you did not know how to do! And what a lot of agony we have *all* had in waiting and watching while you used yourself up with schemes that *never came to anything!* I know, dear, that you're trying to make us rich — but *this isn't the way!* You've been doing *so well* at the University. Now — well — I just hate to think of going through all this again! It really isn't fair to you! And if you don't mind my saying so, *it isn't fair to me!*' ... And a great deal more like that.

The letter was far too long. Composed in haste, it carried many redundant passages, disclosing the untidiness of Marcia's thoughts, and had a tendency to be somewhat shrill in spots.

When Paul received it, next morning at eleven, in the attic where he was cutting threads on the end of a short section of copper pipe, he hastily read all but the last three pages, merely leafing them through with the feeling that their contents — judging from the plentitude of underscoring and exclamation points — were but some more of the same thing, in crescendo. He folded the bulky letter, rather mussily, and tried to thrust it into his shirt-pocket. Failing to find suitable accommodation for it there, he tossed it toward a table which it missed.

Hannah, tarrying to learn his wishes about luncheon, if any — for he didn't always stop to eat — noted the short work he had made of the letter and noted also the dark frown.

'Can't say that I blame her,' muttered Paul, as if Hannah knew.

'No — you really can't,' she said intuitively. 'Mrs. Ward has been very patient.'

'She thinks I'm just wasting my time again. A bit upset,

I fear.' He gave the heavy wrench another vigorous twist. 'I don't believe I'll bother her with any more talk about it until it's done. It won't be long now.'

'How about a cold roast beef sandwich? You can eat that without stopping your work.'

'I don't blame her a damn' bit! She can't be expected to understand.'

'Sandwich?' repeated Hannah, retreating to the head of the stairs.

'Of course — if it's time ... No, no — I don't want any now.'

Hannah returned to the kitchen slowly. For a little while she debated the advisability of writing Mrs. Ward a letter expressing her own enthusiasm over what he was doing; but decided against it. No matter how prudently the letter was written, Mrs. Ward might suspect that Paul had confided something about her feelings on the subject, in which case it would probably have exactly the wrong effect.

The little episode, seemingly unimportant when viewed by itself, distressed Hannah greatly. It wasn't that she had the slightest fear of Paul's suddenly barging out to find — in something or somebody — the equivalent of the stimulating encouragement which Mrs. Ward had not provided. Hannah's anxiety was for the future. Paul Ward was now probably on the way to a kind of success that would make him very well-to-do. It would increase his liberty and his leisure. If Marcia Ward had the good judgment to keep abreast of him and go with him, hand in hand, into their new privileges, she might easily keep his devotion. But if she was going to write him any more scratchy letters, at a time when he was on a tension and fairly killing himself with hard work — well — it might turn out badly.

At all events, she herself could stand by and see that he was fed. He hadn't noticed that she had stayed on without taking her customary Thursdays. The days were all alike to Paul. He didn't know when Thursday came, or Sunday either.

On a Wednesday night in mid-August, Paul came down to the kitchen at ten, and announced that he was leaving the next night for Chicago to consult a patent lawyer who had been strongly recommended to him. He might be gone for two or three days.

'It's all done, then?' asked Hannah, wide-eyed with interest.

'Almost.... Far enough.... I know that I've done it. The rest is very simple — mere details concerning the design of the cabinet.'

'How long would it take to finish the whole job?'

'Oh, a week, maybe.'

'Why don't you finish it?' entreated Hannah. 'You remember what happened when you grew impatient before. It would be simply awful if anything happened to it, this time!'

She was putting things on the porcelain table — sliced ham, cheese, fruit — and the coffee-pot was bubbling.

'Please!' she begged.

'Oh, very well,' consented Paul, half annoyed, but drawing a grin. 'After all — you're mostly right about things, Hannah.'

'Would you mind very much if I took my day off to-morrow?' asked Hannah, after he had stowed away a few mouthfuls.

'Of course not. Run along — and have a good time. How is Peter, by the way?'

'I haven't seen him for a month.'

'You mean — you've not had a day off for a month?' Paul's face wrinkled into an amusing expression of incredulity. Hannah laughed.

'I thought I'd stay by the works,' she said gently.

'Well, Hannah,' declared Paul, with a dramatic gesture, 'when the roll is called up yonder, you'll be there!'

'Thanks,' she replied dryly. 'You, too, I hope.' Her

lips curved into the well-known puckery smile. 'Now that you know how to make your own ice, I don't suppose you need care much where your name is called.'

She did not go to Waterloo that day. Unexpected, Hannah arrived at the lake cottage shortly before noon, having traveled eighty miles by train and ten by bus, carrying along a capacious basket containing a baked ham, a jar of pickled peaches, and several glasses of newly made jelly.

The children were overjoyed to see her, and Mrs. Ward, rather mystified over this visitation, waited with considerable impatience for an opportune moment to ease her natural curiosity. When luncheon was over and the children had gone to the beach, Marcia said, 'Do tell me why you came, Hannah. I know you have some special reason.'

They went out on the veranda and Marcia took up the little tapestry that busied her restless fingers through these days of waiting and wondering.

'Mrs. Ward,' began Hannah soberly, 'I am always poking my nose into other people's business. That's probably because I haven't any of my own. Mr. Ward does not know I have come here today. It's about him.'

Marcia stiffened perceptibly and a slow flush crept up her cheek.

'Indeed?' she said, not very encouragingly. 'I hope it isn't anything you shouldn't be telling me.'

Hannah smiled briefly, confusedly, and replied: 'Yes — I hope that, too. You see — Mr. Ward has practically completed his big invention. Only a few more days of it and he will be going to Chicago to begin business on his patent.'

'You don't tell me, Hannah!' exclaimed Marcia. 'Is it actually going to work?'

'Yes. No doubt about it. He has been keeping it a sort of — surprise for you.'

'Then why are you telling me?' demanded Marcia. 'He'll not like that.'

'Oh — I don't think he'll mind. He has worked very hard. Every day, and day and night, sometimes. It has been a wonderful experience. He has hardly been out of the house for weeks.'

'The poor dear,' murmured Marcia. 'He didn't tell me he was working so hard.'

'And quite lonesome, too. No one to talk with but me.' Hannah brightened and edged her chair a little closer. 'It just occurred to me last night, Mrs. Ward, how fine it would be for him if you were there — even for a day — to be with him and make an awful big fuss over him — when he puts the last finishing touch on this thing.... That's why I came.'

Marcia coolly studied Hannah's eyes for a long moment.

'Are you trying to say to me that I've neglected my duty?' she asked, stressing her words.

And Hannah amazed both Marcia and herself by replying, evenly, 'Yes — Mrs. Ward — that's what I'm trying to say.'

'You're — you're taking a good deal of liberty; don't you think?' Marcia's voice was unsteady.

'I know, Mrs. Ward. I thought of that. Perhaps you'll not be wanting me, any more. But — I thought I ought to tell you. I see that I've just bungled things — but I meant it all right.'

There was a long silence.

'Thanks, Hannah,' said Marcia thickly. 'I'll go back with you.'

'No — if you don't mind my saying so, Mrs. Ward, you'd better let me go first. You can come tomorrow. I think it would be better if you just dropped in — as a surprise, you know.'

'That's good. We were coming in next week, anyway. We'll pack up and go home tomorrow.'

Hannah shook her head.

'No — you come — alone. Surprise him. Without the children.'

'But I can't leave them here alone!'

'You can send me out to take care of them. You get there at noon and tell me to start at once. I can be here by dinner-time. Then you can get Mr. Ward's meals for a couple of days and let him tell you all about everything he has been doing.'

'Thanks, Hannah,' said Marcia softly. 'And forgive me, please, for not understanding. You are a good friend.'

Paul was on his knees, fitting the lower door-hinge when there were steps on the attic stairs. He did not turn from his work but asked absently, 'Time to eat again, Hannah?'

Marcia put down the tray on the table, tiptoed across the room, and put both hands over his eyes.

He reached for them, kissed them, and turning about rose and took her in his arms.

'Darling!' he whispered. 'You came!'

'I couldn't stay away any longer, dear,' murmured Marcia.

'Did you bring the children?'

'No — I have sent Hannah out to look after them.'

'I've done it, Marcia! It's a great thing! We'll be rich!'

'I'm glad, dear. But all I want now is *you!*'

'And we'll travel — and do all the things we've ever wanted to do.'

'It's wonderful, Paul!' She drew him more tightly to her. 'But — just now — I can't think about anything but the happiness of seeing *you!*'

'And we'll be *free!*'

Marcia snuggled close and sought his lips again.

'I'm so glad to be back with you,' she whispered.

'From now on, darling,' said Paul firmly, 'you can have anything you want.'

Chapter IX

WHEN, on the eleventh day of December, negotiations had been completed, Paul and Marcia made a solemn agreement not to commit any more extravagances until the money was actually in hand. The manufacturing firm's name was on the dotted line, but they had been fooled once and were not to be taken in again.

This pledge they made to each other over their champagne glasses in a ritzy speak-easy in Chicago. It was an unaccustomed beverage, esteemed for its ability to inspire optimism and relieve anxiety. But it had not produced that effect on Marcia. She glowed, but it was with the glow of love for her husband who must be protected from any more of the worries that had made his life hard to bear. And Paul, also pleasantly jingled, was in a mood to gratify any wish of his uncommonly attractive wife who had never seemed so desirable as now. So they softly touched glasses across the dinner-table and swore by their love for each other that there would be no unnecessary spending until they could pay cash on the spot.

It didn't occur to either of them that there was anything funny about such a promise made at a little tête-à-tête dinner where the check totaled twenty-three dollars and seventy-five cents, for this event in their fretted lives deserved celebration.

Paul had left home on Friday night. Because he had no classes on Saturday he could conscientiously spend the day in Chicago transacting his important business. And when it was discovered that Monday, too, would be needed for the completion of the deal, he had wired Marcia to meet him.

Long ago they had resolved that come what may they would never jeopardize Paul's life insurance by borrowing against it. On this occasion, however, it seemed imperative — and safe enough. In fact, it was the only way he could raise the thousand dollars required to pay the attorneys' fees and other expenses involved in the securing of his patent rights. While he was about it, Paul made the amount of the loan twelve hundred dollars, to leave a comfortable margin for whatever other costs bobbed up in connection with the momentous affair. In this state of affluence, he wired, she came, and, the business having been concluded at four, the honeymooners dined, communed, pledged, and were immensely satisfied with themselves.

It was just a bit difficult to go back home and take up things where they had put them down. Marcia had insisted — and very properly, Paul thought — that there should be a minimum of talk before the children on the subject of their good fortune. But the topic was hard to avoid. The youngsters could easily remember how nearly the family had come to an achievement of wealth four years ago, and their instinct informed them that this time the thing had been actually accomplished. Indeed, Paul had frankly admitted to them that he had succeeded in his project, warning them it would be 'a long time yet' before there would be anything in the nature of a reward. They were not to talk about it. But the delightful mystery was on their minds, nevertheless.

'When are you going down to look at that car, Dad?' Wallie was inquiring in an impatient tone that made Roberta snicker, for whenever Wallie was exasperated his voice, then in the embarrassing stage of registering in a lower clef, had a tendency to skid. Such minor misfortunes always amused Roberta, whose sense of humor was slightly acidulous.

'No hurry about that, my boy,' Paul would reply with

patriarchal calm, 'and it would please me if you stopped haunting the automobile show-rooms. The dealers are becoming very persistent. It seems that they are under the impression we are in the market for a car, which is entirely incorrect. I hope you will keep this in mind.'

Marcia faithfully kept her end of the bargain in respect to the normal pursuit of their program of frugality, but her trips into the shopping district were more frequent. Her bed, daytimes, was strewn with illustrated magazines devoted to period furniture and interior decorating. Sometimes she would ask Roberta, whose eye for art was precociously experienced, 'How do you like those drapes? Isn't that a gorgeous chair? What do you think of the lamp?' And Roberta, hovering over the pictures, would express an opinion, though it didn't often coincide with her mother's. 'When is all this going to happen?' she would inquire, to which Marcia would reply, absently, 'Oh — sometime — maybe.'

Hannah was not very much surprised over their reticence to confide in her concerning their prospects. Paul had briefly told her that the manufacturing rights had been assigned, also that they were to receive an advance payment on February eleventh, after which there was to be a royalty. But he did not tell her how much. She was not displeased or hurt. There was almost nothing about Paul Ward that she did not understand. When he was worried or beaten, she could depend on his coming to her for counsel and comfort. When again confident and contented, he didn't need her, and it became him to conduct himself with a master-of-the-house dignity in his attitude toward their maid-of-all-work. It wasn't the first time she had sustained that sort of relation to an employer. She remembered how Mrs. Raymond, in a moment of complete letdown over Philip's sorry plight, would cling to her and weep; an hour afterward resuming their mistress-maid relationship, with a little added crispness to assure them both that business was now carrying on as usual. Hannah did not resent it; she thrilled under it. That was the way things ought to be. Otherwise, you couldn't expect to have any discipline in your house, at all. No — Paul Ward didn't owe her a full explanation of his private affairs. He would tell her sometime, no doubt; especially if it didn't work out.

But it was becoming more and more evident that the Wards were about to assume a new mode of living. Mrs. Ward moved about with the self-contained air of a woman satisfactorily related to all her engagements, and, while Paul exhibited no bumptious arrogance, his eyes were now those of a man who could look anybody in the world squarely in the face and suggest a suitable destination. Hannah hoped the children would not be spoiled and was pleased to note that their prospects hadn't altered their habits, so far. Sally had said, one day after school, 'We're going to have a bigger house, some day soon. Won't that be fun?'

'I hope so,' Hannah had replied guardedly. 'But I like this one very well, don't you?'

'No — I want a big yard with trees and lots of flowers and a room of my own. We'll have to get more help, won't we, Hannah? I asked Mother, and she said she supposed so. And I asked her if you would still cook, and she said perhaps not. And I asked her if you would be the house-keeper and she said maybe you wouldn't feel like trying to manage a big house. But you'd know how; wouldn't you, Hannah?'

'We can figure that all out, dear, when the time comes,' replied Hannah, after a reminiscent pause.

'Mother says I mustn't talk to anyone about it, but it's hard not to, 'specially when somebody comes to school with a new dress. I always want to say, "Pooh! — you just wait!"'

'Yes,' sighed Hannah, 'that's the main trouble with having money. It makes people want to say "Pooh." And mostly they're a little too decent to say it, but they keep thinking it and wanting to say it until their mouths and noses get a sort of poohy expression.'

'I'm not poohy yet, am I, Hannah?'

'Come here — and I'll look.'

Sally obediently crossed the room and leaned against the arm of Hannah's chair.

'No, dear, there's no sign of it yet.' Hannah made the announcement deliberately, after pretending a serious examination. She smiled, and Sally kissed her on the cheek.

'Will you tell me, Hannah, if you ever see one coming on?'

'That's not so easy as it sounds, Sally. People can do a great deal to avoid these poohs, but once they come, they're hard to cure.'

Sally was meditative for a while and helped herself to another warm cooky.

'But you really have to be very rich, don't you, before you can pooh enough for people to notice it? Maybe we won't have that much.'

'No,' replied Hannah, after some consideration, 'you can pooh without having any money at all. There are several different kinds. I don't know that I ever thought much about this before, but wouldn't you say that a man who is big and strong might be tempted to pooh at men not so tall and well muscled? That might be called "muscle-pooh."'

'And there's "college-pooh,"' laughed Sally, pleased to assist promptly. 'You get that when you know a lot more than anybody else.'

'Exactly,' agreed Hannah, 'and the "clever-pooh," when you're very quick and witty. When you begin talking about how stupid almost everybody else is, then you're soon going to have a "clever-pooh" fastened on your nose for keeps. I think we've named them all now, dear, and if you eat any more of those cookies you're going to spoil your dinner.'

'You've forgotten the "I'm-very-good" pooh, Hannah. That's the worst one, isn't it — the "being-good" pooh?'

'If it is,' teased Hannah, '*you* won't need to worry about it.'

'I know what you're wanting to say, Hannah. Something about the "pretty-pooh."'

Hannah chuckled dryly.

'You won't need to fret about that one either, Sally, if whoever borrowed your nailbrush doesn't return it very soon.'

'That hurts my feelings, Hannah.' Sally pretended a pout.

'You'd better take them upstairs, then, and give them a good scrubbing, and put a nice clean dress on them. You're dirty as a little pig.'

Paul couldn't remember ever having had quite so interesting an experience as on the day when he deposited his big check in his current account at the Farmers and Mechanics Bank.

He hadn't actually overdrawn his account for all of six months, having been so sharply reprimanded for it the last time that he had determined never to let it happen again. But his balance, when he deposited his monthly checks, was always so small it made him ashamed. He hated to go to the bank. He began to feel wormy and shabby and wretched even before he pushed open the heavy door. The cashier, Mr. Wexler — a lean, stooped, steely-eyed fellow — never quite snubbed him, but his salutation was so dry it crackled.

This February morning Paul entered the bank conscious of an accelerated pulse, carefully on guard against displaying any change in his habitual demeanor, trying to feel and therefore look as small and worthless as usual. The illusion was not so difficult to execute: there had been a heavy thaw, and his soggy, burdensome galoshes gave him the heel-dragging shamble of one taking his place at the end of the bread-line. He went to the second of the tall lobby-desks, helped himself to a deposit-slip, wrote the date, his name, and — opposite the tabulation for checks — '25,000.00.' Then he endorsed his deposit and carried the slip and the check, one in each hand, to Mr. Wexler's window; put them down, fished in his pocket for his passbook, and waited interestedly for something to happen.

He had lived through this moment many times, of late, in anticipation. It was entirely possible the cashier might say, 'Well, well, indeed! And what have we here? Congratulations, Professor Ward, I'm sure! Well, well!' — and push two fingers under the bars for whatever shaking might be done. And Paul had determined not to be cajoled by any of this tardy cordiality. They had made him suffer and cringe and feel like a skunk. All very well. But if they had a notion they could mend their insults by soft-soaping him now that he had some money, they had another guess coming. It had occurred to him that Mr. Wexler might say, 'If you have the time, Mr. Ward, let me take you back to Mr. Trimble's office. I know he will want to shake hands.' And then Paul meant to drag out his watch and beg to be excused. 'Some other time,' he would remark indifferently.

Now he had put down his big check and the slip and the passbook.

Mr. Wexler picked up the check, turned it over, turned it back again, whacked it with a rubber-stamp, and impaled it on a long sharp spike.

''Morning, Mr. Ward,' he rasped, while spiking the check. 'Wet day.'

'And a checkbook, please,' said Paul.

Mr. Wexler tossed one out, and remarked dryly, 'Better not begin drawing on this until it's cleared, Mr. Ward.'

Paul flushed angrily.

'If you think there's something the matter with it,' he growled, 'give it back to me. And I'll not put you to any further anxiety.'

'Sorry, Mr. Ward,' crackled Mr. Wexler. 'The bank has received it for collection.'

'Then I'll thank you, sir, to close my account, and give me the bank's check for what I have in here. I don't like your attitude.'

'I'm afraid you'll have to wait, Mr. Ward,' drawled Wexler, 'until this paper has gone through the clearing-house. If you insist, I can hand you back what you already had in your account here. Please wait a moment.' The cashier left his cage and sauntered back to the bookkeeping department, while Paul drummed impatiently on the window-ledge, scowling darkly. Presently he returned, punctiliously wrote out a receipt, pushed it through the wicket, offered a pen, and Paul scrawled his name on the bottom line certifying that he had drawn out his previous balance in full. And Mr. Wexler, having pushed several levers on his money-machine, handed his irate customer seven dollars and eighty-six cents.

'Thanks,' snarled Paul, turning away.

'Better leave your passbook,' said Mr. Wexler. 'We will mail you the proceeds of this Chicago check when we get it. Good-day, sir.'

'Damned shabby treatment,' protested Paul, his voice a bit unsteady.

'I'm sorry, Mr. Ward. Business is business. Regret to lose your account, but — you asked for your money back. And I gave it to you.'

By this time three or four customers were growing interested while they waited their turn, and Paul, observing their curiosity, left the window and walked out of the place in a grand state of wrath. So — business was business, eh? ... And then it began to occur to him that this was really the first time in his life he had ever *done* any business. The little exchanges of money for food and clothes — that sort of thing wasn't business. Trotting shamefacedly to the bank on the first of every month to deposit a salary of $188.33, and then checking it all out but a handful of small

change by the tenth of the month — that wasn't business
as the insufferable Wexler thought of 'business.' Paul began to wonder if he hadn't been an ass. He was really going
to be in business now, and should be deporting himself like
a business man. Wexler would probably tell the story of his
large indignation to his banker friends and they would
laugh.

After he had walked the half-dozen blocks to the post-
office, where he laid in a supply of stamps, Paul retraced his
steps to the bank, waited his turn at the cashier's window,
and said grimly: 'Mr. Wexler, I made a little mistake here a
while ago. I fear I was rude. I beg your pardon. I've never
had occasion to do very much business. Perhaps I'll learn.
I would like to continue my account here, please.'

Mr. Wexler's thin lips twisted into a fair imitation of a
grin. He pushed a couple of fingers under the grating.

'Attaboy,' he drawled.

Paul squeezed the Wexler knuckles and walked out of the
bank glowing with an immense satisfaction. He was now a
business man in good and regular standing. It did not occur
to him that if Wexler meant to tell the story at all, it was a
still better one than it had been fifteen minutes earlier.
Walking through the slush was difficult, but Paul decided
not to take a street-car. Ordinarily he rode. As he plodded
along, four street-cars passed him, all going in his direction.
It was fun to walk when you knew you had money enough
in the bank to buy a dozen of their damned little street-cars,
if you wanted to. He tried to examine his own attitude in
respect to this matter.

For instance; he needed a new hat. Marcia had been
telling him to buy one. If he had been strapped, the
chances were he would have bought a hat today. Now that
he could have all the hats in town, the old one was plenty
good, for the present. He wondered if having money made
a man stingy and careless about his appearance.

Marcia met him at the door, her face smilingly inquisitive. He kissed her warmly.

'Well — what did they think at the snooty old bank when you turned up with *twenty-five thousand dollars?*' Marcia stressed the words as impressively as if she were saying 'a million.'

Paul chuckled, tossed the old hat aside, peeled off his overcoat, and slipped an arm around Marcia's waist.

'You ought to have seen 'em,' he said, in a tone implying that all the mean little indignities of the past had now been amply avenged. 'Old Wexler poked his fingers through the bars and said "Attaboy!" — just like that.'

They were amazed at the speed with which negotiations were completed for the new home on Marcellus Avenue. Buying a house had always seemed an adventure to be approached with caution and after wide investigation. When the time came for them to buy, they would look at every desirable house in town, weigh and balance them against one another, and arrive at a deliberate decision.

Marcia had called up Mr. Chalmers. She tried to make her query sound diffident to insure against an excess of zeal and anticipation on the part of the realtor, but there was enough confidence in her tone, if not in her actual words, to fetch Mr. Chalmers out in his shiny new car immediately after lunch.

Paul had classes that afternoon, but he could see the house later, Mr. Chalmers said. He wanted Mrs. Ward to inspect it at once because it was really a wonderful buy and would not remain on the market very long. The Haywoods had owned it only a year. Now they had been required to move to Chicago. It was, declared Mr. Chalmers, just the thing for the Wards; eleven-room colonial, four baths, two-car garage, spacious grounds, ornamental shrubbery, exquisite interior decoration practically new. Softly purring the invoice of this remarkable property, Mr. Chalmers conveyed Marcia to it, driving more slowly as they entered Marcellus Avenue, directing her attention to the quality of the neighborhood.

The snow was melted now, except for dirty patches of it on the cold side of walls and trees. Marcia could visualize the beauty of the lawn, the lilacs, the laurel. A little tremor of delight swept her while Mr. Chalmers was fumbling with his huge bunch of keys. The front entrance was most imposing. It was easy to picture Paul and herself greeting their guests in this impressive hallway. She strolled about through the house, her heels echoing on the well-waxed hardwood floors. With her finger-tips pressed thoughtfully against her lips she stood on the second-floor landing, facing the open doors to commodious bedchambers, assigning them to the various members of the family. A guest-room, too. Doubtless they would be having guests frequently now.

'I suppose it's more than we can pay,' reflected Marcia. 'We had not planned on such a large house.' It wasn't true. They had idealized the big house they meant to have, some day, until it was at least the size of the Administration Building at the University. 'I'm afraid to have you tell me how much it costs,' added Marcia, hoping this apprehension of hers might move Mr. Chalmers to be merciful.

Of course you couldn't expect to own a house like this unless you had some money, Mr. Chalmers admitted; but once you owned it you would really *have* something. The steady expense of minor repairs, which one had to expect in a cheap, jerry-built house, usually ate up the first-cost difference between a good house and a bad one. Take this plumbing, for example, and this heating plant; take the extra half-ton of mineral wool in the walls — all these things cost money, to be sure, but once you had them in your house, you were spared the bother and expense of repairs.

'Yes,' said Marcia, 'I see that. How much is it?'

He kept her dangling a little longer and finally announced it was to be had for twenty-three thousand, half of which must be paid in cash. Mr. Haywood needed the money. That's why the price was low. Somebody would be wanting it promptly at that ridiculous figure.

Marcia frowned, shook her head, turned a hopeless little
smile toward Mr. Chalmers, but continued her excursion,
mentally placing furniture — most of which would be new
— and planning window-drapes to match the paper. After
that she spent a long time opening drawers and cabinets in
the kitchen and butler's pantry.

'We'll have to wait and see what Mr. Ward thinks of it,'
said Marcia. 'I'm almost sure he will say it is more than we
should try to invest.' She wasn't sure of any such thing.
In fact, she was quite confident Paul would want to buy the
house on the spot. It never took him long to come to a conclusion.

Next day, Paul having enthused over the purchase, they
signed the papers, drew the check, and were driven home in
a high state of exultation. Now that it was all over and Mr.
Chalmers couldn't boost the price, there was no occasion for
further dissembling: they were almost hysterically gay.

'I have a little surprise for you, Marcia,' said Paul, in a
low tone, when they were back in their room. 'I've bought
a sedan.'

'How wonderful! But can we do it all — house, furniture,
car?'

'Why not? We'll be having more money in a few months.
Might as well make some good use of it. We've waited
plenty long.'

That night Paul strolled out to the kitchen for a word
with Hannah. He had postponed this talk from day to day
until he was having some misgivings over his tardiness to
confide in her. The stark truth was that Hannah had had a
very important part in providing them with their new fortune. Surely she had a right to know something about their
plans.

Hannah welcomed him to her domain without a trace of
rebuke in her tone or manner, even offering him a hand over
the stile by remarking, 'I haven't seen much of you lately,
Mr. Ward, but I know it's because you have been awfully
busy. Are things going all right?'

Once he had decided to tell Hannah where they stood
and what they intended to do, he left nothing undisclosed,
reporting on the purchase of the new house and the automobile, adding, 'And of course we will have to buy new
furniture.'

Hannah put down her knitting when he came to a full
stop, and said: 'I think it's fine for you to have these things.
You've surely earned them. They will bring you a great
deal of pleasure, provided ——'

Paul glanced up anxiously and waited for the proviso.

'Provided you do not let yourself in for a lot of expenses
that will worry you. It has often occurred to me,' continued Hannah meditatively, 'that people ought to decide
exactly what bracket they think they're in, financially, and
then try to — to work in that bracket. For example, if I
want to buy some new spring clothes, and have only twenty
dollars to invest, I'd better not spend twelve dollars for a
new hat and five dollars for shoes which would leave me
only three dollars for a dress. A three-dollar hat might set
off a twelve-dollar dress very nicely. But an expensive hat
worn with a cheap dress not only makes the dress dowdy,
but makes the hat look silly too. Do you see what I mean?'

Paul thought he saw what she meant and nodded approval.

'If this new home,' Hannah went on judiciously, 'is to
cost twenty-three thousand, then the stuff that goes into it
will have to be of the same general quality if you're going to
be happy in it. You can't fill your house with cheap things.
And if you have a large flower-garden and a big lawn, you'll
have to plan on extra expenses for water and work, or it
will shame you.'

'You're on the trail of a good idea, Hannah.' Paul smiled
indulgently. 'You think people should adopt a definite
scale of living and not let an extravagant hat play the deuce
with a cheap pair of shoes.'

'Precisely — only I'm not thinking quite so much about
what the hat does to the shoes as I am about what the shoes

do to the hat — making it look ridiculous. People wouldn't
grin when they looked at the shoes. It's the *hat* that would
amuse them.'

'Think we shouldn't have bought the sedan?' Paul's face
was sober.

'No — I don't think that. But seventeen hundred and
fifty dollars was a good deal to pay for it. I suppose you
were right, though. You couldn't very well leave a cheap car
sitting out in front of a fine house. . . . What worries me is:
Are you going to have enough money left, after buying all
these things, to pay for the cost of running them? Maybe
you are. I hope so. But — I'd keep it in mind if I were
you.'

Paul kept it in mind for a day or two, but realized that he
was now riding a tiger and had better try to stay on.
Marcia was having the time of her life, shopping for the new
equipment of the wonderful house. He couldn't summon
the courage to caution her. After all — you really couldn't
blame her for wanting to furnish the house tastefully, consistently. Even Hannah thought that, and she was a
veritable authority on thrift. Of course Hannah would
have started with a less expensive house and then trimmed
things to fit. Hannah had evolved an interesting philosophy
on this subject. Paul had thought it quite obvious that a
fifteen-dollar chair, flanking a three-hundred-dollar davenport, would look absurd. In Hannah's opinion it was the
davenport that would look absurd. New idea. Very like
Hannah to have such a whimsy. She had even pointed her
views on this matter by adding, 'If a man talks much about
high ideals, and then shows shabby conduct, it isn't his conduct that draws a sour laugh from his friends: it's his *ideals*.'

They moved into the new house in May. Many of the
things had to be ordered, involving delays, and the drapes
and broadloom rugs took time. In spite of all the distractions, Paul was attentive to his University obligations.
He had wondered a little whether his windfall would alter

his relations to his friends of the faculty. They seemed singularly unimpressed, joked him about it briefly, Sandy Laughton observing dryly, 'Now you can have a pair of suspenders for every pair of pants.' The remark, inconsequential as it was, deterred Paul from ordering more than one spring suit. He resolved that there would be no change in his personal mode of living. And it was easy to see, by the attitude of his friends, that his good sense and good taste had been noted.

Now they were making plans for the summer. Marcia had determined to send Roberta to a girls' camp in the Adirondacs. Lucy Trimble was returning to the camp this season, and Roberta, exhilarated with Lucy's report of last year's experiences, talked of little else than her wish to join the camp. Marcia had ventured to call up Mrs. Trimble and was delighted over the cordiality of the bank president's wife, Mrs. Trimble assuring her that there could be no better place for a thirteen-year-old girl than Camp Minnewonkapotamie.

There was so much talk about this that Wallie also became interested in the camp project and was soon booked to go with a score of well-to-do Mid-Western youngsters to a lake in Minnesota. The rates were steep, Paul thought, but Marcia believed Wallie would be in safer company in a camp that cost a little more — a theory which sounded plausible enough, but in fact didn't have a leg to stand on, as they were to discover later.

Paul had already promised his manufacturers that he would spend the first two weeks of July in consultation with their engineers, and it was understood that Marcia would accompany him to Chicago.

Sally, quite carried away with the early results of her planting in the small flower-garden staked off as her exclusive plot, had shown no interest in joining a camping party, considerably to her father's relief; for if they didn't look out there would soon be no money left. It was amazing how rapidly you could dispose of twenty-five thousand dollars if you went about it heartily and had plenty of zealous co-operation on the part of your family.

After everyone had gone away but Sally and Hannah, the house was going to be deliciously quiet. Marcia had experienced no qualms about leaving her youngest in such competent hands. Her sense of maternal obligation, however, prompted her to offer Sally a large portion of last-minute counsel.

The train did not go until ten, which gave her an opportunity to see her baby safely tucked in for the night. Seated on the edge of the bed, energetically stroking the fingers of her new gray suède gloves, Marcia redundantly enjoined Sally to be a good child, to mind Hannah, and not play with children she didn't know. Sally yawned a promise of obedience and remarked that her mother's new silk suit was stunning, which was a fact.

Paul put down the bags he was carrying, entered the room, stooped over the bed; and Sally, having half-strangled him with a farewell caress, begged to go down to the door and see them off. The parental decision on this matter being fifty-fifty, Sally cast the effective ballot, hopped out of bed, tugged on her dressing-gown, and scurried after them, the honk of the taxi having warned the travelers to bestir themselves. Transportation on the banister had been strongly discouraged, but in this emergency Sally felt it was justified. Her prompt arrival in the lower hall coincided embarrassingly with the entrance of the taxi-driver, who had come in for the baggage. Hannah, who had opened the door, endeavored to rebuke her with a not very convincing frown. Marcia was annoyed.

Taking Sally by the sleeve, she led her into the spacious living-room and said firmly, 'I hope you will remember that in our absence you are the mistress of this house and are to act like a lady.'

Then there were hasty kisses, the taxi sputtered away, and Sally dignifiedly climbed the stairs. She was mistress of this house — and a lady. It was a pretty tall order, but

she liked the novelty of it and went to sleep planning a program of behavior consistent with the new rôle she had
undertaken.

When the bell rang next morning, Sally rose with unaccustomed alacrity and dressed with unprecedented care.
Hannah, having heard the child moving about for twenty
minutes, wondered what was up and called to her from the
foot of the stairs, but Sally did not reply. It was, she felt,
unbecoming of a lady to shout that she would be there in a
minute. Besides, it wouldn't be true; for she wasn't ready.

It had been Sally's intention to put on her very best
dress, but on further deliberation this seemed rather affected, so early in the day. Rummaging in the closets she
came upon a dress of Roberta's which hadn't been considered good enough to take along. Surveying herself in
this more mature garment, Sally was pleased to note the
effect of added height, though honesty compelled her to
admit that the lines around the neck left something to be
desired. She corrected this by putting on a large white
jabot of her mother's. While finding the jabot, she had
come upon a pair of long imitation-jade eardrops which,
she felt, would also do quite nicely to set off the ensemble.

With her small tongue bulging one cheek, Sally consulted
the mirror for a report on the progress she was making in the
adjustment of this jewelry, nervously hastening now, for
Hannah had called again and would be popping up here
presently to investigate.

With much dignity Sally proceeded down the stairs and
out into the dining-room where Hannah was in the act of
putting down at her place the customary oatmeal, buttered
toast, and chocolate. Wide-eyed with speechless amazement, Hannah drew back the chair, Sally stiffly accepting
this attention with averted eyes, and sitting very straight.

'Good morning, ma'am,' said Hannah, in a muffled tone
that stirred Sally's apprehensions.

Turning her head slightly, she said, 'Good morning,
Hannah,' kindly enough but remotely. With a deliberate

gesture, suitable to her new calling, she took up her spoon. Feeling that it might be indiscreet to risk dribbling the oatmeal on her mother's jabot, she bent over her dish and one of the eardrops fell in.

Hannah, who had bitten her lip almost to the blood, was determined to play her part in the drama if it killed her, but the misadventure of the insensitive eardrop hadn't been counted on. She retired hastily to the kitchen, aware that if she remained for another instant in Sally's presence there would be an explosion. No matter how well you thought you had yourself in hand, there were a few things that human flesh could not endure without a complete collapse.

Closing the swinging door, Hannah leaned limply against the wall, both hands pressed hard against her ribs, and laughed until the tears ran down her cheeks.

The table-bell tinkled. Resolutely pulling herself together, Hannah attended the summons. Sally glanced up briefly and said, in a low tone astonishingly like her mother's, 'A small dish, Hannah, if you please.'

Hannah said, 'Yes, ma'am,' very respectfully and brought the dish into which Sally scooped a large spoonful of oatmeal-and-eardrop. Then she looked up again, directly into Hannah's eyes this time, for one really couldn't go on like this forever without making sure how people felt about it.

Their eyes having met, Hannah did the best she could, but the affair had now reached such proportions that she couldn't cope with it.

'Oh, Sally, forgive me, darling,' moaned Hannah, when she could speak. 'I wanted to help you play it, dear, but ——' She went off into another hysterical gale of laughter.

Sally put her spoon down slowly and blinked back the tears. Then a self-conscious smile reluctantly curved her lips. And then, to Hannah's joyful relief, the embarrassed little girl chuckled.

'Come here, baby,' murmured Hannah, sinking into a

chair. Sally slipped over into Hannah's lap. 'You *are* a lady, dear. And Hannah's dreadfully sorry to have laughed.'

'It was awfully silly, wasn't it?' said Sally meekly. 'Funny, too, I guess. Let me go, Hannah.'

In a few minutes she was downstairs again, wearing the brown overalls and floppy straw hat which served her as a garden costume. As she passed through the kitchen, she found Hannah deeply absorbed in a letter she had just received.

'How do I look *now?*' demanded Sally, pausing for inspection, but Hannah did not reply. Her face was troubled and her hands trembled. Perplexed, Sally went down the back steps and out to her garden. She hoped nothing unpleasant had happened to Hannah.

The disturbing letter had come by special delivery. It was from Lydia, who rarely had occasion to write. Hannah wondered if anything could be the matter with Peter.

'You will be surprised,' began Lydia, 'to know that I have just heard from your friend Mrs. Adele Cooper Moore. Her husband died last winter in Paris and Mrs. Moore has been in New York for two months. She has somehow managed to trace you to the University Hospital. The hospital people reported the birth of Peter and the fact that I took him, but they were unable to say what had become of *you*. She wants me to tell her where you are. Hints that she hopes you are free to come and be with her. She also speaks of a long cruise: perhaps she wants you as companion. At all events, she requests wired information about you. The letter is rather spluttery and seems to have been written in much excitement. What do you want me to say to her? Wish we could talk this over. Are you coming down Thursday? Peter is well. He and some other boys have a cave in the vacant lot back of the Wyman home. Spends most of his time there and comes in dirty beyond description. Love. Lydia.'

Hannah carried the letter about from room to room,

pausing to re-read it, her forehead wrinkled with perplexity. *Adele* — after all these years. And how had she contrived to follow her movements as far as the hospital? Who could have provided any of that information except Thomas? Her last letter to him had been posted from the Newcomb residence on Lake Shore Drive where she was working as a parlormaid. Had Adele been talking to Thomas?

Considerably shaken, Hannah went out through the kitchen, down the back steps, and slowly crossed the rear lawn to the far corner where Sally, in her brown overalls, was energetically wielding a small hoe.

'Why do weeds grow faster than flowers, Hannah?' Sally's yellow curls were damp and her nose had taken on a fresh consignment of freckles.

'Do they?' asked Hannah absently. 'You mustn't work out here too long at a time, dear. You're *so* hot!... Sally, I've just had a letter from a friend of mine in Waterloo telling me something that makes me want to see her. I really ought to go there tomorrow. And of course I can't leave you here alone. Would you like to go with me?'

Sally dropped the hoe and fanned her sunburned face with the floppy straw hat.

'Sure — I'll go. It would be fun. Would we stay all night? Are we going on a train? Do you think Mother will care?'

After the excitement of boarding the train had subsided, Sally fired a volley of questions to which Hannah replied, measuring her words with deliberation.

'Her name is Mrs. Lydia Edmunds, Sally, and she lives in a big brick house on a shady street. There is a large yard full of tall trees. You will like it, I think. Mrs. Edmunds has lovely flowers. And you will see Peter Edmunds, who is about your age.'

Sally's nose elevated slightly.

'This Peter — does he pull hair and make fun of the way

you throw a ball?' Sally hoped this would sound amusing,
but it was easy to see that the introduction of Peter into
the day's adventures was viewed with some anxiety. 'What
kind of a boy is he, Hannah? Does he carry toads in his
pocket?'

'I'm afraid so, Sally,' regretted Hannah. 'However,
you'll not need to play with him if you don't want to. I'm
told he is very busy most of the day now, in a cave with
some other boys.'

'A real for-sure cave?' Sally's interest was genuine.

'One they dug.'

'Will he let me see it?'

'I don't know, dear. . . . Boys are funny.'

'You mean — Peter wouldn't want a girl around?'

'I think he plays mostly with boys,' admitted Hannah,
'and Gyp, of course. Gyp's his dog.'

'I'll bet you mean he just despises girls,' reflected Sally
hotly. 'Well — I won't bother him.'

Hannah was silent for a while and then said, 'Peter may
not pay very much attention to you, but you'll probably
like him, Sally.'

'Why?'

'Oh — for that reason, mostly,' drawled Hannah. 'Women are made that way.'

Sally giggled a little as she pooh-poohed the idea of being
rated a woman, but showed by her eyes that she enjoyed
the sensation.

'You're so funny, Hannah.'

'I'm quite in earnest, dear. We women are all alike, that
way. If a man refuses to pay any attention to us, we've
simply got to find out the reason.'

'Pooh!' said Sally, shrugging. 'I wouldn't care.'

Mrs. Edmunds met them at the train, Hannah having
telephoned they were coming. Sally was much impressed
by the ease with which Mrs. Edmunds, who was very pretty
and smelled good, handled her car.

'You sit in the middle, Sally,' said Mrs. Edmunds, in a

very soft, drawly voice. 'We'll all three ride in one seat.'

'And where is Peter?' wondered Hannah.

'The cave — as usual. He'll probably spare you a minute or two for a greeting — if he can find the time. I understand they're rehearsing for some initiation ceremonies today. The Owens boy is to be received into membership presently. He was black-balled earlier in the season for being a sissy, but his grandmother has just sent him a fine archery outfit and an Indian suit which seems to have improved his standing in the community. . . . I had to get Peter an Indian suit too, Hannah. It pulls down the corners of his mouth quite a bit and narrows his eyes, but I think you'll recognize him.'

Sally grinned, and decided to like Mrs. Edmunds even if she didn't wish to meet her unsociable child. Mrs. Edmunds said funny things so soberly and smelled so good. Sally was always attracted by nice perfume — not very much, of course, but expensive.

'Did you enjoy the ride on the train, Sally?' asked Mrs. Edmunds, to which Sally replied affirmatively but crisply, resenting the baby-talk tone of the query. And then, feeling she had been curt, she attempted to mend it by asking a question. But it would not be a baby question.

'I am told,' she said thoughtfully, 'that your son has a dog.'

Mrs. Edmunds laughed merrily and exchanged amused glances with Hannah.

'Oh, very much so, Sally,' she replied. 'You'll see him.'

'What kind of a dog is he?'

'Well — that's not an easy question to answer, dear. We never learned much about his family. Sometimes I think he would have been a collie — if he'd had any choice in the matter. At present — now that we're spending so much time in the cave, I think the best way one can describe him is to say that he is a very, very dirty dog.'

'But not much dirtier,' conjectured Hannah, 'than his master.'

They had pulled up in front of the house now, a large, square house with a row of beautiful white pillars and white steps. It smelled cool inside and everything was very still. Mrs. Edmunds took them upstairs to a big bedroom with yellow curtains and a very high ceiling and a bed with tall posts where they laid their hats and coats. Then they went down again and Mrs. Edmunds gave Sally a little tapestry pattern in a wooden frame. The stenciled picture was a basket of flowers and there was yarn in a half-dozen colors.

'Hannah and I will have to be talking — about business — for a little while, Sally. You won't mind. You may go out into the garden if you wish. There is a swing. Come — I'll show you.'

This would be that horrid Peter coming now. He was in an Indian suit, his face smeared with some copperish paint, and had just tossed himself over the fence near the rabbit-pen, followed by the dog. Sally had been much interested in the rabbits and would gladly have remained to watch their clumsy limping about — as if they were nursing a sprained ankle — but felt that Mrs. Edmunds rather expected her to sit in the swing and do the needlework. She was glad now that the terrible boy hadn't found her looking at his rabbits.

Having upended himself expertly over the fence, Peter ran a few steps as one in a great hurry to perform an errand and return to more urgent affairs. The dog, sighting Sally, abandoned Peter and galloped toward the swing, where he stood panting with a large red smile. Peter whistled, but Gyp was still curious about the newcomer who had acknowledged his attentions with a few soft little noises that sounded like the kisses you really didn't have time to give to relatives when starting for school in the morning.

Then Sally wished she had encouraged the dog to obey his master, for Peter, tugging off his hot gaily feathered headdress, was strolling carelessly in her direction.

'Hello,' he growled.

Sally drew a parsimonious smile and said 'Hello,' and, because she was very much occupied with the threading of a needle, she had time only to glance fleetingly in his direction.

'Your name Sally?' accused the Indian.

She conceded this point by nodding, her lips pursed a little.

'You came with my Aunt Hannah?' Peter leaned heavily against the frame of the two-seater swing, bumping it rhythmically with his knee.

'Yes. But I didn't know she was your aunt.'

Encouraged to believe that he might now accept the stranger as a guest in good standing, Gyp put a paw up on the seat beside Sally, who drew away uneasily.

'He won't hurt you,' scoffed Peter. 'Don't be scared.'

'I'm not scared,' retorted Sally. 'His feet are dirty.'

Peter admitted this gruffly. Sally grinned slightly without raising her eyes.

'I suppose you think I'm dirty, too,' he added.

'Well' — said Sally, after a pause — 'if you are' — she looked him squarely in the eyes and smiled — 'I'm sure you must be wanting to go and wash. Your hands, anyway,' she added, displaying her dimples.

Peter grinned amiably and tousled Gyp's ears to cover his confusion. Then he ventured to glance at Sally again. She was bent over her little tapestry, still smiling.

'We've been digging a cave,' explained Peter. 'You gotta get dirty — digging a cave.'

'I suppose so. Are you going to let me see it?' she asked coyly.

'It isn't much.' Peter's eyes registered perplexity as he gave himself to some rapid thinking. 'I'll tell you what: we'll wait until the kids are all at home for dinner. Then I'll show it to you.' He turned and started slowly toward the house. 'I'll be back,' he promised over his shoulder. 'Got to see Aunt Hannah — and wash my hands.'

'If I were you ——' counseled Sally.

'Yeah — I know,' shouted Peter. 'You'd wash *first*.'

He ran up the kitchen steps with a great clatter and disappeared in the house. Sally drew a long breath, smiled contentedly, and resumed her needlework, feeling very grown-up indeed. It was, she mused, a lovely day. And Mrs. Edmunds had the most beautiful roses she had ever seen. Mrs. Edmunds was so sweet. It was odd how a woman as dainty as Mrs. Edmunds could have such a roughneck for a child. She wondered what he would look like if he were clean and nicely dressed.

Once inside the house, Peter suddenly calmed. Tiptoeing up the back stairs, he went to his room, divested himself of the Indian suit; and, locking himself in the bathroom, took the first voluntary bath he had ever undertaken. Then he returned to his room and arrayed himself in the white suit he had never worn but once — and then under protest. There was a moment's indecision between the red tie and the blue one. He chose the red, knotted it with much care, and in this glorified state descended the main stairway.

'That you, Peter?' called Lydia. 'We're in the library, dear. Come in. Aunt Hannah's here.'

Peter hesitated for a moment. It had not occurred to him until this instant that his altered appearance before his relatives might excite their curiosity and possibly evoke smiles. However, it was too late now. He had cut off his retreat.

When he appeared in the doorway, both women looked up and regarded him with a blinking astonishment that twisted his face into a grin. Hannah saved the day for him.

'Why, Peter!' she exclaimed. 'I think this is the sweetest thing for you to clean yourself up so nicely for your Aunt Hannah! Come here, dear, and let me look at you. What a lovely suit! It fits wonderfully!'

'Yeah — I was pretty dirty, Aunt Hannah,' explained Peter, permitting himself to be kissed. She retied the red scarf, Lydia looking on with amazement. Peter always hated to be fussed with.

'There!' said Hannah, patting him. 'It's perfect!'

'Peter,' said Lydia, 'you remember I told you that Aunt Hannah was to bring little Sally Ward along. She's out in the swing. Perhaps you'd better run out and make her acquaintance. I don't suppose you saw her — by any chance — when you came in.'

Pretending reluctance to leave, Peter sidled toward the door. When he was out of earshot Hannah said, 'I don't think that was quite fair, Lydia.' They both laughed.

'Wouldn't it be funny ——?' suggested Lydia, in an undertone.

Hannah's face was suddenly serious.

'*Much* too funny!' she replied.

'But, Hannah! Why shouldn't these children like each other, if they want to? Sally's a dear little thing. Her friendship would be good for Peter. It's easy to see what she has done to him already.'

'No, dear,' protested Hannah, pressing her palm hard against her troubled forehead. 'We've plenty of complications now, without bidding for any more. I want Peter to have a fair chance at life. Now that Adele is determined to locate me, it will be only a question of time until she succeeds. Peter mustn't know that his mother is a servant. That's a secret I mean to keep from him at all costs. . . . But if he and Sally strike up a friendship, it will be almost impossible. . . . Oh, Lydia — how very foolish I was to bring the child here!'

Chapter X

A DOZEN years had wrought many changes at Bar Harbor.
The Gables seemed smaller, duller, stuffier, and had fallen
into genteel disrepair. The beach extended much farther to
the sea. The sand you had to wade was deeper and softer.
The tides seemed always to be out, and when you firmly
took them to task for it, they apathetically ambled in with
almost nothing of the old gaiety.

If you really wanted to find out how old you were, reflected Adele, you should revisit some spot you hadn't
seen since you were up on your toes searching for adventure.
Then you could see not only what had happened to the
cherished old haunt, but to yourself as well.

Once Adele had known everybody who was anybody at
all in The Gables' summer colony. Now the list of acquaintances had been pared down to a frost-bitten little group you
could count on your fingers. The men were grizzled — my
word! how gray and lean Bob Winthrop was — and the
lines in the women's faces were deep. That first afternoon
Adele gave herself to a ruthlessly honest inspection in the
mirror, wondering if she looked as battered as Rosalie Parr,
wondering if her own bobbed hair made her look as silly as
Marie Bryce's, wondering whether it was better sense to
meet middle-age on its own terms or squabble with it to the
probable amusement of the flappers.

Sympathetic friends among the expatriates in Paris had
condoled with her over the 'readjustments' she would be
obliged to make, now that Martin had passed on; but, in
sober truth, there hadn't been much readjusting that she

was conscious of. Martin had been thirteen years her senior, world-weary, frail, drifting about from one sanitarium to another, sometimes with and sometimes without her, eternally muttering about his defaulting viscera and wishing himself dead, which he was, to all useful purposes. The funeral was not an occasion for poignant grief; rather in the nature of a memorial as if it might have been the anniversary of a demise accomplished years ago. No hypocrite, whatever her other weaknesses, Adele hadn't pretended to be devastated with sorrow.

Accompanied by Cynthia Bradford she had gone out next morning to Père la Chaise, and arranged for an inscription on the slab. It had been Martin's wish to put in here when the time came and Adele had cheerfully fulfilled his instructions, feeling that he would be in fairly good company, his resting-place reasonably well insured against any molestation, at least while she lived. Already Martin seemed very remote.

Cynthia had been quite attentive. Her divorce from Thomas had been granted six months ago; and, the luminous novelty of her new freedom having worn through to the iron, she was in the market for diversion. Adele's bereavement provided her a chance to exercise a talent for comradeliness which had become anaemic through disuse. In this mood she had confided more of her own story than might have been possible under any other circumstances.

Part of the serio-comic tale of Cynthia's life with the Bradfords was already known to Adele. It was common talk. Madame Bradford had herself picked Cynthia Rollins as an acceptable daughter-in-law, shortly after Thomas's summary disposal of Hannah, the old lady feeling that if her son really insisted upon marriage, she would arrange it for him as she had arranged everything from his infancy. The Rollins fortune having evaporated, Cynthia had accepted Thomas much as she might have accepted an annuity. And she had earned it — every dime! Thomas had fallen in with the plan complacently, and the jaded trio pursued the established Bradford program — October in Paris, the winter in Cannes, April in Paris, May in London, June in New York (during which time attention would be given to consultations with bankers, brokers, and attorneys), summer at Bar Harbor, October in Paris, winter in Cannes, *ad libitum, ad vitam, ad infinitum.*

At length — it was June — the old lady had died in the New York apartment they had expensively maintained and seldom occupied. Cynthia announced to her sister, an hour afterward, that she was leaving for Paris on an extended vacation.

'I am going immediately, Hortense,' she declared, 'and I have no plans for coming back — that is, not very soon.'

'You'll wait until after the funeral, I hope,' admonished Hortense, who liked to see things done in good form.

'Of course. I wouldn't miss that. I've been looking forward to it for nearly ten years.'

Thomas hadn't protested. Indeed, he had shared her belief that Cynthia needed a long vacation, and while he was much too suave to add that he also could do with a few months by himself, he implied it by refraining to dwell on his probable loneliness during his wife's absence. Pursuant to habit he proceeded to Bar Harbor, settled into a sea-facing second-floor suite at The Gables, and, when apprised of Cynthia's decision to free herself of her matrimonial bondage, picked up the detective story he had put down upon arrival of her letter, and didn't realize what time it was until the bell rang for luncheon.

Cynthia told all, through those days of her girlhood friend's fresh sorrow; and Adele, who had known enough of it to be able to guess at the rest, listened with more patience than interest. Only one new fact about Thomas was disclosed by Cynthia's voluminous confidences. Adele's eyes widened with genuine surprise when she heard it. You would never have suspected that the torpid Thomas entertained any aspiration at all — much less this one! He wanted children, if you can imagine such a thing! Except for this single regret, he lived as unemotionally as a three-toed sloth.

Sometimes it was almost pitiable, declared Cynthia — Thomas's shyly wistful attitude toward the tots they occasionally encountered. And it was quite amazing, too, the way young children responded to his diffident overtures. He would greet some little chap of six with the same reserve that might have been exhibited by another lad of the same age. Cynthia believed it was his very shyness in the presence of small children that encouraged them to share responsibility for the promotion of acquaintance. Thomas would not be seated on a park bench very long before there would be a child or two beside him.

'Of course,' Cynthia had gone on, in that monotonously flat voice of hers that wore you out, 'when you can't produce a child, it's silly to offer any other reasons why you didn't have one, but I was always glad I hadn't brought some unfortunate little thing into the world to live our life, with no home, no permanent friends, no amusement but to trail along after an insufferable old lady. It wouldn't have been right.'

One day Adele had decided, rather impetuously, to return to the States. Oh, yes — she would probably be back in the fall. Cynthia hinted that she might be persuaded to join forces with Adele on this excursion, but, lacking any encouragement, gave up the idea. Sometimes she suspected, from Adele's frank inattention, that their comradeship had relaxed into a merely casual acquaintance. Reluctant to see this happen — for she was no end lonely — Cynthia had all but invited herself to go along. She saw Adele off at the Gare du Nord, saying, 'Do come back soon, dear,' to which Adele had replied, non-committally, 'Don't look for me until you see me. I might find me a man over there.'

'You can't be in earnest,' said Cynthia, a bit piqued by the inference that Adele had failed to confide the real purpose of her journey.

'You'll see,' teased Adele, enjoying Cynthia's astonishment.

The nervous scurry of New York had increased. Crowds like swollen rivers funneled through station exits and swirled fanwise at intersections. The life of the city had been regimented to the point of absurdity and yet its people hurled themselves forward pell-mell as if each was behind his schedule and would surely be reprimanded or fired when he arrived.

Adele suspected that a great deal of this stampede was a mere pose. Men had to pretend they were driven almost to desperation by their tasks. To confess that you weren't hard pushed for time was almost equivalent to admitting you were on the skids.

More than ever, business men (and women, too) were impressed by the mechanical toys they had invented to serve the new god Efficiency. You wanted to talk to Mr. Andrews about that property you owned on 192d Street. Mr. Andrews was on the seventeenth floor of a new skyscraper. Bewildered by the racket and confusion in the main foyer, you took the express elevator by mistake and were shot like a rocket to the fortieth story, returning presently on a local. The girl at the information desk said Mr. Andrews was still in conference. When you finally got to him, the interview was constantly punctuated with bells, buzzers, and every manner of electrified plaything requiring his attention. Earnest-faced secretaries popped in to lay a sheaf of papers on the desk and popped out carrying other papers hastily grabbed up. Adele knew they were bluffing, trying to impress you with the urgency of their large affairs. Old Andrews was attempting to keep up with the pandemonium, but it had made him as jittery as a caged monkey. She tried to tease him a little, but he wouldn't have it.

The odd thing about it was that, although you were confident of your belief that about fifty per cent of this pressure was faked, you yourself soon fell into the feverish trot, pushing and rushing along with the rest. Adele had been away from this madhouse long enough to have forgotten how wearing it was, and in the meantime its rattle and clash, its hurry and worry, had accelerated until it fairly dizzied her.

One day, quite on impulse, she took a late afternoon boat to Boston, hired a car in the morning, and was driven up to the old home on the North Shore. It was for sale again; by a bank, this time. The caretaker was friendly after she had explained who she was and why she had come. She did not enter the house, but sauntered through the gardens and followed the path to the half-timbered cottage where she had so often gone to have a glimpse of Hannah. There had been few changes. It was as if she had been here yesterday. Memories of the thoughtful, deferential, competent Hannah came surging back to fill Adele with an intense longing to see her. What had become of Hannah? Wouldn't it be marvelous if Hannah were free to come to her as a companion? They could travel. Hannah had been so keen on travel. Indeed, it had been Thomas Bradford's enticing offer of foreign sight-seeing that had swept the lonely girl off her feet and into disaster. Adele made a prompt resolve. She would try to find Hannah!

Back in New York by train next day, Adele telephoned the Bradford apartment and was gratified to learn that Thomas was in town. Yes — he would be glad to talk to her. So they lunched together in a relatively calm restaurant on Fifty-Third Street, Thomas — stouter, grayer, nattier — amiably inquiring about Cynthia in the dutiful tone of one asking expected questions concerning the health of one's maiden aunt, and Adele telling him everything she thought he ought to know of his late wife's prosaic life.

'Yeah,' drawled Thomas, 'it was a lucky day for Cynthia when she got rid o' me.'

'*Wasn't* it, though?' agreed Adele heartily, which made

Thomas laugh. 'Lucky for Hannah Parmalee, too, I always thought,' added Adele. 'By the way — I'm meaning to find Hannah if possible. Could you help me?'

By long training in the endurance of embarrassing situations, Thomas had developed a fairly thick crust, but he winced a little under Adele's candid contempt. Defensively he explained that a few weeks after the divorce he had sent Hannah a check for five hundred dollars — the amount of her own money he had used — but the letter had come back marked 'Address Unknown.' It had been sent to her latest Chicago address, a residence on Lake Shore Drive. Yes — he still had it, if Adele thought there was any use trying again.

'You gave it up, after that one attempt? Never made another effort to find out whether Hannah was alive or dead, sick or well? She might have starved.'

Thomas shook his head.

'No, Hannah wasn't the kind to starve. She would make her way, all right. Probably married again. I certainly hope so. I admit I treated her badly, but she would have been treated worse if she had tried to live with me — under the circumstances.' He faced Adele now with a bit of challenge lighting his pale blue eyes. 'But, speaking of indifference and neglect, *you* didn't go to much bother about her, either, until now — now that you need her.'

'I'll grant your point, Thomas,' confessed Adele. 'I had my own troubles to fret about. I hope it isn't too late.'

'If you find out anything, will you let me know?'

'Perhaps. It depends on what I find out.'

'If she is in need, will you let me know?'

'Not likely. Hannah wouldn't want you to do anything about it.'

'That's true,' agreed Thomas glumly. 'Hannah was proud.'

The Newcombs still lived at the Lake Shore Drive address. Mrs. Newcomb, replying to Adele's letter, remembered Hannah very well, and had taken the trouble to inquire of their family physician.

'I was ill myself when Hannah left,' she wrote, 'or I would have shown more interest. Doctor Phelps saw her a few times after we let her go; then sent her to a free clinic. He thinks she went to the University Hospital to have her baby. That is all we know about it.'

Ten days later, Adele had a report from the University Hospital. Hannah Parmalee Bradford, present address unknown, had borne a son there. The child had been taken, likely for later adoption (though they had no record of that), by another patient, Mrs. Jasper Edmunds of Rattoon.... Now we were really getting somewhere, exulted Adele. She wrote to Mrs. Edmunds, careful to request a return of the letter if not delivered in three days. It did not come back. Impatiently she waited for a reply. New York was stifling. Everyone who could do so had gone away for the summer. Unable any longer to endure the heat and noise and loneliness, Adele had packed up hastily and taken herself up to Bar Harbor, resolved that if she did not hear from this Mrs. Edmunds very soon, she would make the trip West and do a bit of sleuthing.

After she had been there three days, Thomas Bradford arrived. He had padded softly into the cool dining-room on rubber soles, passing her table without seeing her, the head waiter preceding him with the attentiveness due a guest of long standing. He nodded to the occupants of several tables, paused to shake hands with the Winthrops and the Parrs; and, when seated, exchanged a smile of recognition with Adele. After luncheon they met in the lounge.

'Heard anything?' asked Thomas, waiving a formal greeting.

Adele swiftly debated a reply and shook her head, Thomas searching her eyes afterward as if not quite sure what her momentary hesitation signified. Then Bob Winthrop came downstairs in his golf togs and lazily called, 'See you out front,' and Thomas had moved away, presumably to dress for the links.

The afternoon mail came. *There was a letter from Hannah*.

DEAR MISS ADELE:

My friend Mrs. Edmunds gave me your letter to her. It is surely good to have word from you after so many years. I have often wondered where you were and if I should ever see you again. You were always very good to me.

I see that you know about my little boy. His name is Peter and he is eleven years old. Some ways he seems older. He is going to be tall and big like his grandfather Parmalee, I think. I see him often, but he does not know I am his mother. Of course this hurts me very much, but I am anxious for him to grow up to be somebody. I don't want him to be held back by his mother's being of the servant class. Not that I am ashamed of it myself, but it would stand in his way at college and after. He has a good home with Mrs. Edmunds and thinks she is his mother. Sometimes it has been hard to stand by and watch him make over her. But I want him to have his chance, as I said. I know you won't tell anyone. Peter calls me 'Aunt Hannah.'

Ever since he was born I have worked in the home of Professor Ward. They have been good to me. They have three children, the youngest born after I came here. They were poor then, but now they live very well. I cannot leave. These people need me now more than ever. Besides, I must stay where I can visit Peter. He will never be mine, but it helps a little to be able to see him. I hope this finds you well. Would you please send me your picture?

Respectfully yours

HANNAH PARMALEE

Adele was pensive. She sat for a long time with the open letter in her hands wondering just how much heart-break would be involved in the sort of sacrifice Hannah was making for her child.

It was odd, but true enough. Here we were in a democratic country that had always blown itself purple in the face over its 'equality' and its derision of social caste, but the facts were that Hannah was right when she believed her boy would have a better chance to succeed if it were never known that his mother had worked in somebody's kitchen.

And, speaking of Peter's chance, when and how was he going to get it? Certainly not in a sleepy little town in the corn-belt, brought up by a kindly disposed widow who had probably never been anywhere in her life. Peter would attend the high school, fall in love with a classmate, spend four years in college, and settle down in Waterloo, likely, to be a country lawyer or a bank-teller or something like that. And Hannah, hoping all the time that Peter would make a name for himself, and going through who knew how much sacrificial agony to speed him on to greatness.

'I won't have it!' declared Adele. 'If it's costing this much to give Peter a chance, I'll come in on it — and help!'

The letter she sent to Hannah was recomposed three times before she was entirely pleased with it. She agreed with Hannah in every particular about the liberty Peter should have and felicitated her on the bravery of her decision to keep herself in the background, no matter at what cost of maternal suffering.

'But, really, Hannah,' continued Adele, shaping the words with her lips as she wrote, 'if this boy is to do the things necessary to justify your painful investment in him, he should soon have a little wider view of the world than he is likely to get in that small town. No reflection on your Mrs. Edmunds at all. A fine woman, doubtless. But Peter needs more room to grow up in. . . . Now I want to make you a proposal. It would please me very much — I'm really frightfully lonesome, Hannah — if you would let Peter come and spend August here with me. I can be an aunt he never saw. He's too young to make many inquiries about that. I'll come to Chicago and meet him. Mrs. Edmunds can bring him that far. I'll show the dear little chap the sea and teach him to swim and find him some pleasant company among the youngsters here. The Winthrops have their grandchildren along. . . . Do humor me in this, Hannah. I'm quite eager about it.'

Mrs. Ward had promised herself to return to Chicago in mid-August for the opera season at Ravinia Park. Paul's consultation work in Chicago was taking him there again. They would be leaving in a week.

Hannah read Adele's special through, voting all of her stock against the project; read it again, still doubtful but interested; read it a third time. The sea, the Winthrops, Adele.

Sally came in for a drink of water.

'Hannah,' she said coaxingly.

'Yes, dear.' Hannah's voice sounded very far away.

'We're going to be alone again.'

'I know, Sally. You will take good care of me, won't you?'

'Will you be wanting to go down to Waterloo again — to see Mrs. Edmunds? If you do, please will you take me?'

'We'll see,' postponed Hannah absently.

After Sally had gone out to the garden, Hannah sat for a long time in earnest thought, her chin cupped in an unsteady hand. In September, when school began again, there would be no occasion for Sally to go along to Waterloo. To refuse to take her there again would unquestionably stir her curiosity. She wouldn't be able to understand. If it was all right — and her mother had agreed it was — to be taken to see Mrs. Edmunds and Peter in July, why not in August? Had she done something amiss to make Hannah refuse her another invitation?

These questions were bound to arise. Sally's feelings mustn't be hurt and her curiosity should not be aroused. How natural if she confided her perplexity to her mother, who would wonder even more about it herself.

Besides — it would be a great experience for Peter, as Adele had said. Adele probably knew what she was talking about. The more she considered it, the more attractive the plan seemed to Hannah. Next day — Sally having been invited to go on a picnic party with the Olivers' grandchildren — Hannah went to Waterloo on an early train and canvassed the whole situation with Lydia, her chief talking-point being the fine experience for Peter.

Lydia listened quietly, not quite prepared to express an opinion, and Hannah rather reluctantly presented the other angle of the case. She didn't want Peter and Sally to be seeing any more of each other. It was very plain, wasn't it, that these children were unusually congenial? Lydia nodded and smiled.

'He talks about her every day,' she said, 'and keeps asking when you're going to bring her again.'

'You see?' demanded Hannah. 'I knew it! We can't have it!'

'Well,' sighed Lydia, 'after all, dear, he's your boy. And I must say you've made very few suggestions about the way you wanted him brought up. If you really think we should let him go, I see no reason why not. I'll arrange to take him to Chicago. We had better wire to Mrs. Moore at once.'

'Thanks, Lydia, you're very good.' Hannah's satisfaction and relief were so genuine that Lydia was glad she had acquiesced promptly.

'Shall I tell him now?' she asked.

'No,' replied Hannah, 'I'll leave you to tell Peter anything you like about his mysterious Aunt Adele. It shouldn't be difficult. She has lived abroad more years than he is old. And he has often heard us speak of her. Peter will be so excited about the trip that he probably won't ask many puzzling questions.' She paused thoughtfully, her eyes troubled. 'I don't like to have Peter deceived, even for his own good, but apparently we can't do this any other way.'

Lydia sighed gently and said she didn't like that part of it either.

'But for his sake,' she added, 'we have already left so much untold that one more small deceit won't matter. It would be quite different if we were planning something that might hurt him. I'm afraid the telling of the literal and complete truth to Peter, at this stage, would be a very shabby act.'

'That's true enough,' agreed Hannah, 'but plenty of good people would say we were doing the wrong thing. I'm sure of that.'

'Plenty of good people,' reflected Lydia, 'are overgenerous with their opinions about problems they don't understand very well. We'll see it through. I shall telegraph Mrs. Moore that Peter and I will meet her at the train she intends to take for her return East. In the confusion of setting off on his big adventure, he will not notice that his mother and his Aunt Adele are not as well acquainted as relatives ought to be. I shall leave him with her and hurry away. The rest of it will be up to her. That sounds practical, doesn't it?'

'I hope so, dear,' said Hannah. 'Thanks for being willing to do it for us. You have been very good to me, Lydia.'

After an hour they went forward to the dining-car, Peter gallantly opening the doors and keeping a weather-eye out for his charming Aunt Adele as they made their way through the aisles of the lurching train.

It had been an exciting morning. Such chuff-chuffing of engines and clanging of bells and rattling of baggage-trucks and people rushing into trains and out of trains! Peter had been so occupied by this complication of new sights and sounds that he had hardly realized his mother was gone and his pretty Aunt Adele was in charge of him until they were gliding out of the gloomy station-shed.

For a half-hour they had slipped smoothly past rows and rows of ugly brick houses that looked very much alike, the track presently rising to a level of the second-story windows. And they had passed several swift trains, so close it made you blink when the big Pullman cars flicked by, whispering a soft little 'Fsst, fsst, fsst, fsst.'

And then came dozens of railroad crossings where the heavy wheels of your train pounded the other tracks, shouting, '*Flat*-on-your-back! *Flat*-on-your-back! *Flat*-on-your-back!' Now there were occasional open spaces with brown-grass stubble where the hay had been cut. Peter hadn't wanted to talk. And Aunt Adele hadn't bothered him with any attentions.

It was open country and the train was going very fast. Peter turned from the window and for the first time recognized his duty to show a polite interest in his stylishly dressed companion.

'I'm hungry, Peter,' she said, and he knew he was going to like her. His experience with women had led him to believe that they never really were hungry; that when they ate it was mostly to accommodate others. If this beautiful woman was the sort to get hungry and was honest enough to say so frequently, he felt that they could easily be friends. Moreover, she hadn't tried to kiss him or hold his hand or smooth his cowlick with a wet finger. He looked up at her amiably and partly closed one eye to let her know that the remark she had made coincided fully with his own feelings. Perhaps, if he had given more thought to it, the wink might have seemed not quite appropriate to the occasion — seeing how recently they had met for the first time — but now that he had done it, Peter knew, from the happy amusement on her face, that his reply had pleased her. Indeed, she seemed so pleased that he half-feared she might put her arm around him or pat him on the knee, but she didn't. It made him feel quite grown-up.... The doors were heavy and hard to pull open, especially the first one they came to at the end of their own car. He tugged with almost full strength, his new Aunt Adele waiting behind him. Now she'd be saying, 'Wait a minute, Peter. I'll help you.' But she didn't say anything; just stood and waited. He had braced himself firmly then and pulled the door open. And she hadn't said, 'That's a big, strong boy!' He knew now that he and Aunt Adele were going to get along together. He liked her. He liked the way she walked. He liked her name. Aunt Adele. He hadn't called her that yet.

Seated now at the table for two, Peter had a chance to inspect his attractive new relative with a sincere frankness that Adele found slightly disconcerting. He made no attempt to disguise his approval of her outward appearance, his sentiments on that subject being fully expressed in the steady gray eyes (Hannah's) and flatteringly confirmed by the puckery little smile (also Hannah's) that lightly pursed his mobile lips.

Adele tried to see as little as possible of Thomas Bradford in this interesting young face, though there was something in the sidelong glance when, gazing out at the window, he unexpectedly let you have it without turning his head — there was something in that half-shy, half-defensive, inquiring glance that was Thomas — Thomas to the life! The shapely ears, too, snugged uncommonly close to the head. That was Thomas. However, Thomas had a very good head — at least on the outside — and Peter might have done worse than to fall heir to it. The forward curve of the hair-line on the temples — Thomas again. It would be the same blondish brown hair, too, when it had darkened a little more in maturity.

'What would you like to have, Peter?' asked Adele casually, training her lorgnette on the menu-card.

'I'd rather you would say, please,' said Peter.

'"Aunt Adele,"' she prompted gently, in the same key.

He grinned companionably and repeated the words after her as her tone had suggested. There was a little caress in it that warmed her heart.

'I hope you're going to like your Aunt Adele, Peter.' Her eyes were intent on the menu so as not to seem too urgent with her proffer of affection.

'I do!' His declaration was so prompt and sincere that Adele's eyes were misty. Quick to observe the alarming effect of his reply, Peter added prudently, 'I like *all* my aunts.'

Adele intuitively understood the nature of this qualifying afterthought.

'That's the way it ought to be, of course,' she commented, 'though aunts can be a great trial.'

'I've never seen but two of mine — Aunt Hannah and you.'

'Your Aunt Hannah is a darling.' Here, thought Adele, was a reasonably safe topic. She hoped that if Peter had any questions to ask about family relationships, they might pivot on Hannah. 'We used to have such fun together when we were girls,' she added truthfully.

'Why didn't you come and see her?'

'There wasn't time, Peter. I was anxious to take you on your vacation at once, for you will have to be back in school presently. I'll try to see Hannah when we return. . . . Do you think you would like an omelet — or some fish?'

Peter's voice was reminiscently obedient. 'My mother said I should let you choose what I'm to eat.'

She couldn't resist teasing him a little with a suggestion that the milk-toast was generally very nice on trains and, noting the slightly apprehensive look in his eyes, added, 'Of course, you needn't have it if you prefer something else.'

'Are *you?*' he asked, wrinkling his face in astonishment.

'Certainly not!' scoffed Adele. 'I'm having lamb chops, creamed potatoes, asparagus, salad, pie, ice cream — almost everything!'

Peter drew a long breath.

'That will be all right for me, too,' he agreed complacently.

'You're very polite, Peter.' She was beginning to write their order now, and having put down two corn soups, two lamb chops, and two peas, she seemed to have difficulty with the lorgnette. 'Will you fill out the rest of it, dear?' She pushed the order-pad and pencil toward him; and Peter, aglow over his responsibility, followed the pattern she had set for him.

'You want coffee, I expect,' he said, without looking up.

'Chocolate, please.'

So, on the last line, Peter wrote two chocolates, rather pleased she hadn't wanted coffee, for he knew he wasn't considered old enough, and it would have made him feel like a baby to have taken chocolate. This made it all right — Aunt Adele's having it, too. He handed back the order, and she signed to the waiter that it was ready for him, without so much as glancing at it to see if it had been filled out properly. Peter's shoulders straightened. He gave her an earnest look with a query behind it and her pretty brows raised slightly in anticipation.

'Did you ever have a boy — Aunt Adele?'

'No, Peter.'

There was a moment's pause.

'That's too bad,' he said gently.

She briefly nodded her appreciation of this spontaneous solicitude, and, observing that Peter wasn't quite finished with what he was trying to say, she asked 'Why?' — in such a low voice that if he hadn't read the word on her lips he might not have heard it. He contemplated a prudent reply, his gray eyes narrowing.

'Because — well — I expect you wanted one.'

'That's true, Peter,' she assented softly; and, after a pause, 'What made you think so?'

He lightly traced a nervous pattern on the tablecloth with his butter-knife and chuckled self-consciously.

'Oh — I don't know,' he ventured, at length. 'Anyway — it would have been pretty nice — for the boy.'

'How very sweet of you, Peter!'

He flushed slightly under this candid tribute and considered the wisdom of changing the conversation. However, the soup had come now to relieve the tension.

'If I could have had a boy,' pursued Adele tenderly, 'I would have wanted one just like you.'

Somewhat disturbed by this endearment, Peter hastened to defend his right to be a problem to his mother, and presently was telling her all about the cave, the club, and the manly sports which occupied so much of his attention.

'I take it that you don't play very much with girls,' observed Adele. 'Perhaps you don't care for them.'

Peter was almost on the point of admitting that this was true when it suddenly occurred to him that Aunt Adele might be offended, for she had been a girl herself and — some ways — seemed a good deal like a girl even now, so he replied, 'Oh — they're all right,' after which he renewed his interest in the soup, trusting that he had squared himself.

'You'll think so some day,' laughed Adele. 'Girls get much nicer as they grow up. I don't think they're very interesting — at eleven.'

The waiter had carried away the soup-plates, leaving Peter without occupation at a moment when he would have appreciated some distraction. Aunt Adele seemed to know exactly what you were thinking. He hoped she wasn't guessing about his thoughts now. He wondered about this for a moment; and, raising his eyes, encountered hers. They were smiling, teasingly. He looked away quickly and felt a sudden warmth creeping up his cheeks.

'Peter,' she accused him playfully, 'you're holding out on me.'

He shook his head guiltily, but would not meet her eyes.

'Funny thing about that,' observed Adele, almost as if she were talking to herself. 'Boys and girls are perfect pests to each other when they're your age — all except one.'

'Yes — that *is* funny,' agreed Peter absently.

The lamb chops had come now and the other things. Very hungry, Peter applied himself diligently, noting, after a while, that his Aunt Adele was more interested in him than her luncheon.

'What's her name, Peter?' she asked softly.

'Sally.'

'Neighbor — I suppose.'

'No — she lives with Aunt Hannah. Sally Ward.'

'So — you like Sally, do you?'

'Well — she's different. You won't tell, will you?'

'No — but I expect Hannah knows. Hannah knows almost everything.'

Peter shook his head.

'Not about that — she doesn't,' declared Peter, a bit brusquely. 'When do we get to Bar Harbor, Aunt Adele?'

'About Friday, I think. We're not going there directly. We will stop in Boston for a couple of days. I have some errands there. And I want you to see a few things that will make school a little more interesting this fall. Would you like to do that, Peter?' Observing that he was only mildly enthusiastic, she went on, 'We will hire a car and drive out over the road that Paul Revere took, when he stirred up the farmers to fight the British. Do you remember?'

Peter remembered, and thought this would be a wonderful thing to do. 'Aunt Hannah doesn't believe in fighting,' he added. 'She doesn't even want to talk about it.'

Adele had forgotten Hannah's odd quirk on the subject of war. Now it all came back to her memory, the frequency of Hannah's comments on combat — all manner of combat, national and individual, public and private. It had been nothing short of an obsession. Doubtless her strange convictions had deepened as she hugged them more tightly through the passing years. . . . And so, Hannah had filled this lad's head with her own queer ideas. It would be interesting to know his reaction to a philosophy so utterly impractical.

'I can't think that Hannah would object to your looking at the Bunker Hill Monument, Peter, or driving out to see Paul Revere's road. After all — that's the way we got our American independence.'

'Aunt Hannah doesn't think so,' rejoined Peter firmly. 'She says any kind of fighting is wrong, no matter who does it.'

'And what do you think?' Adele couldn't help asking.

Peter was sober for a moment, apparently struggling between loyalty to his Aunt Hannah and the necessity to state his own boyish feelings.

'I think,' he said slowly, 'a fellow's got to fight sometimes, whether he wants to or not. You can't let 'em run
over you. Aunt Hannah's wonderful, but I'll bet she'd
find it pretty tough to do that if she was a boy. Don't
you think so, Aunt Adele?'

She dodged this neatly by reminding Peter that she
never had been a boy, and couldn't say just what she
would do.

'That's just it,' approved Peter, pleased with her confession of feminine immunity. 'Men don't want women to
fight.'

Adele drew a disturbingly ironical smile.

'Now you've said something, my lad! Men like to
harness themselves in shiny leather straps with plenty of
bright buttons and go strutting down the street behind
the band. They love the way they look in their uniforms
— so big and straight and strong. They don't want their
women to show off their bravery. They expect the women
to stay at home and fret and lie awake nights and wonder
where their children's next meal is coming from.'

'You talk like Aunt Hannah,' said Peter, wishing now
that the subject hadn't come up — 'except she doesn't
make fun of the belts and things. . . . But — anyway — a
fellow's got to protect himself, don't you think?'

'Yes, Peter, I do think that. Making war is one thing,
and defending yourself is another.'

'Aunt Hannah doesn't think so. It's all the same thing,
she says. I never let her know when I've been in a fight.'

'What does your mother say about it?'

'When I've been fighting?' Peter grinned reminiscently. 'She just asks me how it came out.'

Adele couldn't help smiling over that, and Peter felt
she was on his side, even if she didn't say so.

Thomas had taken a late afternoon dip in the surf and
was sprawled at full length on the sand. He had been
obliged to spend a week in New York attending to cer-

tain stupid matters of business which, he felt, might as easily have been handled by mail. The return trip to Bar Harbor had been hot, dirty, tedious. It was refreshing to be back. Shutting his eyes against the sunlight, he luxuriated in the comforting breeze and the sedative lisp of an outgoing tide.

Most of the bathers had left the beach, passing him as he had come out. Parents were shouting injunctions to their children to come now and get ready for dinner. Drowsily outstretched, he heard the youngsters' prattle receding. Presently he, too, would plod back to the bathhouse, de-sand himself in the shower, and dress. It was very quiet. Thomas opened his eyes, sat up, yawned, and met the gaze of a boy who stood a little way off, feet wide apart, hands on hips, regarding him with interest.

'Hello,' said Thomas pleasantly. 'Were you waiting for me?'

'You were so still,' said the boy, 'and the rest of them were all gone. I thought something was the matter. I beg your pardon, sir.'

'It was quite the right thing to do, I think. We waterspaniels have to take care of each other. No telling what might happen to us. Besides — any sort of flotsam or jetsam lying on the beach is likely to be interesting.' Thomas drew up his knees and folded his arms on them, and the boy dropped down beside him.

'What's flotsam?' he inquired, looking up earnestly into Thomas's face.

'Well — you can't have any flotsam unless you have some jetsam. They always go together like — like cakes and syrup, and each and every, and Sodom and Gomorrah. Now, technically' — Thomas assumed a tone of gravity — 'technically, flotsam is almost anything that washes in from a wreck — and jetsam is stuff the sailors throw overboard just before the wreck — but it all comes to the same thing.'

'Yes, I see,' assented the boy, nodding his head politely. 'Thank you.'

Thomas grinned, partly over his own silly speech, partly
over the seriousness with which it had been received. The
boy drew a brief smile and quickly sobered, his gray eyes
intent on a candid invoice of his new friend. Thomas returned the scrutiny, a bit mystified over the lad's artless
inspection of him. Then they both smiled, and Thomas
said, 'What's your name?'

'Peter Edmunds.'

'Stopping at The Gables, Peter?'

'Yes, sir. I came Thursday. I'm visiting my aunt.'

'Who is your aunt? Maybe I know her.'

'Mrs. Moore. She came to Chicago for me.'

'Oh — so you live in Chicago.'

'No, sir — in Waterloo. My mother brought me to
Chicago to meet Aunt Adele.'

'Thank you for telling me about yourself, Peter. I am
glad to know you. I am Mr. Bradford.'

'How do you do, Mr. Bradford?' said Peter respectfully.
'Do you know my Aunt Adele?'

'Yes, she's a good friend of mine.' There was a considerable pause. 'How old are you, Peter?'

'Eleven. Twelve pretty soon.'

There was another extended silence.

'When?' inquired Thomas quietly.

'November second.'

Thomas's eyes looked far out to sea, meditatively, and
he softly rubbed his thumb against the tips of his fingers,
almost as if he were counting — eeny, meeny, miny, mo.
Peter watched him interestedly.

'Shall we go now?' asked Thomas. 'It will soon be
dinner-time.'

Peter rose and measured long steps. They did not talk
much on the way back. When they parted, Thomas said,
'I'll be seeing you,' and Peter replied, 'Thank you, Mr.
Bradford. I'd like to.'

Chapter XI

THAT was an eventful winter for the Wards. The new refrigerator had caught on instantly, effortlessly. The public had been waiting a long time for it. Salesmen needed only to be order-takers. At the factory, production had been speeded up to three shifts per day. Paul's rewards were exceeding his most lavish expectations.

Hannah's fears that an overstuffed optimism might involve them all in a financial disaster were gradually allayed. For no accountable reason, Paul Ward's luck had turned. Everything he touched ran smoothly. Hannah could well remember the occasion, six years ago, when he had been badgered by an unscrupulous local man to buy a hundred dollars' worth of stock in the Parker Manufacturing Company, engaged in making pumps. He couldn't spare the money. But the chap who had come to see him had pictured such prompt and huge profits that Paul had yielded. The next afternoon's papers reported that the concern had gone into bankruptcy. The very next afternoon! The people who sold him the stock knew the company was broke, knew they were stealing his money. Even Mr. Parker himself, president of the organization, had assisted in making the stock sale. It wasn't much, of course, but Mr. Parker — with his back to the wall — was willing to take what little he could lay his hands on, not caring much how he got it.

Now that Paul's income was ample to take care of every reasonable wish, all his investments proved profitable. Part of this success was attributable to the good advice he received from Sam Trimble, with whom he had become chummy.

Sometimes Paul chuckled about it. He would come to the dinner-table with the evening paper in his hands, folded at the financial page, and say, 'Well, Marcia, we made six hundred dollars today.'

'Why — *Paul!*' she would exclaim. 'How wonderful! What are you going to do with it?'

And Paul would reply idly, 'We'll just leave it there to grow a little more — and then you can buy yourself a new apron, or a new ax, or something.' He was proud of her chance to be indolent.

One would have thought that after the long steady pinch of poverty, he might have become vain, silly, and pompous over what his fortune could do for him personally. Hannah was pleased to observe that this had not happened. He was as indifferent to his swollen income as he had been formerly to his predicaments. An hour's fretting over some humiliation would see him through it, in the old days, after which he would resume his careless attitude toward expenses and obligations alike. Now, true to his nature, Paul would rejoice for a little while over some unexpected increment and then settle quickly again into his normal state of mind.

The new venture had absorbed so much of his time and attention that Hannah often wondered whether he would be able to retain enough interest in his professorship to insure his position at the University. She had so hoped he wouldn't let his new money make a loafer of him. To her delight, September twelfth found him eager to be back in his classroom, and for several days preceding he had been diligent in the Dean's office. Hannah was proud of him when she discovered that his money wasn't likely to spoil him.

It was going to be a bit different with Mrs. Ward. Of course it was not much to be wondered at if this extraordinarily pretty creature, having waded through drudgery, penury, worry, boredom, and dowdiness for all of fifteen years, would now let herself out. Her horizon had been expanded immeasurably and she couldn't be blamed for wanting to stir about a little and see what was going on in a world of larger privileges.

So she was making up for lost time. There was a second maid now — one Bertha — a trim little thing who promptly proved her value by relieving Hannah of the extra work which the new house demanded. Bertha was going to be quite a comfort. Hannah liked her, and felt that the girl heartily reciprocated. At least she acted as if she did. The children were becoming more and more self-reliant. Wallie had his own interests outside. Afternoon and evening absences from home were vaguely attributed to basketball practice and school activities. Roberta didn't need or want very many friends, and spent much time in her room, presumably writing and drawing; an odd youngster who belonged to the tribe mostly by sheer residence. Sally was blossoming; still a little girl, but beginning to show signs of an early development into a rare type of Saxonish loveliness. She was much interested in making exquisite costumes for her dolls; but, having completed a new dress, the thought of mothering the doll seemed tiresome. It would not be long now, reflected Hannah, until Sally would have put her cherished brood up in the attic storeroom.

Marcia Ward had a genuine talent for bridge, and seeing how few gifts she possessed other than her personal appearance, she had gone in for it with an absorption that was only a little northeast of frenzy.

She had also bobbed her hair — one of the earliest in town to venture upon this audacity — and talked about it and fussed with it a good deal, partly because she realized it was amazingly becoming to her girlish type, and partly in self-defense, for the time had not yet arrived when a Mid-Western matron of thirty-nine could do it with impunity. Until very recently the only adult women with

bobbed hair, at least in the hog-and-corn zone, were either
invalids, inmates of lunatic asylums, or out-and-out
huzzies. The University wives not only had long hair, but
wore switches, mostly of earlier vintage to prove they
hadn't always been gray. Mrs. Adams even wore a rat
around which a huge sprayless comber curled as if poised
to break.

So — all of these conditions being as they were — what
time Marcia wasn't talking bridge she was talking hair.
And if she didn't look out, thought Hannah, her conversation would presently become rather irksome to her husband,
who had not shown himself to be keenly interested in
either of these issues.

Eleanor Trimble was now Marcia's closest friend.
Eleanor was the authentic leader of the best social dozen
in town besides holding an excellent position in the esteem
of the better Faculty wives. It was a tricky relationship,
too, for the tie-up between town and gown was as sensitive
as a dancer's corn. On occasions — not very lately, however
— the animosity had blazed until lines had been stretched
for the protection of bystanders. For the past three or four
years there had been no explosions or terrifying conflagra-
tions, but the old feud continued to smoulder like a malodor-
ous spring bonfire nearing extinction.

All the circumstances of Eleanor's life happily conspired
to give her the social precedence she needed for this delicate
job of pasturing lions and lambs in one serene enclosure.
Sam Trimble, as president of the bank where practically
everybody connected with the University cleared his
pittance, was a good man to know, especially when you
hadn't saved enough money for your summer vacation
and must negotiate a loan with little collateral beyond
friendship. Indeed, you would strain a point and consent
to attend almost any sort of party at Sam's house, for
prudential reasons, even if you knew you would have to
meet people with whom you shared very few interests or
experiences aside from the elementary fact that you all

breathed prairie air at approximately the same number of respirations per minute.

But Eleanor Trimble had not come by her social leadership through mere duress. She was born to it. There was no question in anyone's mind about that. She had not been party to the celebrated fights. Her Saturday nights were planned with craft and executed with skill. She would gather up a coterie of top-notch merchants and industrialists and their spouses, and a flock of influential professors, and mash them all together into an outwardly harmonious compound, blandly indifferent to the fact that many a pair of these elements — if left alone together — would have blown off the roof.

Eleanor always knew the right thing to say. Aware that every woman she knew nursed some private vanity, some pet anxiety, some lambent hope, she ministered artfully and effectively to all comers. She was not pretty, but you frequently heard people saying they thought she was. It was because they liked her. She did something to them that made them like themselves. If you analyzed her and then totted her up, item by item, the total was surprisingly short of the aggregate you had previously guessed at. Eleanor was considerably under average height. It required her to gaze up at you, which gave you the satisfaction of looking down. So nobody blamed her for that. It made the women feel important, and as for the men, the distance Eleanor had to look when she gazed up at them made her long-lashed brown eyes wink rapidly and tipped her head back so far that it parted her lips into an expression of childlike adoration. Her eyes and lips were about all she had of physical attractiveness, but they were a plenty.

When Mrs. Hastings arrived on a Saturday night in a new lace gown cut to add seven years to her age and four inches to her girth, Eleanor stood on tiptoe to whisper '*Lovely!*' She was a little liar, but she honestly believed that of such little liars is the kingdom of heaven.

To Mrs. James Blodgett whose son Charles — he had

never been worth the powder it would have taken — was
reported to have landed a job on the *Star*, Eleanor said,
'My dear, what a wonderful chance for that boy! I always
knew he would make you proud, when he struck his stride.'

Even when you knew that what she was saying was
utterly silly, you took it and licked the spoon. She had gone
to the lengths of saying to Marcia, 'What a charming girl
your Roberta is coming to be! So gracious! So lovely!'
This was really carrying things a bit too far, and for an
instant Marcia had eyed her narrowly to see if she might
detect the slightest bulge in her lightly rouged cheek; but,
noting no such symptom of insincerity, purred softly and
thought Eleanor a darling, which wasn't far from the truth.

It was beyond all thought that she who was so gifted in
the arts of comradeship could content herself with the little
conquests she made with her women friends. Eleanor
wasn't above planting a murmured word or two of laud,
honor, praise, and glory into the hairy ear of almost any
broad-shouldered male. She always timed and placed her
seasons of worship in such a manner that the idol could
hardly fail to appreciate her offering. If it was supposed to
be a private matter, she would reach up and detain Bill by
the sleeve just long enough to whisper, out of the corner of
an expressive mouth, 'I heard what a killing you made in
cotton, Little One. Nice work!' Or, she would capitalize
a brief lull in conversation by calling halfway down the long
table, 'Timmy, if you haven't given that seventy-four-
stroke ball away, I'd like it, please, initialed.' And Timmy
would reply, with a booming laugh, 'O.K. Shall I put
"love and kisses" on it?' And then Eleanor would let him
have a half-shy wink as she replied, 'Thank you, Timmy.'

It was fun and she enjoyed it. She enjoyed it so much
that sometimes she was utterly foolhardy, as when she said
to clumsy old Claude Miner, who owned more stock in the
Farmers and Mechanics Bank than anyone else in town
except Sam himself, '*Claude!* You don't mean to tell me
you've worn your *teeth!*' She winked rapidly in happy

surprise. 'Lovely!' she murmured. It was a classic joke that old Claude wore his upper plate only when attending funerals in his Knights Templar uniform, on all other occasions presenting a mouth reminiscent of the widely spaced monoliths at Stonehenge. Sam had said to her that night while they were undressing, 'Sometime you're going to make a pass like that at a fellow who isn't feeble-minded and he'll sock you in the noodle.' And then Sam laughed again until he had another touch of his asthma and had to help himself to a stiff slug of Scotch. Eleanor smiled knowingly and remarked, 'Claude liked it.' And then added, half to herself, as she patted the cold cream on her pretty throat, 'They *all* like it. *You* like it. . . . *I* like it.'

Claude, who had gone north next day for the deer season, expressed them a quarter of venison, a week later. The tag read '*Mrs.* Samuel J. Trimble.'

'You see?' teased Eleanor. 'It pays to be nice to people.'

And so it did. Eleanor was becoming increasingly resourceful in winning friends. It was an amusing game to play; more exacting than bridge, more exciting than golf, more rewarding than either. It wasn't that she merely enjoyed the sensation of conquest. Sometimes her eyes were very sober when she remembered the effect she had produced with certain adroit encouragements and flatteries; for example, the pathetically wistful expression on frail little Mrs. Morris's face when Eleanor told her how very well she was looking. Mrs. Morris was worrying her heart out over that cancer.

Sometimes, of course, you couldn't help chuckling when you thought of the way the eminent Professor Wemble had turned out to be a cunning little kitten when you had dragged him off into a corner to button his sleeve-link. No matter what was being talked of, the Professor was forever sure to be reminded of something that Hegel or Fichte had said, but at this moment he had just breathed heavily and made strange jungle-noises in his larynx. Eleanor thought it was fun.

And so it was — all of it — only fun, until that night when she and Paul Ward had their sudden, unpredictable, unaccountable collision of eyes. There hadn't been the slightest occasion for it. She had looked up at him with exactly the same gaily beaming, friendly, flattering brown eyes that had been radiantly lifted a full half-dozen times into other eyes in the course of the past two hours. This time she found it difficult to get away from the curious mesmerism of Paul's sober, steady gaze. She felt a sudden glow, a hard bump-bump in her heart, and wondered what it was all about.

The evening had drawn to a close. Eleanor had asked Paul to help gather up the tally-cards. Then they had gone into the library to inspect the scores. Laying the cards out on the desk, they had bent over them, touching elbows.

'Alice Patterson, apparently,' said Eleanor. 'I'm glad of that. She's had wretched luck lately.'

'It seems Sam has the best score for the men,' said Paul.

'Sam won't want to take a prize. He hates it, when he's the host.'

'I know — but it's customary, isn't it? Whoever wins it, gets it, even if he did have to pay for it himself.' They laughed — a little more than the pleasantry was worth.

'Very well,' conceded Eleanor. 'Let poor old Sam win a prize once.' She gathered up the cards, one by one.

'I don't feel that Sam is in need of any sympathy,' said Paul quietly. 'He has always been quite lucky — at everything.'

Eleanor glanced up, smiled brightly, suddenly sobered, dropped her eyes, looked up again, became conscious of a little tremor on her lips, flushed slightly, and then said in a throaty undertone, 'You shouldn't look at people — that way. You'll — you might break somebody's ——'

Mr. Blodgett chose that instant to barge into the library.

'I say, Mrs. Trimble, they're calling for you.'

'Righto! We've finished. We'll be there instantly.'

Blodgett retired, leaving them standing a little way apart, facing each other. For a moment they waited in a mutual constraint. Then she smiled and tucked a trembling hand under his arm companionably.

'We must go,' she said.

'Of course,' assented Paul, rather unsteadily.

Just within the door she paused, looked up into his eyes again, and said, 'It's odd — isn't it?'

'Yes,' he replied, 'it is.'

She was in radiant spirits again by the time they rejoined the others. When the last of them had gone home, she said to Sam, 'Mind if I toddle off to bed? I'm tired.'

Seated at her dressing-table, Eleanor studied her eyes. Always, after a party, it was fun to remember the things one had said and done to make people pleased with themselves. This experience tonight was something different. It hadn't been fun. It was too serious.

Reviewing the little episode, moment by moment, she wondered just what she had done, what she had said, how she looked, to provoke this flashing change in their casual acquaintance. What they had been saying to each other was nothing, mere banter and chaff. What Paul had implied when he referred to Sam was all of a piece with the playful compliments he had often bestowed, same sort of pleasantry all the other men liked to think they were good at. What had happened? They had exchanged a look that had given them a strange reaction.

'It's odd — isn't it?' she heard herself saying. Why had she said that? Trying to be frank, perhaps. It was the wrong thing to have said. And Paul had agreed, soberly, that it was indeed 'odd.' But what else could he say? He couldn't very well blurt out clumsily, '*What's* odd?' It was probably all her own fault. Now they would either be stiff and suspicious of each other, or let themselves go again and take the chance of making themselves very restless and unhappy. She had despised these nasty little affairs with all her heart.

Taking up her brush, Eleanor swept it through her black
hair several times, almost savagely. She had been a fool.
There wouldn't be any more of it, she could promise you
that! She would take pains not to see Paul Ward alone,
ever again.

The strokes of the brush were lighter. She laid it down,
propped her elbows on the table, laced her fingers under her
chin, stared into the glass; and, living it all through once
more, frowned witheringly at herself, sighed deeply, closed
her eyes, and smiled.

After that they seemed always to be bumping into each
other at every corner, though this could be easily explained,
Paul thought, by the fact that each of them had become
acutely conscious of the other.

Eleanor was valiantly trying to put things to rights by
being especially attentive to Marcia, who, gladly recipro-
cating these pleasant hospitalities, was planning all of her
social events so that the Trimbles would be not only front-
rank guests, but obviously of the inner circle. The two
women quickly arrived at an intimacy which coupled their
names in the guest-lists of every hostess in their social set.
If either was asked to pour at a tea, both of them poured.

Marcia, fighting a hard bridge battle with doughty op-
ponents — the last hand of the evening — would say
confidentially to Eleanor, whose hand had been laid out on
an adjoining table, 'Would you mind, dear — telling
Hannah to serve now?' And Eleanor would go to the
kitchen, where she was almost as much at home as in her
own house, and start things going. It had become that sort
of relationship.

As this intimacy tightened, Eleanor saw more and more
of the competent, respectful, observant Hannah. Sometimes she surprised herself with the efforts she made to win
favor in the esteem of this resourceful servant of the Wards.
She never felt quite comfortable, much less superior, in
Hannah's presence.

he was proud of her — 'Yeah, Eleanor knows the big board better'n any other man in town. Whenever she says "Sell," you'd better get to a telephone and do something about it pronto 'f you don't want to lose your shirt.'

Eleanor could talk about anything. She was wise, witty, well-informed, clever in repartee. And, plus all that, she was deliciously feminine. It wasn't much wonder that Paul liked her.

But — dear, dear — what were we to do now?

A murky dawn, color of ashes, was threatening to present another sultry day. Jaded by a long night of sleeplessness and worry, Hannah sat up in bed and rubbed her hot eyes. Then she shook her head and made a little gesture of despair. No — there was nothing she could do. Somebody ought to talk to Mrs. Trimble, but that somebody wasn't Hannah. She had a reputation for doing audacious things. She was well aware that the close friends of the Wards considered her a unique character and were amused over the many stories, which Paul often told with delight, of Hannah's odd relation to his household. Sometimes, in her presence, he or Mrs. Ward would make a playful allusion to the high-handed manner in which she had bossed them all for years. The Trimbles had often joined in this friendly teasing. Maybe she could presume a little on that. But no — this was too delicate a matter.

On first thought Hannah felt it might possibly be risked. She had imagined herself going to Mrs. Trimble and saying: 'Please don't break up the only home I have. I am very much alone in the world. You have your home. Let us keep ours.' Of course, she would try to say it kindly and tactfully. But was there any way to do such an impudent thing as that — kindly and tactfully? No — Eleanor Trimble couldn't be counted on to listen patiently to an impertinence so unpardonable, not even from a person like Hannah who enjoyed some unusual privileges of speech and action in the Ward home.

For a while she had figured on the probable effect if she went to Mrs. Trimble with a little gift-basket containing a jar of consommé, a bottle of home-made grape-juice, and a few glasses of jelly. And Mrs. Trimble would say, 'Why, Hannah — did you think I was sick?' And then she could reply, 'Yes, Mrs. Trimble, that was the only way I could account for it.' And then Mrs. Trimble would let her talk about it. But, no — that wouldn't do. Eleanor Trimble was a very gracious person, but she wouldn't consent to a rebuke from Hannah, no matter how richly deserved or how artfully brought to her attention. Hannah drew a long sigh, stood at the open window for a little while, mechanically dressed for the day's work, and went softly down the back stairs. After all, that was where she belonged, wasn't it? How silly even to have dreamed of a heart-to-heart with the banker's wife?

At three that afternoon Mrs. Trimble breezed in to recover her copy of the Wards' itinerary and mailing addresses. She was rather noisily amiable, causing Hannah to wonder whether the errand hadn't been invented. It was a little like the old story about the murderer who returns to the scene of his crime.

'I left it on the desk in the library, Hannah,' she said. 'May I look for it?'

'Certainly, Mrs. Trimble. Shall I help you?'

'I know where it is, Hannah. Thanks.' She disappeared through the library door, returning in a moment to say she had found it and that it had been stupid of her to have forgotten it. She had avoided Hannah's eyes upon her arrival, but now gave her a direct smile. 'I must say, Hannah,' she declared, in the friendliest of tones, 'Mr. and Mrs. Ward are certainly fortunate to be able to pick up whenever they like and leave their home knowing it will be in such good hands as yours. Really, you're a treasure, Hannah! How is little Sally?'

'Thank you, Mrs. Trimble. Sally is out in her garden.

Would you like me to call her? I know she would be happy to see you. The child has been lonely today.'

'I'll go out where she is, Hannah. I can stop only a minute. How nice for you that Sally is to be at home this summer. She's such a dear.' Mrs. Trimble seemed in no hurry to go, after all, and tentatively seated herself on the arm of the davenport. 'I suppose she seems almost like your own, you've had so much to do with bringing her up — from her babyhood. I know how much you mean to Sally. It's a very beautiful relationship, Hannah. You've been just like a mother to these children — almost as good as having some of your own.'

Hannah smiled and said: 'Thank you, Mrs. Trimble. I am fond of all the family. They have been very good to me.'

'Yes, of course,' said Mrs. Trimble, adding, 'That's as it should be. Very pleasant for you all.' This comment was made with a casualness suggesting that enough had now been said on this matter, and Hannah expected Mrs. Trimble would rise and proceed to the garden, but she remained where she was, tentatively swinging one small white-shod foot as if waiting for something.

One thing seemed fairly certain. Mrs. Trimble was here on a little mission of conciliation. Clearly she wanted very much to know where she stood in Hannah's regard. Perhaps if Hannah showed herself to be friendly, that would mean that she hadn't been too much upset by yesterday's little misadventure and would be disposed to forget it. Mrs. Trimble might be wondering whether a bit of coldness and stiffness on Hannah's part, carried forward into the future, would stir Mrs. Ward's curiosity to the point of inquiring why she disliked their friend.

And wasn't it a little strange — Mrs. Trimble's telling Hannah she had been such a good mother to the Ward children? But not so strange, though. Mrs. Trimble was forever saying pleasant things to people, piling it on almost too thickly for comfort sometimes. And hadn't she often said almost the same things to Hannah — about her use-

fulness and how fortunate the Wards were to have her?
But even so — might there not be, in the back of that
canny little head, a wish that Hannah might express, by a
word or an inflection, what she really thought of Mrs. Ward
as an incompetent mother — probably also a doubtful
success as a wife. If Hannah could be made to give her
thoughts away, by so much as a cryptic pucker of the lips,
then Eleanor Trimble could feel comforted in her belief
that Hannah — if not exactly on her side — would at least
condone the affair as thoroughly understandable.

While these queries raced through Hannah's mind, Mrs.
Trimble sat negligently swinging a shapely leg and toying
with the latch of her white leather handbag.

'I must be on my way,' she decided abruptly. 'If there
is anything we can do for you, Hannah, you'll call up,
won't you?'

'Yes, Mrs. Trimble, thank you.' Hannah smiled gratefully, interested to see the genuine relief expressed on Mrs.
Trimble's face as she turned to go. Presently she heard
Sally's voice answering from the garden. Sally would be
glad to receive this little attention. She had been quite
demure all day.

Now Hannah was more worried than ever. Not only had
she no plans for doing something that seemed to need doing,
but she had been unable to avoid an implied approval of
Mrs. Trimble. The woman had given her every possible
chance to disclose how she felt today about the thing that
had occurred yesterday, and Hannah hadn't been the slightest mite disturbed; cordial, respectful, genial. It was
exactly as if she had said to Mrs. Trimble, 'You know
what I saw, but I don't really care. It's your business and
I wish you joy of it.' Hannah was not quite content to
leave the matter stand that way.

She wondered if it wouldn't be a little more honest, and
helpful too, if she should ask Eleanor Trimble back into the
house, after she was through talking to Sally, and say
frankly: 'I have seen you and Mr. Ward wishing you could

be something more than friends. It has been going on for a long time, and I've been so very proud of you both. You were simply wonderful! Yesterday you both slipped a little, but that's easy to understand. He was going away. I know that when they come back, you'll see to it that nothing happens again. Please, Mrs. Trimble. You've been so fine. I like you so much. Don't hurt us. You won't, will you?'

Mrs. Trimble might consent to be talked to in that spirit. And again, she might not. It was a risky thing to try. She was going now, crossing the rear lawn diagonally. She would not come back into the house. Her car was standing at the curb in front. Hannah's heart was in her mouth as she went down the rear steps into the garden, shading her eyes against the sun.

'Good-bye, Hannah!' Mrs. Trimble waved a hand, hesitated, was about to go on.

'I made some red raspberry jam today, Mrs. Trimble. If you wait a minute I'll give you a glass to take to Mr. Trimble. He likes it so well.'

'Thanks so much, Hannah. Shall I come in?'

'Please.... It's cooler inside.'

Eleanor followed, wondering just how much cooler it was going to be inside. Well — she'd asked for it, hadn't she?

Hannah preceded her into the spotlessly clean, white enameled kitchen.

'There!' said Hannah, holding up the glass jar to the light. 'Isn't that pretty?'

'Lovely! You're a darling, Hannah, to want me to have it. If there's any little thing I ever can do for you — will you tell me?'

Hannah tapped meditatively on the white porcelain table with her fingers, her head bent in earnest thought. There was a moment's quite stressful silence.

'Say it, Hannah!' demanded Eleanor. 'I'll listen. Don't be afraid.'

Lifting her misty eyes slowly, Hannah smiled compassionately and murmured, 'Oh — Mrs. Trimble — you had always been so fine!'

Eleanor tugged off her hat and rubbed the back of her hand across her forehead.

'That's the hell of it, Hannah,' she growled. 'Please tell me why — you keep on making — people — *so damned fine!*'

They faced each other — almost challengingly.

'Want to talk about it?' said Hannah quietly.

'Yes!' snapped Eleanor. 'Go right ahead! Get it off your chest!'

'I haven't anything else to say, Mrs. Trimble — really!'

'Yes you have, too!' declared Eleanor fiercely. 'You're disgusted — and disappointed.'

Hannah smiled companionably.

'It's not becoming for a person of my station to speak her mind about anything like that.'

'Well — we'll forget about your station, now. This is to be strictly man-to-man talk.'

Hannah shook her head.

'I really haven't anything to say, Mrs. Trimble, except' — she hesitated for a moment — 'except — I had been so proud of you; so very proud of you.'

Chapter XII

It was something of a shock to Peter when he learned that his Aunt Hannah was a servant.

After the manner of other normal children, he had taken a great many things for granted without inquiring into them at all. For example, it had never occurred to him to ask why his Aunt Hannah lived in the home of Professor Ward or what relation she sustained to that household. Obviously she lived with the Wards for much the same reason that he lived with his mother. People had to live somewhere, and Aunt Hannah lived with the Wards. There was nothing odd or questionable about that.

Now that he had discovered she was the Wards' maid, he had a perplexed feeling about her. He resented the idea. It puzzled him, grieved him, and — to be truthful — it shamed him. And that was because all he knew about domestic servants had been deduced from his observation of Susie Stoup, who had been with them ever since he could remember.

There wasn't the slightest trace of snobbery in Lydia Edmunds. If Peter had ever inquired of her whether Susie was as good as they were, Lydia would have replied promptly in the affirmative. *Of course* Susie Stoup was their equal, at least in the sight of God and the preamble to the Constitution. But, let all that be as it might, Peter would have recognized a sizable difference between his mother's relation to the neighborhood and Susie's.

Albeit faithful and obedient, Susie Stoup possessed about as much initiative as one of Peter's white rabbits. She didn't have nearly as much personality as Gyp, who had just missed being a collie. Susie had no wit, no style, and almost no education. She kept the house clean and was a good, plain cook. Now and then her friend Emma, employed in a neighboring home, would drop in and help her do the dishes so they could go to the movies. Emma was a clumsy, dowdy creature, admirably suited to be Susie's chum. To the best of Peter's knowledge, these two were typical domestics. And now his Aunt Hannah had turned out to be one herself.

He wished it had been someone else who had been appointed to break this bad news to him. Of course Sally had done it innocently enough and by sheer accident, and she had been prompt in her efforts to make repairs when she saw what had happened. He did not hold it against Sally.

Aunt Adele had asked to take him again to Bar Harbor for the summer, and his mother had consented. They were to leave for Chicago on Friday to meet this adorable woman, of whom he had chattered almost too much throughout the year. And at Bar Harbor he would undoubtedly be seeing his marvelous friend Mr. Bradford, who, in his esteem, was a close second to Aunt Adele.

And now — as if he wasn't happy enough — Aunt Hannah had telephoned that she was coming down today to say good-bye to him, and was bringing Sally Ward along! He could hardly contain himself.

Lydia indulgently consented to drive to the station twenty minutes before the train was due, so urgent was Peter's impatience. And when Sally actually appeared in the vestibule of the train and descended the steps, Peter's heart pounded hard. He had tried to remember how she looked last summer, but he realized now that he hadn't done her justice; her gold hair, her blue eyes, her dimples — the dimples were ever so much deeper than he had thought.

Aunt Hannah kissed him and his mother, and then his mother kissed Sally. Peter wasn't quite sure what was expected of him in his greeting to Sally, but it seemed fairly clear that a kiss was not in order. He hated to shake hands with people. Fortunately Sally was carrying a small basket; he took it from her, and they exchanged a smile.

'Hello, Sally,' 'Hello, Peter,' they said. She had the loveliest voice. And Peter liked her coral dress.

'How tall you're growing!' she observed, as they followed along toward the car. 'If you keep on, you'll ——'

'You grew, too,' interposed Peter magnanimously, when it had become evident that Sally hadn't really any definite plans for him in the event of his being taller. It wasn't exactly what he wanted to say. He wished he had the courage to tell her how pretty she was. Without turning his head, he glanced at her out of the tail of his eye, a distinguishing trick of his that people often thought was drollishly grown-up, and Sally laughed a little.

'You haven't changed much, though,' she said judiciously. 'How are the rabbits?'

It didn't seem to matter much how they were, for his mother was telling Sally to sit beside her, and he and Aunt Hannah were getting into the seat behind them. Now that he could look at Sally without being caught at it, he comforted himself with a comprehensive view of her neck, her curls, her coral beads, her jaunty straw hat.

'And how are you this fine morning?' Aunt Hannah was inquiring, affectionately patting his knee.

'Yes, it is, isn't it?' agreed Peter, from afar.

Hannah's face was troubled. Here she was, again involving herself in the risk of throwing these children together. She had done everything she could to forestall it, but Peter's letter to Sally had made it very difficult.

So far as she knew, neither of the children had made much of an effort to further their acquaintance. Sally had received two postcards from Peter during his vacation a year ago, one from Boston and another from Bar Harbor. She had shown them to Hannah without any shyness, and had betrayed no alarming symptoms when Hannah had read her Peter's brief letters.

On Christmas they had exchanged greeting-cards. Sally had kept hers in plain sight on her little desk long after all the other Christmas cards had been put away; but there was nothing sentimental about it — picture of a Scottie, tousling a stocking on a rug strewn with candy. Sally might have kept it because she thought the picture amusing.

When it had been decided that Peter was to go East again with Adele, he had written to Sally.

'Why didn't you tell me, Hannah, about Peter's going away?' she queried. 'Can't we see him before he leaves? You want to, don't you?'

No excuses sounded convincing. The fact was that she did want to see Peter before he left. It was quite impossible to satisfy Sally with some flimsy reason why they couldn't go to Waterloo. So, with much reluctance, Hannah had consented, hoping that Peter would be so much occupied with his own affairs that he would find little time for Sally.

And now here he was, meeting them at the train, and so utterly carried away by Sally that he seemed in a trance. Hannah knew now that she should have been firm in her decision not to let them see each other any more. The thought grieved her. How happy she would have been, she reflected, to see these two — beloved by her above all others — finding themselves more and more closely drawn together. What might have been a promise had now become a threat. If they persisted in their boy-and-girl friendship, it wouldn't be long until Peter would be coming to see Sally, or inquiring why he couldn't. And if he did, he would promptly learn that his Aunt Hannah was something other than he had thought. And on top of that, there was the risk of his discovering that she was his mother. Mrs. Ward would ask questions. She might even suspect there was a slight resemblance.

Sometimes Hannah had moments when she devoutly wished she had never ventured upon this difficult program of trying to insure Peter's social position. Occasionally she wondered whether it would not be a relief to tell the Wards all about it, and to tell Peter, too. And then she would remember how she had spent her life fagging for other people — 'Yes, ma'am,' 'No, ma'am,' 'Thank you, ma'am,' 'Very good, ma'am, if I may say so.' Of course there had been plenty of happiness, too. She was bound to admit that. But Peter must be kept free of this handicap. Peter must go to college and fit himself for something important. He must have influential friends. And — above all — he must never be put to the pain and chagrin of having it known that his mother was not of his own station.

As she watched her boy's intent concentration on Sally's pretty head, Hannah began searching her mind for some excuse to take the late afternoon train for home instead of waiting until night. It would shorten the time, shorten the hazard.

'They've made two tennis courts on the school grounds, Sally,' Peter was saying. 'Want to play this afternoon?'

Sally turned to smile radiantly and nodded a vigorous assent that shook her curls; then, suddenly remembering, she said: 'But I have no tennis shoes. I could have brought them.'

Relieved by the prospect of a game of tennis for them, instead of a dangerous tête-à-tête in the garden, Hannah quickly suggested: 'Perhaps you might borrow a pair. Patty Wyman's, maybe.'

'Huh!' scoffed Peter. '*Her* big feet!'

Lydia laughed merrily, but Hannah drew a little sigh. Peter was so infatuated with Sally that he was slightly out of his head. Feet, indeed! And since when had Sally such remarkably small feet?

'They don't cost very much,' Sally was saying. 'I'll buy some new ones if you'll lend me the money, Hannah.'

Funny, thought Peter, how Sally always called his Aunt Hannah by her first name.

But first, before they went downtown to get the tennis shoes, Sally wanted to see Gyp and the rabbits and the roses; so they strolled across the rear lawn on a tour of inspection.

Conversation lagged a little in the rose arbor, and Peter said: 'I wish you were going to Bar Harbor. We'd have fun.'

Sally nodded and said she supposed they would. And then, for a moment, there didn't seem to be anything else to say. Peter opened his knife and carefully whittled the soft bark from a maple twig.

'We'd better go, maybe,' suggested Sally. 'Hannah will be waiting for us.'

'Has my Aunt Hannah lived at your house always?' asked Peter irrelevantly.

'All *my* life,' said Sally, stooping to bury her nose in a salmon-pink Pandora. 'She came to work for us just before I was born.'

'To *work* for you!' echoed Peter, incredulously.

And then Sally realized that she had said the wrong thing. Peter didn't know! It suddenly swept over her that she had wondered a little at the difference there was in Hannah at home and Hannah here in Waterloo. Dear, dear — what had she done?

'Well, not really *work*,' she amended hastily. 'It's almost as if she was a relation of ours. I love her same as if she was a member of the family. We all think of her that way.'

'What does she do — at your house?' persisted Peter.

'Oh, a little of everything — just like people do, you know. She helps Mother. Really, we couldn't get along without her. Daddy often says that.'

'Does she cook?'

Sally brightened, and exclaimed that Hannah was the most marvelous cook in the world. That was why they let her do the cooking, she supposed, because no one else in the family could do it so well. Peter tried to smile a response to this compliment to his Aunt Hannah's culinary

skill, but it quickly faded. He nervously whittled the stick
to bits, eyes moodily intent on his occupation.

'Does she eat with you at the table?' he demanded, suddenly searching her face.

For a second Sally contemplated a lie, but Peter's steady
gaze disconcerted her. She reluctantly shook her head.

'But she could if she wanted to,' declared Sally stoutly.
'She just got into the habit of not eating with us when we
were little, and she would be taking care of us while Daddy
and Mother ——'

'Huh!' growled Peter. 'You mean she works for you,
same as our Susie works for us. You'd better not say anything about that to my mother. She wouldn't like it. And
you'd better not let Aunt Hannah know you told me.'

'I'm awfully sorry, Peter.' Sally's cheeks were red. 'I
thought you knew. I didn't suppose it was a secret. How
could your mother help knowing?'

'Maybe she does,' muttered Peter, wondering if they
had conspired to keep him in the dark.

'But I don't see why it should make any difference,'
insisted Sally comfortingly. 'Almost everybody works at
something. Perhaps Hannah wanted to. She likes us; I
know she does. It isn't a bit as if she was our maid, Peter.
Really!'

'Well — maybe not,' consented Peter half-heartedly.

'I'm sorry I made you unhappy.' Sally's tone was entreating as she winked back the tears.

He smiled a little at that and assured her it was all right.
At the moment he felt, himself, that he had made too much
of the matter. They sauntered toward the house and entered by the back door. Hannah was in the kitchen, talking
to Susie. Of course she had often done so and Peter had not
given it a second thought. It was just the same as when his
mother talked to Susie. But it wasn't quite the same now.

Presently they all got into the car and drove down to
Baumgardner's Department Store for the tennis shoes.
Peter tried to think of some amiable contribution to the

talk, but nothing occurred to him. He lacked the courage to look up into Aunt Hannah's eyes, fearing she might notice that something was the matter. Aunt Hannah was very quick to see such things. She covered his hand with hers gently, and he gave her fingers a little squeeze. It was too bad about Aunt Hannah. He pitied her. She seemed a different person.

Hannah's thoughts were busy, too. Intuitively she sensed that something had gone amiss. Perhaps Peter and Sally had had a little tiff. She stole a sidelong glance at her boy's sober face. The past year had matured him. Last summer's experience with Adele had made many changes in his disposition; more self-reliant, less childish. She wished she might have a long talk with Adele about him and his future. Adele had been so strongly convinced that Peter needed to be 'brought out.' It seemed so silly to talk about a mere child that way, as one might about an eighteen-year-old ready for college. Perhaps Adele was right. Peter was growing up. Maybe something should be done about it. Hannah wished she might express herself to Adele more clearly in a letter. Letters always sounded so stiff; at least hers did. She could manage to make herself understood in conversation, she believed, but whenever she took up a pen she instantly tightened up and the ink fairly froze as it ran.

Once she had almost decided to ask Adele to come on down to Waterloo this time, and meet Peter here; but that would be too, too risky. Adele was such a featherhead. She might ask the wrong questions, say the wrong things, arouse the boy's suspicions. No — she mustn't be seeing Adele in Peter's presence. Plenty of problems now without angling for new ones.

Peter did not go with them into the shoe department, but loitered along the jewelry cases in the forward part of the store. The day hadn't turned out as it had promised. However, he was resolved to make the best of it, remembering that sometimes a bad worry just cured itself after a day or two. Maybe this one would do that. He hoped so. He kept

repeating to himself the various little consolations Sally
had offered. It wasn't as if Aunt Hannah really worked for
Sally's people. Or, if she did, it was because she wanted to,
because she loved them, and if she worked — well, almost
everybody worked at something. Maybe Aunt Hannah
liked it. If she cooked for them, perhaps it was — as Sally
had said — because she was far and away the best cook in
the house. Why not, then? Peter reviewed Sally's arguments and breathed more easily.

Presently they rejoined him at the front door, Sally
carrying her purchase under her arm. She smiled, and
Peter responded in a way that gratified her immensely.
He had never seen deeper dimples. At luncheon he found
himself trying to think of amusing things to say, so the
dimples would have a chance to show what they could do.

On the tennis court, his spirits rose. Sally played quite
a snappy game for a girl, and kept Peter dancing. He
exulted in her swift service, and was proud of her when it
became evident that he would not have to temper his bom-
bardment of her for courtesy's sake.

Sometimes, when she leaped to reach a high one, there
was a candid display of round pink bare knees — like a
baby's. It made him feel very tender toward Sally. He
felt very much older than she, and thought of her pro-
tectively. The idea lingered in his mind afterward. Often
he day-dreamed about saving her from some danger;
drowning, usually, now that he had become a good swimmer.
In the months that immediately followed, Peter rescued
Sally from all manner of aquatic accidents in which she
stumbled off wharves, tumbled out of canoes, and on one
momentous occasion — from which he woke perspiring —
fell overboard from a ship in the middle of the ocean. It
had been a big job to save Sally that time, but he had done it.

At the station she said, 'Are you going to send me a post-
card when you get there?'

'Sure,' promised Peter. 'I'll write you a letter.'

'Maybe you won't have time to do that,' murmured the

Eternal Woman in Sally, coyly presenting the ancient combination of pensive eyes and a provocative smile.

The train was coming now. Lydia kissed Sally and Hannah too, for she had just decided to go to Virginia in a week, for a visit with Carrie and Henry while Peter was away. Peter shook hands with Sally and said, 'Will you write, too?' Hannah kissed him tenderly, and he responded to it with so much more warmth than usual that her heart bounded and her eyes were wet with happy tears. Peter did not try to explain to himself why he had kissed Aunt Hannah so lovingly. He did so hate to be pawed over, and felt that female relatives should be firmly discouraged from lavish demonstrations of affection. Lydia, smilingly observant, was delighted over the little incident. It would mean so much to Hannah. She also had a fleeting thought that perhaps Hannah had received a vicarious kiss that Peter would have been pleased to bestow on Sally.

The fact was that Peter felt sorry for his Aunt Hannah. He had been ashamed at first. It was a very uncomfortable sensation — being ashamed of Aunt Hannah. Now he was just sorry. But if she had to cook for other people, he was glad she cooked for Sally. Indeed he couldn't blame her much for wanting to live close to Sally where she could see her every day.

Adele had not taken Peter directly to Bar Harbor. They had gone to New York for a week, where he had been turned loose to amuse himself daytimes as he pleased. With a natural talent for self-reliance, Peter found his way to the Battery, the Metropolitan Museum, the Zoo, and even made an unaccompanied trip to the Statue of Liberty. In the late afternoon he would show up at the hotel and escort his attractive aunt to dinner and the theater. Urbanity came easily and naturally to Peter. Adele was delighted with his promptness in adjusting himself to new circumstances. In her opinion this gift was of inestimable value to anyone's successful and satisfying relation to society. *Savoir-faire* — that's what Peter had. He always knew instinctively what to do.

Thomas Bradford's welcome to Peter at Bar Harbor was so warm and tender that Adele was deeply touched by it, and no less by Peter's affectionate response. Almost every day Thomas had the boy with him on all sorts of excursions. They went fishing, sailing, hiking, Adele consumed with curiosity to know what they talked about, but feeling reasonably sure that the most important subject had not come up, or Peter would surely have given her some evidence of it.

One morning Thomas approached Adele in the lounge and said he wanted to have a chat with her alone. They strolled to the swimming-pool, proceeded for some distance away from the bathers, and sat.

'Adele,' he said, 'I think the time has come now to talk about it, don't you?'

'Why *now?*' she queried. 'Have you just discovered something?'

Thomas shook his head.

'I knew Peter was mine the first day I saw him. There seemed nothing to be done about it. I tried to persuade myself that my best course was to let things stand as they were.'

'And now you've changed your mind?'

'Yes. I'm determined to claim my boy.' Thomas regarded her soberly, with something almost like entreaty in his eyes. 'Everyone will agree, I suppose, that I have no right to him after the way his mother was treated. But — *I've got to have that boy!*'

'It's possible,' remarked Adele quietly, 'that his mother feels the same way toward Peter.'

'But she doesn't have him, you know. He thinks this Mrs. Edmunds is his mother.'

'I hope you haven't informed him to the contrary, Thomas.'

'No — and I haven't questioned him much about his

home. Whatever he has told me has been of his own
volition. I can assure you I've done no prying.'

'I believe you, of course. Now let me tell you the whole
story, Thomas, or as much of it as I know. I think you've
a right to that, anyway. Whether you've a right to claim
Peter is another question.'

For the better part of an hour, Adele recited all she knew
of Hannah's story, and Lydia Edmunds's story, too,
Thomas listening attentively. She made no effort to spare
him as she reviewed Hannah's plight when, sick and
penniless, she had applied for work at the home of the
Ward family. And Thomas's eyes were cloudy with remorse when Adele pictured his boy as a baby in the University Hospital. 'A waif!' she declared.

'I didn't know,' he muttered, self-defensively.

'Nor care,' accused Adele. 'Now you turn up, after all
these years, bent on doing your duty. I think your duty is
to keep out of it.'

Thomas shifted his position, faced her directly, and
filled his pipe.

'May I talk awhile now?' he ventured.

Adele smiled dryly and agreed it was his turn.

'Let's assume' — began Thomas, in a tone that promised
a carefully planned speech — 'we'll assume that everything you have charged me with is a true bill. I've been a
piker, rotter, cad — whatever you like. You have said it
is too late to do anything about that now, so let's consider
it a closed incident and think about the situation as it
exists at the moment.'

'Fair enough,' consented Adele. 'Go on.'

'The fact is that Peter — however he may have come
by it — is a remarkable boy. One in a thousand! He has a
bright future. His mother hasn't made much of her life
and, as you say, is determined now that Peter shall have a
chance to make something of himself. And to insure this,
she has concealed her relationship, so as not to embarrass
him; a great sacrifice, no doubt.'

Adele's lips had twisted into a half-derisive grin. Thomas
paused and gave her a chance to comment.

'I was just thinking,' she drawled, 'when you said that
Hannah hadn't accomplished very much with her own life,
that this was a rather odd remark — coming from *you*.
Have you done anything very showy with *yours?*'

'Thanks,' growled Thomas. 'All the more reason why I,
too, might want the boy to be and do something, don't
you think?'

'Very well put, I should say.'

'We're together on that, then. But it isn't quite enough
for both Hannah and me to stand off at a distance and
take no hand in this boy's training. Hannah mustn't let
him know she is his mother, because she is a servant. I
mustn't let him know I'm his father, because I neglected
them. For the sake of perpetuating this hoax about his
belonging to the Edmunds people, I'm expected to say
nothing, do nothing, and watch this splendid young fellow
grow up without advantages.'

'Oh — I'm not so sure about that, Thomas,' countered
Adele. 'I've a little money to spend on him. Mrs. Edmunds
is not poor. Hannah has been accumulating some savings.
It isn't as if Peter would have no chance — if you didn't
come to the rescue.'

There was a long silence while Thomas digested this.
Then he asked, 'Well — what are your plans for him?'

'I don't think it's up to me to make plans for him. After
all, Peter doesn't belong to me, much as I care for him. I
presume he will attend the high school in Waterloo, and
then go to college some place out there. That would be
natural, wouldn't you think?'

'I don't want him to do that,' said Thomas.

Adele pointed an accusing finger close to his nose, and
gave him a knowing smile.

'No — what you want, Thomas Bradford, is easy access
to this boy. I'll bet you've figured it all out: how you're
going to take him with you on long summer vacations —

to France, maybe, and Italy. You want to be the one to show him everything. You want the warm sensation of having him come to you for favors and advice.'

'Exactly!' confessed Thomas impulsively. 'He's my own flesh and blood.' He raised stiffly from his lounging posture. 'And — by God — *I mean to have him!*'

'How are you going about it?' asked Adele quietly. 'I hope you aren't planning to tell Peter you're his father.'

'I haven't thought that far through it yet.'

Peter had sighted them and was coming their way, smiling.

'I hope,' said Adele, 'you'll not say anything to him this summer. Give it a little more thought, won't you? There's a good deal at stake, you know.'

'How about your writing to Hannah? Sound her out. Tell her I'm prepared to give Peter *everything*.'

'Well — Hannah has enough on her mind, I should say. I had a letter from her yesterday. The Ward boy Wallie has been sent home from camp, for breaking rules or something, and she doesn't know quite what to do with him. His parents are abroad. I gather that he's a handful. Try to be patient, won't you?'

'I've spoken for that dory, Mr. Bradford,' called Peter, from a little distance, 'and the bait.'

'Very good, Peter,' replied Thomas. 'We'll start about two. You may ask Bobby Winthrop to go along if you like.'

Peter's face registered a lack of interest in this addition to the party.

'I'd rather we went alone, sir; that is, if you don't care. We'd have more fun by ourselves.'

'Quite all right, Peter.' Thomas's voice was joyous. He turned to Adele as the boy trotted away. His eyes said, 'You see?'

Adele drew a little sigh and laughed.

'It is rather a pity,' she said softly, 'that things are as they are. There's no question about your belonging to each other.'

Hannah had always disliked the whimpering old adage, 'It never rains but it pours.' She couldn't remember ever having said it herself. But there was no question about the extraordinary amount of wet weather she had been experiencing of late.

The first downpour to dampen her spirits, after Peter's departure for Bar Harbor and Lydia's for Virginia, was a long and gloomy letter from Roberta reporting that she and Lucy Trimble had had a falling-out. This was probably a serious matter, for Roberta had no talent for making friends, and without the support of Lucy she would be quite wretched. And she must have taken the quarrel to heart, for she was not one to confide. When things went wrong with Roberta, she had always taken it out in sulking. Judging from the temper of this letter, Roberta's self-pity had developed a case of desperate homesickness.

With much care Hannah composed a reply in which she counseled the sullen child to do her utmost to patch the rift, even if she felt sure that Lucy was to blame.

> When there's spilt milk [she wrote], it never pays to argue very long whether the person was to blame who dropped the pan, or the person who bumped the elbow. The only thing really worth doing, in that case, is to mop up the mess. And always it's the strong one that has it to do. Weak people stick up for their rights. They know how weak they are inside and are afraid others will notice it, so they defend themselves and worry for fear somebody will take advantage of them. The strong people don't go to much bother about defending themselves or their 'rights.' When the milk is spilt, and they're getting the blame for it, and feel sure it wasn't their own fault, they find the mop and say to themselves: 'I'm bigger, I'm stronger, I'm quicker. I'll do it. I'll not be doing it because I'm to blame, but because the others aren't strong enough. It has to be done by somebody. I'll do it myself.'
>
> Now, maybe you'll say that this is a conceited thing for anyone to think — 'I'm stronger.' And perhaps both you and Lucy have been holding back because neither one of

you wants to seem stronger than the other. But, after all, dear, some people *are* stronger than others, not because they've made themselves so, but because they've been made so. And usually when the stronger one goes at it to mop up the mess, the weaker one is willing to help. And then everything is all right again. Sometimes it is even better than it was before. Smallpox is a dreadful thing, but if you have it hard and get over it you'll never have it any more; and then, if some good friend of yours should get it, you can safely be the nurse and maybe help save a life. I think it's wonderful, don't you, to have had something very painful that you know you are never going to have again, and be sure you can expose yourself to it without danger.

It would be pleasant to have you here again at home, Roberta. If you really want to come, we will make things pleasant for you. Of course it is pretty hot here now, and we haven't any mountain breezes, and the grass is brown, and there isn't much to do because almost everybody is out of town. I'm a little afraid that if you came back you wouldn't feel good to remember that you and Lucy had parted on bad terms. If you decide to come home, please be sure to fix that all up with her first, for the nights are sultry and it is not easy to go to sleep here even if one's mind is at rest — and of course yours wouldn't be if you had come home with something unpleasant to fret about.

The next morning Wallie arrived unannounced, in gay spirits, too, until he tried to account for his unexpected return. The explanation was confused and spluttery, and the noise it made increased as it grew more and more unconvincing. It seemed that some of the boys from a neighboring camp — a rival institution — were thought to have damaged one of the canoes belonging to Wallie's camp, and some of the boys from Wallie's camp had gone over and sprinkled oil and tar on the other boys' beach. And so the master of the camp had picked on Wallie and sent him home, and here he was — stormy, persecuted, outraged. Hannah had to repress a smile when she observed the uncanny likeness of the boy's tantrum to Paul Ward's dramatic scene when the Ellises had stolen his refrigerator.

'Well — we're glad you wanted to come home, anyhow,' said Hannah. 'Home's the best place in the world. Much more fun than being at a lake with a lot of rough boys and a cruel camp superintendent. You'll have a better time here, playing with Sally.'

Apparently this was the wrong thing for Hannah to have said, for Wallie began an earnest defense of camp life. As for Mr. Feakins, the headmaster, he had wanted Wallie to go over with the other culprits to the neighboring camp and make it right about the tar — that was all. He wasn't mean about it, and Hannah — he declared — was silly to think of Mr. Feakins as cruel.

'Anyway,' defended Hannah, 'I think those big boys are too rough for you.'

'They aren't any bigger than I am,' growled Wallie.

'Maybe you'd better telegraph to Mr. Feakins, then, and tell him you're coming back to play the game with them.'

'Not on your sweet life I won't!' Wallie was tuning for another grand pandemonium.

'Perhaps,' admonished Hannah, 'you'd better lower your voice. The neighbors might think someone had been spanking you.'

'I'd like to see 'em! Spanking me! Not so's you could notice it!'

One afternoon a week later, while Wallie roamed restlessly about the grounds and deviled the life out of Sally, Hannah was plunged into the depths by a letter from Adele — a long one — reporting the conversation she had just had with Thomas.

And really, Hannah [Adele was saying on page eight], it seems a pity that Peter should be deprived of his inheritance. Thomas is thoroughly honest in his wish to make whatever amends he can. He not only wants to see Peter through college and a professional school, but will take him abroad on vacations, and give him the experience that is so necessary to a man if he is to deal with the people who operate our world.

Of course I see your point too, and am entirely sympathetic, especially after all the unselfish loneliness you have endured to keep your secret safe. It was for Peter's sake that you have gone through all this heartbreak. Now I'm wondering if you shouldn't yield — for Peter's sake. I'm not begging you to do it, Hannah, but I think you should give it serious consideration. You've hoped that your boy might have a chance. Well — perhaps this is the way to give it to him. Do think it over.

Hannah went to her room and sat on the edge of her bed, staring dully at the wall. She felt utterly desolated. Adele had gone over to the other side. Lydia was out of reach.

After an hour she pulled herself together and went to the telephone. Mrs. Trimble presently responded.

'I am in serious trouble, Mrs. Trimble,' said Hannah unsteadily. 'Could I come over tomorrow forenoon and get some advice?'

'Try to come tonight, Hannah. I am driving over to Springfield in the morning to visit some friends, and don't expect to be back until Monday. Mr. Trimble is out of town. No one will disturb us. . . . That's good. I shall look for you a little after eight.'

But Eleanor Trimble did not drive over to Springfield next morning, for she was on the train all day, en route to Bar Harbor.

Chapter XIII

It was a drowsy midsummer Sunday afternoon. Almost everybody had driven up to the cove for better observation of the yacht race, leaving The Gables practically deserted.

Fluffy pearl-white clouds, their heads tucked under their wings, slept motionless in a blue sky Slanting sunshine glinted from lazy sails outside the harbor. On the horizon a southbound coastal steamer slothed under a plume of smoke. Even the ocean was sprawled in a siesta at the turn of the tide, her long-drawn respirations seemingly born of indolence rather than fatigue.

Adele's new book lay open, face down, on the flat granite rock where she had tossed it a half-hour ago. It was a meagerly plotted controversial novel wordily dealing with world politics — past, present, and pending — and she had been deeply interested last night by its discussions, especially by the profound deliverances of one Senator Chester Allaman, who had piled credible facts upon confirmed facts until he had run out of facts, after which he had dogmatized and moralized over the boundless muddle with all the assurance of the apostles of old who spoke as they were moved by the Holy Ghost.

Last night, reading in her room, Adele had been stirred, alarmed, appalled, horrified. The world was quite evidently coming to an end; overpopulated, underfed, the last frontier occupied; eugenically deteriorating, its racial colors clashing, its nationalistic greeds mounting, its mind upset, its emotions unstable, its nerves frazzled. Adele herself would undoubtedly be alive — in terror and tatters — when the ultimate explosion was touched off.

But out here under this serene sky, on this huge durable rock, facing a tranquil sea, with no evidence that the universe was in any manner perturbed and every indication that it was not only solvent but of conscience clear enough to be somnolent, Adele yawned into the crook of her bare elbow, pitched the book away, and remarked to herself that the Honorable Chester Allaman was probably a bag of wind.

She sank back on her leather pillow and gazed hard at the skyline with narrowed, contemplative eyes. After all, wasn't it one's best business in life to be at peace with one's world? Wasn't it at once our most valuable heritage from life and our richest bequest to life — this sense of confidence in the integrity of the Plan? And weren't the old mandarins right when, confronting some sudden declivity in the inevitable ups-and-downs of their pilgrimage, they calmly faced the new vicissitude with their classic phrase, 'This, too, shall pass'?

Tipping back her head, Adele drew the translucent masses of clouds closer. She invoked their serenity, wishing she might hold it and abide in it — forever. Peace! Not as any single era gives it, in grudged handfuls during an armistice, but the permanent peace of the spirit, the peace that is not established by treaty, the peace that nobody ever could define or describe to anybody else because it surpassed all understanding.

How fortunate were the peace-lovers of all generations who had believed in it as confidently and effortlessly as they believed in breathing; and the peace-makers who contrived to live outside the dizzying whirlpool of frets and despairs, ifs and might-have-beens, remorses and revenges — how blest were they!

A few people seemed to have a talent for it. Perhaps it was a gift rather than an achievement. Obviously the wrong way to get it was to struggle for it.

Her thoughts turned to Hannah Parmalee. How often she had chuckled over Hannah's philosophy of non-com-

bativeness. But wasn't Hannah right, in the long run?...
Or was she?

Suppose everybody tried to live that way. Suppose
everybody from the beginning had tried to live that way.
What kind of world would we have had by now? Hadn't
civilization developed through striving, overcoming, master-
ing? It was all very pleasant and restful to lie here on this
sunny seashore under these luminous white clouds and
sleepily cast one's vote for the non-resistant life. Perhaps
the seagulls lived it after the manner of the fowls of the air
who, without sowing, reaping, gathering into barns, or
fretting over their economics, managed to get along somehow. But even they had their little tiffs. And who wanted
to live the life of a seagull, anyway? No — there had to be
striving in the world. Certain audacious and courageous
people simply had to quarrel with life as they found it.

But what were these worried Mr. Fixits getting for their
pains? The Honorable Chester Allaman, for example, who
talked all the way through a novel written to scare people
out of their senses — what reward was his?... Or theirs
who consented to be frightened? Take the whole basketful
of admonitory prophets — antique and contemporary:
mightn't it be found that there was just a trace of the
sadistic in their dire forebodings? The noisy evangelist,
ranting about a future life in hell and despising the econo-
mist for his grubby materialism, and the dismayed econ-
omist, presaging disaster to the present life on earth and
despising the evangelist for his frantic imbecilities —
weren't they both getting a neat little wallop out of their
experience in terrorizing enfeebled minds? And was there
so very much difference in the psychological repercussions
of a burly parent whipping his half-grown daughter, and
the emotional titillation of the pessimistic prophet flogging
a bewildered public? Of course the heavy father was doing
it for his child's good and the prophets were ordained to
arouse and alarm the people. They usually insisted that it
hurt them worse than they who were meeting the hot end

of the paddle, but they had probably lied without meaning to. Wasn't Senator Allaman enjoying the same sweetly painful little spasms of unholy pity for the public's terror that had unquestionably compensated Jonah and Calvin and Cromwell and Edwards for their dour austerities? Senator Allaman, reflected Adele, might spend a profitable hour munching on this nasty probability.

She sighed luxuriously, gazed with wide unfocused eyes into the deep blue above, and marveled that so great a quantity of admonition on the part of the world's savants and seers had contained so little counsel on the desirability of a peaceful life — if not for the turbulent masses, at least for the individual. Hannah Parmalee knew more about the terms and conditions of peace than all the reformers and crusaders put together. They talked about it; she *had* it. They formulated resolutions about it; she quietly accepted it.

Surely it was a pretty sad commentary on our ethical and spiritual leadership if one had to run away from the clatter of their mechanisms and the jingle of their cash collections and the clamor of their fears, to seek peace in communion with the sky and the sea.

The trouble was that you couldn't lie here forever on the warm rocks, consulting the clouds, for the comfort and peace of your soul; and perhaps this soothing experience was a bit deceptive because it floated in a sedative solution of languor and laziness. If the world was to advance, some people had to be up and doing. Some people had to think new thoughts and see to it that the new thoughts were made effective. And the old thoughts had to be dug up and out to make room. Moral and spiritual leaders were, in this respect, engaged in surgery. But were they skilled surgeons? Good surgery left a scar, of course, but not a festering wound. Too many of the moral and political and economic surgeons, though swift and fearless and competent operators, left their patients with a high fever. Maybe they worked too fast. Maybe their hands were not clean.

They said to the public: 'Here, you! Let me cut out what
ails you, and you'll be all right!' So — they cut out what
ailed 'em, but they weren't all right. There was no more
happiness or health or peace for anybody than there had
been before. What the people needed most was a long rest
from the racket and confusion of the forces that had volunteered to save their minds and souls and occupations
and homes. Peace — that was what the people needed.
And to get it they had to go out alone and commune with
the silent sky after the manner of the ancient pagans.

Maybe... Perhaps... But Adele now decided she had
given enough time to this matter and quietly went to sleep,
with the calm expectation that everything would hold
together somehow until she woke up. In spite of the dismal
forecasts, the show would carry on; new plots, new props,
new faces, new masks, new lines — but essentially the same
old show. And by no means an uninteresting old show,
either, if you didn't let the harsh voices of the prompters
annoy you too much.

When she roused, Adele discovered that she was not
alone. Some twenty feet away sat the attractive woman
who had appeared in the dining-room at luncheon — obviously a newcomer, for no one seemed to be acquainted
with her.

The stranger turned her head as Adele sat up rubbing
her eyes, and smiled amiably. She was not pretty, but her
face was engagingly alive. She was simply, modishly
dressed in white silk with a loosely knotted blue scarf. A
white parasol with little blue polka dots lay on the rock
beside her.

'Quiet day,' drawled Adele, feeling that this unattached
person expected a gesture of recognition.

'Too quiet,' agreed Eleanor. 'I'm lonesome. May I
join you?'

Adele replied, not untruthfully, that it would be a
pleasure. For a little while they sat side by side exchanging

inconsequentials and blandly taking each other's measure.
They spoke their names, and Adele casually asked questions ostensibly for courtesy's sake, though her curiosity
had been slightly stirred. Had Mrs. Trimble ever been
here before? She had not. Did she know anyone at The
Gables? Not a soul. There was a pause, while Adele tried
to think of a pleasant way to inquire why in the world
Mrs. Trimble had come here, for surely there were plenty
of summer places where she might find old friends.

'I came to see *you*,' said Eleanor quietly, smiling into
Adele's widening eyes. 'About Hannah, you know.'

'Hannah?' Adele's brows contracted.

'Yes — Hannah and Thomas and Peter.'

'And how are you related to Hannah?'

'About the same way you are, I suppose. Friendly
interest. Want me to tell you about it?'

'Please. Oddly enough I was just thinking about Hannah. It was so restful here, and quiet. Same kind of quietness that Hannah seems to carry about with her. I never
knew so calm a person.'

Eleanor smiled a little. 'She wasn't so calm when I saw
her last. Quite stirred up, in fact. That's why I came.
Hannah's afraid she is going to lose her boy. He's all she
has, you know.'

'But Hannah has already lost her boy, hasn't she? I
mean, so far as their mother-and-son relationship is concerned. If she isn't intending to be his mother, why ——'

'Yes — I see your point, Mrs. Moore,' interposed Eleanor. 'But if Thomas Bradford insists on telling Peter he
is his father, then Hannah necessarily comes into the picture — and she wants to avoid that. Undoubtedly you
know how Hannah feels about her own position, and the
reason she has for ——'

'And it's a rather silly reason, I think,' said Adele dryly.
'I've tried to put myself in her place and be sympathetic.
She was brought up to believe in the high fences that sep-
arate castes. She doesn't want to detain or embarrass

Peter. And if Thomas hadn't shown such an earnest interest in the boy, perhaps her sacrifice might have been justified.' She paused thoughtfully. 'I suppose Hannah feels that I am her enemy.'

'No,' replied Eleanor, 'you're not her enemy, but I think she would like to have her case presented with a little more ——'

'Enthusiasm,' assisted Adele. 'So she asked you to help.'

Eleanor shook her head. 'I volunteered to come, Mrs. Moore. I hope I'm not impertinent in taking a hand in this unusual game. It's a serious matter, I think — or I shouldn't have bothered. Of course, knowing Hannah's queer ideas as you do, you will understand how much she needs support. She wouldn't try to defend herself. Thomas could make off with Peter, and Hannah wouldn't fight or press her claims. All the more reason, then, why somebody should speak in her behalf. It began to appear that it was my job.' She smiled companionably. 'I beg you to believe that I'm not naturally a meddlesome person. I should have preferred to keep out of it.'

Adele said she felt sure of that and appreciated her loyalty to Hannah, adding, 'I'll see that you have a chance to talk it over with Thomas, Mrs. Trimble.'

'Do you think he'll resent my intrusion?'

'Well — if he does he'll not tell you so. You may count on his being polite. Thomas will listen respectfully to everything you have to say. But it won't do a speck of good. This is the only thing he has ever really wanted. I suppose Hannah has told you about his life and how listlessly he went trudging about taking orders without having any personal interests of his own. He's quite a different fellow since young Peter gave him a new reason for living.'

Eleanor smiled and said she would like to talk with him anyway. She felt she owed that much to Hannah.

They met in the lounge next morning. Adele introduced them, presenting Peter also, who seemed disappointed when Thomas said he wouldn't be able to go sailing as he had promised. Clearly it was this new Mrs. Trimble who had upset their plans for the day. Peter dutifully attempted to respond to her smile, but it was a feeble effort. Presently he mumbled an 'Excuse me, please,' and left them.

Adele's explanation was brief. Mrs. Trimble was a close friend of Professor and Mrs. Ward, in whose home Hannah had lived for so many years. In the absence of the Wards, Hannah had confided her anxieties about Peter to Mrs. Trimble, and here she was to ask some questions in Hannah's behalf.

'I suppose it's almost inexcusable — my interference, as a total stranger to you,' said Eleanor, smiling up into Thomas's eyes with all the guilelessness of a little child. 'If you'd prefer not to talk about it, Mr. Bradford, I'll not insist.'

Adele, directly facing Thomas, over the top of Eleanor's well-groomed bobbed head, drew a slightly ironical smile intended for his eye, but he was too much occupied to receipt it.

'By no means,' declared Thomas. 'We shall be grateful for any light you can throw on this matter, Mrs. Trimble. I am glad you came. Shall we take a walk? You'll join us, Adele?'

After a slight hesitation, Adele said she believed they would do as well without her, and Thomas did not press the invitation. The petite Trimble, reflected Adele, really should be given a sporting chance. Thomas would have his way, no doubt, but the Trimble lady would not make it a bit easy for him. Thomas was just a big boy. All men were just big boys; so important, so sufficient, until a pair of curly-lashed entreating eyes looked up rather dazed over the opportunity to solicit a pleasant word from Olympus. Men were all alike. A woman didn't have to carry a very big bag of tricks to achieve her purpose. And as for Mrs. Trimble, she was admirably equipped to disarm Thomas. It was easy to see that he liked the molasses which she was so abundantly prepared to administer. Adele grinned and turned away.

They walked far up the beach and sat, conversation on the way having been restricted to Thomas's queries and Eleanor's replies about life in the university town, their diversions, their occasional pleasure tours.

Seated comfortably, they talked of the Wards and of Hannah, of Lydia Edmunds — and Peter.

'It would be an entirely different matter,' Thomas was saying, 'if this Mrs. Edmunds had adopted Peter. As the case stands, she is under no legal obligation to him. I appreciate all she has done for the boy. But suppose she married; suppose she died. Peter has no claim on her estate — her relatives would see to that. Hannah is not in a position to do anything for him.'

'But there is Mrs. Moore, of course,' observed Eleanor. 'She would gladly come to Peter's rescue.'

'Yes, yes, I know,' countered Thomas. 'But Adele Moore's circumstances are as unstable as the other lady's. Adele might pop off and be married. I'm surprised she hasn't by this time. She is full of whims and hobbies and impetuosities. Besides, Adele is under no obligation to do anything for Peter. Nor is she a rich woman. And moreover ——'

Eleanor leaned toward him and smiled impishly.

'Moreover,' she repeated, '*you want him*. Isn't that what it all comes to?'

Thomas made a faint gesture of defending his argument, but she laughed. It was a silvery, girlish, comradely laugh, and Thomas, finding it decidedly engaging, capitulated with an unwilling grin.

'Very well, then ——' He pretended to be gruff. 'Let's assume that my best argument is located at that point. I want my boy. I want to provide for him and make him my heir.'

'I know,' said Eleanor gently. 'Now let's talk about Hannah.'

'Of course. Why not?' Thomas tried to be casual.

'Hannah will not contest your claim to Peter. It will upset everything she has had in mind for him and mock all the sacrifice she has made, through the years; but she will accept it. That's part of her religion or her philosophy or whatever it is.' Eleanor paused for a moment and then continued slowly, as in a soliloquy: 'That will make it a bit awkward; having one's own way at such a cost to someone else who refuses to contend.'

'I suppose she'll hate me for it.'

Eleanor shook her head.

'No — that's just the trouble. If you could feel that even in her heart Hannah was silently despising you as an enemy, it might be easier to press your claim. She will not do that. And she will keep on hoping, to the very last minute, that you will be generous enough to let things be as they are. Do you know what Hannah said to me the other night when she was telling me about all this? She said that she believed the love you had found for Peter would make you very tender. Somewhere she had been reading about the unusually hard rains that fell last spring in the desert, and how certain flowers bloomed that nobody could remember ever having seen before. The life-germ of them had been buried so deep in the dry ground, and so much windswept sand had been piled over them, that what little water there was couldn't reach down to give them nourishment. And then came this great flood of rain that renewed their strength. But they hadn't been dead; just dormant. Hannah thinks of you that way. And she believes and hopes that Peter's coming into your life will make something bloom in you — something that was always there, but hadn't been given a chance... I hope this doesn't sound too terribly sentimental. I'm afraid I'm not doing Hannah's little allegory full justice. To appreciate it, you would have to hear her say it. But I think it's quite an inspiring idea. Don't you?'

Thomas recalled himself from his reverie, and sighed.

'Well' — his voice was husky — 'suppose something fine did bloom in me, what then? What should I do? Has Hannah a suggestion? Or have you?'

Eleanor's eyes brightened. The opportunity she had been angling for seemed to have arrived.

'Why don't you do everything for Peter that you would have done in the event of claiming him as your own? Let him continue to be Peter Edmunds. Arrange with Mrs. Edmunds for his allowance. Counsel with her about his schooling. And learn Hannah's wishes, too. I think they will both want to conform to your ideas about that. It seems to me it would be such a fine, sporting thing to do. It really stirs me quite deeply to imagine how it would be. A genuine sacrifice for you, no doubt, but something that will make you proud of yourself, every day of your life.'

Thomas toyed with his blond mustache and grinned, a little self-consciously, at this imputation of nobility, but it was plain to see that her tribute to his magnanimity was a pleasant and novel experience. People hadn't ever thought of him as belonging to that category.

'And it would make Peter so proud of you, too,' continued Eleanor in an exalted tone. 'The boy has been brought up to think so highly of good sportsmanship.'

'But he would never know!' Thomas's hands tossed this appeal aside with an impatient gesture. 'How could he be proud of me for doing something for him in secret? As for his sportsmanship, I've noticed that, of course. I suppose we have this Mrs. Edmunds to thank for his ideas on that subject. It isn't likely that Hannah, with her peculiar views on the advisability of sitting still and letting people run over you ——'

'Now that's where you misunderstand Hannah, Mr. Bradford,' declared Eleanor impressively. 'Hannah is a living example of the very highest sportsmanship there is! Private courage! I can't see that there would be anything so very brave and fine about your claiming your son, whom you love and admire. But if you were to give him every-

thing you would have given him as his acknowledged
father, and do it without his ever knowing, *that is the kind
of sportsmanship* Hannah likes best. If she has managed
to fill Peter's head with such ideas, you should be glad
of it.'

Thomas ungrudgingly nodded his consent to this. 'Of
course, of course. Lofty thought. "He best deserves a
knightly crest," and so forth. Everybody agrees to that,
I think. At least everybody agrees it's good poetry and
makes a pretty legend. But, getting back to earth again
where, after all, my own residence is maintained ——'

'Don't be sarcastic, please,' interposed Eleanor with a
reproving smile. 'I dislike satire, especially that kind. It's
so damned insincere — and unfriendly.'

'Sorry. Excuse it, please. What I was trying to say is:
You think such a program, carried out by me, would make
Peter proud of me. Now just what do you mean? The
essence of this plan is its secretiveness. I'm to do something Peter will never know about, and my doing it will
make him proud of me. Doesn't that sound a little bit
silly to you?' Thomas chuckled.

'Perhaps,' conceded Eleanor, 'but it doesn't make quite
so much difference how this idea sounds to *me*. I'm not
presenting my own case or my own views. It's Hannah's
affair. I have been telling you, as well as I know how,
what Hannah believes.'

'Very good, then,' said Thomas encouragingly. 'How
do you think Hannah would explain this dilemma?' His
teasing warned her that she had moved into a difficult
position.

'Hannah would say,' replied Eleanor gropingly, 'that
while Peter would never know exactly what you had done
to make you great in his eyes, he would be aware that
something had happened to make you a very important
person.'

'You mean — it would do something to me, on the inside; something that would flavor all my thoughts and

actions?' Thomas had dropped his bantering mood, and his tone was respectful.

'Exactly! You've said it! Hannah thinks it is the secret renunciation, the giving-up, the letting-go, the sacrifice that nobody understands but the person who does it — Hannah thinks this generates inside you a peculiar power to ——'

'To do what?' queried Thomas skeptically, when she hesitated.

'To do almost anything you like,' replied Eleanor.

'But you yourself,' challenged Thomas, 'don't believe a word of it and privately you think it's a great lot of nonsense. What interests me is: How did you and Hannah ever get to talking in this vein? She is a domestic in the home of your friends. You're not in the habit of discussing philosophy and mysticism with the servants in your neighborhood. I'm pretty sure of that.'

'True enough. But Hannah came to tell me her anxiety about Peter.'

'Yes, I know; but it seems odd that a discussion of this matter about Peter should involve so much talk concerning renunciation and its power to make you over into something grand and noble. Do you mean to say that Hannah expected you to tell me all this in the hope of making an important person of *me*? It sounds very implausible.'

Eleanor did not at once respond to the question but sat with moody eyes intent on the lace handkerchief she was folding and refolding into prim squares. After a long silence she looked up into his eyes, regarded him with a slow, reluctant smile, and said, 'No — you're right — Hannah wasn't trying to make an important person of you, but *me*. When she said these things about renunciation and giving up and letting go — and the glory of private courage — she was advising *me*.'

'And you sat and took it — from a servant!' Thomas's voice was incredulous.

'I sat and took it from a servant,' echoed Eleanor in the

same tone, 'and something tells me it's the truth. I don't
know yet.' Her voice lowered until her words were barely
audible. 'I've promised myself to try it. But the occasion
for experimenting with it hasn't arisen.' She glanced up
and smiled briefly. 'It's one thing to make a good resolution, and quite another thing to enforce it.'

'I don't suppose your problem is anything on the order
of mine,' hinted Thomas. 'It couldn't be, of course.'

'No.'

'You wouldn't want to tell me?'

'No.'

'Apparently you've been doing a lot of tall thinking
about this,' drawled Thomas.

'Yes — it really is an intriguing idea. Naturally, everybody is stirred by stories of secret heroisms performed
without any promise of reward, but I don't believe very
many people consider what sort of effect such acts would
have on the adventurers themselves. I think Hannah
knows that it works. I'm not sure that I'll ever know.
I'm going to try.'

'Good luck, then,' said Thomas companionably. 'I
don't suppose I'll ever know whether you succeeded.'

'Probably not.'

'I should have said that you had been succeeding at it
already . . . You really have something, you know . . .
you're different.' He laughed a little as her eyes widened
with surprise. 'You are so thoroughly urbane, sophisti-
cated, experienced. I hope you don't mind my saying it
has sounded deucedly queer — your serious talk about
these things. They aren't discussed in your world — or
mine. You know that. If anybody of our sort was to have
overheard what we've been chattering about for the past
half hour they'd think we were mentally unhooked. People
like us don't take any stock in such theories.'

'I know,' admitted Eleanor, 'and I wonder why they
don't. People who live in your social world and mine, a
world of privilege and opportunity and easy access to all

forms of culture — why shouldn't we be the very ones to see the reality and value of these spiritual forces? Just look at us! We have a chance to develop our emotions on a very high plane. Grand opera, symphony orchestras, world-wide travel. Everything that can exalt the spirit is ours — dawns in the mountains, sunsets on the sea, great paintings, great sculpture, great drama. Aren't we the people, after all, who should be the quickest to understand the possibilities of our hearts and recognize the power of these mysterious appeals to our emotions? If there is to be any nobility in human life, surely people of your advantages and mine are better equipped to know what it is all about than the underprivileged who have so few chances to be stirred and thrilled.'

'You mean we have to pay for our sunsets in the South Seas by doing something sacrificial,' said Thomas, amused over her long speech.

'Why not?' Eleanor ignored the flippancy of his comment. 'Why not?' she repeated, seriously. 'Don't you think it is really bad for us to experience these gripping emotional appeals and never do anything to justify our right to receive them? Here we go, you and I, stirred by other people's fortitude, moved by other people's renunciations, learning about life at second-hand, and never once trying it out to see what it might make of us!'

Thomas stretched both of his long arms to full length and drew a deep breath.

'Are you trying to sell this idea to me — or to yourself?' he queried, amiably teasing.

'To both of us; especially me.' Eleanor rose.

'Well — I suppose one either believes it, or one doesn't,' drawled Thomas, falling into step beside her. 'Either you accept it or you don't. If you do, you aren't required to sell it to yourself any more.'

'Not the theory — no. As for the practice, that's another matter. I was amused at something Hannah said about that. She has her droll moments, you know.' Eleanor laughed reminiscently. 'Hannah says people sometimes come plop up against a challenge to their skill in bravery and they can't do anything much about it because they had never experimented. She says, "It looks quite easy when a juggler keeps three tennis balls, a frying-pan, and a hatchet in the air at the same time, but I expect he began practicing the act with only a couple of tennis balls."'

When he had come down to earth again after his big surprise, Peter wanted to tell somebody who didn't know about it yet, so he went to his room early that night and wrote to Sally. Perhaps Aunt Hannah had told Sally, but he didn't think so. Aunt Hannah wouldn't really like the new plan very well, and maybe wouldn't want to talk about it to anyone. She hadn't objected to it, but why should she if his mother was agreed?

Dear Sally [he wrote]: I said I would write to you. It is funny to talk about being busy in a place like this but you eat breakfast and then it is time for dinner or somebody wants you to sail. I told you about Mr. Bradford. Well, it is funny but I spend most of the time with him. There is a lagoon near here where we catch flounders. An old man with whiskers rows us in his boat and cuts bait. A flounder is round, not like a ball but a pie in case you never saw one or even if you did. And we play tennis and Uncle Thomas — he wants me to call him that and I do too — plays a fast game for two sets and then his wind gives out, from cigarettes he says and he does smoke a good many. Sally Ive some news for you. I am going to a military school in Virginia for boys on Sept. 13. Uncle Thomas went to school there when he was my age. I am coming home next week alone because Aunt Adele is going to Paris the next day. Maybe I will see you before school begins. Ask Aunt Hannah to bring you. Im afraid she wont like me in a uniform but my Mother will though and Aunt Adele and Uncle Thomas says he thinks it will be bully. He is coming to see me sometimes for he knows the headmaster. How is your tennis now Sally you are pretty good for a girl I think. Ask Aunt

Hannah if you can come down with her. Uncle Thomas is taking me on a hike tomorrow. Last time we saw a red fox. It stood still a long time looking at us before it ran and then not very fast and it looked back once to see if we were coming and Uncle Thomas laughed. Maybe we will see one this time or a deer for there are some. Goodbye for this time. See if Aunt Hannah wont let you come with her.

Your friend

PETER.

P.S. Pleas excuse the blots. Ive a blister on my thumb from bowling. So has Uncle Thomas.

Chapter XIV

THE breach between Lucy Trimble and Roberta, dating from more than two years ago when they were nearing fifteen, had never healed properly. When their misunderstanding had arisen at the Adirondack summer camp, Roberta had taken it too seriously and had sulked over it too long.

With a fair imitation of her mother's accomplishments in repairing damaged feelings, Lucy had cooed affectionate little entreaties in all the dulcet tones of the maternal gamut. But Roberta, morbidly relishing this flattering solicitude far too well to deprive herself of it by a prompt conciliation, continued to brood pensively over her wounds until her brightly buoyant friend grew bored and impatient.

It is possible that their comradeship might have become tiresome to Lucy even if it had not experienced this acute stress. Inheriting Sam Trimble's sunny and equable disposition and Eleanor's talent for making herself agreeable in any company, Lucy's gay gregarious spirit was already chafed by the exactions of Roberta's jealously possessive devotion. Now that this monopolistic adoration had assumed a dourly reproachful air of injury, it was an insupportable burden.

There was no one particular day when Lucy enforced a resolution to let Roberta Ward paddle her own social canoe. Perhaps it would have been a more humane act if an amputation had been performed. In that event Roberta, definitely aware of what had happened to her, might have made an effort to cultivate some promising friendships in other quarters. Instead, she persevered in her morose longing that the fracture might be nursed back to health.

On the surface, relations were amiable enough as the two girls made the journey home together, that September, to enter upon their second year in high school. But the salt of their friendship had lost its savor. Whatever may have been Lucy's brief misgivings over this situation, to Roberta the affair was in the nature of a tragedy. Lacking any gifts for making friends, the quiet withdrawal of Lucy's interest left her in a perilous position socially. It began to be obvious to the unhappy girl that Lucy's patronage had accounted for the place she had occupied, and she was tortured with the thought that nobody had ever really wanted her; that she had been accepted only because of Lucy's ardent loyalty on a 'Love me, love my dog' basis.

It turned out to be an embittering year for Roberta. Always, even from early childhood, a recluse and introvert, she went her own way, becoming less and less communicative at home and more and more distrustful of her rating in the opinion of her acquaintances at school. If the girls were casual in their greetings, Roberta interpreted their attitude as frosty indifference. If they were cordial, she accounted for it as an effort of theirs to show how much they pitied her. She was still invited to the more inclusive parties, but there were plenty of things going on in the inner circle of a dozen or more. These affairs she learned about after they had occurred. She felt utterly outcast.

Once — it was the day school resumed after the Christmas holidays — Roberta had pocketed her pride and asked Lucy why she hadn't been invited to Betsy Partridge's birthday dinner.

'I didn't know you weren't,' Lucy had replied, making a brave attempt to look dismayed. 'I noticed you weren't there, but I supposed something had turned up to — to keep you away.'

'No, you didn't,' protested Roberta, sullenly. 'You couldn't have helped knowing that I wasn't asked.'

'Well, after all' — Lucy shrugged slightly — 'it wasn't my party. I asked you to mine, didn't I?'

Roberta grinned feebly and commented, 'Yes — the skating party for the whole class; everybody in town.' She winked back the angry tears.

'Betsy's mother arranged that little dinner as a surprise, Roberta,' explained Lucy gently. 'Almost any sort of slip can happen in an affair like that. I wouldn't fret about it if I were you.'

'You wouldn't have to,' muttered Roberta. 'Everybody likes you.'

The bell rescued Lucy from the necessity of any further dissembling in Roberta's behalf. The constraint between them, now that it had been mutually discussed, was an established fact. Neither of them knew how to deal with it. Lucy was sorry enough, but what could you do with a person like Roberta? 'Now I *ask* you!' she said to herself in exasperation.

As the year wore on, Roberta drew more snugly into her shell, comforting herself with her drawing, and taking but scant interest in the few social events to which she was invited.

Marcia worried about it, but lacked the capacity for finding a remedy. She suggested a Valentine party for Roberta, here at home, or at the City Club, or wherever she wished. Roberta had no interest in the plan, so they gave it up. Marcia was at her wits' end. The fact was that she herself had been accustomed to beating a retreat when events became too complicated for her. Her favorite method of dealing with a predicament was to go to her room, bury her face deep in the pillows, and cry until she had a red nose and a headache. With a disposition like that she was at a disadvantage in her efforts to counsel Roberta to be of good cheer and tackle her problem with a courageous smile.

'I'm terribly anxious about Roberta,' she confided to Eleanor. 'She feels so — so out of things, this year; has it in her head that the girls don't like her; thinks Lucy isn't friendly.'

'Nonsense!' scoffed Eleanor. 'Some childish disagreement, maybe. You remember how such things used to go when we were of that age. Whatever it is, you can depend on its blowing over presently. Why, Roberta was at our house only yesterday.'

'She was there on an errand,' said Marcia obdurately. 'It has been a good while since Lucy was over here. I know Roberta is too sensitive and reticent — but really ——'

'Well, do you want me to speak to Lucy about it?' Eleanor's tone hinted that this procedure might be considered as a risky last resort not to be highly recommended.

'No, no, no!' Marcia shook her head vigorously. 'I'm sure Roberta wouldn't want *that!* If she can't have Lucy's friendship of her own free will ——'

Eleanor drew her chair closer and lowered her voice confidentially.

'These children,' she began, 'are all too preoccupied with their own affairs to have the least bit of sympathy or understanding for each other's peculiarities. I suppose we were that way too at fifteen. My Lucy is a heedless youngster who just lives from moment to moment in a grand state of excitement. Your Roberta is inclined to be aloof and unaggressive. Temperamentally they are as opposite as the poles. Your Sally is like Lucy — impetuous and full of ginger. Those two, if they were of an age, would hit it off. We'll just have to make up our minds that Lucy and Roberta represent different types.'

The speech had promised more comfort than it was able to deliver, and when it was concluded there was a moment's silence.

'I suppose so,' murmured Marcia at length, drawing a deep sigh. 'Sometimes I think we should send Roberta away to school; give her a chance to make friends in another environment.'

'It's a good thought,' agreed Eleanor quickly. 'A change

like that might solve the whole problem for her.' But they both knew, and each of them was aware that the other knew, how difficult it was going to be for Roberta to find contentment, no matter where she lived.

Most of the children who came to the Wards were Sally's friends. It seemed to Roberta that the place was constantly jammed with noisy girls who clattered up and down the stairs, invading the pantry, banging the piano, slamming the doors — obnoxious creatures sticky with perspiration and forever smelling like apples and butter. Nor were they any too considerate of Roberta's thin-skinned sensitivity when they encountered her, perhaps because she made no bones about her distaste for them; and, besides — though Roberta was too taken up with her own sorrows to make any reasonable allowance for this — they were at that abominable phase of disheveled, rattle-headed, muddy-footed adolescence in which no normal child is distinguished for reverence.

Sometimes Sally felt sorry for Roberta and made awkward little excursions into her moody sister's confidence, where she had always been unwelcome. Late on Saturday afternoon, she was likely to tear loose from the fudge-making bedlam in the kitchen and go plunging up to Roberta's sanctuary with an exuberant invitation to come down and share in the fun.

'Now *wouldn't* that be jolly?' Roberta would reply scornfully. 'With that bunch of animals!'

Each member of the family, in his own way, was distressed about Roberta. Wallie, who had never drawn any prizes for altruism either inside the house or out of it, had long since given up trying to be gracious to her and rarely had anything more winsome to say than 'Aw, snap out of it, can't you?' But he had his moments when he would have been glad enough to think of something he might do, without too much effort, toward the reconditioning of his sister's broken spirit. Privately it had annoyed him when Roberta and Lucy Trimble were no longer intimately associated; for he greatly admired Lucy, and missed her visits more than he cared to admit. Paul, now loaded with extra responsibilities since his elevation to the deanship, had nothing constructive to offer. Always volatile as a weathervane, with an amazing capacity for bouncing from the Slough of Despond to the Heights of Pisgah without an intermediate stop for refueling, he could hardly be expected to understand his daughter's chronic dejection. Sometimes he pitied her from the bottom of his heart and resolved to leave no stone unturned in an effort to divert her, but when he approached her with his suggestions she exasperated him with her stubborn refusal to consent or even to appreciate his generosity. One day he would try to impute some grace to her by commending her on being such a thoughtful, quiet, dutiful daughter; the next day he would be likely to inquire acidly, at breakfast, whether friends were being requested to omit flowers. As for Marcia, she cried about it for hours on end, and then drove downtown to a beauty shop for repairs.

None of them gave as much consecutive thought to the case as Hannah. Her worry was somewhat complicated by her misgivings, for it troubled her to remember that she had never given Roberta the affection she had bestowed on Wallie and Sally. Of course, she told herself, the spiritless child had always resented her overtures of friendship, but, even so, she might have made her preference for Sally a little less conspicuous. Through that winter and spring Hannah fairly racked her brain trying to think of something she might say or do to enliven Roberta, went to endless bother to plan the meals with Roberta's tastes in mind, catered to every little whim, and made special efforts to dignify and defer to her infrequent comments. But you positively couldn't do anything for Roberta.

She was nearing seventeen now, and her isolation was becoming increasingly difficult to bear in the face of the inevitable pairing of her high-school classmates. Roberta

thought them sickeningly silly, and said so with such
withering contempt that nobody any longer bothered about
inviting her to anything.

Her drawing now served to compensate for her social
losses. There was no question at all about Roberta's
artistic talent. Her themes were decidedly unpleasant, but
she handled them with astonishing skill and fidelity. By
way of her father's influence she contrived to engage for
private instruction at the hands of Andre Gallet, head of
the Art Department at the University, who promptly
reported that Roberta — if she applied herself — might be
expected to go far.

It was a pleasant relief to have these good tidings about
Roberta. The family was unanimous in applauding her.
She was as cloistral and touchy as ever, but these unhappy
distinctions could now be readily understood and condoned.
As a genius, Roberta was to be pardoned for her eccen-
tricities. The household was cheered, and much pains were
taken to see that the artist was shielded from unnecessary
shocks, jolts, abrasions — and intrusions upon the privacy
which had become more and more insular.

Twice a week, on Wednesday and Saturday afternoons
from four to six, Roberta sat at the feet of M. Gallet, her
deep melancholy eyes intent on his impulsive gestures, her
drooping lips parted a little in admiration. She worked for
Gallet as she had never worked at anything before. And
because she was the most gifted and indefatigable student
he had ever taken on, he gave her the best he had to offer,
now yelling at her until the big dark eyes swam with tears,
now repentantly healing the bruise with encouraging little
pats on her angular shoulder which made her habitually
sluggish heart thump hard against her boyish chest.

One day she slipped quietly out of the house, returning
two hours later to announce casually to her mother that
she had visited a tailor. Marcia was both amazed and
delighted that Roberta, who had been so appallingly indifferent to her appearance for nearly two years, had

actually taken the initiative in improving herself. In
a few days the suit was delivered, a most severe brown
whipcord, with highly built shoulders and plenty of man-
nish pockets. There was also a brown hat which a boy
might have worn without explanation, and flat-heeled snub-
nosed russet shoes. That afternoon she wore the rather
startling ensemble to her session with Professor Gallet, who
tactfully felicitated her on having adopted a costume at
once so *chic*, so *distingué*, so — so *tout à vous*; and Roberta,
coloring a little, shyly murmured, '*Merci.*'

She had hoped he would approve. The family, of course,
could be counted on to deride her. That's what families
were for — to frustrate originality and offer special pre-
miums for conventionalized dullness.

When she arrived home shortly before dinner, Roberta
encountered them all, one by one. Paul grinned as he
appraised her in the new rig and drawled, 'We'll make
a man of you yet.' Sally gaily shouted, 'Lookit!' Wallie,
meeting her in the upper hall, laid the back of his hand
against his forehead, reeled weakly, and said, very deferentially, 'How do you do, sir?' Thoroughly frenzied,
Roberta told him where he could go, after which she turned
angrily to her room and banged the door in his face. Her
savage retort made Wallie laugh; and she, interpreting it
as further ridicule of her revolutionary garb, refused to
come down to dinner.

Hannah went up with a tray, but was not admitted.

Roberta was something of a problem.

There was nothing unusual about the crush. Neglected
at school and misunderstood at home, Roberta devoted all
her pent-up affection to Professor Gallet. He was too warm-
hearted to snub her, too canny to make capital of her in-
fatuation. Whatever moral scruples he may have had or
lacked, he was not disposed to jeopardize his job by giving
any encouragement to this sort of thing.

Roberta's starry-eyed adoration became rather embarrass-

ing to the arty Gaul, who, twice her age and comfortably
domesticated with a roly-poly wife and four attractive
children, had no notion of taking advantage of Professor
Ward's prematurely neurotic daughter.

She brought him flowers, an incomprehensible modern-
istic etching, and a couple of tall thin vellum-bound volumes
of lower-case poetry composed under high emotional
pressure by a frustrated soul who disapproved of the
universe, denying the existence of God on one page and
blaming Him on the next for having done a bad job.

He thanked her pleasantly for the poems, and promised
he would read them; and, when cornered a few days later
for an appraisal, remarked shrilly that they were 'tripe.'
Professor Gallet was proud of his American slang. Roberta
wept, and accused him of not liking her any more, which
was true.

'It is the artistic temperament,' consoled Professor
Gallet. 'We both have it! We suffer. Shall we now proceed
to our work?' he added more practically.

They proceeded to their work. The lessons were continued. But Roberta had lost a little more of her moral
underpinning, and became quite a pitiable object as her
self-confidence was drained of its few remaining red
corpuscles.

In this state of mental torture, she began to feel acutely
unfriendly toward people who seemed happily adjusted to
their environment. The chief object of her envy was Sally.
Sally had everything. She was remarkably pretty. At
fifteen she was flowering early into a vital maidenhood.
Everybody loved her. She knew what to say, what to do,
how to dress. She was athletic, clever, well balanced.

Ever since Peter Edmunds had gone away to school,
a correspondence had been maintained. At first it had dealt
mostly with school affairs. Sally had written about the
high-school sports and games. Peter had sent her his picture
in uniform. Sally had hidden it. She had never resented
the family's friendly chaffing about the local boys who

showed her their shy and clumsy attentions, but she didn't want to take the risk of being teased about Peter. Bland and open about all her friendships and social engagements, her feeling for Peter Edmunds was a different matter. Nobody knew of it but Hannah, and it was not now a frequent topic of discussion, even between them. And when, rarely, Peter's name was mentioned, Sally realized that Hannah — so comradely on all other occasions — was increasingly distrait and eager to have done with the subject, almost as if she thought Sally had no right to talk about him.

At first this had given Sally some anxious moments. It was so evident that Hannah quietly but firmly resented the friendship and wanted it discontinued. She searched the record of her own conduct to see if she could recall something she had said or done to bring this about. Had Peter reported to his mother that Sally had inadvertently let it slip — about Hannah's being their servant? Would this account for Hannah's attitude? Or was it something else?

If Hannah heard from Peter, it was through the letters she received from his mother. These letters from Waterloo came frequently, and Hannah seemed always on the lookout for mail. But so did Roberta, if it came to that. Sometimes there seemed to be a race on, between Hannah and Roberta, who should meet the postman.

One day Sally wrote to Peter that she hoped to come East next fall, to a preparatory school in Northampton. He would like that, she believed. It took more than a little courage to tell him, and she awaited the reply with a nervous impatience that slightly slowed her rackety gallop up the stairs. And as the days passed, she refused a second helping at the table. Weeks went by — and there was no letter from Peter.

At Christmas time, Mrs. Edmunds went to Virginia to visit her relatives and Peter. This much Sally extracted from Hannah. The lovely Christmas card she had sent to Peter (it had been selected with much care and had cost a dollar) brought no response. After two weeks had gone by, Sally ventured to tell Hannah of her perplexity. She tried to make it sound casual, and chuckled a little, as if it didn't really matter much, but her unsteady voice quite gave her away. Hannah seemed rather touched over it as she replied: 'I'm sure I don't know, dear. Boys of that age are very careless. I expect he's pretty busy.'

In March, Sally's mother noticed her listlessness and Doctor Bowen ordered her to take halibut liver oil, a table-spoonful of which was dutifully poured into the wash-basin every night before retiring. Sally made a resolute effort to be gay, but it was hard to do. Sometimes her pride had its innings for a few days, especially when they were rehearsing for the class play and the extra work distracted her mind. When that was over, she drifted again into the unaccountable periods of abstraction and inattention which everybody in the house knew 'weren't a bit like Sally.'

The postman for the Marcellus Avenue district began his morning route at the corner only three houses away. He usually rang the bell while the Wards were eating breakfast. Some time ago, Roberta had developed the habit of meeting him at the door. Hannah would start from the kitchen, but Roberta usually intercepted her.

Once Wallie had remarked, as Roberta laid her napkin aside and hurriedly pushed back her chair, 'I don't see why you've got to break your neck every morning to grab the mail. You never get any, do you?'

Paul remarked that this was an unnecessarily discourteous speech, and added that we could jolly well get along without such comments. Marcia sighed deeply. Sally's finely modeled brows contracted a little. A very unpleasant thought occurred to her, but she instantly dismissed it. Roberta was a difficult person to live with, but she wouldn't do a thing like that ... and — of course — Hannah wouldn't! ... No — Peter had found someone he liked better. He had been willing to write her an occasional letter so long as she was a thousand miles away, but when she had threatened to come East to school he had thought it high time to drop their friendship before it became embarrassing — and made some demands on him.

Hannah felt that *she* needed some halibut liver oil too. She had never been confronted with the apparent necessity for showing disloyalty to someone she loved, in the hope of serving what she believed to be a worthy cause. It was going to be better for Peter — and Sally, too — if their friendship was not allowed to develop into affection. She had devoutly hoped it might be broken off before it became serious. If something intervened between them now, they would get over it.

But she felt very uncomfortable. Peter would write inquiring how Sally was. Sally would ask shy questions about Peter. Once, when Sally was particularly inquisitive, Hannah was all but on the point of tossing the whole case away, for she was carrying in her apron pocket a letter containing some pathetically wistful queries. How Sally's blue eyes would have sparkled, thought Hannah, if she had known the depth of Peter's continuing interest in her. But Hannah had gone through too much heart-breaking sacrifice in Peter's behalf to risk jeopardizing it all now for the sake of humoring Sally in her girlish fondness for this boy. Doubtless she would recover. She would forget it. In any event, Hannah had firmly decided to do nothing to aid them in promoting their friendship. There was too much at stake.

The past twenty months, in spite of anxieties about Roberta — and Wallie, too, for he was not doing a bit well in the university and spent most of his time tinkering with a decrepit motor chassis — had brought at least two great satisfactions to Hannah.

She had half dreaded to see Paul come home from Europe. As for Eleanor Trimble's probable attitude toward the problem of their relationship, Hannah believed she would make every effort to re-establish their friendship on a sound and safe footing. But there was still Paul's feeling to be reckoned with.

In her imagination Hannah had followed Paul and Marcia on their tour. Marcia would not be a very comfortable traveling companion. She had indulged herself at home in indolent habits, rarely breakfasting before ten, and had developed her natural talent for wasting time until the log of her journey through a typical day, had it been honestly set down in ink, would have made the laziest dog laugh. Marcia would be a ball-and-chain to Paul on a sightseeing tour.

Of course it wasn't quite fair to think of Mrs. Ward as an unintelligent person, for she had had college training, and her associations were mostly with people whose interests required them to keep abreast of serious thought, but it surely must have irritated Paul sometimes to note the inattention in her bird's-egg blue eyes when conversations of importance were actively astir. Hannah could easily picture her toddling along beside Paul through the spacious and venerable halls of Oxford, and occasionally saying 'Really!' but wishing it were time to take the train back to London.

So far as the Paul–Eleanor problem was concerned, it would be much more simple, reflected Hannah, if he had gone abroad by himself. Returning, he would be so pleased to see his wife that nobody else, not even Eleanor Trimble, would have counted for very much. He would have idealized the pretty creature during his absence. His homecoming would be quite another matter with a weary and fretful Marcia in tow.

But whether Eleanor Trimble's firm grip on her own emotions was so compelling as to be contagious, or whether Paul had resolutely determined on his own account to stay on the reservation at all costs to his personal feelings, Hannah was delighted to see what promised to be the happy outcome of an affair that had been brimming with danger.

She often wondered whether the two of them had contrived to find a little time by themselves for an honest appraisal of their mutual attraction and a resolve to make it serve them rather than ruin them. This much Hannah never knew, though she strongly suspected that Paul and Eleanor must have talked it all over deliberately, judging from the considerable constraint between them on the occasion of their first evening together and the easy freedom of their contacts afterward.

Of course, the chief reason for Hannah's happiness over this matter was undeniably practical. Now there would be no menace hanging over the Ward-Trimble friendship and no threat of scandals and separations. But — these considerations aside — it thrilled her to the very marrow as she watched the drama skillfully staged. After all was said that could possibly be said about the few outstanding acts and events which had a flavor of nobility, the most stirring experience anybody could expect to have in the course of a lifetime was the serene satisfaction of exerting a complete self-control under circumstances demanding that no outward sign be given of one's inner struggle.

It was one kind of fortitude to grit one's teeth and silently sweat while the surgeon plied his trade. That sort of courage was good, and blessed were all they who had it. But the type of heroism that sent deliciously chilly little quivers twitching up and down Hannah's spine was the apparently effortless and tranquil demeanor of people who could endure hardness as good soldiers without turning a hair. Her admiration for Eleanor Trimble was so intense that she had difficulty in restraining it. And as for Paul, Hannah was of the opinion that there were very few people in the world like him, and impulsively told him so at midnight one Sunday when he came out to the kitchen after the Trimbles had left for home.

'Thanks, Hannah,' he had replied, a bit surprised by her frank remark. 'But what made you say that?'

'You know very well,' she said, without looking up.

'I came out for a box of matches,' he explained.

She reached a damp hand into the cupboard and gave him a match-box. He lingered for an instant, and Hannah smiled into his inquisitive eyes.

'I'm proud of you!' she said, barely above a whisper.

A little embarrassed over this impetuous tribute, Paul filled his pipe to provide himself some occupation while sparring for an appropriate rejoinder. Presently he said, 'Hannah, you're a remarkable woman.'

'Well — if I am — some of it's your fault.'

Paul patted her on the shoulder affectionately and turned toward the door. Tarrying, he drew a slightly diffident grin and drawled, 'You see almost everything, don't you?'

Hannah said she was glad she couldn't.

'It's rather odd,' he remarked reflectively. 'You have always known so much about me — and I have known so very little about you.'

'I'll tell you some day,' replied Hannah soberly, 'if you really want me to.'

'Truly?'

'Truly!'

'Now?' He sauntered back.

'No — not now. It's a long story . . . it can wait.'

One of the most trying experiences of Hannah's life had arisen when it became evident that — in spite of her own wishes — Peter was to be sent to a military academy. If there was a principle worth sacrificing for above another it was the everlasting rightness of non-combative living. It had cost her heavily to practice that belief. If she had any one pet aspiration for her boy it was the hope that he might want to live without fighting. Now we were going to send him to a place that gave you scientific training for war. Lydia had calmly said that Colonel Livingstone, the head of the academy, was reputed to be a hard-boiled professional soldier of the old school. Hannah had seen his picture in the catalog; stern, steely-eyed, a long scar on one bronzed cheek and a deep crease in the other where an early dimple had turned out to be a scowl — and jaws like a fox-trap.

'Rather cross-looking, isn't he?' observed Hannah.

'I'll wager,' said Lydia calmly, 'that this gentleman could bite the head right off of a hammer and pffft it clear across the Rappahannock.' Hannah had been demure and unreconcilable for an hour, and Lydia had hoped to say something droll enough to beguile a pensive smile.

Hannah had made an earnest effort not to be resentful, but it did seem as if Thomas had willfully done the one thing to their boy that she would have avoided at any price. She had tried to be understanding, but surely Thomas might have been a little more considerate of her feelings. Of course there were extenuating circumstances. Thomas and this Colonel Livingstone had prepped together at this academy when they were youngsters, forming an acquaintance that had outlasted the years. Later the colonel had gone to West Point and Thomas to Yale, but they had not forgotten their early days together in Virginia. It was natural, of course, that Thomas should want his boy to go there. Hannah had grieved when she saw her tall son in a cadet uniform, but there was nothing she could do about it.

Thomas had promised he would not tell Peter about their relationship, at least until he was out on his own. He would furnish ample funds for Peter's education, to be deposited to Lydia's account and administered by her, with the proviso that Peter was to attend the preparatory school and college which Thomas chose. Whatever information Lydia cared to pass along to Hannah concerning plans for Peter was to be considered her own business, and if Hannah wished to offer suggestions she might do so through Lydia.

Occasionally Thomas wrote to Lydia, when posting remittances, offering such reports of Peter's progress as he had learned through Colonel Livingstone.

One Thursday morning in March, Hannah was met at the door in Waterloo by a very exuberant Lydia.

'Lots of news for you,' she exclaimed. 'Just arrived. Fat letter from Thomas. Peter's been very bad. They've had to punish him. I'll tell you all about it. It's wonderful! You'll love it! I'm so thrilled! Take off your coat. Come out to the library.'

Thoroughly mystified, Hannah had followed Lydia, sinking weakly into a big leather chair and murmuring: 'Don't tell me anything serious has happened to our boy. Oh — we shouldn't have let him go there, Lydia. Tell me — what has he done?'

'It's a long story. Thomas says Peter let some other youngster copy from his paper in a trig examination, and when Peter was brought up for it he told the professor he didn't know the other chap was copying. But unfortunately the culprit, in confessing, had declared that Peter knew all about it and had pushed the papers under his nose so he could see them better.'

'I suppose Peter wanted to do his friend a good turn,' said Hannah, rising to his defense. 'I'm glad he wasn't a tattle-tale.'

'Of course — but it was against the rules, and our Peter seems to have lied a little. So they cancelled his privileges — whatever that means — for ten days. One of the features of his punishment was that he was not to leave his barracks for any reason during that period.'

'But he wouldn't!' Hannah's face was troubled.

'But he did! You see, Thomas was having a birthday. And he had written to Peter to meet him that next Saturday night, in Richmond. They would have dinner together and go to a show and Peter could return to school on the midnight train. And Peter didn't want to confess to Thomas that he was under punishment. So he sneaked out late that afternoon, in the face of orders not to leave the campus, and went to Richmond, where he spent the evening with Thomas, never breathing a word to him about the dreadful thing he had done.'

'Oh, Lydia! What did they do to him?' moaned Hannah.

'Now don't hurry me, please. I'll tell you everything. He got back to the campus a little before two and hung about in the shadows of the trees until the sentry had passed, and then he edged his way along the buildings until he came to the Administration Hall. And there he smelled smoke. He looked into a basement window and saw a blaze.'

'How awful for him!' interposed Hannah. 'I suppose he turned in an alarm and then they found out that he had been away.'

'No, he broke the window and let himself down into the basement, found the fire furiously burning, and while putting it out he singed his clothes and burned his hands severely. Then, instead of going to the hospital, he went to his room and tried to do something for his injuries by himself.'

'Lydia! How badly was he hurt?'

'Badly enough so that explanations were in order. Next morning they discovered all the evidences of the fire, and found Peter's fountain pen, and when he came to class they saw his bandaged hands. So, naturally, he was brought before Colonel Livingstone. Here is the letter that the Colonel wrote to Thomas, and also the report of his interview with Peter. You can read it for yourself.' Lydia handed over the papers and sat gently rocking, as she waited with expectant eyes.

Dear Thomas [wrote the Colonel]: I have been obliged to demote that young rapscallion Edmunds of whom you think so highly. I hope his punishment and humiliation will do him some good. He is a very headstrong youngster. I enclose a copy of the official stenographic report of my conference with him.

Hannah turned to the impressive document with nervous fingers.

Peter Edmunds, Major Sergeant in Company G, was then called:

Colonel Livingstone: 'Sergeant Edmunds, I understand you were under orders not to leave your barracks under any circumstances on the night of March thirteenth. Is that correct?'

Edmunds: 'Yes, sir.'

'Where were you on the night of March thirteenth?'

'In Richmond, sir.'

'What were you doing there?'

'Spending the evening with Mr. Thomas Bradford, sir.'

'You knew you were violating a command of a superior officer?'

'Yes, sir.'

'Did Mr. Bradford know you were absent without leave?'

'No, sir.'

'You knew the penalty for such conduct, did you not?'

'Yes, sir.'

'It becomes my duty, then, to enforce the regulations. You lose your standing as a junior officer and are reduced to the ranks. You also forfeit all campus privileges for thirty days. You will also spend five days in the guardhouse, effective upon the adjournment of this conference. Is there anything you wish to say?'

'No, sir.'

'That will do, then. You may go.'

'Yes, sir.'

'Just a moment: what is the matter with your hands?'

'I burned them, sir.'

'I have had a report of that incident. Do you wish to make a statement about it?'

'No, sir.'

'I am informed that on the night of March thirteenth you single-handedly extinguished a fire that might have destroyed this building. Is that true?'

'I do not know, sir.'

'You do not know *what?*'

'Whether the fire would have destroyed the building, sir.'

'But you put it out?'

'Yes, sir.'

'Have you been nourishing the hope that your gallantry or your injuries might give you immunity from punishment for your disobedience?'

'No, sir.'

'Private Edmunds, when you have learned to obey orders you will probably make a good soldier.'

'Thank you, sir.'

'The Academy is deeply in your debt for a courageous act.'

'Thank you, sir.'

'I personally like you very much.'

'Thank you, sir.'

'Is there anything further you wish to say?'

'Yes, sir. I like you very much too, sir.'

'That will be all, then, Private Edmunds. You may report immediately at the guardhouse.'

Hannah's face was shining as she winked back the hot tears. Then, when she could speak, she said exultantly: 'Lydia, I'll take back everything I've said about that place. Colonel Livingstone is wonderful! And *Peter!* My dear — I'm so proud! I've been repaid for everything — everything!'

'And you won't fret any more about Peter's being in a school where they teach boys how to fight?'

'Not if they teach that kind of fighting, Lydia.' Hannah's wet eyes were radiant. *'That's the kind of fighting I believe in!'*

The whole country was passing through a phase of unprecedented prosperity. Factories were running three shifts. Speculative stocks had fattened until their own grandmothers wouldn't have recognized them. The refrigerator business was booming. Paul Ward was well-to-do. He had been very successful in his adventures with the market.

For some time it had been occurring to him that Hannah looked tired and drawn. One day late in May he said to her: 'You need a vacation — not two weeks, this time, but a couple of months. How would you like to take an ocean voyage? Go back to England. Visit your relatives. See your old home. You've had this coming to you for a long time.'

Hannah tried to think of many reasons why she couldn't do it, but was overruled. Marcia, who had worried a little about Hannah's health, joined Paul in pressing the project. In a few days they had talked her into it, and now Paul was going down town to arrange for her ship accommodations.

'June sixteenth — the *Jefferson*. How's that?' he asked, hat in hand.

Sally was in the kitchen chatting with Hannah when her father stepped in to make his inquiry.

'Thanks, Mr. Ward,' said Hannah. 'That will be fine.'

'We'll miss you dreadfully,' said Sally.

'I'll miss you too, dear. I wish you were going along. I know it will be a lonesome trip.'

Paul stroked his jaw thoughtfully.

'Well,' he said impulsively, 'why not take Sally along?'

'Do you mean it, Daddy?' she shouted, clutching at his sleeve. 'Really? Could I, Daddy? Oh, would you, Hannah? Please!'

Marcia drifted in to see what all the excitement was about. It wasn't a bad idea, she reflected. Perhaps Roberta could be handled more easily if she had her alone for a few weeks. And Roberta had been making things so very difficult for Sally lately. Hannah would take good care of the child, no question about that. Marcia approved the suggestion without debate. The whole affair was settled in fifteen minutes, Hannah's happiness shining in her eyes.

Sally was so beside herself with joy that she ran up to tell Roberta.

'I wish you were going too,' she exclaimed, realizing as she said it that it wasn't quite true.

'When I go abroad,' sniffed Roberta dryly, 'I'll hope to have more pleasant company than the family cook.'

'How can you say such things?' demanded Sally hotly.

Roberta shrugged deeper into the pillows of her *chaise*

longue and grinned contemptuously. She always enjoyed the sensation of getting a rise out of her amiable sister.

'Well, it's so, isn't it?' she muttered. 'Hannah is our cook, isn't she? Go along with her, if that's your idea of a congenial traveling companion.'

Wallie, who had a talent for earing-in on choice bits like this, laughed raucously from the hallway outside her open bedroom door and called: 'Speaking of congenial traveling companions, I'd pity whoever went with *you.*'

Roberta scrambled to her feet. Sally, assuming the door was now to be vigorously closed against Wallie's badgering, decided that her absence was probably desired and left the room. At Wallie's door she paused.

'You mustn't yell things like that at Roberta.'

'Why should you care?' growled Wallie. 'She's certainly been mean enough to you.'

'Cross, maybe,' Sally admitted. 'Not mean — any other way.'

Wallie elevated one eyebrow mysteriously.

'She's jealous of you.' He lowered his tone to a confidential warning. 'I wouldn't trust that gal around the corner with a bag of peanuts. Not any more.'

Sally stood for a moment with troubled eyes pondering this remark and was about to ask Wallie just what he meant. Then, deciding not to pursue the painful subject farther, she turned slowly away and went downstairs hoping to revive her spirits with Hannah.

She was counting the days now. School was out. Two weeks from Saturday was to be the great day! It was hard to wait.

One morning Hannah seemed much disturbed about something. She had had a letter. Sally sincerely hoped it wasn't anything that might interfere with their plans. She lingered in the kitchen and tagged Hannah about through the house hoping to learn what was up, but no confidences were forthcoming.

As the days passed, Hannah's abstracted manner persisted. Sally would endeavor by her own exuberance to re-enlist enthusiasm for the delightful voyage; and Hannah, rallying, would go through all the emotions of ecstatic anticipation from which nothing was lacking — but genuineness.

Hannah would have given much to have been able to cancel the trip, but couldn't get the consent of her own mind to disappoint Sally. Besides, she was not in a position to offer a satisfactory explanation. The letter that had perplexed her was from Lydia, enclosing one she had just received from Peter. 'Uncle' Thomas was taking him abroad for the summer. They were going to France first for a couple of weeks but would spend most of their time in England. They were sailing on the *Faversham* on the twelfth.

Hannah was glad enough that her boy was to have this interesting experience, but it troubled her to consider the possibility of a chance encounter over there. She did not want to see Thomas. Above all, she did not want to meet Thomas in company with their son. The situation would be more than she could deal with. And she didn't want Peter and Sally to find each other.

During their brief married life Thomas had often encouraged her to talk of her childhood home near Reigate in Surrey. What if Thomas should decide to tour with Peter in that neighborhood? It was unlikely that he would want to do that, but it was hard to predict what Thomas might want to do.

She went to Waterloo and talked it over with Lydia, who laughed at her apprehensions.

'Don't be foolish, Hannah. There isn't a chance in a thousand that you will meet them. And why should Thomas think of taking Peter to visit your old home? He has promised to keep your secret and I believe you can trust him. He hasn't told Peter anything — about their relationship, or yours.'

'Are you quite sure of that, Lydia?' urged Hannah for
the dozenth time. 'How can you know?'

'For the simple reason that Peter has never asked any
questions. Do you suppose that boy would carry on as
usual, saying nothing to me about it, if Thomas had confided?'

'Then you think I'm entirely safe to go — and take Sally
Ward with me?'

'Of course!' Lydia dismissed Hannah's fears with a toss
of her hand. 'We needn't tell Peter you are going over.
He'll not be looking for you. I wouldn't give it another
minute's thought.'

There were plenty of young people aboard the *Jefferson*,
most of them in touring parties directed by teachers. Sally
was instantly drawn into their deck sports and social affairs.
But there was also much time for leisurely chats with
Hannah. It pleased her to see that there was a marked
change in their relationship since leaving home for this
voyage. Hannah wasn't treating her as if she were a child.
Sally had been a bit anxious about that. It was comforting
to feel that she had grown up.

One afternoon, seated in their deck chairs reading, Sally
glanced across to say, 'Did you see Peter last week, when
you were in Waterloo?'

Hannah shook her head and after a little pause explained
that Peter hadn't come home from school.

'Did you write him that I was going to England with
you?'

'No, dear — I don't believe I did.'

Sally pretended to read another page.

'I wonder why you didn't,' she remarked softly, half to
herself.

Hannah reminded her that her decision to come along
on the trip had been arrived at suddenly. 'There were so
many things to think about,' she added.

'Oh, well,' said Sally, her eyes returning to the novel,

'it probably wouldn't have interested him. I haven't heard from Peter for ever so long, you know.'

For a little while Hannah privately debated whether to let the matter drop without risking further discussion. But this seemed a rather cold-blooded attitude to take, in view of the singularly close comradeship they sustained.

'Peter doesn't write to his Aunt Hannah very often, either,' she replied quietly. 'Their hours at the Military Academy are well filled, I suppose.'

'With doing what?' Sally wondered, half-querulously. 'Marching and dressing-up and playing at being soldiers. Or maybe he doesn't tell you much about it.' She laughed a little, teasingly. 'He wouldn't want to annoy you with talk about such things, knowing how you feel about fighting. You didn't want him to go there, did you, Hannah?'

'No — not at first.'

Sally's eyes widened, and suddenly sitting up very straight in her steamer chair she said, 'You mean — you approve of it now?'

'Well' — Hannah faltered, not finding it easy to define her sentiments — 'I could have wished that Peter was some place else than in a military school, and I still dislike fighting as much as ever, but I'm grateful for the discipline he's getting. People have to train carefully to keep themselves well in hand — if they're to live without fighting — and I think Peter is getting that kind of experience.'

Sally laughed.

'That's funny,' she declared. 'I never thought of boys going to a military school to learn how to keep from fighting.'

Hannah was silently thoughtful for some time. Then she laid her hand on Sally's and said:

'I'm going to tell you a little story, dear, so you'll understand what I mean. I don't want you to think that I have changed my mind about war or the things that lead to war. But it is important, I think, that people should learn early how to control their feelings and take their medicine.

This story is about something that happened to Peter last spring.'

Sally's eyes brightened attentively.

Hannah told it slowly and in detail, and when she came to the point of the formal interview between Colonel Livingstone and Peter she unlatched her handbag and handed Sally the much-folded document, silently observing the girl's increasingly serious face as she followed the typed lines. Presently Sally's eyes swam with tears.

'Wasn't he marvelous?' she murmured, deeply moved.

'Wonderful man,' assented Hannah.

'I mean Peter!' declared Sally. 'Colonel Livingstone was an old meanie.'

'No — not a meanie. Peter's performance was grand, of course, but I don't think he would or could have done that the first day he was there in school. He had to learn that kind of control by associating with men who believed in it. It's a great thing for Peter just to be able to see Colonel Livingstone every day, and breathe the same air.'

There was a long pause.

'Did Peter write to you about it?' asked Sally.

'Not a line,' replied Hannah proudly, 'nor to his mother. We found out about it through his — uncle.'

'Don't you suppose he was pleased with himself, though, over the way he carried on? I should have thought he would want you to know all about it — and his mother, too.'

'That's just it!' declared Hannah. 'That's where the fineness of the whole thing comes in! Somehow they've managed to teach Peter the importance of private bravery — bravery that isn't bragged about. Sally, the greatest thing anybody can do is to build himself up strongly *on the inside*. The trouble with most people is that they don't think enough of the value of their own inner selves. If they do something courageous, they want credit for it, want to be flattered, want to tell it to others. And then, you see, the real value of it to themselves is gone.'

'You mean — because they've collected all their pay for it in their family's oh's and ah's?'

'Exactly! They get all their reward from the outside instead of privately storing it up on the *inside!* It means a great deal, Sally, to have a lot of strength under lock and key, strength that nobody knows about but *you — only you.*'

Sally sighed and smiled wistfully.

'I expect,' she ventured, groping for the words, 'that people who go about with a lot of proud secrets about themselves, all locked up on the inside, are awfully lonely.'

Hannah shook her head decisively.

'They're the people who are *never* lonely! Their memories are good company. It's the people who have no proud memories who are lonely, dear. They don't like to be by themselves because — well, there's nothing interesting there. The place is empty. *They have told everything away!*'

Chapter XV

CYNTHIA BRADFORD had become a very restless and discontented woman. Considering with what reptilious patience she had waited for the bright day when she might legally detach herself from Thomas without jeopardizing the bequest promised by her crotchety old mother-in-law, it was unfortunate that her freedom had not afforded her a higher degree of satisfaction.

For years Cynthia had been envious of women friends who, finding life with their husbands irksome or upsetting, had 'taken the cure' in some liberal-minded court. But no sooner was she herself at full liberty to do exactly as she pleased than it dismayed her to discover that she did not know exactly what it would be her pleasure to do.

After six months of it, she heartily wished she was still Thomas Bradford's wife. He did not love her and never had, nor did she love him, but he had been considerate of her comfort, amiable, courteous, kind. And now she was missing him more than she had previously longed to be free of him. Every scrap of news about his movements was interesting. At Christmas time and on his birthday she sent greetings to which he graciously but briefly responded, with a remote formality not calculated to encourage a renewal of their broken ties.

Always a nomad, Cynthia's mileage had soared to dizzying figures. Had she been a de luxe motor-car, she would have been junked by now. She had gone to India and stayed until it was too rainy, and on to China until it was too dusty. She knew more about Egypt than the Egyptians. Sometimes she would spend a month in Florence and sometimes she would visit old friends in Cannes. She liked spring in England and fall in Sorrento.

But eventually she always came back to Paris. If you were obliged to live alone, said Cynthia, Paris was the least undesirable place in the world to do it in.

There had been a brief period after the death of Martin Moore when it seemed that Adele might become a confidential comrade. But their intimacy had not lasted very long. Adele became inattentive to Cynthia's self-piteous chatter, and felt under no obligation to accept the receivership for her tangled heart affairs. They did not quarrel; they just drifted apart. Whenever Cynthia returned to Paris after an extended absence she would call up Adele and they would have luncheon together. And that would be all for a while.

Adele found these infrequent reunions difficult to handle. A couple of years ago, returning from a summer in the States, she had imprudently remarked that she had seen a little of Thomas at Bar Harbor. Cynthia confessed that she wished she had the courage to spend some time there, but couldn't take the risk of having her friends think she was sparring for a reconciliation.

Yesterday, as they had sat together at Prunier's, Adele, weary unto death of Cynthia's monotonous prattle about Thomas, reflected that if she wanted to she could give her tiresome friend some amazing news. She wondered what manner of fit Cynthia might have if it were suddenly blurted out that Thomas was now spending the best of his time and thought on the education of his idolized son. They ate their filet of sole Marguéry with a little bottle of Barsac and promised to see each other again very soon, privately aware that their next engagement would probably not occur for months.

Adele was a bit annoyed, therefore, when she heard Cynthia's voice on the telephone next morning.

'Have you seen today's *Matin*?' inquired Cynthia excitedly.

'No. What about it?'

'Thomas is here — at the Ritz.'

'Really?'

'And his nephew is with him — a Peter Edmunds. Thomas has no nephew. What do you make of it?'

Adele wished she had a little more time to organize a reply. Surely Thomas had been indiscreet in bringing Peter to Paris. Perhaps he hadn't realized the depth of Cynthia's interest in his movements.

'Well,' she drawled, 'I suppose it is just one of those mistakes that newspapers insist on making.'

'Will you be seeing him?'

'That depends on Thomas.'

'You aren't going to call him up?'

'Why should I?'

Cynthia's curiosity was rapidly devouring her. She telephoned to the Ritz for a reservation, packed a couple of wardrobe cases, summoned a taxi, and within an hour was giving herself little errands in the lobby, at the information desk, in the lounge, all over the place, indeed, changing her mind about lunching in the grill after she had made a careful invoice of it, and proceeding to the more imposing dining-salon, where she ate without appetite, her eyes attentive to the door.

As for Adele, her interest had been stirred too by the news of Peter's presence in town. Doubtless Thomas would want to bring them together for a brief visit. Thomas knew where she lived — at the Crillon; or did he? Perhaps he had wanted to locate her, but had forgotten her address. She decided not to take the chance of missing a glimpse of Peter.

Dear Boy [she wrote]: I see you are here with Uncle Thomas. For how long, and am I going to see you?

Lovingly

AUNT ADELE

Calling a messenger, she dispatched the note, and was much excited when the reply came at seven while she was dressing for dinner. Peter was anxious to see her. They had arrived only yesterday. Uncle Thomas hoped she could dine with them tomorrow evening.

Three hours later Thomas telephoned to confirm the invitation. He was cordial, but it was easy to see that he had something perplexing on his mind.

'I hadn't counted on seeing Cynthia,' he remarked, in a tone that gave away his anxiety. 'It's just a bit awkward. She is here at the Ritz. We encountered her in the lobby this evening. Naturally I had to introduce Peter. I'm not at all keen on their knowing each other. They're both fairly good at asking questions, you know. Perhaps it would be more sensible if Peter and I pushed along to London. I should like to have a little chat with you about it.'

'Why don't you run over here now?' suggested Adele. 'I'm quite at liberty.'

Thomas said he would do so. Tapping on Peter's adjacent door, he told him he would be out on an errand for a while. Peter had been tramping about all day at Versailles, and was glad enough not to have been included in whatever it was Uncle Thomas wanted to do. A few minutes after he had been left alone, he decided to go down and buy some French magazines to pass the time.

There he met this Cynthia person again. Uncle Thomas hadn't said her last name; or, if he had, Peter had muffed it. She was extremely affable as she plied him with the usual questions asked of newcomers. How was he liking Paris, and was this his first time? ... And where did he live, and was Mr. Bradford really his uncle?

Cynthia quite took Peter's breath away with the volume and velocity of her queries. They were expressed, however, in a rather disarming manner. It was obvious that this lady was eager to talk with almost anyone from her native land, and doubtless this was just her way of showing a friendly interest. She suggested — moving toward the lounge as she did so — that they sit down and have a little chat if Peter wasn't rushing off to do something else — and he couldn't think of any good reason for declining. In fact, it was difficult to disoblige her. Apparently she was the kind of a woman who took things in her own hands and merely permitted you to watch while she had her own way. So they strolled into the almost deserted red and gold lounge and sat together on a divan.

Deciding that there was no occasion to be secretive with this lonesome woman who wanted to talk, Peter briefly replied to her questions, told her where he lived, where he went to school, how he had met Mr. Bradford, who, having no family, had taken an interest in him probably because his own father was dead.

'What an interesting story!' commented Cynthia. 'I suppose Mr. Bradford really seems like an uncle, now that you've seen so much of each other.'

Peter smiled and admitted that this was true. Cynthia laughed a little and gnawed her lip, her cryptic expression hinting that she might be about to impart some interesting sidelights on this matter.

'Well,' she continued, after a meditative pause, 'if Mr. Bradford is almost your Uncle Thomas, I think I could be considered almost your Aunt Cynthia. Perhaps you don't know that I was your Uncle Thomas's wife, once upon a time.' She laughed again, rather nervously, and studied his face with amusement.

'N-no,' admitted Peter, slightly flustered. 'But he never talks much about himself.'

'Perhaps I shouldn't have told you. Maybe he didn't want you to know, though I can't see why not. There isn't anything private about it.'

Peter was finding it a warm evening, and patted the perspiration on his forehead with his handkerchief, Cynthia regarding him attentively. She chuckled, and laid a light hand on his arm.

'You love him very much, don't you?' she said gently.

'You've picked up so many of his little tricks.' She leaned forward as if about to rise, noting that Peter was growing restless and quite at a loss for suitable rejoinders to her personal comments. 'Well, now you've an Aunt Cynthia, so perhaps you'll let me call you Peter.'

He smiled briefly and nodded. It occurred to him that if he wasn't to be considered absolutely tongue-tied, it would be to his advantage to make some sort of remark.

'Thanks,' he said, with an effort to be pleasant. 'One can always make room for another aunt.'

'Sounds as though you had quite an assortment,' she observed invitingly.

For a split second Peter was on the point of mentioning Aunt Adele, but his intuition warned him that this might lead to complications, for Aunt Adele lived here in Paris. Maybe Uncle Thomas might have some reasons for keeping his Cynthia out of their affairs. He decided not to say anything about Aunt Adele.

'Yes,' he replied — adding gallantly, 'and they're all very nice.'

Cynthia rose.

'Perhaps it would be just as well if you didn't say anything to Mr. Bradford about our talk, Peter. I can't think of any reason why he wouldn't want you to know about me, but maybe it would be better to let him tell you when he gets around to it. Agreed?'

Peter was prompt to oblige her with a promise. Indeed, he had fully decided not to mention the incident. After all, it was none of his business, and it occurred to him to say so now, without realizing that his remark really implied a reproof to Cynthia for being so free with her chatter.

'No, I'll not tell. Anyhow, it doesn't concern *me*.'

Cynthia blinked rapidly a few times and flushed a little under her rouge. It had irritated her more than she was disposed to admit to herself that Thomas's indifference to their former relation was so bland he hadn't even troubled to mention her name to Peter.

'Of course not,' she replied crisply. 'Thomas wouldn't bother to speak to you of his wives.'

Peter's brow arched a little, inquisitively, but he did not ask for any further light. They were retracing their steps to the lobby now, Cynthia with the uncomfortable sensation that the handsome young fellow's silence — after her last catty comment — had left her holding the conversational bag in the awkwardest possible manner.

'There were two of us,' she continued, hotly, clipping her words. 'There was a Hannah somebody before me. Hannah Parmalee, or some such name . . . Well — I hope you have a good time here, Peter. I may not be seeing you again. I'm leaving in the morning.' She extended her hand and Peter took it mechanically.

'Good night,' he said, with eyes averted. Then he turned away toward the elevator, forgetting that he had wanted the magazines.

He did not see Uncle Thomas again that night. Uncle Thomas had come in late, and hearing no stir in the adjoining room had probably decided that Peter was asleep.

For a long time he sat by the window, his thoughts in a grand state of confusion. It was difficult to know where to begin in this almost unbelievable tangle of relationships. This Cynthia was really a quite terrible person, bent on having some kind of revenge. If she had been married to Uncle Thomas, which was probably true, he had done very well to be rid of her. Now she was going to get even with him by attempting to prejudice Peter against him. So much for that.

But *Aunt Hannah?* Was this the reason why Uncle Thomas had taken so much interest in him? Because, once upon a time, Aunt Hannah had been his wife? Why, if this were true, Uncle Thomas really *was* his uncle! Peter grinned and then chuckled a little. This explained a great many things. Maybe Uncle Thomas felt badly about it and wanted to make it up to Aunt Hannah; had decided to be good to her nephew.

And then he fell to thinking about Aunt Hannah's being a servant. Was it possible that Uncle Thomas — so generous and tender-hearted — would leave her in such a plight? Maybe he had wanted to help her and she wouldn't accept it. There never had been a person as independent as Aunt Hannah. The whole affair was very baffling indeed. He wished he dared talk to Aunt Adele about it, but that wouldn't be quite loyal to Uncle Thomas. Obviously, Uncle Thomas didn't want him to know anything about it, or he would have told him. But there had never been any secret about Aunt Hannah's being his aunt; why should there be a mystery about Uncle Thomas? Why hadn't they told him?

Peter undressed and got into bed, but he was not sleepy. The intricate web refused to disentangle itself. The more he thought about it, the more perplexing it was. Well, he would have to wait until somebody who knew all about it was ready to tell him. He wasn't going to make Uncle Thomas unhappy with questions. Uncle Thomas was the grandest man alive, and he wouldn't annoy him. Their affection mustn't have the slightest strain put on it. It was too precious.

And if Aunt Hannah hadn't wanted him to know about Uncle Thomas, that was her own business. She must have had some reason, and it wouldn't be anything to the discredit of either of them; he knew that.

He finally dropped off to sleep wondering what Sally would think if she knew that his Uncle Thomas, of whom he had so often spoken and written, was indeed his real uncle. How her blue eyes would open in surprise! And why had Sally stopped writing to him? He wished he knew. Of course it couldn't have been because she had discovered some secret that disturbed her. That was nonsense. Sally had seen another boy that she liked better, and had forgotten him.

They went down to Reigate in a motor-bus. London was

just another great city to Hannah. She couldn't remember
anything about it. But as they neared Reigate her childhood memories were stirred. Sally thought it better not to
bother her with too many questions, for Hannah seemed
wholly occupied with the attempted recovery of impressions
received when a little girl.

Howard Hall, where Dan Parmalee had learned about
trees and shrubs and flowers, was on the easterly lip of the
picturesque Holmsdale Hollow valley, within easy sight of
Reigate. The highroad that served the massive old pile of
weatherbeaten stone was an authentic strip of the storied
Pilgrims' Way.

Before they had left home, Sally's father had given her a
book about Canterbury and the pilgrimages, knowing that
Hannah would be taking her down to Reigate.

'Maybe I had better read the "Canterbury Tales" too,'
said Sally.

'That will hardly be necessary,' advised Paul. 'Not much
in that book about Canterbury — or the pilgrims, either.'

They alighted from the motor-bus at the great wrought-
iron gates of Howard Hall, and Hannah made inquiries of
the lodgekeeper's wife.

'Is anyone working here now,' she asked, 'named
Parmalee?'

'Yes,' said the woman. 'James Parmalee is the head gardener. And his daughter Hannah is a maid at the hall.
And young James works in the garden too.'

Sally was bright-eyed and excited. Imagine! Hannah
had a namesake she had never seen. Wouldn't it be fun to
see their meeting? Hannah explained their errand, and the
lodgekeeper's wife told them to follow the drive. James
would probably be found in the rose garden.

'Does it look natural, Hannah?' asked Sally. 'Won't it
be interesting to see the little house you lived in? And
Peter's mother, too. She was a little girl here, wasn't she?'

'No, dear. Peter's mother is just a very good friend of
mine. She never lived here.'

'Then you're not Peter's aunt?'

Hannah, wholly occupied with the familiar old scenes, replied absently, 'No — we just taught Peter to call me aunt.'

'And you're no relation at all?'

'See, Sally! There's the rose garden, and some men working. I think we'd better inquire of them.'

They were regarded with interest as they approached. An older man, standing a little apart from the others, walked toward them slowly.

'I am looking for James Parmalee,' said Hannah. Her voice was unsteady. Sally wondered if this might not be he, and whether Hannah didn't suspect it.

'I am James Parmalee, ma'am.' He was a tall man, with huge shoulders and big hands and deep-set gray eyes.

'I am your sister Hannah.' The words were spoken quietly.

James Parmalee's face was a study in mystification. Then he drew a smile that established their relationship beyond all question. He advanced, rubbing a large hand on his brown smock, and offered it.

'Glad you've come, Hannah. Is this your little girl, maybe?'

Hannah explained Sally briefly.

'I hear you have a Hannah, too, James. We will want to see her.'

'Yes, we'll be finding her. Here's my boy.' He beckoned to the youngest of his crew. 'Come here, James.'

Sally's heart thumped as he approached. *He looked like Peter!* If they had been brothers they couldn't have resembled each other any more closely!

It was an eventful afternoon, with tea at the cottage. Hannah hadn't been able to remember Mrs. James, whose people had lived down in Tunbridge Wells, but they were not long in getting acquainted. The girl Hannah resembled her mother. Sally was made much of by the family. She was delighted over the friendly way they accepted her into the party. It was difficult for her to keep from showing too much curiosity about young James. After a while he seemed to realize that Sally was invoicing him with unusual interest, and the half-shy glance he gave her made him look more than ever like Peter.

They spent the night at the cottage, and returned to London the next afternoon. After they were well started, Sally roused Hannah from a reverie by saying, 'Isn't it funny how much James looks like Peter?'

Hannah regarded her soberly for a moment and then said, with a smile, 'Peter seems to be much on your mind, Sally... But — James really is a very handsome boy.'

They rode in silence for a while.

'Hannah, did you ever wish you had children?' asked Sally irrelevantly.

'Well, I have *you*, Sally. You're almost like my own.' Hannah's tone was tender.

'And Peter,' assisted Sally.

Hannah turned her face toward the window again and nodded. Then they were busy with their own thoughts, not speaking to each other again until they were slowing down for Bromley. Sally couldn't help feeling that she had stumbled into a mystery.

Once Peter had determined not to pester his Uncle Thomas with any questions based on the impertinent assault that had been made on him by the awful Cynthia person, it was not a difficult matter to view his hero with the same feeling of admiration he had had before. How much of it was true he didn't know and had no means of finding out. He would forget it. Above all other objectionable organisms in the natural world, Peter loathed a tattler. Uncle Thomas had often said that tattlers were always cowards at heart, and invariably liars to boot. Perhaps that's what this Cynthia was. Uncle Thomas should have the benefit of all the doubts.

The dinner with Aunt Adele hadn't been quite as much fun as he had anticipated, mostly because Uncle Thomas was very quiet and seemed on a strain. As soon as they had left Paris he cheered up and was quite himself again. Peter was much pleased.

Uncle Thomas knew London so well that he never had to inquire his way. Day after day he thought up new excursions, and he seemed to take delight in watching Peter's enthusiastic reactions to everything he was experiencing for the first time. They wandered along the Embankment searching for the old Water Gate. They spent hours in the Abbey. They went by underground miles and miles to bob up in fantastic old-worldish suburbs, each crowded with relics of important historical significance. They made short work of the famous art galleries and a long job of inspecting the Tower.

One afternoon they went, in carnival mood, to the Regent Park Zoo. Uncle Thomas had been postponing this pleasure on the ground that monkey-cages in midsummer were something he could jolly well do without, but he finally yielded to Peter's importunities, specifying that he himself would spend most of his time out-of-doors communing with the penguins.

Peter was in an hilarious mood that day. When they came to the fenced enclosure where a patient elephant sleepily plodded around a half-acre circle carrying loads of sightseers for a sixpence, he dared Uncle Thomas to take a ride with him.

'You may,' consented Uncle Thomas indulgently, 'but I've quite passed the time of life when people do such things.'

So Peter lined up in the queue and waited his turn, Uncle Thomas strolling on toward the penguin pool, where, he said, he would meet Peter when he was through with his silly adventure. Most of the passengers standing in line were younger than Peter, but he didn't much mind that. Presently he climbed the steps, took his seat on the wooden housing, and was soon being bobbed along on the elephant, feeling rather foolish as he looked down into the amused faces of the spectators.

When they were halfway around the circle, his heart almost stood still. Sauntering along the path were Sally and Aunt Hannah! He called 'Sally!' and the English lad on the bench beside him glanced up with an expression suggesting that this wasn't the way well-behaved people acted in London when they rode on elephants. He would have to wait until the stupid old monstrosity completed the journey back to the little mounting-platform.

The business of unloading was exasperatingly tedious, something like docking a steamship. At length Peter was on the ground again, pushing through the crowd.

Hurrying around the enclosure to the place where he had seen Aunt Hannah and Sally, he stood for some minutes anxiously looking both ways. Then he joined the crowd moving in the direction they had taken, eagerly scanning faces and trying to see over the tops of people's heads. With mounting panic, he carried on, debating his course where paths diverged, and finally bringing up at the penguin pool, where he found Uncle Thomas sitting on a bench.

'Well! Judging by the heat you have stirred up,' observed Uncle Thomas, 'it looks as if the elephant might have been riding *you!* What's all the excitement?'

'I'm looking for Aunt Hannah,' said Peter breathlessly, 'and Sally. I saw them. Will you wait here, please, while I find them?'

Uncle Thomas seemed suddenly perplexed.

'I'd rather you didn't, Peter,' he said, soberly. 'Your Aunt Hannah may find it embarrassing.'

'But Uncle Thomas, *I just have to see Sally!*'

Chapter XVI

So now Peter wasn't going to amount to anything, after all. Life had poured out some very bitter medicine, probably good for what ailed you at the moment, but this particular dose seemed unnecessarily distasteful.

For twenty years no personal desire had seriously engaged Hannah's attention but the one constant hope for Peter's future. At all costs, this dear boy must be given a chance to make an honored place for himself in a world for which his mother had obsequiously fetched and carried ever since she was a little girl.

Hannah hadn't asked Life to grant her more than that, the assurance that her son's path might be cleared of obstacles. And to her Spartan mind, the chief obstacle to be cleared away was herself. It had not been easy to do, but she had done it.

She was ill-prepared, this morning, to brace her disciplined emotions against this sickening blow. The letter from Lydia found her thoroughly exhausted and in mental turmoil. For the past five days, Paul Ward's critical condition, as he lay broken to bits and half delirious in the University Hospital, had worried her into a state of utter collapse. It was an unfortunate hour for the receipt of more bad news.

Now the dream that had sustained her for so long, through all weathers, had vanished. It would be almost impossible, she felt, to carry on any further without the girding of that one bright hope. The whole world had suddenly lost its meaning. The thing Hannah had lived for had been destroyed: Peter was not going to amount to anything, after all.

The pages of Lydia's letter — and Thomas's — rattled in Hannah's agitated fingers as she reread them. How could Lydia bring herself to the point of writing calmly of a disaster so complete and overwhelming? Thomas was arranging that Peter should be a genteel loafer like himself. He had planned it with crafty care.

As I am intending to make Peter my heir [Thomas had written to Lydia], he will have no occasion to work. Now, at the close of his sophomore year, he faces a decision on this matter. As you know, Peter has always been interested in chemistry and has done very well indeed with his elementary study of it. He has talked much about his ambition to pursue this subject seriously with a view to a practice of chemical engineering as a profession.

But it isn't important that every man should undertake a profession. The few who find themselves able to live without a gainful occupation ought to be contented with their destiny and grateful for their freedom from toil. I have tried to explain to Peter that it isn't very good cricket for a man of independent means — as he will be if he follows my suggestions — to insist on elbowing some less fortunate fellow out of a chance to earn his living. Every time a well-to-do trains himself for a remunerative job, he is taking bread out of the mouths of people who need that work and would gladly perform it if they had a chance. This, in my opinion, is decidedly unethical.

For some time I have been seriously considering the purchase of a seagoing yacht. It would give me an enormous amount of pleasure to have Peter with me on an extended cruise. We would be gone two years, probably. On our return, if Peter wishes to resume college work either here or abroad, for leisurely study of history, aesthetics, the humanities, philosophy, and other subjects which embellish a gentleman's life, I shall be quite agreed to his doing so. But I am firmly opposed to his entering upon a grubby experience of the noxious stews and stinks of a chemical laboratory, with nothing to come of it but hard work in some job that he doesn't need — and by rights shouldn't ask for. Aside from my personal wishes for Peter, there is a little

matter of morals involved here which I hope will impress
you — and Hannah, too.

Hannah read this part of it dully. Her mind was too
tired to consider it with any degree of fair judgment. She
could think of no immediate arguments to refute Thomas's
theories about the immorality of work performed by people
who didn't have to. All she could see in this dismaying proposal of Thomas's was the ugly, stark-naked fact that he
was planning to make a worthless nobody of their son. She
closed her hot eyes, hung her head, and let the whole tragedy engulf her like a tidal wave.

She had never given way to self-pity, and in the course of
the long, difficult years she had shed very few tears in her
own behalf. But really, wasn't this impending calamity too
serious to be borne without putting up an uncompromising
struggle? Was there any merit in sitting quietly and
silently while this crime was committed? Was it for a disappointment like this that she had given up her child in his
babyhood and waived all rights to his affection? And was
it for this that she had practiced all manner of little deceits
to spare his pride and speed his way toward an honorable
and respected career?

The house was very quiet. Occasionally Hannah caught
the sound of Mrs. Ward's soothing tones as she tried to con-
sole Wallie, who had been lucky enough to come through
his motor crash with no worse injuries than a fractured arm
and a few clean gashes made by broken glass. It wasn't
Wallie's physical hurts that distressed him: he would get
over them in a couple of weeks. Wallie's aches now were
in his heart, an apparently sincere regret over the reckless,
smart-alecky driving that had put his father's life in
jeopardy. Hannah couldn't remember ever having seen
Wallie candidly repentant over any of his blunders. This
one seemed to have sobered him.

His mother was up there in his room now, telling him for
the hundredth time that he mustn't brood over this any
more; that he wasn't to blame; that he didn't mean to do it;

that he hadn't realized how fast he was going; that it wasn't his fault if the tire was defective.

Hannah wondered whether that sort of consolation was constructive. She doubted if it was even kind. If Wallie was having a thoughtful hour, observing himself as a heedless menace to other people's lives, surely his painful injuries had brought him a right to whatever benefit he might now derive from his self-inspection. Doubtless Marcia Ward was getting a measure of comfort out of the sweetly maternal murmurs she was bestowing. 'There, there!' she was cooing, gently. 'Now, now!' But what Wallie needed most was a chance to look himself over in private. The fact was that the comfort Marcia offered him wasn't effective because it wasn't true. Wallie always drove too fast and had liked to brag about it in the face of admonitions, police warnings, arrests; and on one humiliating occasion a whole night in jail at Kankakee, where he had been gathered in too late for bail to be arranged.

Tinkering up old cars and driving them like a demon had been so much more interesting than the university that he had dropped out in the middle of his senior year, and hadn't done anything profitable since, to Paul's chagrin, disgust, and sorrow. They had had many bitter words about it.

'Leaving your own future out of it, if that doesn't interest you,' Paul had stormed, 'how do you suppose it makes *me* look — a university dean — enforcing discipline on refractory students? I try to tell some impudent youngster that he is a worthless cub who deserves a spanking, and I know he is grinning inside and wishing he dared say to me, "Maybe you'd better trot off home and give your own cub a licking!"'

Hannah sat inert, conscious of the endearing tones of Marcia's voice absolving Wallie of all blame and bidding him stop his worrying over something he couldn't help. She wished she had a right to say to Mrs. Ward, 'If Wallie is having a little session with himself, why interfere with it?'

And for a while she pondered the subject. If Paul wanted to forgive Wallie and say, 'That's all right, my boy. Don't fret any more. We'll both forget it now,' he had every right to do so; but did Marcia have the right to step in between Wallie and his remorse? It was a nice little point and deserved a lot of thinking about. There was a good deal of that going on. So many people thought they were doing a service by saying to their remorseful friends in some crisis of their own concocting: 'Do quit worrying about it! You couldn't help it! Don't torture yourself any further!' But what right had *they* to be offering absolution so cheerfully and cheaply? Wouldn't it be ever so much better to let people torture themselves into some valorous decision to make things right, if possible? Take Wallie's case, for example. The catastrophe he had caused might almost pay for itself if it demanded that he mend his ways and make a decisive right-about-face into a useful life.

'A useful life!' whispered Hannah. 'Dear Peter, I wish I could do something for *you!* . . . But maybe' — she reflected — 'maybe Peter will be strong enough to resist this temptation.' Then she shook her head hopelessly. What could you expect of a twenty-year-old boy confronted with an alluring offer like that?

She returned to Thomas's letter.

Of course [he was saying now] I haven't said to Peter that he must choose between a fortune and a profession. I haven't cared to put it that way. But the fact remains that if Peter proposes to earn his own living, there seems no good reason why he should inherit a legacy. If he wants to provide for his own future, that is his privilege. In that case, however, I should be disposed to leave my money to some worthy institution. I should not take such action to compensate for my own disappointment, or to penalize Peter for failing to conform to my wishes; I should be doing it because I think it would be the right and just thing to do under the circumstances. Peter now has this momentous matter under advisement. Naturally he is a bit upset over the necessity for making a decision. I do not wish to press him too urgently, but the fact is that I am not growing any younger, and if we are to take this cruise we should do it now.

Peter may or may not solicit your counsel. After all, it is a personal matter; and regardless of whatever influences are brought to bear on him, the decision will be more satisfactory to him in the long run if it is made without too much help. I do not intend to coax him. I have stated my proposition. It is now up to him to accept or decline. I have given him until June first to scrap it out with himself. It has occurred to me that it was only fair and sportsmanly for me to give you this information.

Hannah reviewed Lydia's letter. It said:

I'm afraid you're going to be disturbed about this, Hannah. You've always been so keen on Peter's making a great name for himself. But really, if he had this fortune he might do more actual good with it than he could by working in chemistry. Anyhow, it seems a pretty big thing for a young fellow to throw away, doesn't it? Do write and tell me how you feel about it.

It was easy to see how Lydia felt about it. Hannah could hardly hope for any assistance from that quarter. Was there anything she could do?

Sally had been so fond of Peter. What would she be likely to think of the problem he was facing? Perhaps she wouldn't care very much now. She never talked about him any more. Of course that didn't mean that Sally had left off thinking about him. There had not been much opportunity for a confidential chat with Sally recently — not since she had gone East to college.

Hannah often wondered whether she had done the right thing that day at Regent Park when, glimpsing Peter on the elephant, she had impulsively decided to hustle Sally away before she too saw him. It was a cruel thing to do, but what else could she have done? She dared not risk a meeting that would involve not only a renewal of Peter's and Sally's friendship but an inevitable collision with Thomas also.

No — too much heartache had already been invested in this dilemma. Hannah had cried herself to sleep that night. She had so longed to see Peter. She had felt traitorous, running away from him.

It was noon now. Sally would be coming back presently. She had been over at the University Hospital since early morning. There was nothing she could do but sit in the tiny lounge a few feet from her father's door and anxiously watch the faces of the white-robed people who went through it. They would smile sympathetically into Sally's worried eyes as they passed. The young internes would probably have errands in that neighborhood, hopeful of an introduction. Sally was growing more beautiful every day. Her childish chubbiness was gone, and the round little face had ovaled, but the wide blue eyes and the yellow-gold hair and the deep dimples remained to remind Hannah of those enchanted days when, yearning for her own child, she had cuddled Sally close to her breast.

Paul's serious condition had been very hard on Sally. She had been summoned home from Northampton by an inexcusably frantic telegram. Mrs. Ward had dictated it over the phone, and it was as shrilly hysterical as she herself. So Sally had gone through all the agonies of losing her father, that night, on her lonesome journey.

Hannah glanced at the kitchen clock. Sally had telephoned at eleven to say there was no change. She would come home for luncheon, she said, though she wasn't hungry. Hannah had received the message and relayed it to Mrs. Ward, who, having found it impossible to sit over there and be stared at when there wasn't anything she could do, had decided to give her time to Wallie this morning. Wallie, she declared, needed her more, just now, than Paul.

The front door opened, and Sally came in softly and went on through to the kitchen. Hannah glanced up inquiringly. Even in her worry and weariness Sally was, she thought, the most charming creature she had ever seen.

'Doctor Lansing says it's about fifty-fifty, Hannah. But oh, he looks so tired and drawn — and so little, too, as if he'd been sick for years.' Sally laid her pale cheek against Hannah's. 'I'm awfully afraid. I don't see how he can possibly get well.'

'Your father,' said Hannah, steadying her voice, 'has always been a very strong man, with a remarkable power to pull himself through all sorts of trouble.'

'But that's just it! He isn't pulling! He's too badly hurt to try.' Sally's voice was breaking. 'Even when he's fully conscious he acts as if he didn't care. I said that to Doctor Lansing and he thought so too. He said it would certainly help if Daddy had any interest in getting well. I tried to be cheerful — and encouraging — but he just smiled a little and shook his head. I'm afraid he has given it up. It's so unlike him, Hannah. That's what frightens me.'

Mrs. Ward and Sally had driven over to the hospital at about two-thirty. Hannah had promised she would go up to Wallie's room occasionally and see if he wanted anything. At three, she had taken him a glass of iced pineapple juice and some freshly made ginger-snaps. Wallie had been lying with his face to the wall, but turned his head disinterestedly when Hannah came in.

'Something to drink, eh?' he muttered, trying to be gracious. 'Put it down there, Hannah. I don't believe I want anything now.'

'Rather not talk?'

Wallie shook his head.

'There isn't much to talk about, is there?' he said dully. 'Feeling pretty wormy today, Hannah.'

'That's encouraging,' remarked Hannah dryly.

Wallie drew a sour grin and muttered that she was a great comfort, to which Hannah replied, 'I think I *could* be, if I had a chance.'

This seemed to stir his curiosity slightly, and he sat up in bed, wincing as he protected his broken arm. Hannah helped him stack up the pillows, and handed him the cold glass.

'Very well,' he said, after he had drained it. 'If you've something you want to say, Hannah, say it. You've a chance now. Perhaps you're wanting to tell me I'm no good. If that's it, you'll be wasting your time — for I know it.'

Hannah sat down on the edge of the bed and faced him with sober eyes.

'I'd like to tell you a story, Wallie,' she said, in the same tone she had often used when he was a child. 'It's about yourself when you were a small boy.'

'That ought to be diverting. I was very good, I think, and showed a great deal of promise — when I was a boy.'

'Well, not always, and certainly not on the occasion I am thinking about.' Hannah's eyes strayed to the window, and her reminiscence took on the mood of a soliloquy. 'You had insisted on keeping up when you should have been in bed. It was one of the very bad colds you used to have. You were determined to go to a basketball game ——'

'Yeah, I remember; and had pneumonia and nearly died. I wish to God I had!'

Hannah nodded a tentative agreement to this statement.

'I've wondered, too,' she said, reflectively, 'several times, during this past year, whether the costly investment your father made in you, the night of the crisis in your pneumonia, was really worth all the thousands of dollars he was willing to risk on you; for you were so very sick that ——'

Wallie's dull eyes widened and his lips parted inquiringly.

'I don't think I heard about that,' he growled. 'Father didn't have thousands of dollars to risk on anything then, did he?'

'Well, I'll tell you all about it. It's time you knew. You should have been told before. It might have saved **your** father's life — if you had known. Of course I don't know how much effect it might have had on you, but it might have been worth trying.'

'Well,' said Wallie, frowning impatiently, 'carry on!'

Hannah quietly carried on. She told it all. There was no effort to dramatize it, no necessity for dramatizing it; the strange chronicle furnished its own dramatics. And it was a long story, too, prefaced by a prologue that recited Paul's desperate struggle to help himself out of debt, his discouraging work with the refrigerator, his happy completion of his task, his frantic rage when his rights to it were stolen. And then came the stirring tale of that night when, with his little boy's life hanging by a fragile thread, he had promised to give up his sole remaining chance to save his fortune in the hope that some power beyond himself might save his son.

Wallie's eyes were cloudy when Hannah paused.

'I don't believe in such stuff,' he muttered.

'Neither did he,' said Hannah gently. 'That, I think, was the brave part of it. He didn't take any stock in it. But your life was so precious that he — he took a chance — anyway.'

There was a long silence.

'He never told me,' said Wallie.

'No, he wouldn't . . . It isn't the sort of thing people talk about very much — especially when they're well and everything is running normally.'

Wallie leaned forward attentively on his good elbow.

'Do you think my father believes that his final success with his refrigerator was related to that affair?'

'I don't know, Wallie.'

'But you do think he got some sort of — what you call "power" out of it that helped him to his success?'

Hannah nodded.

Wallie was thoughtful for a while. Then, his own part in the whole wretched tragedy sweeping over him, he closed his eyes tightly and shook his head as when a swimmer

shakes the water out of his hair. Suddenly his eyes were
suffused with tears.

'Do you think he still has it?' he asked earnestly.

'I don't know, dear. If he has, he may be too far gone to
lay hold on it.'

'Why don't you go over there and talk to him, Hannah?'
Wallie's tone was firm, commanding. 'You know more
about it than anyone else. You two understand each other.
Go there and tell him he has simply got to take hold! Tell
him!'

Hannah shook her head slowly; then, looking him steadily
in the eyes, she said; 'I'm not the one to tell him, Wallie.
It wouldn't rouse him, coming from me.'

Impetuously, and for all the world like Paul's impulsive-
ness in moments of stress, Wallie swept back the sheet with
his sound arm, thrust a well-muscled leg over the edge of
the bed, his face twisted with emotion.

'Then, by God, *I'll* go and tell him!' he shouted. 'Get
me my clothes.'

Hannah had hastily risen to clear the way for this unexpected outburst. Standing before him, she laid an outspread hand firmly on his forehead, tipped it back, and
searched his agitated eyes with a look that stilled him.

'*What* are you going to tell him?' she demanded huskily.
'What do *you* know about the power your father found?
Do you think it would help him for you to gallop into his
room and put on a scene, when you wouldn't know what to
say to him, and wouldn't know what you were talking
about?'

Wallie's shoulders slumped and he hung his head de-
jectedly.

'You're right, Hannah,' he muttered. 'It would be
nothing but noisy impudence. I'm not the one to do it.'

Hannah sat down on the bed beside him and took his
good hand in both of hers.

'Whatever is said to your father, Wallie, must be spoken
very quietly. This power we have been talking about is not

boisterous. You don't shout it at people. He wouldn't recognize it if you brought it to him that way.'

There was a long pause.

'I wonder' — Wallie turned to face Hannah contritely — 'I wonder if it would do any good if I went over there and said, quietly, so as not to upset him, "If you'll only get well, I'll go back to school and — and try to pay up for what you did for me when *I* was sick."'

Hannah's sudden intake of breath sounded like a sob.

'I think he'd like that, Wallie,' she said brokenly.

'That would make him know I was in earnest — about wanting him to get well, wouldn't it?'

'Yes — and it would be a comfort to him.' Hannah hesitated for a moment. 'Now, if you were able to go just one step farther with that, you might make him think of his power.'

'Tell me, Hannah. I'll do *anything!*'

'Well — don't dicker with Them. They might not like it. Come the whole way with your promise. Burn all your bridges! He did that for *you!*'

Wallie's fingers tightened on her hand.

'Very well, Hannah,' he said firmly, 'I'll tell him that no matter what happens I'm going back to college, and I'm going to play the game straight with him from now on — whether he lives to see me do it, or not!'

Hannah lifted his hand and pressed it hard against her breast, then laid her wet cheek against it caressingly. There was a long moment of silence. Then, dashing the tears from her eyes, she rose, walked steadily to the clothes-closet, opened the door, and turning, said, 'What suit do you want to wear?'

'You mean you want me to go?'

'Yes,' said Hannah. 'You're the one to tell him.'

'You think he'll know what I'm talking about?'

'Yes — and he'll know that *you know* what you're talking about.'

Sally was starting back to Northampton on the eleven
o'clock train. It was eight now. Hannah had been helping
her with the packing. The door stood open. Mrs. Ward,
tenderly solicitous, fluttered in occasionally to show her interest, and restlessly fluttered out again to keep company
with Wallie in his room across the hall.

Upon each of her returns to him, Wallie dutifully put
aside his mathematics and the drawing-board — he was
boning to take a calculus examination that he had flunked
while in process of completing his education two years ago
— and greeted her with an amiable smile.

Marcia couldn't quite make Wallie out. Of course it
was to be expected that Paul's definite improvement would
take a heavy load off Wallie's heart. He had been so remorseful. Indeed Marcia had worried more than she liked
to admit to herself over the ghastly possibility of his impulsively destroying himself. Now that his father had
taken a new lease on life, Wallie's dour mood would be lifted.
Doubtless in a day or two he would resume his normal
habits of thought, a half-cynical, half-flippant attitude
which, while it exasperated her at times, was ever so much
better than his recent state of sullen self-scourging.

But the Wallie who had risen from his sackcloth and
ashes upon the announcement that his father would recover
was a new Wallie with whom Marcia had had no previous
acquaintance. The adolescent cockiness and bravado
seemed to have been suddenly outgrown. Her pampered
boy had become a man.

The kinks in Marcia's world were straightening out. Paul
was going to get well. Wallie was going back to school. In
spite of her satisfaction, however, the Paul she had recovered seemed changed somehow; and as for Wallie, she
was almost shy in his presence. Suddenly remembering
something she must do, Marcia would leave his room, presently darting back again to see if she knew him any better.

As for the interview Wallie had had with his father, she
knew nothing more than that the boy had made some

promises and Paul had reacted favorably to them. Now
Paul wanted to be well again, and Wallie wanted to mend
his conduct. All this was natural enough. But it had done
something to both of them that wasn't quite explained by
the simple facts in the case. They both seemed so thoughtful, so uncannily alike in their quiet seriousness. Marcia
wondered if they were going to remain that way; and if so,
whether she was going to understand them and like them
as much as before. It was as if they had seen the same
ghost, and it had laid the same tranquilizing finger on their
lips.

'Is your calculus interesting?' asked Marcia.

'No,' admitted Wallie, 'I can't say that it is. I'm not
studying it because I like it, but because I have to pass an
examination in it.'

'I think colleges are silly,' said Marcia sympathetically.
'The idea of making people learn things they don't want to
know — just to accumulate a required number of credits!'

Wallie grinned.

'Hannah says a little drudgery is good for you,' he
drawled.

'Well, Hannah ought to know,' observed Marcia, daintily
dealing with a yawn. 'She's had plenty of it. You and
Hannah,' she added, after a pause, 'have become quite
well acquainted lately. Whatever do you find to talk
about — her hobby, maybe?'

'Peace, and that sort of thing, you mean?'

'Yes — letting people use you for a doormat.'

'Quite to the contrary. Hannah likes to talk about good,
hard, stern discipline. She's an odd number, Mother. She
thinks people ought to deal very gently with everybody but
themselves. I rather fancy she wears a hair shirt herself.'

'Maybe. She never told me. Hannah keeps her own
counsel better than anyone I ever met. I know little more
about her past than she told me the first afternoon she came
to us — when you were four. Perhaps she has told your
father about herself. I don't know. They have always

seemed to understand each other — rather better, I have
sometimes felt, than I have understood either of them.'

'I guess you and Dad understand each other, all right,'
consoled Wallie. 'I think I understand him, too, a little
better than ever before. He's a wonderful person, you
know. There's a lot to him that doesn't show up on the
surface. But of course you know that.'

Marcia nodded, and wondered what Wallie was talking
about. Paul was an open book. You could read his thoughts
at a thousand yards. That had been one of his troubles, his
inability to keep his plans to himself. She smiled.

'Well,' she remarked knowingly, 'I never thought of
your father as a deeply secretive person. He mighty nearly
ruined himself one time, offering confidences to a man who
was almost a stranger — that Ellis person — the one who
stole his first refrigerator . . . and then he just backed down
and let the fellow make off with it. There wasn't anything
very deep about that. No — one of your father's chief
charms has been his boyish enthusiasms. They have got
him into trouble a few times, but I'd much rather see him
that way than — than mysterious.'

'Hannah thinks it's a pretty good thing for a person to
have a few little tricks tucked away.'

Marcia chuckled, and pursed her lips half derisively.

'Like the smart fellow in the advertisement who studied
French privately and amazed his girl by parley-vousing
glibly at a restaurant?'

Wallie laughed. 'Hannah would have the fellow study
French privately, I think, and then do all his parley-vousing
without an audience.'

'I call that smug selfishness,' said Marcia impatiently.

'Well, Hannah believes in selfishness — of a sort. She
thinks it's more important to be concerned about your relation to yourself than your relation to anyone else.'

'Including members of your own household, I presume.'

'Yes,' agreed Wallie, 'including them, too.'

Marcia smiled a bit reproachfully into Wallie's eyes.

'I hope you're not going to adopt that program, Wallie, and — and leave *me* out.' Marcia wished she hadn't said it. She had implied her observation of a change in his general attitude, and now had solicited an explanation which he might not wish to make. She hoped it would not cause any constraint between them. Wallie had made no response. So, finding the conversation perilously perched high and dry, with the tide going out, Marcia said she would run over and see how Sally was getting on with her packing. Finding the door closed, she went on downstairs slowly, feeling suddenly lonesome. Strolling to the kitchen, she halved a large grapefruit, painstakingly dug out the seeds, found two plates and spoons, and returned to Wallie, resolved to avoid the theme that had closed, unsatisfactorily, on a diminished seventh. As she passed Sally's door she heard the quiet murmur of Hannah's voice, and wished she knew what they were talking about.

'Brought you something, darling,' she said brightly.

'Thanks, Marcia.' Once in a great while he called her that and it made her almost foolishly happy.

'I'll kiss you for that,' she said — and did.

'You're very pretty,' said Wallie softly, which made everything all right again for Marcia. Wallie hadn't escaped her, after all.

'You needn't have bothered to press that old foulard, Hannah,' Sally was saying. 'I haven't been wearing it anywhere but in my room.'

'I love this new white satin gown. It's exquisite.' Hannah caressed it with fingertips that were slightly dismayed over their roughness.

'So do I, Hannah.' Sally's tone was very tender. 'Special reasons,' she added, giving Hannah a comradely wink.

'Wore it to a party, I suppose, where you found a very nice boy. Is that what you're trying to say? Want to tell me about him — or is it too sweet a secret?'

Sally strolled across to the door and quietly closed it.

'Yes, it really is too sweet a secret, and I want to tell you about him. First of all, he is a sophomore at New Haven.' Sally paused and met Hannah's eyes soberly enough, but inwardly amused a little over her expression of sudden interest. 'He has dark hair that must have been quite curly when he was a little boy, and rather deep-set gray eyes. He is tall and athletic. There is a deep cleft between his lower lip and his chin, and when he smiles his lips have a funny little pucker as if he had thought of something more that he didn't intend you to know. And when he looks at you sideways — like this — quite seriously, you wonder if he approves of you, and just as you're beginning to feel a little annoyed over this frank itemizing of you, and maybe are about to say, "So, what?" as saucily as you can, his lips pucker into that smile again that does things to your breathing. And the worst part of it is that you can't keep him from knowing about it. At least you feel that he does, and that doesn't help you any. But we haven't said a word.'

'Why, Sally!' murmured Hannah. 'Imagine your falling in love. You're only a child.' She sat down in a low chair, still holding the party dress folded across her arms. 'I thought it was odd, your bringing this gown along when there wouldn't be any use for it. Wanted to be able to look at it occasionally; was that it?'

Sally nodded, and sank down on the cushion beside Hannah's chair.

'Partly,' she confessed shyly. 'And partly because I wanted to show it to you.' She traced a pattern on Hannah's knee.

'That's sweet,' said Hannah unsteadily. 'I suppose this boy will be seeing you now, every chance he gets.'

Sally's eyes were downcast as she continued to follow the little design on Hannah's dress with a nervous forefinger.

'I'm afraid not,' she said demurely. 'I think he means to go away — to be gone for a long time.'

Hannah swallowed hard and hoped her heart wasn't pounding so Sally could feel the beat of it.

'Have you seen him often?' she asked huskily.

'Yes.'

'And now he's going away?'

'He says he's afraid he can't do otherwise.'

'And you think he loves you?'

'No,' said Sally slowly, 'I don't think he does — or he wouldn't go.'

'But of course you couldn't say that to him.'

'No — certainly *not!* He hasn't said anything that would give me a right to object to his going — clear to Timbuctoo — and staying forever!' Sally laid her cheek against Hannah's knee.

Marcia tapped lightly on the door now, and came in to inquire how they were getting on, and could she do anything? It was nearing time for Sally to go.

Hannah went downstairs to call a taxi, and Sally presently joined her in the kitchen. She seemed to have something important on her mind. Slipping an arm around Hannah she said confidentially, 'Do you know that Peter was in London when we were, and saw us at Regent Park, and lost us in the crowd?'

For an instant Hannah hesitated, debating a reply.

'Peter was riding the elephant,' Sally went on. 'He saw us and as soon as he could he set out to find us. Hannah, I remember how flustered you were, and how anxious you seemed to get away from there. Tell me truly — did you see Peter?'

Hannah nodded, without looking up.

'Why did you do that, Hannah?' Sally's tone was very serious.

'Because — because I thought it ever so much better if you and Peter didn't see each other any more.'

'Why?'

'I'm afraid I can't tell you.'

There was a momentary silence.

'I've always felt that you would rather we kept apart, and I've often wondered why. You are so fond of Peter, and I think you are of me, too.'

'Maybe that's the reason, Sally.'

There was another pause.

'But it wasn't you who kept Peter's letters from me; I know that Hannah . . . Please tell me it wasn't you.'

'No, dear.'

'You're not offended — my asking?'

'No, I'm glad you asked, so I could tell you.' Hannah drew Sally close to her, and lowering her voice almost to a whisper said: 'If I were you, I would try now to forget all about Peter. He's a dear boy, and I don't blame you for liking him, but — Sally, you mustn't count on him now.'

'How do you mean, Hannah — I mustn't count on him?'

'Well, it's just a bit hard to say, for I love him very much, but I'm afraid that Peter isn't going to amount to anything after all.'

Chapter XVII

It was an unexpectedly gorgeous Sunday morning in mid-May, the first really warm day of the season. Yesterday there had been a chilly rain and Peter had feared their visit would have to occur indoors where there might be small opportunity for the confidential talk he wanted to have with Sally. This morning's blue sky and sunshine furnished a pleasant surprise.

The sporty gray coupé which Uncle Thomas had given him on his last birthday industriously but quietly devoured the miles, leveled the hills, and straightened the curves on the scenic road to Northampton, where, in a little downtown park, Sally would be waiting at noon sharp for his arrival. It had been a month since he had seen her.

A sudden inspiration had descended on Peter. It was an ideal day for a picnic. That would be ever so much more fun than a dingy booth in some wayside eatery swarming with holiday motorists. There were a few things on his mind which could be discussed more satisfyingly out in the open. It had been difficult to have an uninterrupted talk with Sally.

Pausing at a delicatessen shop in Hartford, he picked up the makings of an out-of-doors lunch. Sally would probably laugh when she unwrapped the things he had bought — the leather-bound edition of a roasted chicken, a dismaying quantity of big dill pickles, a huge bag of potato-chips, and a bottle of olives which he suspected would have to be opened like champagne at the christening of a ship.

Stowing his purchases, Peter resumed his journey, the
balmy breeze swirling about him in the open car and tipping
up the flat brim of his soft gray hat after the manner of
Napoleon's. But he did not feel much like Napoleon. His
perplexities of the past few weeks had done something to
his spirit. He was aware that this was a golden day and he
knew he ought to be very happy, for he was going to see
Sally, but he wished he might meet her in a less perturbed
state of mind. It might be the last time they would meet
for a couple of years, and who knew what might happen in
the meantime? Certainly he was in no position to stake
off a claim to Sally, but to take the risk of letting someone
else make off with her, while he was indolently ship-ahoying
on the other side of the globe, was unthinkable. He had
already tossed and fretted enough at night, worrying over
his present problems, to realize what life would amount to,
in far-away waters, brooding over the probability that he
had lost her.

It wasn't quite fair to be confronted, at his age, with the
fateful decision Uncle Thomas had asked him to make.
The majority of his classmates had no definite ideas about
the professional courses they might elect and felt under no
compulsion to declare what roads they meant to travel.
Uncle Thomas wanted him to say, within the next six weeks,
whether his proposal would be accepted. Begging for more
time, Peter had wangled a small concession out of him, as
to the date, but it mustn't be later than July first; for the
yacht was ready, the crew already signed up, and Uncle
Thomas restlessly pacing about, tugging his short mustache,
and watching for the postman.

Of course, Uncle Thomas had meant it all in the kindest
possible way, and for that affection and generosity one
must be deeply grateful. He had counted on this round-
the-world voyage with such earnest expectation that it
would be almost a crime to disappoint him. Uncle Thomas
was the sort of person you wanted to humor in all his
whims. He was such a helpless, pathetically lonesome

creature, with not one interest in life except his devotion to Peter. It did no good to reflect hotly that Uncle Thomas was taking entirely too much for granted when he bought that yacht for the express purpose of the cruise, without consulting Peter's wishes. No — Uncle Thomas mustn't be hurt. You simply had to do what he wanted even if it ran counter to your own best interests.

Examining his motives, Peter honestly believed it was this sense of duty to requite Uncle Thomas for his devotion that was driving him to an acceptance of the proposal. To be sure, it was — as his mother had written — no small matter to throw away a fortune. But he felt very sure that it would have been easier to forgo the promised legacy than endure the thought that he had proved himself ungrateful and inconsiderate of Uncle Thomas's feelings.

The gray coupé insisted on passing a big truck on a hill; then, thinking better of it, lagged behind and loitered all the way up until the crest was reached and the coast was clear. Peter, suddenly free to speed on his way, wished the visibility on his problem would similarly lengthen and show him the road. That was the trouble: you couldn't estimate the future possibilities of your choice in this thing, no matter how you chose. Had it been a clean-cut decision between pleasure and duty, it might be easier to handle. But the duty part of it was not very urgent. He felt under no strong obligation to prepare himself for chemical engineering. Nobody had asked him to, not even his mother. She would be pleased, for sentimental reasons. But the fact that his father, whom he couldn't remember, had been a chemist, did not demand his espousal of the same profession. And he wasn't even sure that he had any marked talent for it. He liked chemistry above all other subjects, but one might work in a laboratory for a lifetime without accomplishing anything very important. No — it was just one of those awkward problems that you couldn't deal with spiritedly. It offered no challenge, either one way or the other.

Peter glanced at the clock and reduced his speed to forty-five. There was plenty of time. But it was difficult to idle along. One felt oneself under severe time-pressure, these days. You had a decision to make promptly — promptly!

Naturally, Sally would think it quite dreadful for him to quit college now. There had been no chance to talk about it seriously. He had told her of Uncle Thomas's proposed cruise and she had simply said, 'How interesting!' Brought up in a professor's family, Sally would undoubtedly feel that a failure to finish one's course was next thing to a tragedy; or would she? It might be interesting to find out how strongly she felt on the subject.

He devoutly wished he knew exactly where he stood with Sally. That might help him to a decision. It was clear enough that she liked him. They were thoroughly congenial. But, so far as he could see, their warm comradeship — in her own regard — was nothing more than a continuation of the childhood friendliness that had lapsed through no fault of their own.

If only she hadn't been so blandly, guilelessly forthright in her attitude toward him! When she introduced him to her friends, you would have thought he was her brother. Even on the occasion of that first meeting, after they had been separated for so long — that purely accidental meeting at the tennis tournament in Boston — she had held his hand tightly in both of hers and, smiling up into his eyes, had exclaimed, '*Peter!* I thought I would never see you or hear from you again.' There hadn't been anything coy or shy about it.

Late that afternoon she had insisted on his joining her party of a half-dozen, presenting him to them without the slightest trace of bashfulness or diffidence, and when she left — the Northamptonians were taking an early evening train — she said, 'Will you answer my letters now, Peter, if I write to you?'

'I like *that*,' he had countered, 'after the way you let me down.'

'You mean — you did write to me, Peter?' she asked soberly.

'Of course! Dozens! You didn't get them?'

'Sorry, Peter.'

'But they were sent to your home address, Sally.'

And then Peter had been on the point of inquiring if anyone was living there who might not want them to write to each other, but decided that this wasn't the time or place to introduce so delicate a subject. Besides, it was time for her to go.

Next day he had written to her. It was the beginning of a correspondence that had delighted him, and perplexed him, too; for Sally's candid interest in him was so open and aboveboard that he felt she would be amazed if she knew his own sensations in regard to her. She was his grown-up playmate; that was all.

Then there had been the sophomore party at Northampton, with Sally showing him off to her friends, her arm slipped through his companionably, her fingers tightening on his sleeve, her wide blue eyes beaming up at him as artlessly as if she were his twin sister! She couldn't have the slightest speck of romantic affection for him — and do that!

Thinking it all over, late that night, he pictured himself taking Sally out of the crowd and saying tenderly, 'I think you're a darling! I think you're the most wonderful girl in the world!' And then Sally would unquestionably reply, without a bit of restraint, 'I'm so glad, Peter. I think you're wonderful, too. Isn't it fun to be together?'

Then there had been another party when he had actually contrived a moment alone with her, conscious that his heart was beating loud enough to be heard and finding his voice unsteady when he spoke to her.

'You look simply stunning tonight, Sally,' he had said, and she had replied instantly, 'I hoped you would like me in this dress, Peter. It's the nicest one I ever had. Makes me look tall, don't you think?'

It did make her look tall, but that wasn't half of it. The white satin gown modeled every lovely curve adorably. Sally didn't seem to know that.

'I like my new shoes, too,' she added, naïvely inviting his inspection as if he might have been her mother. *That*, reflected Peter, later, was the hell of it. She was so deucedly innocent and ingenuous. She took him for granted. Their relationship was the same as when they had played the hotly contested game of tennis on the school court in Waterloo. To Sally, he was still that boy with the friendly dog and the limping rabbits.

Sometimes he grinned when he thought of the astonishment she might display in her startled eyes if he were to blurt out, suddenly, 'You belong to me and I want you! Do you understand? I want you for mine — forever!' That would be something different, something that had never crossed her mind. He would not be surprised if she winced, and pressed the backs of her fingers hard against her pretty mouth, and replied thickly, 'Oh, Peter — you've spoiled everything! Why, my *dear*, I never thought of you that way!'

She ran out to the curb, slammed the door that he had opened for her, slipped over very close beside him, and said softly, 'Isn't it going to be a lark?'

'It's worse than that,' warned Peter, with a sidelong wink. 'We're having a picnic.'

'On what?'

'I brought some stuff along.'

'How wonderful!'

'Better wait till you see it. . . . How did you leave your father?'

'He's getting well. It will take some time. Wallie's going back to the University has bucked him up a lot. Daddy's so elated. But I wrote you that. Thanks for all the nice letters. . . . I know just the place for our picnic, Peter. Carry on until I tell you where to turn.'

'How was Aunt Hannah?'

'Fit as a fiddle — except she doesn't want you to go
cruising. She is fretting about it, a little. You know she
takes a tremendous interest in everything you do. She
wishes you wouldn't give up college.'

'I know — but she doesn't understand. Aunt Hannah'
— Peter hesitated, not quite sure what he had intended to
say — 'doesn't understand.'

'Well — I don't suppose you need to worry about what
she thinks,' said Sally comfortingly. 'It's your own affair.
It isn't quite the same as if she were your really truly aunt.
In that case ——'

'But she is, you know,' contradicted Peter, eyes steadily
on the busy road. 'What made you think she wasn't?'

'Because she told me,' said Sally casually, 'and I don't
think she meant it as a secret. She said that she and your
mother had just taught you to call her "aunt" when you
were a child. I should have thought you knew, by this
time.'

The gray coupé had slackened speed until it was barely
moving. Peter turned to face Sally with bewildered eyes.

'But that can't be true!' he declared soberly. 'You see,
it's her being my aunt that explains everything about
Uncle Thomas — and what he is doing for me.' Peter drew
the car to the side of the road, turned off the motor, and
proceeded with his story. 'I had expected to tell you all
this, anyway. It clears up a lot of things. It will help you
understand how I'm fixed. When I was in Paris, I learned
accidentally that Uncle Thomas really *is* my uncle. And
that accounts for everything he wants to do for me. My
Aunt Hannah, once upon a time, was his *wife*.'

'Peter! Are you sure? Did you ask him?'

'No,' he muttered, rather reluctantly. 'Uncle Thomas
hadn't told me about it and I didn't like to worry him with
questions. He isn't the sort of person you feel free to examine about his own business.'

'You could have asked your mother,' suggested Sally,

in a tone of gentle reproof. 'Surely she would tell you anything you want to know about it.'

'Yes — I suppose you would think that, Sally.' Peter's face registered uncertainty about the reasonableness of what he was going to say. 'But it's this way. Ever since I can remember, my mother and my Aunt Hannah have had a lot to talk about that apparently didn't concern me, at all. When I was a little boy, they used to sit and talk by the hour in low tones. I never thought there was anything strange about it. It was grown-up conversation that I wouldn't understand. In fact, I think it pleased me that my mother and my aunt were so devoted to each other, and I knew they were to me. There were plenty of things that adults had to say to one another that small children weren't expected to know. If Aunt Hannah and Mother had secrets, there wasn't anything unnatural about that.'

'And so you never asked any questions,' observed Sally comprehendingly.

Peter gave a little shrug and grinned.

'There weren't any I wanted to ask, really. I think the first time I ever felt any curiosity about Aunt Hannah was when I found out that she worked at your house.'

'And I told you that,' murmured Sally self-reproachfully. 'I was awfully sorry, Peter. I'm always talking first — and thinking afterward. And now I've done it again today, it seems. But I don't see why you should be kept in the dark about your own family relationships. That isn't quite fair!'

'Maybe not. But it is just as I told you, Sally. I was brought up in an atmosphere pretty heavily charged with secrets. I assumed that the same thing was true with all children. I was discouraged from asking questions. And even now I hesitate to prod into my Aunt Hannah's story. There seems to be no doubt about her having been the wife of Uncle Thomas. They separated and he married again. It was his second wife who told me.'

Sally wondered how she had happened to do that and Peter told her the circumstances in considerable detail.

'What a horrible woman!' exclaimed Sally. 'She must have had a lot of brass.'

'That's one reason I couldn't get up the courage to say anything to Uncle Thomas about the incident. I felt he'd probably had enough trouble with her. I didn't want to worry him with any mention of her — a quite killable creature.'

'Perhaps what she told you was untrue.'

'I think ——' Peter deliberated for an instant. 'I think I wanted to believe her — after the first shock of it, for it cleared up Uncle Thomas's affectionate interest in me. I gathered that he hoped to square with Aunt Hannah by befriending her nephew — his nephew, too, by marriage. . . . And now it seems that I'm not his nephew, or Aunt Hannah's, either. The whole thing is very queer.'

Sally impulsively laid a hand on his arm and gave it a playful little push.

'Then I think we had better forget it and have our picnic,' she advised maternally. 'It's this next country road to the left, Peter. There's a lovely pond and a grove and maybe we will find some trilliums. Let's stop fretting about your Aunt Hannah.'

'But she isn't my Aunt Hannah, after all. That puts everything haywire again.' Peter mechanically snapped the ignition on, spun the engine, and slipped in the gears. 'What business has Uncle Thomas — making me his heir — if Aunt Hannah is no relation of mine?'

'Maybe he likes you,' suggested Sally gently. 'I don't see how he could help it, really.'

Peter regarded her fleetingly with one of his oddly pursed smiles.

'You like to spoof me, don't you?'

'I'm not spoofing. If I were a man, like Uncle Thomas, and had no dependents and a million dollars, I'd give it all to you, Peter — just because you're so nice.'

'Thanks, Sally,' he said dryly, expectant of some whimsical rejoinder. Upon her failure to reply to this, he glanced toward her with a half-reproving smile and encountered eyes that seemed sincere. 'Poker face!' he grumbled. 'You ought to grin when you say things like that.' He chuckled a little, and pretended a warning look. 'Sometime you'll tease me and I'll — I might take you seriously.'

'And then what?' inquired Sally lightly. 'Box my ears?'

'Which way do we go from here?' asked Peter, slowing down as a fork in the road approached.

'I'm sure I don't know,' said Sally, half to herself. Then, suddenly attentive, 'Oh — it's the one to the right, Peter. Not very far now. Over this little hill. . . . Don't be so serious, old owl. We're going on a picnic.'

'Was I so serious?' growled Peter.

Sally nodded.

'And funny, too,' she added cryptically.

'You don't mean — witty.'

'No,' said Sally — 'just funny.'

They drove on in silence for a little while, Peter attentive to the narrow road which had deteriorated to a mere grassy lane.

'Cute hat,' remarked Peter, after a brief appraising glance. 'The pink ribbon brings out the blue in your eyes.'

'You're growing quite observing, little one,' remarked Sally. 'Fancy your knowing I have blue eyes!'

'I like the pink sweater too,' he continued courageously. 'It fits you so well. I mean,' he amended quickly — 'it suits you exactly.'

'Then I'll wear it — always,' she declared — 'just for you.'

'Better remember what I told you,' warned Peter, 'about teasing me — with a straight face.'

'There it is, Peter! Isn't that lovely?' The placid little lake had suddenly come into view. 'And only two cars. We'll have the place almost to ourselves.'

'Will you like that?' Peter heard himself saying, a bit unsteadily.

'Of course! What a silly question!'

Peter drew a deep sigh, gave her what he felt was a good imitation of a brotherly smile, and drawled, 'Yes — it was, rather; wasn't it?'

He sat, arms clasping his knees; and, at her request, making no move to help her unwrap the packages containing their luncheon. Seated there beside her on the steamer-rug, Peter was stirred to a feeling of inexpressible tenderness for Sally as she busied herself with the occupation that accented her womanhood, her potential wifehood. As he watched her pretty hands competently preparing the food he had brought, the act seemed to symbolize a natural bond between them. Peter wondered if such a thought had occurred to her, too, but doubted it.

'Had you any plans,' she asked, 'for demobilizing this chicken?'

'Let's be savages,' said Peter, 'and tear it to pieces with our bare hands.'

She passed it to him.

'You do it, Peter. You're much more savage than I am.'

'Was I cross?' he asked, proceeding to dismember the chicken.

'N-no — just glum — and remote.'

'I was thinking, Sally. I've a lot to think about. I'm going away.'

'Well — you're not going today. Let's enjoy ourselves together, this once more. Do tell me all about this cruise, Peter.'

Half-heartedly, he repeated what Uncle Thomas had said about their voyage, south to the Canal and into the Pacific; south, again, touching at Guayaquil, Callao, Iquique, Valparaiso, and on to Desolation Island ——

'Desolation Island sounds quite jolly. I suppose you'll be desolating there about the time of the tennis match in

Forest Hills. We'll miss you, Peter.... Well — please go on. Then, from Desolation Island you sail to ——'

'New Zealand. It's a long haul, too, forty-five hundred miles; and then to Sidney, and then down to Tasmania——'

'I don't like your going to Tasmania, Peter. I've heard the girls down there are so forward. By the way, how do you happen to be missing Tahiti? If I were a boy with nothing to do but cruise around with my uncle, I'd ——'

Peter gave her a reproachful look.

'You're saying it the worst way, aren't you?'

'What would you like to have me do, Peter?' She lifted sober eyes, and then smiled a little. 'You aren't hoping I'll try to make your trip sound glamorous, are you? That would seem as if I really wanted you to go.'

'And you don't?' he asked, so wistfully that it made Sally laugh.

'Of course not, stupid!' Then, suddenly serious, she added pensively: 'I'll be quite lost without you, Peter. We've been friends so long. Even when we were not hearing from each other, I knew we should meet again sometime and play together. But now you're going so far and to be gone so long. I'll be awfully lonely.'

He glanced up to study her face. There was no question about the sincerity of what she was saying, but — '*play* together.' That was her thought. They wouldn't be able to play together any more. Just good chums, that's what they were.

'So many things might happen, Peter, in two years,' she was continuing.

'I know,' he ventured. 'You might fall in love with somebody and be married. And then we couldn't play together any more, without dragging the other fellow along.' He tried to make this sound amusing, but Sally's smile was not spontaneous.

'Peter, dear' — her voice was self-consciously unsteady — 'I *am* in love.'

For an instant her confession fairly sickened him. It was as if he had been struck a sudden blow. Then, realizing the implications of any delay to felicitate her, he attempted a comradely smile, and said, 'I'm glad you wanted to tell me, Sally.'

'I didn't want to really,' she admitted, with averted eyes. 'It wasn't easy to do.'

'It shouldn't have been so hard to tell *me*,' muttered Peter. 'Almost like telling your brother.... College fellow, I suppose.'

Sally nodded, and began gathering up the fragments of their luncheon.

'Just finishing,' she said, casually enough.

'But he'll let you complete your course, won't he?' demanded Peter, his tone imputing a large selfishness to this unworthy beggar, whoever he was.

'Oh, yes,' said Sally, without looking up. 'We haven't begun to think about marriage. He's not in a position to make any plans.'

'You mean — money?'

Sally nodded; then, swiftly abandoning her reflective mood, she glanced up, smiled, scrambled to her feet, and said, 'Enough on that, Peter! Let's run down to the lake and pretend it's a finger-bowl.'

The trip back to Northampton was distinguished for the long pauses in their conversation. Most of the talk was done by Peter who seemed anxious to justify himself in Sally's eyes.

One little incident, as they were leaving their picnic ground, had temporarily confused them both. It had been a full five minutes afterward before either of them could think of anything sufficiently casual to disguise the emotion suddenly stirred.

The air was growing chilly. Peter had asked Sally, when they were making ready to start, if she was warm enough, and she had confessed a wish that she had brought

a coat. Unlocking the back deck of the coupé, Peter drew
out a camel's-hair overcoat and invited her to slip into it.
She turned, held out her arms, and he put it on her. His
hands touched her neck and lingered there for a moment.
Then, without releasing her, he drew her around until she
faced him. For a moment he held the lapels of the coat
close to her throat, with a pressure that couldn't possibly
have been mistaken for anything but a caress. Sally looked
up steadily into his eyes, and smiled. And he smiled into
hers. His heart speeded. He had never been this close to
Sally before. Her lips were parted, as if she might be about
to ask a question.

'I'm afraid,' he said rather huskily, 'the sleeves are going to be a little long.'

She held them up, shook her hands free, and laid them
gently on Peter's forearms. He proceeded to button the
coat, seemingly reluctant to have done with his task.

'It feels good, Peter,' she said softly. 'I'm glad you
thought of it.'

There was a momentary pause, Peter's eyes narrowing
a little as he regarded her indecisively. The pink tip of
Sally's tongue moistened her lips, as she looked up with
almost childish inquiry.

'It has been such fun,' she said.

'Yes,' replied Peter, with a deep-drawn breath. 'Shall
we go now?'

They had been very quiet for nearly a mile. Then Peter
wanted to talk again about Uncle Thomas. You see — it
was *this* way. Uncle Thomas mustn't be hurt. Whether he
was a real uncle or not didn't alter the case very much now.
The fact was that he had invested heavily in the yacht for
the express purpose of this voyage with Peter.

'He should have asked you first, I think,' commented
Sally.

'Of course — but that isn't the way Uncle Thomas does
things. He assumes that everybody else likes what he
likes. It was to be a wonderful surprise — don't you see?

Uncle Thomas never dreamed that I might have some opinions on the subject.'

'And — when you come back,' said Sally, 'I suppose there will be another plan made for you — another voyage, maybe. Will you like that sort of life?'

'Perhaps not,' admitted Peter glumly. 'But it might be regarded as an education — of a sort. And there's nothing to keep me here. I mean' — he added — 'I've no obligations. My mother is independent. And I've no other ties.'

They had agreed that it would be more prudent if Sally were let out in the downtown district. Drawing up in front of the favorite hotel, Peter reluctantly opened the car door. Sally slipped out of the coat and laid it on the seat.

'Good-bye,' she said. 'I suppose we shall not be seeing each other again. Examinations — and everything.'

Peter joined her on the pavement, signing to the doorman that he was not stopping. A small group of loungers regarded them with mild interest.

'I don't like to say good-bye, Sally.' Peter's tone was tender. 'I'll be thinking about you — every day. I'll send you my addresses, if you don't think this bird of yours will object to your writing.'

'He won't care.'

'Maybe you'll not let him know,' suggested Peter, hopeful of compounding a small intrigue to preserve their comradeship.

Sally tipped her head in doubt about the fairness of this duplicity. 'I'm afraid he'll have to know,' she said dutifully.

Peter reached out his hand and drew a dour little smile.

'Seems a very formal way to part,' he muttered.

'Isn't it?' she agreed — 'with everybody looking at us.'

He grew suddenly reckless.

'I almost kissed you,' he growled, 'when I helped you on with my coat.'

Sally's eyes wavered for an instant.

'Yes,' she said softly, 'I know.'

'What would you have thought?'

Sally laughed.

'It might not have done me any good to think,' she answered quietly. 'You're ever so much bigger and stronger than I am. . . . 'Bye, Peter! Don't forget me!'

Wallie met her at the train when she arrived home the second Friday afternoon in June. He had Lucy Trimble with him. The girls greeted each other amiably. Sally was surprised and amused over Wallie's proprietary attitude toward Lucy. There seemed to be a great deal of understanding between them.

'You children,' said Sally, while her baggage was being stowed in the car, 'seem to have become very well acquainted since I saw you last.'

'You don't know *nothin'*,' declared Wallie mysteriously.

'In that case,' drawled Sally, 'I'll sit in the back seat with the freight, and you two cooing doves can hold hands.'

'You can see that college has broadened her experience, Wallie.' Lucy turned around to bestow a companionable wink on her pert young friend.

They teased each other pleasantly all the way home, with brief intervals for Sally's queries about the household. Her father was coming home from the hospital next week; spending most of his time now in the solarium, growing more and more restless to be up and doing. Roberta wasn't returning this summer. Yes — Mother was well and playing an enviable game of golf. Hannah? — Well, Hannah hadn't been quite up to grade, lately; losing weight; something the matter.

'She needs another vacation,' thought Wallie.

Sally made no comment. Poor Hannah — fretting her heart out over Peter's going away, and stopping college. But why should she let it trouble her so? After all — she wasn't responsible for Peter. And it wasn't quite like Hannah to be dismal very long about anything.

Marcia was waiting for them at the door, bright-eyed

with happiness. Sally gave her a bear-hug and they exchanged the murmured endearments customary at reunions, after which Marcia automatically patted her yellow curls back into their proper places.

'Where's Hannah?'

'We don't know,' said Marcia, a little concerned. 'She
left the house shortly after luncheon. Always tells us when
she goes away. Hannah has not been very well. I'm rather
anxious about her.'

'If she hasn't shown up by dinner-time,' said Wallie,
'I'll do a little scouting for her — though I'm afraid I
wouldn't know where to look. Hannah isn't very gar-
rulous about her goings and comings.'

'She may have gone to see a doctor,' suggested Lucy.

'I don't think it's that,' said Marcia. 'She's worrying
about something.'

'Well — don't people worry about their health?' demanded Wallie. 'How about calling the hospital? She
might have gone to the clinic.'

'Here she comes *now*,' exclaimed Sally, who was facing
the open door to the street. 'I don't see there's much the
matter with her.'

Hannah was coming up the walk with a steady stride, a
smile on her face, chin up, shoulders high.

'Well, I'll be damned,' muttered Wallie. 'Whatever it
was that ailed her, she's got rid of it.'

'And I don't think it was at the hospital,' observed
Sally.

Hannah's decision to visit Paul had not been arrived at
on impulse. She had been debating the matter for days.
Something must be done to save Peter; and if so, it must
be done promptly, for he was coming home on the twelfth
to bid Lydia good-bye. He would be returning East within
a week.

There was no question about the renewed grip on life
and hope and happiness that had come to Paul Ward.

Wallie's report of his interview with his father — one of
the most touching and stirring experiences Hannah had
ever heard of — assured her that Paul had invited and
received some revitalizing energy not in the keeping of
medical science.

And at the same time that Paul was renewing his courage
and his health, Hannah's spiritual resources had run low.
The goal she had pursued was now quite inaccessible.
Everything she had worked for and sacrificed for had been
destroyed by forces beyond her control. How often,
through the years, Paul Ward had leaned full weight
against her, in his various predicaments. Now *he* had the
strength. She wondered if she might warm her chilling
faith at his reinvigorated fire. It would be a comfort to
talk with him.

Hannah hoped for a private interview. It was not going
to be an easy matter to arrange. You never knew when
Mrs. Ward or Wallie would drop in at the hospital for a
visit; not infrequently two and three times a day.

This afternoon she could account for their movements.
Mrs. Ward would remain at home waiting Sally's arrival.
Wallie had the car and was over at the Trimbles' for
luncheon. This seemed to be the occasion she had been
waiting for. Slipping quietly out of the house, she walked
to the street-car and made the long, jolting trip to the
hospital. There she had asked to see Professor Ward, and
apparently his consent had been phrased enthusiastically;
for, instead of a mere nod from the desk, Hannah was personally escorted to the door of Paul's room.

'Hannah!' he cried. 'I'm so glad you came!'

She stood by his bedside, holding his hand tightly, intently studying his face. His experience had aged him,
she thought; not into feebleness, though; into stability;
into a new phase of — of refinement.

'I have thought so much about you since I've been here,'
he said. 'Thank you, Hannah, for putting my boy on his
feet again — and his father, too. I have had an interesting

demonstration of "the will to power."... Do sit down.
Tell me about yourself. I'm afraid you're looking a bit
fagged. Are you well?'

'That's what I came to tell you, Paul. I am in trouble.'
She drew up a chair and tugged off her gloves. It wasn't
going to be easy to tell him, for she intended, this time,
to tell him *everything* — or almost everything. She couldn't
bring herself to report the friendship of their children. It
would have involved a violation of Sally's confidence.

'It's about Peter,' she began. 'You remember, don't
you, the boy you met, many years ago, the time we rode
home together on the train from Waterloo?'

'Certainly. What's he doing now? Must be of college
age. Fine lad, he was. He called you "aunt," I remember.
Isn't his mother able to handle him?'

'No,' said Hannah, 'she isn't.'

'But why are you fretting about it?'

There was a long pause.

'Because *I* am his mother.'

Paul stared into her heavy eyes and muttered an ejacula-
tion of amazement.

'Well — I'm bound to say you've done a very good job
of keeping this a secret for twenty years. Go on, Hannah.
Tell me all about it. Why didn't you want people to know?
He's legitimate, isn't he? You told me you were married.
Why didn't you own him?'

The nurse came in then and Paul told her he was not to
be disturbed for any reason whatsoever until he sent for her.

'It's a long story,' said Hannah. 'I hope I'll not wear
you out. But I've carried it as far as I can. I must confide it to someone very much stronger than I am, and get
some help. That's why I came to you.'

Paul settled back into his pillows and signed to her to
continue. She began in Surrey and told it all. Some of it
went rapidly, sketchily; some of it brought tears, as when
Philip died, and some of it brought smiles — Adele's comments on the risk involved in marrying Thomas. Paul's

eyes were indignant when Thomas left her stranded in
Chicago, and he muttered, 'The cad!'

'But I cannot join you in calling him that,' said Hannah.
'He was weak, self-indulged, spineless, but — not a cad.
At heart, a pretty fine fellow.'

The story proceeded; the visits to Waterloo, the decision
to have the boy brought up as 'Peter Edmunds,' the circumstances of Adele's return to the extraordinary drama,
Thomas's quick identification of his son at Bar Harbor
and the promise Eleanor had wrung from him that he
would not disclose his relationship to Peter.

'Do you mean to tell me that Mrs. Trimble has known
all about this? How did she happen to get into it?'

And then Hannah related that part of the story, rather
diffidently, for it was a delicate subject. Paul's eyes were
averted.

When she paused, he cleared his throat, and said huskily,
'Eleanor told me she felt deeply indebted to you, Hannah.
And — for the same reason — so should I.'

'It was the other way about,' insisted Hannah, shaking
her head. 'Mrs. Trimble was a valuable friend to me.'

But now it must be made clear that young Peter was no
weakling. Proudly, Hannah reported the little episodes
which testified to the sort of boy he was. It gratified her
immensely to tell Paul about the time Peter took his
punishment gallantly at the Military Academy, and showed
him the cherished paper containing the interview with
Colonel Livingstone.

'A youngster like that is well worth saving,' agreed Paul
stoutly.

So now we had come to the root of the matter. Hannah
went into full details about Thomas's proposal, which
would wreck every ambition she had nourished for her boy,
so moved by the distressfulness of it that she often had to
stop and collect herself before proceeding.

'And now I've come to you, Paul, because I think you
have laid fresh hold upon the power that I'm very much

afraid I've lost. I still believe in it, but I'm not strong
enough to use it.'

'Hannah' — Paul sat upright and laid his hand on hers.
'Are you willing to make a little investment?'

She smiled through her tears.

'I persuaded you to do that, once, didn't I?' she remembered.

'And it worked. Now you've a notion that I have regained some energy from "the Outside." Are you willing
to let me try to deal with your problem — and not ask me
how I'm going about it — or ask me, afterward, what I
did?'

'You mean — you're going to talk to Thomas?'

'You're not to ask questions,' repeated Paul firmly.
'Are you willing to trust me?'

Hannah regarded him soberly for a moment; then her
eyes brightened, and she smiled.

'Will you stop fretting about it?' he persisted.

'Yes, Paul,' she murmured. 'I think' — Hannah drew a
deep sigh — 'I think I feel relieved — already. But —
how are you going to get to Thomas — in your condition?'

'That's my affair!' growled Paul, 'and I'll thank you to
keep your promise — now and hereafter.'

Hannah drew a puckery smile.

'Remember the day you tried to break *yours?*'

'Yes — and you didn't let me. Keep that in mind. I
can be hard, too!'

She rose, and drew on her gloves.

'Put up your right hand!' demanded Paul. 'Repeat
after me: — "I believe that Peter will fulfill my dreams
for him."'

With uplifted face, and eyes that took no account of
Paul, Hannah raised her hand and said, almost exultantly,
'I believe that Peter will fulfill my dreams for him!'

'"I am not going to worry about him — any more!"'

'I am not going to worry about him — any more.'

Paul sank back and closed his eyes. 'There!' he muttered. 'Now go — and see that you keep your word! It won't make much difference if you break your promise to *me*. I'll forgive you. But see to it that you keep your word with *Them!* — or Him — or It! I'm sure you know more about that part of it than I do.'

Chapter XVIII

PETER had driven home. He would leave the coupé in Waterloo for his mother to use or sell as she liked. Then he would return by rail to New York and join Uncle Thomas for the cruise.

Lydia noted many changes in him. The boyish sparkle and enthusiasm seemed stifled. It wasn't that Peter had taken on an air of gloom or grimness, nor was he inattentive or taciturn; but what he had to say lacked spontaneity.

He talked freely about the contemplated voyage; exhibited maps, pictures, and the detailed shore itineraries which Uncle Thomas had toiled over with the expert assistance of the National Geographic people and other seasoned travelers.

'He must have gone to endless trouble,' reflected Lydia.

'I think it was mostly the bother and expense he has invested,' said Peter, 'that finally brought me to a decision. I couldn't let him down.'

'But you really do want to go, don't you, Peter?' Lydia put down the group of pictures of Tamatave in Madagascar, lowered her lorgnette, and regarded him earnestly. 'You're not doing this just to please Uncle Thomas, are you?'

Peter toyed with his watch-chain and meditated a fair reply.

'Well — that weighs heavily. Why shouldn't it? Perhaps, if I were entirely free to consult my own wishes, I might have postponed this trip until later. Naturally, Uncle Thomas feels that if we put it off until I have finished college, he might be too old to do it without fatigue, or I might find myself absorbed in my work — and not care to go, or —— '

'Or you might fall in love,' assisted Lydia, smiling. 'Maybe you have,' she added. 'I don't want to pry, but something tells me there's another reason for your tardiness in deciding to go. Almost any young fellow would grab at the chance, I should think.'

'No — it isn't that, Mother.' Peter dismissed the suggestion with a brief gesture. 'I don't mind telling you there is a girl who might have detained me, but — well — she's spoken for.'

'You met her in the East, I suppose?'

Peter nodded, feeling that it was near enough to the truth.

'I used to think you were fond of the pretty Ward girl. What was her name — Sally?' Lydia was trying too hard to make this sound casual and had overdone it a little, as she immediately suspected from the puzzled look Peter gave her.

'I'm surprised you had any trouble recalling her name,' he said meaningly. 'Surely Aunt Hannah has talked enough about her to you.'

'Forgive me, Peter. I'm afraid it really was a leading question. But you can't blame your mother for being interested.' She laughed softly. 'Anyway — that's about all a woman has to think about.'

'I don't mind telling you,' said Peter impulsively. 'I am fond of Sally; have been always; but she is in love with someone else. I should have thought Aunt Hannah knew. Sally has always been so confidential with her.'

'I've been led to believe,' said Lydia slowly, 'that Sally Ward liked you tremendously. Your Aunt Hannah says she is always talking about you.'

'That's the trouble,' muttered Peter. 'She's just a mighty good friend — on a sort of "pal" basis. Brother-'n'-sister kind of business.'

'Your Aunt Hannah, Peter —— '

'By the way, Mother' — Peter's voice was unsteady —
'there's a question I should like to ask you.'

Lydia suddenly tipped her head to listen, rose quickly,
and started toward the kitchen, explaining, as she went,
'Sorry, Peter, something's boiling over out here.'

Peter listened, but couldn't hear anything. He grinned,
rose, sauntered out into the hallway, lighted a cigarette.
The old fashioned front doorbell raised a loud clamor. He
answered it, and took in a special-delivery letter addressed
to himself and marked 'Personal.' It was brief, succinct,
mysterious, dated from the University Hospital, but written on official University stationery.

> DEAR MR. EDMUNDS:
> I wish to have a private talk with you on an urgent matter
> of mutual concern. I would come to see you but am unable
> to travel. May I suggest that upon receipt of this you come
> to me at your earliest convenience, informing no one. If
> this letter seems strange, be assured that it is no more un-
> usual for you to be in receipt of it than for me to be writing
> it.
>
> Very truly yours
> PAUL WARD

Peter's heart raced. What could Sally's father possibly
want with him? Would it be something about Sally? He
thrust the letter back into its envelope and into his pocket,
retraced his steps to the library.

'Didn't I hear the bell?' asked Lydia, who had again
busied herself with the cruise pictures.

'You just imagine you're hearing things this morning,
Mother,' drawled Peter. He gave her a slow, knowing wink,
but she blandly refused to be flustered. A very well-
balanced woman, he thought.

'I suppose you'll be prowling back into the jungle — in
Madagascar,' she said, intent upon a photograph of natives
in fantastic barbarity.

Peter's eyes brightened.

'That reminds me — I've to take some typhoid shots.'

Might as well run over to the University Hospital and have one today; get the business over with. Haven't any shopping you want to do, have you? I'll take you along.'

She studied him for a moment with brooding eyes, and shook her head.

'I must stay here and supervise dinner,' she said. 'The Wymans are coming, you know. Don't be late.'

'Very well — I'll start now, if you don't mind.'

Lydia went to the window and watched him go. From the same window, a few minutes before, she had watched the gray uniform of a postal employee receding down the street shortly after the doorbell had rung. Typhoid shots! Surely Peter was ingenious, and mighty quick on the trigger. The letter was from Sally, no doubt. She chuckled softly. Sally was going to give him some typhoid shots.

Patty Wyman drove slowly by the house, looking very lovely in the green ensemble that matched her swanky little roadster. She had called Peter on the telephone yesterday and he had said, 'I'll be seeing you.' But he hadn't — yet. Patty would be looking for him this afternoon, doubtless. Lydia sighed, smiled, drew the lace curtains together, went out through the kitchen into the garden, and clipped a basketful of roses. She wondered whether Peter would give himself away when he returned. Probably not. He was pretty deep. She would say, 'I hope they didn't hurt you.' And he would rub his arm, and wince a little, maybe, and reply, 'Not very much.' And she would say, with a wink, 'I hope you'll be able to eat your dinner, son.' But he probably wouldn't tell her what she wanted to know. Well — why should he? She'd always had secrets from *him!*

Peter felt that he would have recognized Professor Ward, but he had certainly changed a great deal. Of course, his recent illness would account for much of that. The Professor Ward he had met and instantly liked when he was a small boy had seemed so youthful. It had been difficult to

think of him as a professor. The graying man in the wheeled
chair was the same person, frosted. The eyes were as
friendly, the mouth as mobile, the dimple in the chin —
Sally had one, too — was as deep.

The greeting was without constraint.

'Sit down, won't you? Thanks for coming. Much water
has gone over the dam since I saw you last. You've grown
to be quite a stalwart fellow.'

'I hope you're nearly well, sir. It was good of you to ask
me in. If there's anything I can do for you, I'll be glad.'

'Peter, I am about to intrude upon your private affairs. It is not my custom, and I am not quite sure where to
begin. But if you will be patient, I'll try to be brief.'

'Take your time, sir.... And thanks for your interest
in me. I'm sure it will be to my advantage.'

'I hope so.... Some twenty years ago there appeared at
my home a woman in distress. She had just been dis-
charged from this hospital where she had borne a child.
I was not informed of that fact at the time, though my
wife knew. Perhaps she felt it might make some difference
in my attitude toward our new maid if I were told. At all
events, I did not know; nor would I have cared had I known;
for the woman was capable, honest, clean, and extraordinarily kind.'

'My Aunt Hannah,' said Peter.

Paul Ward smiled, bowed slightly, and went on.

'Hannah found us poor as church-mice; poorer, for
church-mice do not borrow money they cannot pay, and
aren't humiliated with monthly bills they aren't able to
meet. This remarkable woman took us all in hand, helped
us organize our home on a self-sustaining basis, saw us
through every conceivable predicament; and, in short,
made herself so indispensable that to have lost her would
have been little short of a tragedy. Now she is in trouble,
and it amounts almost to a personal grief to me. I thought
you ought to know about it. Perhaps you might think of
something we could do.'

'Anything, sir,' declared Peter. 'I'm very fond of my Aunt Hannah. What's the difficulty, please?'

'It's this boy. You see — it was quite impossible for her to keep him, so he was given to other people.'

'And they have mistreated him?'

'No — no, that isn't it.' Paul shook his head, gazed for some time out at the window, and then returned to his narrative. 'Perhaps I should say — though you unquestionably know this — that Hannah Parmalee was brought up with the most inflexible ideas on the subject of social caste. Her father was a gardener. She had spent her early life as parlormaid, housekeeper, general servant. I don't think she ever rebelled against it, but it was her earnest hope that her child might grow up to take a less difficult place in the scheme o' things. I think this is about the only ambition she has ever cherished, the hope that her boy would achieve rank, position, honor.'

Peter was listening attentively, his lips parted a little. He leaned forward in his chair, resting his weight on his elbows. Paul lifted a hand with outspread white fingers, as to say he was not quite ready for questions.

'And so — she never disclosed herself as the boy's mother, feeling that if the relationship were known, it might prove to be an obstacle to his social and business success. . . . Now — neither you nor I are in a position to realize just what manner of heart-breaking sacrifice this would entail, because we have never been mothers, and aren't going to be. There has been omitted from our nature all the machinery for understanding that sort of mental anguish. But I think we have enough imagination to guess what it must have meant to Hannah, all through the years, to see her boy caressed by and caressing another mother, while she stood by, wistful, silent, hopeful ——'

'How do you mean — "stood by"?' Peter's voice was husky. 'Was she able to see him?'

Paul nodded.

'And he never knew?'

'No — not until now.'

Peter stared hard at the floor, swallowed convulsively, and muttered, 'Incredible!'

'It *is*, rather.'

'But — but ——' Peter shook his head decisively. 'You see, sir, this can't possibly be true. I know who my mother is. There really couldn't be any mistake about *that*, you know!'

'All the more credit to Hannah for the way she kept the faith with you.'

Peter lifted almost indignant eyes.

'Why are you telling me this if she didn't want me to know?'

'Because, you see, Hannah has dreamed for all the years of your amounting to something important. It was for this she gave you up; for this she sacrificed her rights as a mother. She does not know I am telling you, and I strongly suspect she would feel I had done her and you a grave injury. But you've a right to know what it has cost your mother to see you grow up to a point where you might live a useful, perhaps eminent life — and what unutterable grief it has caused her to see you throw that opportunity away!'

Peter dug his finger-tips hard into his temples.

'Aunt Hannah is *my mother!*' he muttered. 'Uncle Thomas is *my father!* So — *that* accounts for it! It's true! ...*God!*'

'It is a severe shock, naturally,' agreed Paul, after a little silence. 'But it might be ever so much worse, you know. You're not making the discovery that you are illegitimate, nor are you confronted with a bad heritage. I know almost nothing about your father, beyond the fact that he is a person of large wealth, wide travel, and university training. But any young fellow who would be ashamed of having a woman like Hannah for his mother wouldn't deserve to have any relatives. Peter — of all the people I have known intimately, your mother is one of the bravest, one of the wisest.'

'I know she is all of that, sir,' Peter assented in a barely audible voice. 'It isn't that I have any wish to disown the relationship. But — it does bowl one over a bit.'

'Obviously — and it will take a little time before you can be expected to accommodate yourself to the idea.'

Peter glanced at his watch.

'I suppose I should go and see her at once. Is that your wish, sir?'

'No, no, Peter! This is something that needs to be thought through with care. I learned about it only yesterday. I have had no time to give the problem my considered judgment, whatever that might be worth. But I doubt the wisdom of your rushing off to see Hannah.'

'Did she come here to tell you the story?'

'Yes. Hannah had carried her burden of perplexity as far as she could bear it. She came to me because — well, there wasn't anybody else available. She was reluctant to begin it; but, once fairly launched, she told it all.'

Peter found himself wondering how much discussion there had been on his friendship with Sally, but decided not to inquire.

'Did she tell you how I happened to meet Uncle — my father? Did my Aunt Adele take me to Bar Harbor purposely to bring us together?'

'No, that was an accident. And, by the way, Mrs. Adele Moore is not your aunt. Your mother was employed in the home of her people when they were both young women.'

'Aunt Adele is no relation to me?' Peter's face was a study in mystification. 'Then why did she bother with me at all?'

'The most interesting part of your mother's career, Peter, is the quality of her friendships and the lasting impression she has made on the lives of many people presumably not of her station. Did you ever hear of Philip Raymond?'

Peter vaguely remembered the name as one of his Aunt Hannah's childhood friends.

'Perhaps I would better tell you a little about that,' said Paul. 'It helps to an understanding of Hannah. You know all about her peculiar views on non-combativeness, non-resistance, and everything that goes with that state of mind.'

Peter smiled a little.

'And she means it, too,' he commented. 'It hasn't been a mere academic theory with her.'

'She means it,' echoed Paul seriously, 'and she has some very excellent reasons for believing that her theory is sound. Perhaps that is why she has felt so utterly forsaken over your plan to be a person of leisure. Hannah always knew that if she didn't fight back, didn't enforce her rights, she would ultimately get what she wanted — and more — through the personal power generated by this passive attitude toward antagonisms. The one great reward she sought was to be realized through *you!* And now it had begun to appear that this reward would not be granted. The disappointment was breaking down the very structure and digging up the foundation of the faith upon which she had predicated every action of her life! It wasn't only that *you* were slated to be a failure — according to her estimate of success; it was going to be a demonstration that her whole philosophy of life was an indefensible sophistry.'

'And this Philip Raymond?'

'That's what I mean to tell you. Philip Raymond was responsible for Hannah's views. She loved him devotedly, believed everything he said, ordered her whole life after that pattern. It's a tender story, and I think you ought to hear it.'

Paul Ward had been deeply touched by Hannah's narration of that idyllic romance and its pathetic dénouement. Quietly, but impressively, he recited the little epic while Peter listened with brooding eyes. When it was finished, they both sat silently for a moment. Then Paul said, 'The question you are facing now, Peter, seems to be reduced to the simple proposition: which one of your parents are you going to disappoint? It is obvious that you must disappoint one of them.'

Peter slowly nodded his head, without looking up.

'You will have to balance the importance of your father's prospect of a cruise with you,' continued Paul soberly, 'against the importance of your mother's twenty years of sacrifice for you.'

'I see that,' muttered Peter defenselessly.

'You have your mother's faith to look out for, too, my boy. That's decidedly important, I think.'

'To *her*, yes — of course,' agreed Peter.

'It might become important to you, too,' declared Paul. 'It's an odd thing, but — you know Hannah has something, don't you? It is infectious. Once you've experimented with it, a little, you'll discover that it's by no means a mere theory!'

Peter lifted his eyes and searched Paul Ward's pallid face.

'You don't mean,' he demanded, 'that *you* believe in it!'

'Yes! *I* believe in it! I am not a mystic, Peter. I do not consider myself a religious person. I know nothing about theology. I haven't any convictions on the subject of Deity — as to how He, They, or It subsist. But it has been definitely proved to me — thanks to Hannah — that there is a peculiar power available to those who are willing to accept it — and make use of it.'

Peter drew a long breath — and smiled.

'I'm — I'm surprised,' he said, after a little delay.

'Well — if you ever have urgent occasion to try this out, and do it honestly, making some genuine investment as a suitable certificate of your sincerity, you'll be *still more surprised!*'

'If you don't mind my asking, sir — did you ever get what you wanted — by this process?'

'Yes!'

'It's hard to believe, sir. My mind doesn't behave that

way at all. Everything in me simply bristles at the thought
of any practical reliance on the supernatural.'

'So did mine, Peter. I thought it was a mess of precious
nonsense.'

Peter rose, thrust his hands deep in his pockets, and paced
the length of the room.

'Well — be that as it may — I must not let my — my
mother down. I'll tell her I'm going back to college in the
fall. I may never amount to much, but I can try.'

Paul had a sudden impulse to reach out his hand and con-
gratulate Peter on his decision; then thought better of it.
Peter was not the sort to relish applause. He was Hannah's boy.

'I presumed you would adopt that course,' said Paul.
'However — if you are agreeable to the suggestion, be in no
hurry to talk to your mother. It occurs to me that Hannah
might be seriously embarrassed if you went to her with an
open acknowledgment of your relationship. Indeed, that
will be exactly what she does *not* want! She has gone
through a great deal to keep her secret; she thinks it would
be to your serious disadvantage if it were known she is your
mother. I think you would far better let it remain a secret,
for her sake. Convey the information to her, any way you
like, that you have decided to continue your college course
and your professional training; but don't upset Hannah by
telling her you know you are her son. I'm afraid that would
spoil it all! She doesn't want you to know. Better respect
her wishes.'

'Perhaps that's wise, sir,' admitted Peter.

'Don't tell *anybody*,' urged Paul.

'Not even my mother?'

'Meaning your foster mother? No — not even Mrs.
Edmunds. Hannah kept this costly secret for your sake.
Now you continue to keep it — for her sake.'

'I'll do as you say, sir, at least for the present.'

'I think this is all going to work out very happily,
Peter.'

'I hope so, sir. I'll go now. My mother has guests this evening. She will be expecting me home.'

'You'll be entering Sheffield, this fall?'

'Yes, sir — majoring in Chemistry.'

'Your mother said that was your pet interest. I wish you well, Peter.'

There was a tap on the door, and it was pushed open a little way. Paul glanced up, frowning slightly.

'Come!' he said, not very hospitably.

She had never looked so thoroughly adorable in her life. It was a very simple, girlish, white frock, the blue scarf matching her eyes.

Hesitating in the doorway, she glanced from one to the other mystifiedly.

'Oh, it's you, Sally,' said Paul. 'Come on in, dear. Perhaps you remember Peter Edmunds. I think you played with him, a time or two, when you went with Hannah to Waterloo. Mr. Edmunds has been talking to me about his college course — this fall.'

For a moment Sally stood staring at Peter. Then her lips parted in a radiant smile. She walked toward him, holding out both hands.

'Peter!' she said softly.

He extended his hands to hers, but she did not take them. Instead, with outspread fingers she reached up and laid them on his shoulders. Putting his arms around her, he drew Sally very close. She looked up earnestly into his face.

'You're not going away?' she murmured, shaking her head childishly.

Peter's hands were trembling, as they tightened their hold.

Paul Ward watched the strange tableau with open mouth and astounded eyes. They had forgotten his presence.

'I didn't suppose you cared that much, dear,' said Peter huskily.

Sally's arms encircled his neck.

'Care?' she whispered. 'Oh — Peter!'

He gathered her tightly to him and kissed her — a kiss that threatened to become permanent. Then, flushed and breathless, Sally drew away, and suddenly became conscious of her father. She glanced toward him, the tears sparkling in her eyes; and Peter, considerably flustered, turned to face him, wondering what manner of explanation was in order.

Paul grinned, and scratched his head.

'Well' — he drawled, 'I'm glad I had the forethought to introduce you to each other.'

Then they laughed, almost hysterically.

'Come here, baby,' said Paul.

Sally stooped and kissed him. Peter, standing by with her hand clasped tightly in his, wondered what her father might be thinking about all this. It was one thing for Professor Ward to extol his housekeeper as a woman of courage and wisdom; it would be quite another thing for Professor Ward to welcome the housekeeper's son into his family circle. Peter wished that Sally's father might have been given a chance to digest this a little. It seemed like taking him at a disadvantage.

With one arm around Sally, Paul Ward extended his hand to Peter, looking him squarely in the eyes.

'I believe you can be trusted,' he said firmly, 'to take good care of my girl.'

Peter's heart bounded with gratitude. It was not going to make any difference to Sally's father that he was Hannah's son. His eyes lighted with happiness.

'Thank you, sir!' he exclaimed. 'I'll do my best.'

Paul sank back into his pillows, smiling wearily.

'Now, you two had better run along,' he said, in a voice that betrayed his weakness. 'I've had about all of you that I can take — for one session.'

'Sally, what are you doing, for the rest of the day?' asked Peter impulsively.

'Whatever you say, dear.'

'How about driving home with me for dinner? I want my mother to know. I'll bring you back afterward.'

'May I, Daddy?'

'Of course,' consented Paul. 'Quite the thing to do. Peter's mother will be glad to know you are both happy. Will this be a surprise to her?'

'Very much so,' said Peter. 'It was to me, too, sir. You see, Sally and I have been close friends for a long time, but I didn't know she cared — not the way *I* cared.'

'Daddy, he's the stupidest boy in the whole world.' Sally slipped her arm through Peter's and teased him with an impish smile. 'Will you tell Wallie, when he comes to pick me up, that I'm provided for? ... Peter, perhaps we should drive around by our house and let me get my coat, if we're to be out late. Mother will want to see you, too, I know.'

Peter's brows contracted a little.

'You may wear mine, if it's chilly. I think I'd rather meet your mother when there's more time. Is that all right?'

Sally nodded.

'*Everything*,' she replied softly, 'is all right — now.'

There was a light in the kitchen when Sally quietly entered the house shortly after midnight. It would be Hannah waiting up for her. She meant to confide her great happiness to Hannah, of course, but had hoped she might be allowed to go directly to her room tonight without encountering anyone. The joy of this moment was too tenderly sweet to be shared.

She expected to remember every detail of that evening's experience as long as she lived.

They had left the hospital at four, decorously avoiding each other's eyes and hands until out of the building and safe in Peter's coupé.

'It's wonderful, darling!' murmured Peter. 'I can't believe it!' He took her hand in both of his and searched her eyes.

'Come, Peter,' she had said gently. 'Push that little button and start your engine. Let's not do anything silly in plain sight of all these windows.'

They had carried themselves with great dignity until the town had been escaped and the open road was before them. Sally slipped over very close beside him.

'I'll bet you haven't had a glimpse of Lincoln Lake since you've got home,' said Peter. 'It isn't far out of the way.'

'Sure we shan't keep your mother's dinner waiting?' wondered Sally dreamily.

They had followed the gravel road then to the lake, stopping in the shade of a clump of maples. He had drawn her into his arms.

'Darling,' she had said, after a long sigh of contentment, 'tell me about it. How did you happen to decide not to go away? Why did you come to see Daddy?'

Peter had been silent for a moment, apparently trying to make up his mind how much to confide.

'Sally, dear,' he said, measuring his words, 'it seems that my whole life has been a tangle of secrets that have been kept from me, for one reason and another. But there aren't going to be any secrets between *us!* Your father sent for me today. He wanted to tell me why he thought I should carry on with college and try to make something of myself.'

'I wonder if Hannah had been talking to him.'

'Yes — she had.' Peter's voice was unsteady.

'That was odd. I'm awfully glad she did, Peter, dear.' Sally had laid her palm caressingly against his cheek. 'But — really — she didn't have a right to interfere in your affairs.'

Peter nodded his head.

'Yes — she had a right to, Sally. She is my mother.'

Sally knew she would never forget that moment; Peter's far-away look, her own sense of having been stunned to speechlessness. She had looked up into his sober face with astonished eyes.

'Who told you?' she whispered.

'Your father.'

'So — that's why your Uncle Thomas ——

'Yes — that's why he wanted me to be with him.'

'I can't believe it, Peter. How did Hannah ever manage to keep this a secret?'

'Well — the circumstances all seemed to conspire. My mother took me when her own baby died.'

Sally had smiled sympathetically.

'Mrs. Edmunds is still your mother, I see.'

'Yes — we decided today that it would be better not to let Aunt Hannah know that I have been told. Your father thinks it would make her unhappy. Do you think you can carry it off, with Aunt Hannah, and treat her the same as ever, Sally?'

'I'll try. It won't be too difficult. Hannah has always seemed like another mother to me, dear.'

'And you're not disappointed — now that you know?'

Sally had tightened her arm around his neck.

'No, Peter. It won't make any difference. I'm glad you told me. And — I'll keep your secret. Shall I tell Daddy that I know?'

'As you like, darling.'

'Perhaps I'd better wait until he brings it up.'

'Maybe that would be better.'

'I don't believe I'll tell my mother, Peter. She might find it difficult to avoid letting Hannah know. It might spoil everything.'

'Maybe. You ought to know. Perhaps you're right.'

'Do you see what time it is? We must go.' Sally had sat up straight, patting her tousled hair. 'Your mother will think me a fright, Peter.'

'You can blame it on me. Shall we forget everything now, except that we have each other?'

And so — they had forgotten everything, except that they had each other. Peter had driven the rest of the way to Waterloo at a speed that did not encourage conversation.

They had arrived a little late. Mrs. Edmunds had met
them at the door.

'Sally Ward, Mother,' said Peter. 'You remember,
don't you?' He stopped and kissed her; then whispered
something in her ear.

Mrs. Edmunds had seemed very happy about it. She
had kissed Sally tenderly.

'Peter has always wanted you, dear,' she said softly.
'I'm very glad for you both.' She smiled into their eyes.
'You make a handsome pair. There can be no doubt about
that.... Come, now. The Wymans are here. Dinner is
waiting. Peter, show Sally up to my room.'

'I'd forgotten,' said Peter, as they ran upstairs arm in
arm. 'Patty Wyman's here. Be specially nice to her,
darling.'

'Is she the girl you once said had big feet?' laughed Sally.

'You remember everything, don't you?'

'Perhaps Patty would have preferred I hadn't come.'

Peter dismissed Patty with a shrug and a flick of the
fingers, and they went down to the old-fashioned parlor
where introductions were had, Mrs. Edmunds announcing,
quietly, 'Sally Ward — Peter's fiancée.' They had all been
very cordial, Patty almost boisterously so.

'Why, Peter!' she exclaimed. 'What an old meanie you
are — not even to have told the neighbors!'

And then Peter had grinned and confessed, 'I've only
known it myself since about four o'clock.' How amazed
they had been!

She couldn't remember much about what they had had to
eat. Peter had carved the roast and had done it expertly.
She had sat at the other end of the table beside Mrs. Edmunds, who had leaned close enough to say, while Susie was
brushing crumbs, 'It will be sweet to have a daughter.'
And Sally had tried hard not to think about what she had
heard, fearing her puzzlement might show in her face.

The drive home — how tender! She wanted now to slip
up to her room and be alone with the day's ecstasies.

But Hannah would know she had come and would think it very queer if she went up without pausing to speak. Her heart raced a little. Hannah was such a knowing person. She always guessed what you were thinking about. You didn't have to tell her. She knew.

'Not gone to bed yet?' called Sally, from the kitchen doorway.

Hannah put down her book on the table and smiled a welcome.

'Wallie said you had gone away with somebody — for dinner. I was a bit anxious about you, dear. It's late.'

'You can't imagine where I've been. I accidentally ran into Peter. He'd driven over on an errand — something for his mother. Then he wanted me to go home with him for dinner.'

Hannah's eyes widened with surprise.

'How was Peter?' she asked, trying hard to keep her voice steady.

'Wonderful!' Sally leaned on the back of Hannah's chair; and, bending forward, laid her flushed cheek against Hannah's ear. 'Got something to tell you, darling,' she murmured childishly. 'Give you three guesses.'

She could feel a little tremor run over Hannah, a succession of stifled sobs.

'You — and — Peter?' asked Hannah thickly.

Sally pressed her face hard against Hannah's and nodded her head.

Then Hannah turned, put an arm around Sally, looked up in perplexity, and said, 'But — Peter can't take care of you, dear. He's — going away.'

'Peter has changed his mind, Hannah. He's not going. He expects to carry on in college — and be a chemist — and everything, just the way you'd hoped.'

Hannah drew a deep, shuddering sigh that seemed to throw off an insupportable weight. Then she clutched Sally's hands hard.

'Did he decide that — because — because he didn't want to leave *you?*'

'Well' — Sally smiled archly — 'perhaps that did have something to do with it.'

Hannah rose, clasped one hand tightly with the other, and slowly paced the room, apparently anxious to control her pent-up emotion.

'I wanted Daddy to see Peter. I had expected to go to the hospital anyway, you know.'

Hannah leaned a hand against the wall and went suddenly pale.

'Well,' she said hoarsely. 'Did your father see him?'

'Daddy's crazy about him!'

'Does he know you and Peter are engaged?'

'Yes — we told him. He's glad.'

Retracing her steps unsteadily to the table, Hannah sat down and cupped her face with both hands. She was deeply moved.

'Aren't you pleased, Hannah?'

'Yes, dear; I'm pleased. I'm glad you told your father.'

'He was wonderful about it.'

'Your father,' said Hannah fervently, '*is a wonderful man!*'

Chapter XIX

It had turned quite cold in the night, and when Lydia was roused at seven by the exasperating racket Susie was making at the furnace a powdery snow was being driven aimlessly about by a crazy gale.

She stood by the window for a moment, shivering and depressed; then went back to bed to wait until the heat should begin to come up attended by the inevitable whiff of noxious coal gas.

So — winter had come again, dismayingly prompt with its sullen gray sky. The winters, reflected Lydia, were growing longer; arriving earlier — this was only the thirteenth of November — and hanging on tiresomely through what had used to be spring. She wished this might have been a bright morning. A streak of genial sunshine would have lightened her mood. She felt old, and a bit terrified.

Yesterday afternoon Mr. Jennings had seemed so pessimistic about the country's financial condition. It hadn't been so much what Mr. Jennings actually said as the spent manner in which he betrayed his forebodings with the beaten eyes and jerky gestures of an old man who has just missed the last train.

'Are things as bad,' she had asked, 'as the papers have been saying?' And Mr. Jennings had scowled grimly, rubbed his chin hard with shaky fingers, and replied, 'Well — it hasn't reached the proportions of a panic yet; except, of course, for people who had been playing the market.'

Lydia had tried to be comforted by that, even in the face of the banker's gloom, for she hadn't played the market.

She wouldn't have known how. The whole business was as incomprehensible to her as the jargon of polo.

'It's just a Wall Street mishap, then?' she had observed brightly.

Mr. Jennings had pulled an indulgent grin.

'A Wall Street mishap, Mrs. Edmunds,' he solemnly replied, in the tone of the committal service, 'is always an inconvenience to large numbers of people. And so far as playing the market is concerned, that has not been distinctly a New York recreation. Almost everybody is involved in it.'

'I didn't know,' Lydia had confessed.

'Of course not — and it's to your credit. You see, Mrs. Edmunds, the whole country has been spending money that had no existence in fact. Wages have been good, credit has been easy. It has become a settled habit, with all sorts of people, to be pleased and contented with possessions on which they had paid a mere pittance. Almost nobody owned anything outright. Most of the nation's business was done on paper. Everybody had his safety-deposit locker stuffed with pretty pictures of large sums of money. Now that the bottom has dropped out of this picture business, they're all scared. Credit has suddenly closed up like a steel trap.'

'Are my bonds — all right?' she had inquired anxiously.

'For the present — yes. You are fortunate not to have owned any speculative stocks.'

Mr. Jennings had been buzzed to the telephone then and she had taken a rather unceremonious leave when it became obvious that he had said everything he was likely to say to her and had more important problems on his distracted mind.

She had left the bank then, mentally calling the roll of the people who were probably wondering what was to become of them. Hannah had often spoken of the Trimbles' keen interest in the ups-and-downs of stock speculation. They had lived extravagantly. It would be difficult for them to alter their habits. And there was Thomas Bradford! Peter had often remarked that Uncle Thomas grew very fidgety if the market was cutting capers. It would be too bad if Thomas lost his money, for he didn't have much else. She wondered if her brother Henry — but no; it wasn't likely that Henry would be involved. Henry didn't even carry coins loose in his pocket, but kept his change in a little purse. Before he spent a nickel, he had to unbutton the flap on his hip-pocket to get to the purse. She felt satisfied about Henry's immunity from the disaster that had overtaken the gamblers.

Then Lydia had paid the gas and electric-light bills and walked home, haunted by the first sensation of insecurity that she had faced in her whole lifetime. At the old home, when she was a girl, they had rigidly economized, but she couldn't remember that they had ever been frightened. Jasper had turned a few sharp corners, early in their married life, but if he had fretted seriously over it he hadn't let her know. As a widow, there had never been a moment's concern about money. Sometimes when she was lonely and blue she would comfort herself with the assurance that at least there would always be a good living. Life wasn't always so rich and full as she might have wished, but she would be sheltered and fed and comfortable if she lived to be a hundred.

Arriving home at three-thirty she had found a letter from Peter. He was well, happy in his work, and grateful for the check. He hoped her affairs were in good condition. Everyone was worried about the crash. How did she feel about her funds? Perhaps she had better plan an economy program. 'I can do with much less than you have been sending me,' he had continued. 'I have been very frugal lately; quite miserly, indeed, now that I've opened a savings account.'

Lydia had smiled at that. Peter was thinking of marriage.

> I am unhappy about Uncle Thomas [he went on]. He has lost heavily. Of course, it won't be poverty. I mean —

Uncle Thomas will still eat, and buy two tickets so he can travel in a Pullman drawing-room. But he has lost enough to make him sick. He wasn't very well, anyway. I didn't want to worry you, so said nothing much about it at the time, but Uncle Thomas was dreadfully let down by my refusal to go with him on the cruise. He wasn't cross or indignant; just inconsolably hurt. Maybe I did not handle it considerately enough. I was so hilarious over Sally that I fear I talked more about my own happiness than his disappointment. Then came this crack-up in the stock market. He seemed dazed, incredulous. It will be hard for him to reorganize his habits.

I have a letter from him today. He is at Asheville for what he calls 'a little recuperation.' But it's more serious than that, for he writes from a sanitarium, and I know you couldn't drag him into that sort of place unless there was something the matter. I'm undecided what part I ought to play. If I go down there to see him, I know he will be embarrassed. It will only add to his discomfort if I leave my work to go popping in on him with my pity when there's really nothing I can do. But he has been so kind, and I have seemed so ungrateful. What do you think? Shall I go to him?

Lydia had sat for a long time gazing dully at the letter, wondering what would become of Thomas. People who had nothing but money were in a very awkward position if they lost much of it. But the last thing Thomas Bradford would want was anyone's pity — Peter's least of all. It would make him feel old and helpless.

She was glad now that Peter did not know just how deeply he was indebted to Thomas. For years the monthly check had arrived early, to be deposited to the account set aside for Peter. The June remittance had been the last one. Thomas had not written to explain that there wouldn't be any more, doubtless taking it for granted that Lydia would understand.

Well — it wasn't as if Peter would have to leave college because Thomas had stopped paying for it. Lydia knew she would not be able to continue remittances in the same figures, but she could give him all he actually required. It comforted her to note Peter's suggestion about a reduction of his allowance. She had been wondering how she was going to tell him.

The bedroom was warming now and Lydia dressed to go down. The ground was white. It was Hannah's customary day to come. Perhaps she would change her mind when she saw the weather. But maybe not. Hannah had taken on new energy ever since Peter had decided to go back to school. It was amazing; she was a different woman. And she had seemed so unaccountably elated over the engagement of Sally and Peter. That was odd, for Hannah had never enthused over the prospect of the match; not that she didn't like Sally, but she wanted Peter kept away from the Wards. And now that Peter had done the very thing Hannah had been at such pains to forestall, she was fairly sitting on top of the world! Lydia had quizzed her about it, half-playfully, and Hannah — a little flustered — had said, 'I suppose it was destined to happen, and we may as well make the best of it' — but she didn't have the appearance of a person resigning herself submissively to an inexorable fate. She was pipping with joy! There was something more, back of all this, believed Lydia, that she herself hadn't learned.

Hannah literally blew in at eleven, rosy and out of breath. Susie was ordered to make a pot of coffee and give the furnace another punch.

'I surely needed you, dear,' said Lydia, stirring the grate-fire. 'I feared you might not come.'

'Why not? It's a very bracing day.'

'I'm glad somebody thinks so.'

Hannah laid a hand on Lydia's shoulder.

'What is it, dear?' she asked gently. 'Money — maybe?'

'Not mine. It seems to be safe enough. But so many people are in trouble; friends of ours.'

'Who — for instance?'

'Well, there's Thomas, for one. I don't suppose it's part of my job to worry over Thomas, but ——' Lydia paused. 'What about him?' demanded Hannah. 'Tell me.'

The porter had made several trips to the vestibule, staggering through the swaying car with heavy bags and cases. It had begun to look as if almost everybody on the train would be getting off at Asheville. He had come now for Hannah's baggage. There wasn't much of it — a suitcase and an overnight bag. The porter insisted on rubbing her shoes, and when she inquired nervously whether they were almost there he said, 'Yas'm; in five minutes.' Hannah's query was entirely superfluous, for the passengers were pulling on their coats; but she had wanted to try out her voice to see if it would sound as hollow and indecisive as she had feared. And it fulfilled her forebodings, sounding as if she were guilty of some crime and expected to be met by the police at the station.

Ever since wakening, long before daylight, Hannah had been growing more and more stampeded by the thought of her errand. When the conductor stopped to return the unused portion of her ticket, she would have been very glad if he had said, 'Sorry, madam, but you're on the wrong train. Your transportation reads to Asheville, and we're not going there.'

It wasn't as if her decision to see Thomas had been arrived at impetuously. The idea of going to him had not begun to take on tangible form until she was on the way home from her day with Lydia. Peter had wondered, in his letter, whether he ought to visit his Uncle Thomas. Lydia and Hannah had both agreed with him that this might have the wrong effect. It might only add to Thomas's humiliation and sense of defeat if Peter, who had so idolized him, made a journey to witness his hero's collapse.

But *someone* should have a friendly talk with Thomas. He was sick, worried, lonely. It was not right to neglect him. Gradually the conviction deepened in Hannah's mind that she herself should go. The fact that Thomas had once neglected her at a time of her most urgent need of him was quite beside the point and could be forgotten.

Next morning, Hannah had sought a word with Paul. She found him in the library studiously intent upon the paper which he had carried with him from the breakfast-table, contrary to his usual custom. Briefly she had confided her dilemma while he listened only half attentively.

'By all means,' he had urged, with a businesslike promptness that discouraged any extended debate. 'By all means go, Hannah. It will be a great satisfaction to you both. Thomas's illness provides a very good reason for a friendly interview.' His eyes wandered again to the newspaper. 'You should plan to go at once.'

'I'm not quite sure,' Hannah replied uncertainly. 'It isn't enough to go there in a friendly attitude. I ought to have something helpful to say to him. I should like to be able to do something for him.'

Aware now that Hannah was seriously pressing for advice, rather than his mere consent to her journey, Paul had put down the paper, carefully polished his glasses, and deliberated.

'You might not be able to do anything — directly,' he announced judicially. 'But in the face of your efforts to conciliate, Thomas may be able to do something for *himself*. Obviously, what he needs now is a restoration of his self-confidence, his self-esteem. Doubtless the memory of his bad treatment of you has been a very sore and sensitive spot in his mind, all through the years. You're the only person who can help him heal that old lesion.'

'Is it so very important that the old lesion be healed *now?* Perhaps it doesn't bother him any more. It has been a long time.'

'Yes — but there have been plenty of distractions. Now that Thomas has plenty of time for reviewing his mistakes, the thing he did to you will loom large and hurt very painfully ... Hannah, it might be interesting to inquire'—

Paul's eyes narrowed thoughtfully as he paused to find the right words for a new idea — 'It might be interesting to inquire whether the person who has been dreadfully wronged, injured, defrauded, is not morally obliged to assist the other fellow in relieving himself of his intolerable remorse.'

Hannah nodded an agreement to this, adding, in a tone barely audible, that not many people would find it easy to do.

'No, not easy — but far easier than for the aggressor to make peace with the person he has wronged. This is part of your own philosophy, Hannah, and that philosophy is sound. See here! You have always maintained that the person who, having been injured or defrauded, makes no effort to avenge himself or reclaim his losses, achieves a peculiar strength of spirit. That is a demonstrable fact. You and I both know it's true. Now! — isn't it just as logical that the person who has perpetrated that fraud and inflicted that injury — and has been permitted to do it without hindrance or threat of redress — is *weakened* in spirit? And, if so, is it not the duty of the strong one to come to the rescue?'

Hannah found herself deeply stirred.

'Oh, Paul,' she exclaimed, 'that's magnificent!'

He tipped back in his chair, interlaced his fingers behind his head, and, smiling into her eyes, said slowly: 'I suppose that this might be called the highest, the costliest, the final degree in the practice of personal disarmament, personal peace, private courage. You can do it, of course, for you've trained yourself in that school. Go to Thomas, Hannah. Then — I think you can feel that you've — *graduated!*'

There was a considerable silence. Hannah rose and walked toward the door, where, with her hand on the knob, she turned to say, 'That was quite distressing news, wasn't it?'

Paul's brows contracted into a dark frown. He tapped the paper with his glasses.

'I suppose you mean — about Ellis's financial smash — and attempted suicide?'

Hannah nodded.

'Well?' growled Paul, deep in his throat.

Hannah drew a puckery little smile.

'Got what was coming to him, didn't he?' demanded Paul gruffly.

'I was just wondering,' said Hannah gently. 'Perhaps *you* might earn one of those diplomas, too.'

For the first few moments they hardly realized what they were saying to each other, so occupied were they in their candid appraisals of the graying hair and the deeply chiselled lines which mapped the long journey they had made through the years since the day of their separation.

Hannah would have known him anywhere. The things she had admired most had remained practically unchanged — the quadrant of spider-webbish crow's-feet that had always added a touch of maturity and something almost like sagacity to the sidelong look he gave you; the rugged temples, where, under the pallor, a blue vein now pulsed ominously; the square chin that had always lied a little when presenting Thomas as a man of determination; the close-set ears, finely modeled, patrician — the ears he had bequeathed to Peter in such an unmistakably identifiable manner that Hannah had sometimes wondered if the ears wouldn't some day tell the secret of their relationship to the most indifferent observer; the soft, drawling voice that seemed always to be saying, no matter by what words, 'After all, what's the difference ... Why bother? ... Forget it ... Take the cash and let the credit go.' There had been times when it had seemed a very comforting voice.

'This is an unexpected pleasure, Hannah,' Thomas was saying evenly. 'I wish I were in a position to show you about. It is quite beautiful here. I shall arrange some drives for you — if you will permit me.'

It wasn't going to be easy to talk about the things that

really mattered. Thomas quietly, courteously directed the conversation for an hour, avoiding any mention of his misfortunes. The years, he declared pleasantly, had been very kind to Hannah, adding, 'Some people have a talent for combating Time,' and when she smiled her appreciation, he continued playfully, 'I observe that your theory of non-resistance did not insist on your submission to the ravages of oncoming age.'

Hannah was growing a bit restless. Thomas was taking pains to see that none of his inconsequential remarks tossed her a cue for some serious comment. Besides, there were plenty of interruptions which Thomas apparently welcomed. The nurse came and went on trivial errands, almost as if she had had instructions to do so. The doctor came, and Hannah was amiably presented as a long-time friend, 'practically a member of our family.' The daily papers came. The librarian came. The chauffeur came. The mail came, followed presently by a special-delivery letter. Thomas asked to be pardoned while he read it. Hannah was beginning to feel superfluous.

'I mustn't tire you,' she said, when there was a brief undisturbed interval. 'I had thought we might both be glad for a quiet talk. We parted under circumstances that made us sorry. I felt that it might ease our minds if we met again and assured each other of our friendship.'

Thomas, with a gentle gesture, dismissed any suggestion that there had been ill-feeling between them.

'It is fine of you, Hannah,' he declared companionably. 'Surely you have no cause to regret your own attitude. It was most magnanimous.... As for me — well ——' He shrugged a shoulder slightly. 'Perhaps it's too late to talk about it. I've always been sorry.'

'I didn't come to discuss that,' said Hannah reassuringly. 'I understood the predicament you were in — when you left me. I have not harbored any resentment. It gives me pleasure to tell you that. I thought you might be glad to know it, now that you aren't very well and have need of a peaceful mind. . . . There's really nothing,' she continued, after a pause which Thomas hadn't been disposed to make use of — 'there's nothing to compare with a peaceful mind, particularly when one is alone — or ill.'

Thomas's face clouded.

'You're right,' he said crisply. 'That's my trouble now. I'm not sleeping. I can crowd the daytime with little distractions, but at night, when everything is quiet, my mind is a riot. All the people who have done me up come to taunt me. I've been robbed by men I trusted, men I'd known for years. I get to hating them — at night.' He nervously slipped a hand under the sheet and fumbled in the vicinity of his heart. 'It isn't good for me. But, somehow, I can't stop it.'

'Must you let them keep on robbing you?'

'No,' snapped Thomas obtusely, 'they can't take anything else. I've been practically cleaned out.'

'Of money — you mean?'

'Money — of course!' he growled, in an impatient tone that charged Hannah with stupidity. Then, suddenly sorry for his rudeness, he added less irascibly, 'There's nothing left now to steal.'

'Except your peace,' said Hannah quietly. 'You couldn't help their taking your money. Now that they've got it, let them have it. But — please, Thomas — don't let them hurt you any more.'

He stirred restlessly. The nurse came in and he dismissed her with a jerk of his head toward the door. 'See that we're not bothered for a while,' he said, as she went out.

'It's easy enough to say, Hannah. Perhaps it might even be easy enough to do — for a person of your fine caliber. But ——'

Hannah leaned forward, resting her elbows on the arms of her chair, and regarded Thomas compassionately.

'May I tell you a strange story, about the man in whose home I have been employed for many years?'

'Case like mine, I presume,' surmised Thomas.

She made no effort to speed or abridge her narrative. For a time it was evident that Thomas was listening for sheer courtesy's sake. But when the invention was ruthlessly stolen, after Paul's hope had been so radiantly illumined and a fortune was all but in his hand, it was gratifying to see Thomas growing keenly attentive. Thrusting a bent arm under his head, he followed her lips with absorbed eyes.

'And then,' continued Hannah, 'the poor fellow went literally crazy, hacked his machine to fragments, and yelled to high heaven that he would get even if it took his last cent.'

'And not much wonder!' approved Thomas. 'He could have put them all behind the bars for a rascally job like that. I hope he did.'

'He didn't,' said Hannah serenely. 'And that has to be explained by another story.... Am I wearying you, Thomas?'

'Not at all. Go right on. What did Ward do about it?'

'Well — before I tell you that ——' And then Hannah proceeded to the almost incredible incident of Paul's promise made at the time of Wallie's desperate illness.

'Religious fellow, eh?' commented Thomas dryly, at the end of it.

'No — not the least bit.'

'Umm — perhaps not in the conventional way — but he did believe in a faith-cure.'

'No — I don't think he had any faith at all. But he loved his child and was willing to gamble on *my* faith.'

'You really believed in it, I suppose.... Of course, I can see that you did.' Thomas drew a grin. 'Ward put up the votive offering of money, and you put up your faith, and together you worked a miracle: is that it?'

Hannah refused to be disturbed. She smiled indulgently, and went on.

'That's one way of saying it. But Mr. Ward didn't actually "put up the money." It had already been stolen from him, you see. He simply consented to let them have it — and not fight back. The curious thing about it was that he didn't even hate the Ellises any more. He seemed to have possessed himself of some new energy to do things he had never been able to accomplish before. He became more important at the University, did twice the work with half the effort, and then — one day — he resumed his interest in the old invention and made another machine that completely surpassed the one they'd stolen. It made him very well-to-do.'

Thomas laughed unpleasantly.

'And so — his God paid him off in cash. That was nice of Him. . . . Forgive me, Hannah,' he added, quickly sobering when he saw the pain in her eyes. 'I'm afraid that wasn't very courteous.'

'Oh — that's all right, Thomas. I'd much rather you'd be honest than polite. Paul did become wealthy, but that was only incidental. The really important reward he received was the gift of *personal peace*. From the day he decided not to make war on the Ellis brothers, he left off hating them. They did not trouble him any more — at night. He couldn't have bought that — not for a million!'

'But he had to invest something to get it,' observed Thomas thoughtfully. 'I assume that you've been telling me all this because you think my case is similar. Perhaps it is. But I'm quite empty-handed, Hannah. Ward had something to offer — when his boy needed it.'

'I was just about to speak of that, Thomas.' Hannah's voice was very tender. 'Paul Ward was prepared to make almost any sort of sacrifice for his son. All that was to his credit, of course. But when he did it he knew that if his adventure was successful, he would have his boy restored to him. You and I both know what it means to give up something for the sake of a child — and never to experience the

happiness of actually claiming him as our own. You say
you have nothing to offer. My dear, you have already made
your offering. Year after year, you have hidden your
identity as Peter's father, permitting his foster mother to
take full credit for giving him his education, travel, luxuries,
advantages of all sorts. You asked nothing in return. I
think you deserve something for this investment.'

Thomas's eyes softened.

'How about *you*, Hannah?' he said gently. 'Surely your
sacrifice was much greater than mine.'

'I've had my pay,' said Hannah.

'In — in what you call — *personal peace* — you mean?'

'Yes.' She laid her hand gently on his and smiled into
his eyes. 'May I not share it with you, Thomas?'

They regarded each other silently for a little while. Then
with a deep sigh, Thomas shook his head doubtfully.

'You've earned it, you know,' persisted Hannah softly.
'It's there — waiting for you — whenever you want to
claim it.'

He smiled his appreciation of her solicitude, but gave no
sign of belief in what she had been saying. Presently he
reached up for the cord that dangled at the head of his bed
and pressed the button. The nurse appeared.

'Kindly serve luncheon here — for two,' he said. And
when the door had closed again, he remarked animatedly,
'Hannah, it has been immensely good of you to come. How
long can you stay?'

'Until tonight. I'm leaving at ten. I've my work to do.
I shall go home much happier for having talked with you.'

It was nine o'clock. Hannah had dropped in for a moment to say good-bye, and had left in high spirits. The
nurse was busying herself with the customary duties of preparing her difficult insomniac for another restless night.

'You have had a very active day, Mr. Bradford,' she
remarked half-testily. 'Much too much excitement.'

Thomas made no reply.

'Well — how about it? Shall I give you a sleeping-powder, or do you want your detective story?'

'Neither,' said Thomas, as from a considerable distance.

'You'll ring — if you want me?'

'I'll not be wanting you. Turn off the light, please.'

Chapter XX

SALLY tossed the flowers down toward the uplifted white arms of her bridesmaids, blew them a kiss, and continued up the stairs, Peter following closely.

In the upper hall she tightened her fingers on his arm and whispered, 'Let's go down the back way, darling, and find Hannah.' It was dark in the narrow passage that led to the kitchen. For a long moment they paused before opening the door, and were a bit breathless when they emerged into the crowded service quarters where Hannah was calmly supervising the swarm of extra help. They waved a hand to her and she came quickly to meet them, her eyes shining.

'Thanks for everything, Hannah,' said Sally. 'The dinner was simply perfect! The only thing lacking was you. We wanted you — sitting beside us. I wish you had been willing to do it, dear. We must run now. We came down to say good-bye.'

'And we love you — very much,' added Peter, slipping an arm about her. He lowered his tone and bent to murmur into her ear, 'We'll be thinking about you — always.'

'I'm so proud of you both.' Hannah's voice was unsteady.

They came into a tight little circle, entwining their arms.

'Will you take good care of Sally, Peter?'

'You know I will, Aunt Hannah. And when we're settled in Schenectady, you're to be our first guest. Promise? We've definitely planned on that. Haven't we, Sally?'

'And you're to stay as long as you can stand the rations.'

'We must be off now,' said Peter. He drew Hannah into

his arms and kissed her tenderly. She reached up both hands, pressed her palms against his cheeks, searched his eyes earnestly, and whispered, 'Oh — my boy — I'm so happy for you!'

Hot tears welled up into Sally's eyes.

'We'll be writing you, darling,' she promised.

Hannah clung to them for another moment.

'You both — belong — to me,' she said brokenly. 'I'll be — awfully lonesome.' Then, resolutely brightening, 'Run along, now. Be good to each other.' She followed them to the door, nervously stroking Peter's sleeve.

Marcia, never more stunningly beautiful, turned to Mrs. Edmunds.

'Did you ever see a more handsome pair? We may as well admit it, just between us, my dear. They are absolutely incomparable! I think Peter is really the most divine-looking thing I ever saw; and, of course, I think that Sally ——'

'Is adorably lovely,' agreed Lydia. 'But why shouldn't she be, if you don't mind my saying it to your face.'

Marcia didn't mind.

'I'll be calling you Lydia now, may I? We'll be wanting to see much of you. Not just because we're related — but because we really want you.'

Lydia smiled her thanks. Marcia glanced toward the hallway, noted that the crowd was moving out onto the veranda, and turned to say, 'I think I'll run up and see if I can do anything for Sally.'

'They'll have to hurry, won't they?' said Lydia.

Wallie gave Lucy Trimble's hand an affectionate squeeze as he passed her, and called to Roberta, slim and slinky in black satin: 'Better get your coat, young fellow. You haven't enough on. It will be chilly down there.'

'I'm not going,' drawled Roberta. 'There'll be enough of a mob without me.'

Wallie screwed up his face reprovingly. Roberta grinned, nonchalantly patted an elaborately sleek black curl that circled the huge red eardrop, withdrew the long red cigarette-holder, and blew a leisurely exhalation into Wallie's eyes.

'But what will Sally think?' he muttered.

Roberta shrugged an angular shoulder.

'Sally,' she replied dryly, 'won't be thinking.'

Sam Trimble, playing a next-of-kin rôle, gave the belated messenger boy a quarter and signed for the telegram.

'Guess I'll read it,' he remarked. 'Make sure it isn't something that might upset anybody.' He winked to Adele wickedly, and opened the message. 'Ah — it's from Peter's Uncle Thomas. Congratulations — and so forth. . . . Well — as I was saying, Mrs. Moore, it's the utilities that's going to get a sock in the jaw.'

'You mean — another bigger sock?' queried Adele complacently.

'Sure!' Sam hooked an elbow over the banister and prepared to elucidate. 'You see — it's this way ——'

'Give me a light first, won't you? This sounds as if it's going to be hard.'

There was a commotion above, and Peter and Sally, hand in hand, came racing down in their going-away clothes. The congestion about the front door eased to let them pass.

Lydia opened her arms as Peter neared her and was gathered into an affectionate embrace. Then he kissed Marcia, a bit shyly, all but muffing it in the jostling pack. Sally hugged her parents. Paul slapped Peter on the back.

'Come on!' commanded Wallie. 'You'll miss your train!'

They scurried out. Car doors slammed. Lights gleamed. Motors churned. Marcia and Lydia joined the racket outside and were showered with confetti.

Hannah slipped quietly, quickly up the stairs.

Paul and Eleanor, in the front doorway, followed her with their eyes; then exchanged an inquiring glance.

'Run along up with her,' said Eleanor soberly. 'She ought to have someone with her. It's damned pitiful — if you ask *me*.'

'Why don't *you* go?' Paul studied her eyes. 'You know all about it.'

'About *what?*'

'About *everything*.'

Eleanor's lips slowly parted in astonishment.

'Do *you?*' she whispered.

Paul nodded.

'Are you sure? — *Everything?*'

'*Everything!* And it isn't pitiful at all. And Hannah will prefer to be alone — to watch them go. She'll see it through. You can depend on that. Hannah is at her very best when there's a demand for — for private courage. . . . Well — there they go, God bless 'em!'

Hannah turned off the light in Sally's disordered bedroom and ran to one of the front windows. She drew aside the curtain, her heart pounding hard. The cars were moving down the driveway and out into the street.

She pressed her knuckles deeply into her trembling lips, dabbed at her eyes with the corner of her white apron, drew a whimpering little sob, bowed her head, and leaned limply for a moment against the casing.

Then she straightened, wiped her eyes, took a deep breath, squared her shoulders — and smiled.

THE END